THE SPLIT

A Satirical Dystopian Fairytale Comedy Political Thriller

Steve Radlauer | Ellis Weiner

Exasperated Media
New York • Los Angeles

www.exasperatedmedia.com
info@exasperatedmedia.com

The Split

ISBNs:
Trade Paperback: 979-8-9928044-0-9
Hardcover: 979-8-9928044-1-6
Ebook: 979-8-9928044-2-3

THE SPLIT

By the Same Authors

Monsters of the Ivy League

Books by Steve Radlauer

Nonfiction

The Historic Shops & Restaurants of New York
(with Ellen Williams)
Cyndi Lauper (as K.K. Willis, Jr.)

Humor

Special Moments (with Joe Bodolai)

Nonfiction Humor

Townie Planet
Dan Quayle: Airhead Apparent (with Paul Slansky)

Books by Ellis Weiner

The Joy of Worry
Drop Dead, My Lovely
The Big Boat to Bye-Bye
The Templeton Twins Have an Idea (middle-grade)
The Templeton Twins Make A Scene (middle-grade)

With Barbara Davilman

Yiddish with Dick and Jane
Yiddish with George and Laura
How to Raise a Jewish Dog
How to Profit from the Coming Rapture
Arffirmations: Meditations for Your Dog
Cat-echisms: Fundamentals of Feline Faith
The Big Jewish Book for Jews

To Lucy and Phoebe

—SR

To Elaine, for her fine counsel, good times together, and great laffs.

—EW

1 *In which we meet our heroine and her dainty little gun.*

THE CAMPAIGN TO elect the next CEO of the Confederation of Conservative States of America was in high gear, and no one who listened to the radio could avoid knowing all about it. "If we have to execute the woman to save the baby, then that's exactly what we're going to do. God personally told me that's what he wants," shouted Oliver M. Waldrip, the candidate of the Divine Party, who was, against all odds, trying to wrest supreme leadership from the popular incumbent CEO.

Lorinda Moon, in an elaborate cowgirl outfit with fringe everywhere, would have changed stations had there been another station to change to. She was alone in her ratty old Ryonbong DragonFire, rapidly approaching a uniformed Perfecton police officer standing in the middle of her lane, arms akimbo, his mirrored sunglasses nearly blinding her. "Damn it," she said. "Just what I need." She turned off the radio, glanced at herself from the nose up in the rearview mirror, decided she looked sufficiently cute, hit the brakes, and tried to remember the little speech he would require her to give. Behind him, the rotating beacon on the roof of his official pickup truck flashed red and blue as the oversized chrome exhaust stacks spewed a fat plume of black smoke into the fetid air. Leaning against the truck was a hand-lettered sign reading "GUN CHECK".

As he approached with his wary-cop plod she rolled down her window, ignoring the sooty heat blast, and said, cheerily, "Good afternoon, officer."

"Loyalty oath, please," he barked.

She closed her eyes, took a breath, and said, "I re-pledge my loyalty to Jesus Christ, to the sacred memory of Donald J. Trump, to the mighty Republic of Texas, to the Confederation of Conservative States of America, and to our beloved Chief Operating Officer, Mr. Ezra Ferrell McWeeny."

Shaking his head sadly, the cop said, "Try that again, ma'am."

She forced a girlish giggle. "Oops. I always mix those up. Okay. Umm… 'I re-pledge my loyalty to the sacred memory of Donald J, Trump, to Jesus Christ, to the mighty…'"

"That's better," interrupted the cop. He pulled a scanner from the bristling array of gear around his belt. "Your Citizen Card, please."

She grabbed her purse from the passenger seat, fished out her wallet, removed a plastic card, and handed it over. He scanned it, looked at the screen of the reader, and sniggered. "Miss Lorinda Moon. Please show me your Lady SIG Sauer .22. Your *pink* Lady SIG Sauer."

Rummaging in her purse, Lorinda said, "I'm sure I packed it when I changed bags… I do have my Bible!" she said, holding up a tiny book.

"Your gun, please."

Lorinda found it and passed the small pink pistol to him. He dropped the magazine, pulled back the slide, and shook his head. "It's not loaded. That's a serious violation of the law."

"But I have the bullets." She plunged her hand into her purse and shoved aside the lipstick, the hairbrush, the bag of hard candies, the sunglasses, the tissues, the phone, the tiny bottle of ibuprofen, the tube of ultra-high-SPF sunblock, the gunshot first aid kit, and the HEPA face mask. Then she touched the little pack of condoms and realized she had a problem. "It's amazing how much junk I have," she said flirtatiously, hiding the condoms in a side pocket. "Look," she said, holding her purse open so he could see the tiny projectiles rattling around the bottom of the bag.

"They're not going to protect you in there."

"If it's loaded it might take a bad bounce or something and shoot my foot off."

"That can't happen."

"It definitely can," she laughed. "There are two people in my neighborhood it happened to."

The cop shook his head. "I'll let you off this time," he said, winking at her as he handed back the gun and the card, "but don't let it happen again."

"Yes sir. I'll load it right now."

"You can wait till you get wherever you're going."

"Yes, sir, I will. Thank you, officer. I'll load it at work."

"Where do you work?"

"I tend bar at PumpJack's." Another giggle. "PumpJack's Oil-Fired Grille and Sports Bar."

"Yeah, I recognized the uniform. Great burgers. Maybe I'll see you there sometime."

"I'm there every day, just about."

"Well, all right then." He turned toward his truck, then turned back to her. "You need a bigger weapon. That thing's a joke."

2 *In which Lorinda demonstrates her bartending virtuosity.*

IT WAS A busy Friday afternoon, just the way Lorinda liked it. Aside from the tips, she liked the way she always rose to the occasion, got into the groove, gliding back and forth behind the bar, spinning to the back-bar, grabbing even the most obscure bottle in a fraction of a second, having an encyclopedia of cocktails in her brain and backup resources close to hand if she needed them, cultivating her customers — her fans, as she thought of them — telling stories, telling jokes, flirting, knowing their names and sometimes even their parents' or children's names, never losing track of an order or spilling a drink, knowing exactly how to get somebody to have one more, or to cut them off — nicely — if they'd had one too many. She sometimes wondered how she'd managed to find such a great job.

A good-looking man in his mid-twenties squeezed into the only vacant barstool. She'd never seen him before. Well-dressed for PumpJack's: a sports jacket over an open shirt with a collar. "Howdy, stranger," she said. "What can I get you?"

"Can I have a Johnny Reb?" the new guy said. "With a lime?"

"One Reb," said Lorinda, instantly fishing up a bottle from below the bar top, popping the top, stuffing in a wedge of lime, and sliding it to him. "I'm Lorinda, by the way. Welcome to my bar."

"Ooooh, Lori's in love," said a big guy in a black tee-shirt sitting three stools over.

Chapter 2

"Leave her alone, Benjie," said the pretty young woman in sage-green scrubs sitting next to him. She loudly drained the dregs of a raspberry-red drink through a straw. "He's cute."

"Benjie, you just shut up and mind your own business. Thank you, Nurse Emmie."

"She never talks to *me* like that," muttered the guy in pseudo-military duds and a buzz-cut who sat between the nurse and the new guy.

Benjie snickered. "News flash, Elijah — nobody talks to you like that."

Lorinda frowned at him. "Benjie? Maybe shut the hell up for a second?" She looked at Buzz-Cut. "Any luck with the ladies, Elijah?"

He shook his head morosely. "Nah. You meet any possibilities for me?"

"I don't know, honey," she said. "A gal came in last week who looked like a Maybe. But I haven't seen her since."

"Hey, Elijah," Benjie said. "How about maybe thinking about joining the Virgins?"

"It's not called the Virgins," Lucas, the short, slightly simian-looking man on the far side of Benjie, jumped in. "It's the UnVirs. Short for 'Unwilling Virgins' — get it?" The UnVirs was a social-media group of men unable to find a woman to have sex with. Or, really, to do anything at all with.

"Well, it should be called the Virgins. UnVirs is, like, the opposite," Benjie said, not without a certain amount of logic.

"I can't believe you think I'm one of them," Elijah said. "Nasty."

"Why not? It's free!" Everyone looked at Benjie in disbelief. "What?" he said, all innocence. "I'm not kidding. I hear the government has a program to help those guys get… you know. Find partners."

"That's a rumor," Nurse Emmie said.

"Hey, yeah, I heard that, too," Lucas said. "They're bringing in women from, like, Russia. Those babes are hot."

Benjie gestured toward him in agreement. "Right! Thanks, Lucas." He turned to Elijah. "So. Whattaya say, 'Lije?"

"I say fuck you," Elijah said, mustering up some dignity. "No way I'm joining up with that bunch of losers."

The new guy laughed. "You got *that* right."

Lorinda took stock. The mood was deflating, and it was up to her to bring it back up. It was exactly the kind of challenge she relished.

"You know what, guys?" she said. "Let's play a little drinking game." She reached under the bar and came up with a chubby volume whose pages seemed on the verge of falling out and whose tattered dust cover identified it as *The Savoy Cocktail Book*. "Give me a minute," she said, riffling through it.

"Taking a little reading break?" asked Benjie.

"I'm looking for … oh, this is a good one."

She set the book down under the bar top where only she could see it and quickly lined up a cocktail shaker, two booze bottles, two tiny bottles of bitters, and a small container of some clear liquid.

"Just what do you think you're doing?" asked Benjie in his best imitation of an authority figure. It was his effort at retribution for her having called him out earlier, and was nothing new.

"I'm consulting my Bible," she said. "I'm looking for a cocktail with a really long, confusing name." She closed her eyes for a few seconds, then said, "Okay, I know how to do this. I'm going to whisper into Lucas's ear — just once — the name of the drink I'm making. He's going to write it down on this — " she tore the top sheet off a pad of restaurant receipts — "and give it to me, without letting anyone else see it. Got that, Lucas?"

He nodded, not very convincingly.

"Then he whispers it to Benjie."

"What do I whisper?" Lucas asked.

"The name of the drink! You whisper it to Benjie. He writes it down and whispers to Emmie, she writes it down and whispers to Elijah, he writes it down and... I'm sorry, what's your name?"

"Brad," said the new guy. He was clearly smitten with Lorinda and making no effort to hide it.

"Hi, Brad. Welcome to my world. So Elijah whispers to Brad. Then Brad writes it down, and then I collect the drink names..." She gave each of the other four a receipt to write on. "... and make the drinks. Drinks that go with the names you give me."

"Have you ever done this before?" Emmie asked. "Whatever it is?"

"Nope. Just thought of it."

"It's like that game — Telephone?" said Emmie. "And everyone gets it wrong?"

"Maybe," said Lorinda. "So these'll be regular-price drinks. And you'll pay and you'll drink them. Except Brad. He gets comped this time. But you still have to drink it, Brad."

"See? Special treatment!" said Benjie.

Brad smiled. "Yes, ma'am."

Lucas winced. "When you say 'regular-price' — "

"Same as always for cocktails. Ninety-eight dollars."

Ninety-eight dollars was on the low side for a good cocktail in Perfecton, and in any case they were all — the regulars and the new guy — under Lorinda's spell.

"Everybody in?" she asked. They all nodded in assent. "Okay then, here we go." She whispered in Lucas's ear and handed him a pen. Looking mystified, he wrote on his slip of paper. Lorinda grabbed it and said, "Now you whisper to Benjie. Don't let anyone else hear it."

Lucas turned and whispered to Benjie, who gave him an "are you insane?" look as Lorinda handed him the pen. He wrote, then turned and whispered to Emmie. "What?" said Emmie.

"No cheating," said Lorinda, handing her the pen. "You get one chance." Emmie shrugged, wrote down what she'd heard, and slid the pen to Elijah while whispering to him. He chuckled, wrote on his piece of paper, and gave Brad the pen and whispered in his ear.

After she'd collected the notes, Lorinda looked them over and laughed. "Hoo boy." She put them down in sequence under the bar top, and got to work. Grabbing new bottles and ingredients and vessels as she needed them, the fringe on her fake-suede jacket flying, her cowgirl hat flopping on its tether against her back — she quickly whipped up five very different looking concoctions. She set the first one — milky and bubbly in an oversized wine glass — in front of Lucas. Then she picked up her old book, flashed it briefly at her audience, and read aloud: "Nineteen-Twenty Pick-Me-Up Cocktail. Anisette, gin, two kinds of bitters, sugar syrup, soda. Lucas thought this was called — " looking at what he wrote — "Ninety-Three Pickup." They all laughed. "So this one's real, from the book. It's a drink that's meant to take you back to the 1920s—or maybe now it's 1993? or 1893?—in your mind. Very calming, relaxing, away from all this modern stress. How is it?"

Lucas took a sip, closed his eyes for a moment, and said, "It's good, I think."

Lorinda set the second drink — green, in a tall highball glass, with some kind of sprig sticking out the top — in front of Benjie. "Your Nightly Tree Backup, sir."

"That's not what I told him," Lucas laughed.

"It's what I heard," said Benjie defensively. "I'm partially deaf in my right ear."

"Gin, Chartreuse, orange bitters, orange zest, and a Texas parsley sprig," Lorinda said proudly. "It'll take you to a cool pine forest of the mind. Your Nightly Tree Backup. How is it?"

Benjie lifted his glass, poked himself in the eye with the sprig, dramatically tossed it on the bar, and took a gulp. "That's ... really different," he said. "Nightly Tree Backup." He took another sip. "Not bad. Put it on the menu."

"And now," said Lorinda, passing Emmie a martini glass containing a two-layer drink, red on the bottom, clear on top, with white powder around the rim and a cherry on top. "Your Mighty Free Track. Grenadine, vodka, gin, and a maraschino cherry. Oh, and sugar on the rim. If that doesn't set you free, nothing will."

Emmie took a sip and cringed. "It's a little strong for me," she said.

"You'll get used to it," said Lorinda. "Next time you're here looking to be set free you'll be craving one. And for you ..." She read Elijah's piece of paper and laughed. "This one makes no sense: Mind If We Lack." She set down in front of Elijah a small glass pitcher filled with water, a bowl of ice, and a tall glass containing a couple of inches of blue liquid.

Elijah looked baffled. "What's all this?"

"This," said Lorinda, "is your Mind If We Lack. In French they call it 'pastis.' A couple of these and you'll completely lack your mind. Even more than you do now. Which is very liberating, you know.'" She dropped two ice cubes into the glass, then filled the glass with water. The blue had vanished; the liquid that filled the glass was white.

"How'd you do that?" asked Elijah.

"Magic," said Lorinda. "That could be the last bottle of blue pastis in the CCSA. You'll never see it again. Drink that and one day you'll take a magical cruise across the blue ocean to France."

"Why would I do that?" said Elijah, only half kidding.

"And finally," said Lorinda, reading the last drink name, dropping the piece of paper on the bar, and locking eyes with Brad, "Mighty Fine Rack."

"That's what I thought I heard," said Brad. He sounded defiant. Or like he was trying to sound defiant.

Emmie said, "Oh, Christ," as the other lads hooted. Lorinda stared them down, then set Brad's drink on the bar—a big mug topped with a tall peak of whipped cream.

"Hey, no fair," said Benjie. "How come he gets to have one that looks like a big tit?"

"This," she said, ignoring him, "is very special. It represents a snow-topped mountain that's the home of the king of the forest, a giant stag with an enormous rack"—she glared in feigned anger at Benjie—"*of horns* on his head. And under the snow is a river of delicious coffee, coffee liqueur, and a little shaved chocolate. Now drink up, y'all."

"So," said Benjie after taking another sip of his drink, "what's the point of all this?"

Lorinda was about to say something flip—maybe, "To use you guys as guinea pigs while I invent new drinks"—but she hesitated. The real answer was, "to keep the party going." But for some reason she took the question more seriously, for once, and thought for a moment. Was it to impress the new guy? Yeah, maybe—but not really. Then what? She improvised. "It's...it's like life, isn't it? We're all individuals. So we say things, and hear things, in our own way.

And sometimes we get things wrong. But if you allow people to do that, and don't boss them around and tell them what's right and wrong and what 'reality' is, things work out."

"Yeah, well, they worked out this time because you knew what you were doing," Emmie said. She hoisted her drink. "Here's to Lorinda, our favorite bartender."

The others joined with raised glasses.

Then Brad spoke up. "I know y'all just met me, but my buddy's having a big party at his house later. It'll go all night long — and you're all invited." He picked up the pen and wrote on the restaurant bill next to his drink name. "Here's the address. Anyone else want it?" He slid it to Lorinda, who jammed it into her pocket without looking at it.

3 *In which our heroine receives a promotion and prepares to celebrate.*

AS SHE CLEANED up, Lorinda was thinking about how much she liked talking to people, entertaining them. And how much they seemed to like it: The crowd around the bar was always bigger when she was behind it. It was 10:10 PM and Linette, the night girl, had checked in. Lorinda stopped by the office in the rear, beyond the kitchen, to say good-night to the branch manager.

"See you tomorrow, Mrs. Barker."

"Can I have a word with you, Lorinda dear?" Mrs. Barker was in her forties or fifties — it was hard to tell — and, as usual, was dressed like an off-duty lady rodeo champion. She waved Lorinda in toward the visitor's chair.

Uh, oh, thought Lorinda as she sat. "Busy tonight, huh?"

"Lorinda," said Mrs. Barker, "I think you know we appreciate your work."

"Thank you, Mrs. Barker. You know I like it here." What's the catch, Lorinda wondered.

"Bless your heart. And that's why I'm not going to call you Lorinda anymore, but . . . Miss Head of Bartending Operations!"

It took a second for it to sink in. Lorinda's eyes went wide. "Oh my gosh!" she said. "I mean, that's fantastic! Thank you! I can't believe it."

"You're on your way to big things, Missy. I wouldn't be surprised if you're sitting in this chair in a year or two. You've got a good head on your shoulders."

"But," said Lorinda, "What about you? We need you. Where would you go?"

"Oh, don't worry about little old me," said Mrs. Barker. "I've got my eye on a corner office at headquarters."

"In Dallas?"

"That's right."

"And your husband?"

"Old Charlie loves Dallas. Or," she whispered even though no one else was in range, "he will by the time I get done with him." She really made herself laugh with that one.

"Wow, Dallas," said Lorinda. "I'd love to travel. I've only been out of Perfecton once. My parents took us to New Orleans. And of course I was born up north."

"Where did your people come from?"

"Upper State New York," said Lorinda. "They left during the Great Moratorium."

"That was sure a crazy time," said Mrs. Barker. "Well, they were smart to get out of that diabolical hellhole while they could. And I can see their smartness rubbed off on you. You're a lucky girl to be here. If you were still there, you'd probably be a prostitute or a drug addict. Or both. Or you'd be mentally ill from all…" Here she whispered. "…*the abortions*. Or a communist. Praise God for Texas! CCSA! The best!"

"I know!" Lorinda smiled. "Perfecton is so nice!

"Nice is what Perfecton is all about, my dear. It's why our founders created it. You know the motto: 'A serene, wholesome place to live the modern conservative lifestyle —'"

"'— away from the temptations of Satan.'" Lorinda sighed. "It's great. Not too much traffic, no potholes, usually. Good weather except for tornado season…"

"We're very blessed to live here. And I think *you're* going to be a star as Head of Bartending Operations. You'll start at the beginning of the month. You'll get an orientation between now and then. Oh, and I didn't even mention." Mrs. Barker paused for dramatic effect. "You'll be getting a two-hundred-dollar a week raise!"

"Wow," said Lorinda, with as much fake enthusiasm as she could muster. As a regular, non-supervisory employee she was making PumpJack's standard starting wage of two-hundred-fifty-six-thousand dollars a year, so the extra two-hundred wasn't going to make that big a difference. But it was definitely a nice gesture, and a vote of confidence in her work.

"So," said Mrs. Barker, wrapping up their meeting, "what are you going to do to celebrate your new position?"

Lorinda thought for a second. "I don't know. Maybe I'll go to this party a friend invited me to."

"Oooh," said Mrs. Barker conspiratorially. "Fun! Don't do anything I wouldn't do."

They both had a good laugh over that one.

Lorinda studied herself in her bathroom mirror, touching up her makeup, giving her hair a little toss, checking out her tight-as-legally-permitted jeans, her sweater, her boots. She was glad to be out of her PumpJack's uniform and into clothes that made her feel — she blushed slightly when she found the word she was looking for — *sexy*.

"Are you sure this is a good idea, honey?" said her mother, poking her head into the bathroom and using her I'm-concerned-but-I'm-not-being-pushy voice. "Seems awfully late to be going out." In her early-forties, Mrs. Rita Moon was on the young side for the mother of PumpJack's most popular bartender. On the other hand, with her short graying hair, saggy eyes, and baggy pink terrycloth bathrobe, she could pass for a good ten years older.

"Yes, mother. It's a great idea. I'm celebrating my promotion with some of my friends. If I can't celebrate that, what can I celebrate? I'm twenty-two years old. I'm not a baby."

"That's what we're worried about," said her father. Mr. Robert "Bob" Moon was also in his early forties. With his brush-cut dark hair, his well-worn khaki cargo pants, and his faded olive-green tee-shirt, he had a vaguely military look about him.

"Nothing to worry about, Dad," said Lorinda, putting away her supplies and giving herself one last look in the mirror. "I'll report any and all bad behavior to the Perfecton Police Department — or to the Security Bureau if it's really bad. Like I always do."

"When did you ever do that?" asked Mrs. Moon.

"Never," said Lorinda. "That's because I've never once seen any bad behavior. But I know who to call if I see any!"

"Don't be a wiseass," said her father. "And don't forget — there are cameras everywhere."

"Thanks, Dad."

"And I just saw that there's a heavy smog rolling in, so drive carefully. And if you can't see, pull over and wait it out."

"Okay, Dad."

"Don't stay out too late, dear," squeaked Mrs. Moon.

"I don't need to be at work until six tomorrow night. Saturday. Gotta go — I'm picking up Emmie. Love you guys."

"Maybe I'll be able to afford a new car once I get my raise," said Lorinda.

"Two-hundred dollars a week? No way," said Emmie, riding shotgun. She had traded her hospital scrubs for loose-fitting jeans and a blousy pink top.

"Yeah, I know. But you gotta dream."

"You gotta dream," echoed Emmie.

Rounding a curve, they came face-to-face with a pulsating billboard in bright LED lights, alternating between the headline "OLIVER M. WALDRIP — THE ONLY FUNDAMENTALIST CANDIDATE FOR CEO," Waldrip's grinning, unctuous puss, and his motto: "EDUCATION IS THE ENEMY." Inevitably — it happened whether or not the car radio was on — they heard the sign's audio, broadcast via the CCSA's Short-Range Billboard Channel (SRBC): *"Jesus has assured me He favors my candidacy. I know you voters will do the right, Christian thing."*

Suddenly, before the audio was even finished, the billboard disappeared behind an ashen charcoal cloud. "Oh dammit," said Lorinda, hitting the brakes and slowing down to a crawl. "My dad warned me about this. Is your window closed all the way?"

Emmie checked. "Yeah. You don't want to breathe it. That shit'll kill you. You know how many people we get at the hospital every time there's a smog event? A lot!" she said, not waiting for Lorinda's guess. "And some of them always die. And the worst part is, the government blames *us! The hospital staff!* For not doing our part to Maintain the Population. *You* try to maintain the population when the air is like this!"

It was a familiar campaign, promoted by the government from the federal level on down to the states: "M.P.! Maintain the Population!"

The truth — which the government never acknowledged, and about which every national and state official lied when asked — was that, during the two-year Moratorium after The Split, when anyone from either the CCSA or the USA could move from one to the other with a minimum of bureaucratic red tape, many people had fled the so-called "red", mostly-southern-and-midwestern nation for the so-called "blue", mainly-northern-and-west-coast country. ("We reject the term 'fled,'" announced CCSA Secretary of Citizenship Laura Larsen. "We prefer 'emigrated from.'"). What started out as a welcome, even triumphant "cleansing" (as it was unofficially referred to, even if the mass migration was entirely voluntary) of liberals, progressives, gays, trans, feminists, Jews, racial minorities, Muslims, Catholics, and other undesirables, ended up as a crisis of manpower. Yes — real conservatives, patriotic believers in freedom, and good Christians from up north resettled in the south. But the bulk of the traffic flow was in the other direction, by an order of magnitude or two.

The result, in the newly birthed nation, was simply not enough bodies: a shortfall of workers for the fields and factories of the country's crucial agricultural and dirty-energy sectors, a dearth of laborers to man (or woman) the nation's factories (whether locally or foreign-owned), and a distinct lack of sufficient consumers to drive its hyper-capitalist economy. Sure, a national ban on abortion, with no exceptions, helped. But once the employment and economic numbers were in, the CCSA government found itself in the unfamiliar position of having to assist its citizens in the business of staying alive.

The question was: How?

Improving the material conditions of life — fixing dangerously unmaintained roads, mitigating industrial pollution of air and water, regulating the manufacture of food and drugs — required outlays of money, which in turn required the raising of what few nominal taxes there were, or even creating new ones. This was considered politically unfeasible and morally reprehensible. And, of course, interfering with the private sector to improve people's working lives by establishing a minimum wage, enforcing safety standards, or permitting unions and collective bargaining, was deemed traitorous, "communistic", and un-Christian.

Instead, the government turned to persuasion. It mounted a continuing and ever-evolving series of ad campaigns designed to encourage the citizens of the CCSA to do everything they could to remain alive, to help others remain alive, and — how to put this delicately? — to get married, have sex, and produce babies.

There had been another campaign — hotly debated, uncertainly executed, and quickly abandoned. It involved spending money in other countries on advertising that touted the charms and benefits of life in the CCSA, in the hopes of encouraging immigration. Sadly, what the nay-sayers predicted came to pass: No matter how carefully targeted the ads were, no matter how narrowly targeted to the "good people" of Western Europe, Scandinavia, Canada, Australia, and Russia and it satellites, the citizens of those countries most susceptible to the CCSA's promise of total freedom, untrammeled individualism, and Southern hospitality turned out to be a mob of non-white, non-Christian minorities whose lives in their home countries left much to be desired. "We don't want Germany's Somalis," one politician railed. "We want Germany's *Germans*." After a few months of watching Africans and Muslims de-plane at Dallas-Fort Worth, the Confederated government scuttled the campaign, fired all those responsible, and sent the dusky immigrants back to their shit-holes.

So there were no immigrants—just the domestic push for making more citizens the hard way. Was it working? It was difficult to say. Just last year the government had tried to assess the robustness of the population by conducting a nationwide census; but most of the fiercely independent citizens of the country—holding to their principles of Christian faith, conservative self-reliance, and proud disdain for "nanny state" meddling—refused to answer census workers' questions.

Emmie was reflecting on her own sarcastic response to a mail-in census questionnaire ("How many people reside in your home?" "Does the dog count?") when she found herself lurching forward as Lorinda smashed the brake pedal to the floor.

"What?!" Emmie was glad she'd remembered to use her seat belt, even though it wasn't required by law.

"Something in the road. Lucky I saw it. Hold your breath for a second. I have to see what it is." As Lorinda engaged the parking brake, both she and Emmie inhaled deeply. Lorinda got out of the car with a pause and a lurch, as though diving into a lake. She closed the door and carefully moved forward. Emmie watched until her friend walked around the large object in the road and disappeared from headlight range about a dozen feet beyond the front of the car. In a few seconds Lorinda came back.

"It's a roof," she said, closing the door behind her.

"A roof?"

"You know, those big things with shingles? On top of houses?"

"Tornado?"

"Must be. I didn't see a tornado warning, but—"

"Hey, they can't warn us every time there's a little tornado. They probably didn't even know about it. I can't tell you how many tornado victims we get in the hospital when we didn't even know there'd been a tornado."

"All right," said Lorinda, "I can drive around the side, I think." She released the parking brake and slowly eased the car past the roof, occasionally running over who-knows-what — some shingles? A chunk of roof beam? Then, as suddenly as it had appeared, the smog lifted as she steered the car back to the middle of the road.

"I haven't been out this way before," said Lorinda.

"Really nice houses," said Emmie. "You think that guy Brad owns one?"

"It's his friend's place, he said. Probably his friend's parents' place. I mean, come on."

Without missing a beat, Emmie looked at the restaurant receipt in her hand. "Righteous Pathway. Number three-fifty-five. Too bad the GPS satellite is broken."

"Here we go," said Lorinda, spotting the street sign and turning right. "Righteous Pathway. Dumb name for a street."

"Shhh. Someone might hear you."

4 *In which our heroine proves herself an immoral citizen of the CCSA.*

LORINDA DROVE SLOWLY in order to read the address numbers and ogle the fancy houses. "Three-fifty-nine," said Emmie, "three-fifty-seven . . . here we are."

There were several cars parked on the street and in the driveway, but Lorinda easily found a spot. The house was big, like the others on Righteous Pathway: two stories, a grand portico, lots of glass, a couple of chimneys, yard space on the sides to distance it from its neighbors. It looked brand new: no broken windows, no bad paint, no dangling gutters. They could see people inside dancing. They could hear the pulse of the music.

Lorinda saw Brad as soon as she walked in. Standing by the door, a Johnny Reb in one hand, a joint in the other, his gun hanging from a holster on his belt, cowboy style, he was hard to miss. His face lit up as she entered. "You're here!" he said. "I didn't think you'd come."

"Of course I'm here," she said. "Shall we dance?"

"Good idea. Let me introduce you to my friend Finn. It's his house. His parents' house."

"First let's dance."

An hour later the lights were down low and the music had evolved from jumpy rhythmic numbers to slow, romantic ballads. Lorinda and Brad were pressed against each other, swaying to the music.

She was halfway through her third beer and trying to remember if her limit was usually one or two. Emmie, slow-dancing with a guy she'd met a half-hour earlier, made eye contact with Lorinda and winked. Lorinda winked back, but her joy was interrupted by a sharp pain in her side. "*Owww!*" she blurted.

"What?" said Brad, who had turned to fetch his beer from a nearby table.

"You just smashed me with your gun," said Lorinda, rubbing her hip. "That hurt."

"Sorry," said Brad, setting down the drink and attempting to resume full-body contact. At that moment the lights went bright, the music stopped, and the television on the wall lit up. "Shit," said Brad. "What's he up to now?"

"Who?"

"Finn. That's him."

Finn was a tall, skinny, teenage-looking man in his mid-twenties, with curly red hair, plaid shorts, a black tee-shirt, and flip-flops. "Hey, everybody, thanks for coming," he said. "Sorry to interrupt, but I figure none of you saw the debate earlier — you had better things to do, I'm sure — so I recorded it. I thought I'd show you the first ten or fifteen minutes of it now, cause it's important to know what's going on in the world. It's the CEO debate. It's important."

This elicited a round of boos and good-natured attacks on Finn's character from the people on the dance floor. "No, really," said Finn. "Just a few minutes of it. People! The election's in only three months! Okay, Murray! Play TV." Most CCSA citizens assumed that the "Murray" in the ubiquitous command was simply a random, sort of amusing, sort of semitic name, a first name appearing on the birth certificate of virtually no actual inhabitant of the country. In fact, it was an homage — paid by the engineers who adapted some legacy remote-control software for use in the CCSA — to Charles Murray, author of the classic racist book *The Bell Curve*.

As the partygoers grabbed their drinks or went for a refill, the show began, cued to the moderator's first question: "Mr. Waldrip, why are you and the Divine Party better qualified to rule the CCSA than the incumbent, Mr. McWeeny, and his White Christian Party?"

"First," said Ollie Waldrip, "we're better Christians, despite the name of his party. Second, we're absolutists. *Fundamentalists.* For instance, if we have to execute the woman to save the baby, then that's exactly what we're going to do. God personally told me that's what He wants."

"That's exactly, word for word, what you always say," Ezra Ferrell McWeeny interrupted. "Praise Jesus, we know better. We want those women to live. We *need* them."

"Those are the words God implanted in my brain," yelled Waldrip, "and who are you to contradict God?"

"You need to be hospitalized," McWeeny shouted back. "You're mentally ill. That's not God talking to you. You're hearing voices."

"And third — "

"Third is, you're a lunatic. Completely out of your mind — "

"I didn't come here to be insulted like this!" Waldrip said.

"No problem," McWeeny said. "It's free of charge." To the moderator he said, "Come on, Earl. Next question."

"All right! Gentlemen! Please." The moderator took a breath. "CEO McWeeny. You're on record as having called for the re-unification of the CCSA with the USA. What — "

Lorinda had trouble hearing the rest of the question over the boos and jeers of the partygoers. Finally she heard, "— think that's a good idea?"

McWeeny's bulldog face went mild and blasé as he held up a cautioning hand. "You're mis-quoting me. As usual. No, I don't call for re-unification. I said it's something we should study —" More boos from the revelers. "— so that when the USA comes crawling back to us and begs us to re-join the nation, we know what our terms will be."

"That's not what you said, God damn it!" Waldrip began.

"Nice. Nice blaspheming, you fraud."

"You said, 'I look forward to the day we can knit the two halves of the country back together' —"

"*Under our terms*. Is that too subtle for you? Earl, explain it to him."

"Gentlemen!" The moderator banged his fist on the table. "All right, let's talk about the North Dakota Purchase."

"It's a damn disgrace," Waldrip said. "Our country is not for sale!"

"Spoken like someone who hasn't the faintest idea of what our government is facing," McWeeny said. "All I can tell you is that it's still being negotiated..."

Lorinda had only a vague idea of what they were talking about. Apparently, during the fifteen years since The Split, even after the Moratorium, millions of undesirable people — not to mention a surprising number of white so-called Christians — had left the CCSA, some by climbing, burrowing under, blasting through, or hiking around The Wall, and emigrated to the USA — so many, in fact, that the other country found itself in need of real estate in which to allow them to settle. This coincided with the discovery by the CCSA that it was spending the bulk of its gross national product on building and maintaining its various border walls with the USA, Canada, and Mexico, and in a few years would be bankrupt. So a deal was in the works to sell North Dakota to the USA. The relatively small number of people living there would be free either to remain and become USA citizens, or to move to God's Country at CCSA expense. Lorinda, when she thought about it (which was pretty much never) didn't know whether she was for or against the idea.

There was a brewing hubbub on the other side of the living room. Lorinda looked in that direction. She couldn't see what was going on, but she did hear the growled names "Waldrip" and "McWeeny."

"We didn't engineer The Split in order to sell our own country for parts!" Waldrip shouted from the television.

"Do you even know what the word 'default' means?" sneered McWeeny. Just as Ollie Waldrip leapt out from behind his lectern, the hubbub across the room escalated to a loud kerfuffle.

"Okay, Murray! Freeze!" shouted Finn. The image froze on an airborne Waldrip in the middle of tackling McWeeny — and things were getting just as raucous across the room as they were on the screen. People were yelling. Fists were flying. Guns were being waved.

"Hey!" yelled Brad, which had no effect whatsoever on the escalating melee. Sweeping Lorinda behind him, Brad yanked his gun out of his holster and pointed it up, not knowing what else to do with it.

"Don't shoot the ceiling!" yelled Finn. "My parents will kill me."

Lorinda spun Brad around, kissed him long and hard on the mouth, and said, "Put that thing away." He obediently re-holstered the gun. She then took his hand, pulled him away from the fracas and toward the stairway, and led him up the stairs. In the upstairs hallway she looked around for a likely doorway.

"Finn's room," said Brad, pointing to a closed door. Lorinda led him there, opened the door, pushed him inside, closed the door behind her, and clicked the privacy lock. Had she remembered to stash the condoms in her pocket? She felt for them. She had.

"Take that gun off," she said.

"Make me."

"Do it, or I'm out of here."

He laughed. "This isn't your bar, where you get to be the boss." He reclined on the bed, half-sitting up, his back against the headboard and fingers laced behind his head. "You're not going anywhere. You're just happy you're with someone who obviously isn't one of the UnVirs."

"Uh-huh." She turned toward the door and unlocked it.

"Okay, okay!" he said. "I'm taking it off. But I was going to do it anyway."

She locked the door again.

No shots were fired during the half-hour they spent together in Finn's room. Brad was now asleep on his stomach, his head buried in a pillow, his pale ass zebraed by the moonlight sneaking in through the slats of the blinds. Lorinda, moving slowly so as not to wake him, gathered her clothes, dressed, and quietly opened the door. She took a moment to turn back and look at Brad. She wanted to feel something for him, the second man with whom she'd ever had sex. In fact, this was only the second time she'd ever had sex: once with Duke Simmons in high school, and now with Brad. But she felt nothing except relief that she could slip out without having some icky conversation with him.

Downstairs, the party was circling the drain. Two couples danced, without enthusiasm, to some ancient rock-and-roll tearjerker. Emmie, talking to Finn on the sofa, looked up at Lorinda as she came downstairs. "Look who's back," she said.

"Let's go," said Lorinda.

"Right now?"

"Unless you don't need a ride."

"Ohhhh-kay," sighed Emmie.

"You can stay," said Finn. "My parents aren't coming back till Monday."

"You're sweet," said Emmie, "but I've got to go."

"So?" They were already halfway back to Emmie's house, and it was the first word either of them had spoken.

"So nothing," said Lorinda. "Yes. I'll answer the question you want to ask. Yes, we had sex."

"Whoa," said Emmie. "That was quick. Are you all right?"

"Yeah, I'm fine."

"And Brad?"

"He's fine." She hesitated and added, "... Although he wasn't *that* fine." That cracked them both up.

"Did he use a thingy?"

"A thingy? Are you trying to say condom, Miss Nurse?'"

Emmie laughed. "Yes, that's it. Condom. Safe. Protection."

"Yes. He did. Because I brought one."

"Really?" Emmie seemed truly surprised. Of course condoms were illegal. But, like so many illegal things in the CCSA, you could obtain them on the black market. "Where'd you get it?

"I don't know. A friend of my brother's? Who remembers? Why?"

"Just . . ." Whatever Emmie was going to say, she thought better of it. "Never mind. I'm glad you had one."

"Me, t— "

"What color was it?"

Lorinda stole a look from the road ahead to make eye contact with her friend. "White. Why?"

Emmie fluttered her hands dismissively. "No reason." She settled back. "You sober enough to drive?"

"Well, I am now.

5 *In which our heroine goes to church.*

"OH, LOOK, EMMIE'S here."

Normally Lorinda said whatever she had to in order to avoid attending Sunday church services with her parents and brother Zeke. She "hadn't slept last night and was tired." She "had bookkeeping work for the bar to catch up on." Whether skeptical or not, her parents gave her a pass. It wasn't that she wasn't a believer — or, rather, yes, she wasn't a believer, but she was a believer in belief. She approved of and respected, and maybe even envied, her parent's commitment to evangelical Christianity. It was just that the prospect of sitting in the theater-in-the-round pew of the Liberated Independent Church of the Cause, listening to Pastor Doug orate and chant and declaim, while everyone around her nodded and wept and swayed and sang, was usually too much to bear.

Not today, though. For some reason, Lorinda had felt an atypical urge to accompany her family to church. Maybe it was last night's encounter with Brad, and its weird emotional residue, a combination of thrilling transgression and faintly depressing disappointment. Or maybe it was the slowly-germinating implications of her job promotion and Mrs. Barker's benediction about its possibilities. Maybe she was looking for some spiritual solace. Or maybe she just didn't want to stay home alone and brood.

Now, as they pulled into their reserved parking space in the sprawling asphalt lot, she spied Emmie's car.

"Yeah?" her brother said. "Cool. Emmie's hot, Lor."

"Zeke!" Lorinda said, grossed out. "Ew!"

"I'm just sayin'!"

"We're going to church, Ezekial," their mother said. "Mind what you say."

"I'm just sayin' what I'm sayin'." He cackled. "I'm sayin' what I'm sayin' and I'm playin' what I'm playin' and I'm okayin' what I'm... prayin'."

Lorinda rolled her eyes. She might have known. Zeke was on manna again. She surreptitiously glanced at his nostrils and was pretty sure she saw a few flecks of green powder he had missed when he cleaned himself up for the ride to church.

Manna was its street name. Lorinda didn't know the drug's official chemical name, but she did know — pretty much everybody knew, in spite of its illegality and notorious reputation — that it combined the energizing and attitude uplift effects of cocaine with the euphoria of ecstasy, along with a weird imperviousness to fatigue and physical pain. As a result, most (if not all) of Zeke's co-workers on the Citizens Construction Corps were fond of it — if not completely addicted to it.

The CCC was the new nation's employer of last resort — a battalion of men and women ages 20 to 40 who were sent like a SWAT team of manual laborers to farms and factories and construction sites in desperate need of workers. With no minimum wage and no unions (in keeping with the breakaway nation's proclaimed philosophy of freedom for workers as well as for entrepreneurs), CCC personnel salaries were rock-bottom, but supplemented by the (field-ration-type) food and (tent-based) lodgings provided at each job. How these proud, hard-working citizens were able to obtain, let alone pay for, a drug the manufacture, distribution, and sale of which was against Confederal law, was just one of the many mysteries characterizing life in this Confederation of Conservative States of America.

Lorinda and her family shuffled through the happy throng of congregants milling in the churchly equivalent of pre-game tailgate festivity outside the sanctuary, Bob nodding affably to colleagues from his logistics office at Gotfried Lenz Pharmaceuticals, Rita waving to paralegal colleagues from her law firm. Zeke spied a CCC buddy and the two ran toward each other and commenced a complicated ritual of hand-slaps and finger-wiggles that made Lorinda certain that both were high as drones on manna.

Crowds clustered around the various barbeque and fried chicken and hamburger trucks, while dozens of barely visibly loudspeakers, hidden amidst the immaculate landscaping, enhanced the lively, upbeat mood with the country-and-western stylings of The Saved, the church's house band. Lorinda spied people she knew from high school and couldn't decide whether to say hello and be seen. But she didn't see Emmie.

Finally, the melodious (if pre-recorded) voice of Kendra, wife of Pastor Doug, could be heard announcing, "Service time, y'all," and the crowd made its orderly way through the various entrances, bringing their food and drinks with them. By the time Lorinda, Bob, Rita, and Zeke reached their usual reserved seats, most of the ten-thousand pews (so-called in spite of the fact that they more closely resembled the plush, fake-velvet maroon recliners of a fancy movie theater, complete with cup-holders) were filled.

As she settled in, Lorinda at first wondered if she would, as she often did, end up falling asleep during the sermon. But suddenly her mood brightened. She remembered the promotion, and the career pep talk Mrs. Barker had delivered. What a lovely topic to think about, fantasize about, and use as a distraction from the tedium to come!

The sanctuary was designed more like a regional theater-in-the-round than a traditional church, so that the preacher had full 360-degree access to all those seated around him. The band and the choir occupied a raised platform behind one of the sections of ranked seats. Giant video screens hung from the ceiling. Pastor Doug, in chinos, a white linen shirt, and a navy-blue blazer, all under an off-white Cattleman cowboy hat, stood at the ready behind his trademark swiveling lectern. The Saved (lead singer, guitar, bass, drums, keyboard) brought their entrance music to a close. Pastor Doug held up a Bible as the chattering crowd quieted down into an expectant silence.

"Question," he said. "How many words are there in the Bible?" He looked around as though waiting for a reply. "I'll tell you. Seven-hundred eighty-three thousand, one hundred and thirty-seven." He gave a wry little smile, knowing it would be visible to all via the mammoth television screens. "I'd like to say I counted them myself, but... well, let's just say, thank *Gah*-duh I didn't have to."

As the faithful shared an amused chuckle, Lorinda focused on what she'd probably have to learn in order to step into and master the job of Director of Barkeeping Operations: Bookkeeping, probably; despite what she told her parents, she didn't do any real bookkeeping in her present job. The ordering of—well, everything. Liquor, mixers, glasses, snacks. But she could learn that. She would make it her business to learn that.

"That's a lot of words," the preacher continued. "And there's a lot of good ones in there. Words like 'righteous.' And 'blessed.' And 'holy.' And there's some not-so-nice ones, too. Like 'perdition.' And 'sin.' And 'hypocrites.' But I'll tell you what words aren't in this book." He suddenly slammed the book down onto the lectern with a bang that brought a surprised jolt to many in their seats. "What you don't see are words like 'antibiotic.' And 'steroid.' And 'beta blocker.'" He slowly turned his head from the far left to the far right of his visual field, taking in about half of the assembled. "And you don't see the word 'drug.' Now —"

"Drugs!" A young man across the arena from Lorinda had leapt up as though celebrating a sudden home run or touchdown. *"Yes!"*

Others around the church came to their feet, cheering and shouting and waving to each other as their parents or partners tried to shush them and get them back into their seats. Most were men, but there were a few women, too, all in their twenties. Manna-heads, Lorinda thought. She turned and looked at Zeke. He had the same avid, burning-eyed look as the others, but Bob had his forearm in a tight grip, and her brother remained seated. Suddenly, bursting out of him like a reflexive scream, he shouted, "Man-NUH!" A ragged cheer arose from the others.

Pastor Doug, vexed, snapped directly to the camera, "Put 'em up there." The image on the screens suddenly lurched away from the pastor and focused on one side of the house. It sought, found, and quickly zoomed in to focus on a pair of the shouters, whose faces appeared up top, magnified and in lurid color. The pair saw themselves and went silent in awe.

Lorinda barely noticed. She was thinking about what could follow once she learned all those bar-management tasks and skills. *You could get a bar going from a standing start. You could walk into a PumpJack's that hadn't opened yet, where the paint was still wet, and in a week or two have a functioning bar in operation. That would be so cool! But then what?*

6

In which Lorinda contemplates her future, ignores Pastor Doug, and gets something unexpected from Emmie.

THE PASTOR SAID, "Tommy? Keep shooting. Ed? Round 'em up."

The image of the two shouters froze, shrank to a small box, and slid into the upper left-hand corner of the screen. The video shooter, pivoting with his camera as though dancing with a very skeletal robot, found another screamer and sent her face onto the screen, at which point, Ed in the control room shrank her face and set it alongside the first two. This went on at an impressively rapid clip, the shooter spotting and picking off faces all around the sanctuary like a sniper, until almost all the young people yelling "Drugs!" and "Manna!" had their shouty, frenzied faces captured, frozen, and on display in a checkerboard-like array of still images. Lorinda wondered what the point of this was, but it soon emerged: The shouters all stopped to gaze at and admire themselves, and the hall fell silent.

"Y'all happy now?" the pastor said. "Okay, then. Kindly be seated and I'll continue."

Where, Lorinda wondered, *would she go from there? Specialize in the bar end of the business, or learn to manage the kitchen, too?* Immediately, she knew: Stick to the bar. Chefs and cooks, as she knew only too well, could be tyrannical, picky, petty, and domineering. *Why look for trouble and heartache? Focus on the bar biz, and take it up the ladder... All the way to Dallas!*

Raising fists in triumph, applauding for each other and themselves, the unruly drug fans, one by one, sat down and shut up. Pastor Doug adjusted his hat and continued. "Three-quarter of a million words in the Bible, and not one of them is about viruses or inoculations or vaccines. Not one of them has any blessed thing to do with statins, or blood pressure, or KO-LESS-TER-ALL good, bad, or indifferent!"

He paused for a laugh, and he got one, accompanied around the sanctuary by a flurry of knowing nods and murmured agreement.

"So," he said, and with his trademark panache suddenly swiveled round 180 degrees and addressed those who had hitherto only seen his back. "Let me ask you good people something. If GAH-duh himself did not see fit to talk to us about pharmaceuticals, why in Heaven and on Earth would we let mere men — and women! — tell us which of those chemicals we can and cannot put into our own bodies, and those of our children?" Whether it was a rhetorical question or not, he didn't wait for an answer. Instead, he went on, "Because they went to some fancy school? And read some fancy books? I'll tell you something, my friends. You know what they *didn't* read in those schools? The only book that matters." He seized the Bible and slammed it down again on the lectern. "This one. The Good Book."

Or, Lorinda thought, *become an expert in cocktails! Start a consulting business. Develop a line of cocktails of her own!* She reminded herself that PumpJack's wasn't the only chain of restaurants in the CCSA. There were more upscale places, too. Some with tablecloths! Who knew where all this could lead?

"Now. It's true…" Pastor Doug continued. "We all know someone — in our family, or over in… Austin…" He said the name with the distaste he usually reserved for Sodom and Gomorrah and New York. "… who talks about 'science.' Well. Science, as we all know, is un-Christian. It was thanks to science that we got the atomic bomb, and the COVID epidemics and their wicked vaccinations, and so much else. And, of course, we all know that science is mostly conducted by... well, let's just call them 'the Unsaved.'"

Lorinda figured, What the hell, and started to think about what kind of new car she wanted. *Maybe a Toyota Savior. Granted, it was said they weren't as good as the Toyotas sold in the USA. But they looked the same. And she was sick of driving a North Korean piece of shit she couldn't even pronounce.*

"What I'm saying, my friends, is: Why did we even start this New Country? Why did we campaign for, and insist on, The Split? I'll tell you why, although I'm sure y'all know: It was to restore godliness to the free states of America. Because, when it comes to a showdown between science and GAH-duh... well, I know who I'm betting on, every time. Science without GAH-duh is like a car without a driver. Better get out of its way. And that brings me to our special guest here this morning." Pastor Doug gestured gracefully toward a man in the front row. "Jackson, come on up here."

"That's your boss!" Rita Moon excitedly whispered.

"My boss's boss's boss," Bob Moon whispered back.

A short, bald man in a noticeably elegant charcoal gray suit stood and slowly mounted the four shallow steps to join Pastor Doug at the lectern. He stood beside the pastor and gazed mildly into the middle distance, as though happy to be admired and on display. Either that, or he was uncomfortable commingling with ordinary, church-going people, and was essentially holding his breath until it was over. "This is Jackson Howe," the pastor said. "Some of you know him. He's CEO of Gotfried Lenz Pharmaceuticals. And if you don't know him, you probably know some of the drugs his company has developed and blessed our new country with. Such as — " The pastor shrugged and shook his head. He handed the executive a cordless microphone. "Jackson, you tell 'em the such-as. I can never pronounce those things."

Howe took the mic and said, "Thank you, Pastor Doug. I just want to say, it's great to meet and greet all you good people today. At Gotfried Lenz we've worked hard to develop state-of-the-art pharmaceuticals for any number of medical needs. Things like Zelzah, and Fershterasis. Also Delbasid, Flummox, Luftsid and Estupor. Also — "

"Whoa, Jackson, we get it!" Pastor Doug gently relieved the executive of the mic and said to the crowd, "I brought him up here because he's been a very good friend of this church — and by 'good friend' I mean, he's written us some good checks, big checks. And they always clear!"

Knowing chuckles bubbled around the hall as the two men exchanged a brief comment off-mic. Addressing the crowd, Pastor Doug said, "Now I wanted you good people to meet Jackson, here—and you can talk to him after the service—because he's come to me with an idea that I find very exciting."

To Howe he said, "Thank you, sir." He gestured toward an amply-upholstered armchair several yards away on the stage. "Y'all be seated in the Chair of Honor and I'll take it from here."

Howe waved to the crowd, who responded with appreciative applause as he made his way to the special chair. When the pastor resumed, it was in his trademark declamatory-orator style. "Drugs…" He paused dramatically. "…are a life-saving miracle! Even if they were omitted from the Good Book!"

A few manna-heads yelled, *"Yes!"* and *"Dude!"* but were immediately shushed.

"A life-saving miracle sent by *Gah*-duh," the preacher went on. "Because He loves us and wants us to *thrive*."

This time the shouts were from the older folks. *"Amen!"* "Praise Him!"

"Amen and Praise Him indeed, my friends." The pastor then executed one of the moves for which he was well-known: He spun on a single heel and suddenly addressed those to whom his back had been turned. "But how can we *thrive*... How can we *avail* ourselves of the *miracle* of these *pharmaceutical blessings*... if we have to depend on so-called *doctors* to write us little *permission slips* to *obtain* them?"

This — a rhetorical question with an arguably obscure reference — left the crowd bollixed. Some yelled, *"Yes!"* and others, *"No!"*

The preacher held up his hand. "I agree. And so does Mr. Jackson Howe, who came to me with an idea. 'Doug,' he said. 'I've been thinking about how we can make life-saving pharmaceuticals available to all people, all the time. About how to *help* people. Which is what *Jee*-zuss would have wanted. And I prayed on it. And I think *Gah*-duh may just have shown me the way.'" The pastor paused. "Do y'all want to hear about Mr. Howe's idea?"

Cries of *"Yes!"* arose from around the hall. Lorinda saw her mom wave a fist and shout, "Amen!"

Pastor Doug held up a calming hand. "All right, then. Here it is. He proposes that all drugs be made available *over-the-counter*. You walk into a drug store, you say, 'Give me a bottle of twenty X pills or a tube of Y ointment,' and you get it. *no* prescriptions. *No* mandatory visit to any doctor or... what's the word... oh, yes: *specialist*." He somehow made it sound obscene. "Now, I know some of you have a doctor you *trust*. And that's *fine*. You can talk to him, and get his recommendations and suggestions, no *problemo*. But you all know what's good for yourselves — and for *your children*. So I think — and I think you all think — that what we're talking about here is an idea whose time has come. Now that we're free of the Old Country, let's keep making this a New Country!"

This triggered the loudest applause yet. Even Lorinda joined in, although out of distracted, mechanical politeness. Her thoughts focused on appreciating just how thrilling these career plans were. Mrs. Barker had lit a fuse in Lorinda's soul — a fuse Lorinda had had no idea even existed. It now burned steadily toward a fireworks explosion of accomplishment and advancement she had never even conceived. She had always been adaptable. But now she realized that she felt — and she savored the word — *ambitious*.

Pastor Doug nodded all round, and pointed a finger at Jackson Howe in his seat, followed by a thumb's-up. Then the pastor waved the crowd quiet and resumed.

"Now I've got two things to add before we get on to today's lesson. First is, when I say 'all drugs,' I'm not talking about *all* drugs. I'm not talking about heroin. I'm not talking about crack or cocaine. I'm not talking about ecstasy or fentanyl. And I am sure as heck not talking about contraceptive pills or day-after murdering pills or A-BORT-O-FAY-SHINTS." He paused for more applause, and got it. He nodded, shushed the multitude, and said, "And the second thing is this. It's no secret we got a campaign going on to see who will lead our sacred Confederation for a new term as its Chief Executive Officer. Well, my friends, if you want to see the realization and the implementation of Mr. Jackson Howe's brilliant idea — vouchsafed unto him by *Gah*-duh — then there is only one candidate you can vote for. I am of course talking about Reverend Oliver M. Waldrip — the godliest, whitest man running, the only real Christian capable of leading this Christian nation, and the man I personally am hoping will be our next CEO." Then, with a big, benevolent smile on his face, he did a slow three-sixty rotation on his left heel, taking in every section of the auditorium. His flock knew exactly what was coming: Pastor Doug's trademark signoff. "Now," he grinned, "always remember: We're right and they're wrong, no matter who they are or what they say. Amen!" A thunderous "AMEN!" came back at him. Nodding with satisfaction, he turned his gaze upward, toward the raised platform where the band stood, waiting for their cue. "Cody?"

The Saved, with Cheryl Zink, its sexy lead singer, broke into, "He is Coming and I Am Ready" as the pastor went over to where Jackson Howe was seated. The executive rose and the two men shook hands, after which Pastor Doug escorted Howe over to the steps and ushered him back down toward his seat.

And that, apparently, was the sermon of the day. The pastor encouraged all to sing along, then cued another upbeat, light-rock hymn, and ended with the altar call. With a congregation of ten thousand, a gathering of even ten percent of the faithful at the foot of the stage would have been unruly and absurd. So Pastor Doug called for "an in-place altar call," exhorting anyone and everyone to stand, give free voice to their acceptance of Jesus, and be sanctified by his group benediction.

As usual, this form of worship seemed slightly odd to Lorinda, who had several clear memories of church services in New York State fifteen years earlier, before her family emigrated to the CCSA. She had been seven at the time, but perhaps that fact accounted for her impression of colorless, intimidating solemnity of those Old Country services.

Whatever. It didn't matter. Her parents, now as always, seemed refreshed by the service, and chatted happily as they shuffled among the crowd leaving the sanctuary. Out on the plaza fronting the entrance, a large group of people clustered to meet Jackson Howe, while another flocked around Pastor Doug and Kendra.

Lorinda's father had just said, "So. Ice cream?" when Lorinda heard her name called.

She looked around. There was Emmie, pointedly standing still and not approaching. Emmie waved her over with a look of mischievous excitement, as though bursting to share some red-hot bit of gossip.

"Be right back," Lorinda told her family.

Lorinda had just managed to say, "Ems! What — " when her friend grabbed her hand and essentially dragged her through the crowd, toward one of the broad uprights that supported the portico above the plaza. On the far side of the upright, shielded from Lorinda's family, Emmie said, "Okay. God, I'm glad you came. Here." She withdrew from an inside jacket pocket a small white paper bag, inside of which was a cardboard box. "Take it. And don't let anyone see it. I mean *anyone*, Lor. Put it in your bag right now."

Lorinda did as she was told. "What is it?"

"A pregnancy test," Emmie whispered.

"Pregnancy test?!"

"Shhh."

"Where'd you get it?" whispered Lorinda.

"It doesn't matter. I'm a nurse. Medical things come my way."

"But . . . I don't need this. . . ."

"Honey, you do. Look, if it's negative, you throw it away and that's that. But what if it isn't?" Lorinda rolled her eyes. "You need to listen to me," Emmie said, with an unexpected seriousness. "I can't get into it here in the church parking lot, but you need to take that test."

Lorinda sighed. If she didn't want to contemplate that dire possibility, she was nonetheless grateful to her friend for caring so much, and taking some risk to act on her behalf. "Okay. I'll do it."

"Soon," said Emmie.

"Okay. I promise." She kissed Emmie on the cheek. "Thanks, sweetie."

"You're very welcome."

"Hey," Lorinda said, looking for a way to change the subject. "What did you think of that Jackson guy? And his idea? He's my dad's boss's boss's boss, you know."

"That all drugs should be over-the-counter?" Emmie pursed her lips and shook her head. "It's insane. It's *fucking insane*. But that's who runs this country, right?"

Lorinda had never thought of it that way. "Is it?"

"Believe me, it is. And when people start taking the wrong drugs, or the right drugs at the wrong dosages, or in combination with other drugs that don't mix well, and they end up in the hospital, we're the ones who have to deal with it in the emergency room. Fucking insane. Anyway. Gotta go. See you at the bar tomorrow?"

"Tuesday," said Lorinda. "I'm off Monday. Monday's fun-day."

Emmie gave her an encouraging little smile, and in few seconds was lost in the crowd.

7

In which Lorinda learns something that threatens her big dream.

LORINDA WOKE UP early Monday morning after a rough night during which, when she did manage to sleep, she dreamed about being lost in a forest at night, or forgetting how to make the simplest cocktail, or being so hugely pregnant that she was unable to stand up. After she sent her parents off to work with kisses, she locked herself in her bathroom — her brother was still asleep, but better safe than sorry — picked up the box Emmie had given her, read the instructions and did as she was directed. The ten-minute wait for the results was excruciating, filled with thoughts of losing her position at PumpJack's and being forced to live forever in her parents' house, with no way to afford the childcare that would allow her to have a job.

When the ten minutes were up, she carefully opened the little envelope that contained the piece of shiny cardboard on which the results would appear. The circle in the middle had turned a deep, rusty red.

She gasped. *She was pregnant.* Immediately, one of humanity's more recently evolved survival mechanisms kicked in: denial. She hurried to her bedroom, grabbed her phone, and returned to the bathroom. Emmie picked up after one ring.

"Lor —"

"It says I'm pregnant," Lorinda said. "Which is impossible."

Emmie sighed. "I was afraid of that."

"But... these tests can't even work this fast. It takes weeks —"

"Not this one," said Emmie. "It's brand new. Uses a new hormone. And it's made in — "

"But I told you!" Lorinda blurted, as though arguing on the phone would help. "We used . . . " — she lowered her voice even behind the closed door — " . . . a condom!"

"You said it was white? Did it have a gold star on it?"

"Ems . . . Jesus Christ, I don't know. I wasn't exactly looking carefully."

"Did you see the little wrapper? Was it — "

"Red? Yeah. It had 'Freedom' printed on it. Look, couldn't this just be a . . . whatchmacallit?"

"A false positive? No. That test is state-of-the-art. Listen . . . " Emmie took a breath. "Those Freedom condoms, they're made by the government — "

"What government?"

"Your government. Our government. The CCSA. It has some fake company name on it but it's the government."

"So?"

"They've been making them for a couple of years," Emmie said patiently. "And for a couple of years there have been reports from all over the CCSA that women using that condom are getting pregnant."

Lorinda groped for a reply. "How . . . how . . . "

"A journal article I read says that a third of them, maybe more, have little pinholes in them."

"*What?*"

"It's deliberate. They're made to fail. And PS, that journal story was taken down three days after it went online. And the government denies everything. Of course."

Lorinda fell silent.

"Lor — ?"

Lorinda felt as if someone had hit her on the head with a shovel. She tried to wrestle her brain back into focus by staring at the pregnancy-test box on the counter next to the sink. "How can you be so sure this test works?"

"Look at the bottom of the box," Emmie said.

Lorinda looked, but in her growing anger and disbelief she could hardly read the words. "What am I seeing?"

"You're seeing 'Made in USA.' It's in the small print down at the bottom."

"So?"

"It means the thing is real, Lor. Those condoms are made-in-CCSA crap. The test is real. Brand new. USA. State of the art. I'm sorry, honey."

Lorinda's hands were shaking. She thought she was going to drop the phone. "Yeah. Look, Em, thanks. I gotta think..."

She ended the call, then screamed louder than she knew she could scream: "Fuck those fuckers!" Scooping up the test box with her phone hand, she opened the bathroom door, stomped to her room, and slammed her door so hard that the framed picture of herself at age ten in her ceremonial baptism gown, accompanied by Pastor Doug and her parents grinning down at her, fell off the wall and crashed. Shards of glass flew across the floor. Again she screamed: "Fuck!"

"What's going on?" Zeke groggily called from his room.

"Nothing!" she yelled. "Go back to sleep!"

She knelt down to deal with the mess and instantly cut her finger on a piece of glass she didn't even see. Her eyes filled with tears. She had come so far! In envisioning her future life of excitement and possibility, she had dared to fantasize things that a year ago — a year?

Two weeks ago! — would have been unimaginable. And those fantasies hadn't been just some romantic teenage daydreams. She had *earned* them. And she was ready, she was *eager,* to keep earning them, and to make them come true.

But now all that was over.

8 *In which our heroine freaks out.*

"FUCK!" SHE YELLED again as she realized she was bleeding all over the picture. She found an old pair of socks in a drawer, wrapped one of them around her bleeding finger, and sunk onto the bed.

How can they do this to me? she thought. Oh, she could probably proceed with the training for her new managerial post, and even put a month or two into the job. But soon enough, her pregnancy would be noticeable, and there would be no way anyone — not at the PumpJack's where she worked, and certainly no one farther up the corporate ladder — would want to groom her for responsibilities she would be unable to fulfill. The demands of late-stage pregnancy (not to mention motherhood itself) would act as a lead weight, tethering her ballooning ambitions to the earth. She'd have to take weeks, if not months, off, and there'd be no assurance she'd even be welcomed back to PumpJack's if, somehow, she could find childcare.

All of this was immediately self-evident to Lorinda because she was a loyal, educated citizen of the Confederation of Conservative States of America. She appreciated — indeed, she treasured — her country's dedication to freedom, and to liberty, and to self-determination and self-sufficiency. Those virtues were what separated the CCSA from the socialist, nanny-state USA; that's why The Split happened in the first place. Lorinda had been taught this history, both at home and in school, from the day her family arrived in Texas, fifteen years before.

It wasn't that conservatives believed people shouldn't help each other, as she'd been taught foolish liberals claimed. It was, rather, that helping others was a private thing, a church thing, a family thing. When you tried to institutionalize help, and assign it to the government, something always went wrong — starting, of course, with the theft-like imposition of taxes to fund that overreaching, meddling government. And so, in exchange for the blessing of living in this paradise of individualism, her country asked only two things of its adult citizens over the age of 16: First, that each one carry a firearm, in order to protect themselves, their loved ones, and their property from every other person carrying a firearm to protect themselves, their loved ones, and their property. And second, that everyone be "pro-life."

This, she had been taught in eleventh grade social studies class, did not mean an unquestioning sentimental reverence for all life forms, or even all human beings. After all, people created their own fate, for better or for worse, and usually deserved what they got.

No, being pro-life meant respecting, revering, and protecting womb-bound zygotes and fetuses. Whether or not they were actually "people" — whether or not they were actually conscious — who could say? But one thing could be said: They were souls, bundles of pure innocence sent by God Who, for whatever reason, was unable to protect them Himself. Once they were born, of course, they were subject, like all people, to the unquestionable rigors and justice of the marketplace, and one hoped they were assisted in that struggle by their parents, relatives, and kindly strangers. But up to the moment of birth, it was every citizen's duty to protect them. *Life*, in the CCSA, began at conception and ended at birth. Then began *living*, which was an entirely different matter.

This, Lorinda knew, was not only what Jesus believed (and the CCSA was nothing if not a Christian nation), it was also a fine way to Maintain the Population. This was the sense of obligation that came crashing down onto Lorinda like a giant wave, washing away the dream of her career.

"Fuck that shit!" she screamed.

"Fuck that shit!" Zeke yelled from his bed.

"Shut the fuck up!" Lorinda yelled back.

Still in her schlumpy sleep clothes, sniffling, puffy-eyed, a bed-headed mess, she looked down. On the floor, amid the glass shards, was the box the pregnancy test had come in. She picked it up and looked at the back. In bold blue letters it said "Proudly Made in Philadelphia, USA." The package was nice. Shiny cardboard, good colors, interesting graphics, including a few simple, cartoony pictures that explained how to administer and read the test. She flipped to a side panel, where she saw a similarly cartoony figure — a "girl" in a triangular "skirt" — dropping the box into a bin with a triangle composed of arrows, and the caption "PLEASE DISPOSE OF THOUGHTFULLY."

Staring at it, she thought: That's weird.

First, what on earth did it mean? Be kind and polite when tossing this thing in the trash? She had never seen any product from the CCSA display that kind of message. "Please be nice"? And what did that triangle-of-arrows mean? Then she read the fine print: "Remember, our beautiful Planet Earth belongs to all of us. We trust that you will do your part to protect and preserve its beauty. This package and its contents are Universally Recyclable and may be deposited in Group 1, Group 2, or Group 3 Recycling Bins. We thank you and the Earth thanks you." The word "recycling" rang a bell, but she might not have heard it since before her family immigrated to Perfecton.

Lorinda's eyes filled with a different kind of tears. She turned again to the package back and studied it. She knew that Philadelphia was one of the major cities of the USA, not too far from where she grew up. And now here, in her hand, was an artifact from that faraway place, that place derided and criticized and dismissed and warned against by every teacher she had ever had since her parents brought her here. It was like a meteorite from another planet — a planet where, she had been taught, everyone was both lazy and hysterical, brashly un-Christian and perennially fearful, where the men were all gay and the women were all lesbians, where "African-Americans" routinely committed crimes or rioted over nothing, and whites were too cowardly or too absurdly guilty to stop them.

Suddenly it didn't add up.

She couldn't square the notion of a sick, weak, collapsing society with this useful, pleasant, friendly object (no doubt more trustworthy than its CCSA counterpart, if there even was a CCSA counterpart), considerately asking its users to be considerate. For the first time she thought that maybe she had been wrong about the USA.

It took exactly one second for her to have the next thought: What else could she be wrong about?

And the answer to that was obvious. If Emmie was right — and the evidence pointed to exactly that — then Lorinda had been wrong in her thinking about her country and her government. She had come of age accepting the stern but properly conservative principle that the CCSA was not responsible for her *welfare*, but it was — and it boasted about this — responsible for protecting her *freedom*.

But it had lied. Her freedom was now completely and absolutely compromised—destroyed!—by this pregnancy. And this pregnancy was not her fault. (It was not even the fault of that jerk Brad.) It had come about through deception and trickery on the part of the CCSA itself.

This instantly gave rise to another question: Why should she remain loyal to a system that had betrayed her in such a fashion? Why should she be forced to have a baby for the benefit of a system that deliberately subverted her ability to live as she chose? Individual liberty was the one thing everyone bragged about! And urged everyone else to be thankful for! It was, supposedly, what the country was invented for and founded upon. It was what made the CCSA superior to the Old Country.

But here was that very nation deliberately derailing the lives of women (and a lot of men) just to manufacture more *bodies*.

She thought about tearing the box into tiny pieces, to prevent anyone in her family from finding it, but decided to wait a while: It was too nice. Anyway, she ought to show the result to Emmie for confirmation. She found the piece of cardboard with the test result, slipped it into the little box, slid the box under her pillow, picked up her phone from the floor, and hit Emmie with a message: "See U soon?"

Emmie got back immediately: "You OK?"

Lorinda: "Just need to see U."

Emmie: "Bar tomorrow? I have stuff today."

Lorinda: "Sure. Early if U can."

Emmie: "OK. Seeya."

Then Lorinda carefully crossed her room, avoiding the broken glass, and went down to the kitchen to get the broom and dustpan.

9 *In which our heroine says the forbidden word as an unwelcome visitor arrives.*

TUESDAY AFTERNOON. LORINDA lined up the bottles and glassware at PumpJack's just the way she liked it. Then she went over the shelves and racks again in an effort to keep busy. When she saw Emmie approaching in the mirror she gave a fake, forced expression of delighted surprise. "Hey, stranger," she said, turning around, as her friend settled on the corner stool.

She leaned over the bar as if to give Emmie a peck on the cheek but instead whispered, "Thanks for coming. Don't say anything: the cameras."

"How many cameras?" Emmie whispered back, trying to look like she was just exchanging a warm hello.

"Two," whispered Lorinda, rolling her eyes first to the left, then to the right, to indicate their locations. Like every CCSA citizen over the age of seven or eight, Emmie was good at tracking down the nearest cameras and quickly picked them out over the back bar. "I can disconnect them," Lorinda said. "Hold on a second," She grabbed a cloth from under the bar and, as if looking for a glass to polish, turned to the back bar and bent down below what she knew was the sightline of the cameras. She quickly found the socket, unplugged the cameras and, as an afterthought, grabbed a bourbon bottle from a higher shelf and placed it on its side on top of the unplugged wire before turning back to Emmie.

"Are you sure about that condom thing?"

Emmie nodded. "Pretty sure. I mean I read it in *RN*. Which is a pretty dependable journal. They began to get all these reports of women becoming pregnant when they really shouldn't have been, so they had their contributors all over the country buy a bunch of condoms and examine them. Like I said — not all of them were ... fucked with. But a lot of them were. They came that way right out of the box."

"Unbelievable." Lorinda looked away. Had she really made this decision? She had. Turning back to Emmie, she said as softly as possible to still be heard, "I can't have a baby now. I just can't. It can't happen. Maybe some time, but not now." She shuddered with disgust. "I can't believe our fucking government is sabotaging condoms to" — making air quotes — "maintain the population."

"Plus," Emmie said. "I mean, it's none of my business. But I gather you're not crazy about having a baby with Brad."

"Oh, God!"

"Although," Emmie said. "It's nice to know he's got the goods. And so do you."

"Stop!"

They both laughed. It came as a relief. Lorinda set about mixing Emmie's usual red drink. As she set it on the bar, she leaned toward her friend and said, again quietly, "So I need to do something. You were telling me about those pills?"

"Yeah," said Emmie. She sighed. "Well, that's a problem. It's like with the condoms. Our lovely government — don't tell anyone I said this — they're still putting out fake pills. Placebos. They don't do anything. And they look exactly like the real ones. They're packaged the same. It's really fucked up, but there's nothing we can do about it. Every now and then some good ones show up, but if you need ..." she whispered the next two words " ... *a termination,* then you can't wait for something that might never turn up. I mean, I can tell you if I hear of anything. Medical people are usually the first to know. But don't hold your breath."

Emmie took a thoughtful sip of her drink, then patted Lorinda's hand. "There are things you can do. I can help. I may know someone. And it's very early. You have plenty of time."

"I need..." Lorinda couldn't quite get through the sentence. Teachers in the CCSA, starting in kindergarten, were supposed to put a great deal of effort into insisting to their students that there was one thing that was the worst thing a woman could do. In fact, the latest standardized national curriculum explicitly contained lessons in every subject — from English to social studies to home economics to math — in which students were to be instructed that it was the worst word in the English language. Many teachers had been fired, and worse, for not hammering these lessons hard enough. "What I need," Lorinda said with effort, "is an *abortion*."

Emmie winced but nodded. "It's not impossible," she said softly.

Lorinda, looking past her, said, "Oh, shit."

Emmie turned to see why Lorinda was frowning. "Oh, hi, Brad," said Emmie. "Look who's here, Lorinda."

10 *In which two unpleasant men perturb our heroine.*

LOOKING GRIM, BRAD approached the bar. "Ladies! Mind if I sit?"

Emmie shrugged as Brad sat next to her.

"What can I get you?" said Lorinda, coolly. She wasn't thrilled to see him and didn't particularly care if he knew it.

"How about a Reb," said Brad. As Lorinda fetched the beer, he glanced at Emmie and decided he had no choice but to say what he had to say in front of her. "I've been trying to get you," he said as Lorinda set down his bottle. "You never pick up, you never call back. You're supposed to be mine now."

"Yours? Like you own me? Because we — " Lorinda lowered her voice. "Because we fucked once?"

Brad winced. It was strong language, especially from a girl.

Lorinda quickly calmed herself down. "Look, Brad," she said, deciding she might as well unload now rather than postpone the inevitable. "I've been busy. And, honestly, I don't really think we have anything to talk about." She picked up a cocktail shaker, took off the lid, and looked inside as if searching for manufacturing flaws.

"But," Brad started, "we..."

"We had a little fun," Lorinda interrupted, putting the lid back on the shaker and setting it down on the back bar. "Maybe someday, you know... but, now's not the time."

Brad looked stricken. He tried to say something, gave up, slid off the stool, took out his wallet, found a fifty-dollar bill, and slapped it down on the counter. "Keep the change," he said as he strode away.

"What change?" said Lorinda under her breath.

"That went well," Emmie laughed.

"That's a free Johnny Reb if you want it," said Lorinda, dryly. "He didn't touch it."

After Emmie left, Lorinda poured Brad's beer down the drain and went back to tidying the place up for the evening rush. She was facing the back bar, polishing a glass and brooding about her dilemma, when her thoughts were interrupted by a heavy knock on the bar. She glanced at the mirror and saw a tall, paunchy, middle-aged man in a government-issue white shirt and black suit jacket, holding at arm's length a badge in its wallet. It stopped her cold.

"Bureau of Investigations, Agent Morrow," he snarled. "Why did you turn off your cameras?"

Lorinda had heard about this sort of thing. Thinking quickly, she turned around and said, "What cameras?"

"Don't get cute with me, honey. How do I get back there?"

"Customers aren't allowed behind the bar," said Lorinda.

"I'm not a customer. I'm the government."

"Okay. Just come around this way."

Despite his height and his paunch, Agent Morrow was surprisingly agile. He slipped easily through the cutout under the bar, produced a small government-issue com-pad from an inner pocket of his jacket, tapped the screen, stared at it for a couple of seconds, and went straight to where it said the cameras were supposed to be plugged in. He bent over, saw that his information was wrong, then popped right back up. "Goddammit," he spat. "Technician faggots can't be bothered to do their job." Bending low, he crept along the back bar until he found what he was looking for. "Well, lookee here," he grinned momentarily, thrusting the bourbon bottle she'd tipped over toward Lorinda before setting it on another shelf, then waving the cord at her before plugging it back in. "You don't store bottles next to where cameras are plugged in. Don't they teach you people anything?"

"I'm sorry, sir. I thought I heard something fall over earlier but I didn't know where the sound came from. I didn't even know there were cameras here."

"There aren't any cameras here," he said as he plugged the cameras back in. He then made his way to the cutout, ducked gracefully under the bar, and turned to glare at Lorinda. "It better not happen again."

"Okay, it won't," she said as he hurried away. It occurred to her that putting the bourbon bottle over the wires may have been the smartest thing she did all week.

When she left PumpJack's later that evening, she was preoccupied with memories of that rusty-red bullseye on the pregnancy test, and her conversation with Emmie, and that weird little encounter with Brad, and that really weird little encounter with the government guy, and, looming over it all, her promotion. Her career.

She didn't notice the shiny black Zhiguli pickup truck that followed her at a discreet distance all the way home from the bar, peeling off after she parked in front of her house.

11 *In which our heroine seems to have found a solution to her problem.*

LORINDA KNEW ENOUGH not to set off an alarm at a government surveillance agency by searching online for "pregnancy termination" or "abortion" or "abortion drug" or "abortifacient." Although even if she'd decided to live dangerously and search those terms, there was no knowing what could pop up: Just as they did with radio and television broadcasts from the USA, and however much the government denied it, everyone knew — or assumed — that the authorities limited the reach of internet searches, and kept a tight rein on content it deemed "acceptable." Sometimes, of course, you got lucky, and a search might yield as many as 10,000 results. But that only happened with approved topics, such as "rights" or "miracles" or "Trump." Best not to tempt fate by searching radioactive subjects like "termination."

Which didn't mean she wasn't becoming obsessed with solving her problem. Over the next two weeks, her inability to envision a realistic plan sent her into an increasingly disturbing mental roundelay of desperate remedies she'd heard about (in cautionary public health talk shows) or read about (in lurid fiction) or imagined: violent exercise, staircase, bleach, wire hanger, mugwort, caffeine pills, parsley, vitamin C, ladder, staircase... bleach, wire hanger...

In the meantime, Emmie had started insinuating herself into the daily routine of a doctor she occasionally worked with, Dr. Henry Holman. He was the oldest doctor in the hospital, the head of OB/GYN at Perfecton General, and rumored to be a liberal originally from someplace in the USA. As far as Emmie could tell, he enjoyed speaking with her. Sometimes she even imagined he was flirting with her, despite being older than her parents.

She had been wondering how to discreetly arrange a tête-a-tête with him when she suddenly found herself assigned to assist him in a routine C-section. As they were wrapping up, it was simply a matter of saying, "Hey, can we have lunch tomorrow? I have something I need to ask you. It's . . . kind of private."

He agreed immediately.

And now there he was, alone at a table at the far end of the cafeteria, in a corner by the windows, the day's special ("Tex-Mex Chipped Beef") plated before him on a tray. He was short and stocky, with a white fringe of hair outlining a bald pate. He wore the usual white lab coat over a white shirt and dark blue tie. It was a little early for lunch and the place was nearly empty. Toting the sandwich she'd brought from home, Emmie grabbed a can of soda and a coffee and headed for his table. He didn't look up until she was a few steps away, then smiled and gestured for her to have a seat.

"I hope you don't mind meeting at this time," said Dr. Holman, softly. "I've made the assumption that we'll want some privacy. We'll talk in low voices and smile a lot. I picked this table because it's the farthest from the cameras and microphones, but you never know."

"Okay," said Emmie, smiling in a way that she hoped didn't seem too fake.

"I'm seventy-three years old," said the doctor. "I never thought, when I was in med school, that one day I'd want to avoid... surveillance in a hospital cafeteria. I would have retired already, but it's not so easy these days."

"The doctor shortage," said Emmie with an inappropriately bright smile.

"That's right. In any case, I'm a dinosaur here. All the younger staff seem used to the cameras and mics." He laughed. Emmie wasn't sure if the laugh was real or for the cameras. "I got into my specialty because — I know this will sound naïve at best — I wanted to help people. I wanted to help women. And their babies. Long before The Split I was recruited to run OB/GYN at the Sealy in Galveston — "

"Back when there was a Galveston," said Emmie, trying but failing to look upbeat.

He nodded. "This was before it was underwater," said Dr. Holman. "Obviously. Before that I was working in Boston. Galveston was a great opportunity, I thought. And it was, for a while. Then the laws changed. No more... procedures for women who needed them. Then Hurricane Claude and no more Galveston. Then they moved me to Austin. Then came The Split." Dr. Holman forked a bite of chipped beef into his mouth and tried to look like he was enjoying it. "Then they moved me here to establish the department. Which I did."

"It's a great department," said Emmie, eagerly.

"Well," said the doctor, "it's not bad considering what we've had to work with. You wouldn't think it was so great if you'd seen the department at Brigham & Women's in Boston." He smiled. "But enough about me. You said you wanted to ask me something?"

Emmie realized she hadn't had a single bite of her lunch. Wondering if that looked suspicious, she raised the sandwich to her mouth and took a healthy chomp, then washed it down with a bracing slug of NoLa Cola. She had rehearsed obsessively what she was about to say, but now her mind was entirely empty. "Okay, Doctor Holman —"

"Please. Henry."

"— Henry, I, um, know someone... who knows someone who, um —"

"Finds herself in a certain state?"

Emmie stopped dead. The man was a mind-reader. "Yes!" she whispered, eyes wide. "How —"

He waved away her amazement. "It was an easy guess. And if I had been wrong, you'd correct me. But..." He scrutinized her closely. Gone was the crinkly-eyed amusement. Now he looked like a tired, wary old man.

"But what?"

"Can I trust you, Emily?"

She nodded solemnly.

He seemed to debate something within himself for a moment. Finally, he sighed. "All right. I have to say this carefully."

"I understand," said Emmie.

"Women have the same... issues they've always had. And it's much harder now for them to deal with some of those issues. They can end up in prison, along with the doctors who are just trying to help them live their lives."

"I know. And —"

"Oh, but wait." He contrived an expression of naughty mischief, as though telling her a dirty joke. "Are we talking about you?"

Her laugh wasn't all that fake. "Uh, no."

"Okay. Look," said the doctor, having another taste of his lunch and a sip of his bottled water, "I'm not going to be here for much longer.

As far as I know I'm the only one here who is..." He stopped to think about how to phrase it. "Who is capable of directing a woman to someone who can help her," he said. "Sometimes, medical ethics, and just plain compassion, may conflict with the law. Do you agree?" He leaned back and, in a sudden weird shift she realized was for show, chuckled theatrically.

Emmie tried to laugh back, but her emotions were moving too fast. This whole exchange was leaving her relieved, and excited, but also anxious and a little paranoid. Of course, no one had actually said anything bad, and he seemed trustworthy. So she figured, "Fuck it," and said, "As a matter of fact, my friend... my friend's friend may need to find... something that isn't legal, and that many people think is unethical, but that I think would, um, be very important to her physical and mental health."

The doctor smiled at her, had another bite of his lunch, chewed it thoughtfully, then hit the table and chuckled as if he'd just thought of a good joke. "Then you know what I'm saying. Women need options they can't get here in Perfecton. Or in most of this..." — he almost spat the word — "country."

"Yes," said Emmie. "It's difficult."

"It's beyond difficult. Before I retire I need to know that women here won't be trapped. At the mercy of these barbarian... pious... *hucksters.*"

Emmie was suddenly worried that the doctor was getting carried away. His voice was rising, he was gesturing broadly, he was no longer smiling. To break the spell, she leaned back and laughed, and then laughed some more. Dr. Holman hesitated for a moment, then joined her.

"Thank you," he said as his laughter subsided. "I'm passionate about this. It's hard to keep it bottled up."

"I agree with you," said Emmie. "I'm afraid. But I agree."

"I'm going to give you the name of a contact, a doctor in Austin. A former colleague of mine," he said softly. "As far as I know there's not a single doc between here and there who can provide…help." He directed his eyes to the table. She followed his gaze and saw, next to her sandwich, a tattered business card. When he'd dropped it there she didn't know; it was a sort of magic trick, a sleight of hand. She looked back at him. "You'll be very careful with that, won't you?"

"Of course," she said, forcing a big camera-ready smile.

"I'm going to miss this place," he said. "You…my other colleagues… Tell you what I won't miss, though." He looked down and frowned at his plate. "This food."

As Lorinda finished her booze inventory that afternoon, a message from Emmie popped up: "Hey! Wanna go for a little drive after work tonight? I'm on a double shift."

"Sure," Lorinda responded immediately. "I come straight to the hospital?"

"Right. See U then."

It was a tiring evening for Lorinda. None of her favorite regulars, lots of weird drink orders, some guy complaining about her "piss-poor pour." She stopped at the parking-lot exit and thought about which way she wanted to drive to the hospital. She looked down the street to the right, then to the left, as if that would help her decide. Aside from a shiny black Zhiguli pickup truck parked on the left, the street was deserted. She headed right.

Although it was a dark night and the brown haze was particularly thick, as soon as she turned into the hospital parking lot Lorinda spotted Emmie, in her dark green scrubs, standing outside the main entrance.

"Take you home?" she asked as Emmie closed the Ryonbong's flimsy passenger door.

"I have my car here. Let's just drive around for a while."

"You got it," said Lorinda, heading back out of the parking lot. "What's going on?"

"I've been hanging out a little with this old doctor, Dr.... I won't say his name. You don't need to know his name. Anyway, they say he's, like, a liberal from up north, the USA. Been here forever, head of OB/GYN."

"And?" said Lorinda eagerly, turning out of the parking lot. "Does he... you know?"

"Him? No way. Last time a doctor performed a termination in Perfecton the whole town knew about it in a few days," Emmie said. "They both went to jail, the doc and the woman. And the laws are stricter now."

"Yeah, I remember that."

"Anyway," said Emmie. "This doctor. He gave me the name of someone who does that procedure. An old colleague of his. In Austin."

"Austin! That's really far."

"Yeah," said Emmie, "but think about it. Big city, lots of people, people don't know each other. It's not like Perfecton. Here's her business card." She dropped the card on the seat next to her.

"You're my hero, Emmie. Thank you," said Lorinda. Then she shuddered.

"What?"

"I've been thinking about falling down a flight of stairs. Or off a ladder. Drinking poison. Playing football. Doing gymnastics. I can't have a baby now, Ems." Then, glancing at her rearview mirror and squinting through the haze, "That's weird," she said. "I think the same truck was parked down the street when I left PumpJack's. What are the odds?"

"There are a lot of trucks around here," said Emmie.

"Hang on," said Lorinda, making a sudden turn into a driveway, backing out, and heading rapidly in the direction from which they'd just come, toward the pickup. The truck, now only ten or twelve car-lengths away, responded by doing the same thing, speeding off ahead of them and squealing down the first side street. By the time they reached the street, all they could see was a cloud of black smoke hovering in the fetid air.

12 *In which that black truck follows our heroine all the way to Austin.*

IF SHE WAS going to turn around and head back home, better to do it sooner rather than later.

Before she'd even crossed the border out of Perfecton, Lorinda reviewed the series of thoughts that had led her into her car at such an ungodly hour. The starting point in her logic: She figured she'd have to make a face-to-face appointment with this doctor and come back another time for the procedure. Contacting her by phone, for this sort of thing, was out of the question. There was no telling who could be listening in, either from the hospital or the government. Or both.

Which meant two round-trips to Austin. It was a ton of driving, yes, especially in her crappy old Ryonbong DragonFire, but there was really no other way. Even when everything is legal and above-board, you don't just walk into a hospital and get what you need. And this was anything but. She'd decided it would be best to arrive first thing in the morning in case she had to wait around to see the doctor, make an appointment, fill out forms, whatever. To avoid missing a day's pay, she left on a Sunday night — Monday morning, really, at 3 a.m. — so as to arrive first thing Monday, her day off at PumpJack's. Leaving at that hour also meant she wouldn't run into her parents and have to come up with a lie to explain where she was going and what she intended to do there. Yes, she concluded, this was probably the best way to do what she needed to do.

Each of the few times she'd driven long distances in Texas she was amazed at how big the state was. The drive from Perfecton to Austin was going to take five hours — maybe more, at Ryonbong speeds. And Austin wasn't anywhere near the eastern border, where Texas meets Louisiana. That old feeling of Lone Star pride snuck up on her. *We're so big. We're so great. Don't Mess With Texas. Remember the Alamo.*

But something was different. For the first time these yay-Texas, boosterish feelings made her uncomfortable. Which was strange. Why, she wondered, would she question herself about a little good old Texas chauvinism? It was something she shared with literally everybody she had ever met since the age of seven: that quiet — and sometimes noisy — conviction that, as Texans, they were . . . just *better* than people from the other states of the CCSA. Of course this sort of friendly competitiveness was encouraged at every level of the New Country's society, and the citizens of every state thought that *they* were somehow superior to those of every other state. "Our national character," Lorinda's eleventh grade history teacher had once said, "Is equal parts Revolutionary War, the War of Northern Aggression, medieval chivalry, and football." Then she had added, "Of course, everybody thinks they're superior to everybody else. Our secret here in Texas is, we *know* we are." The class had burst into cheers. And who could deny it? Texans were louder, bigger, sexier, funnier, braver, and just all-around more magnificent than —

Lorinda gave a little derisive snort and pressed hard on the gas pedal, which didn't really make the car go faster but it did help her escape those old thoughts. For the first time, the adjectives failed her, and the inner pep talk felt desperate and hollow. She remembered where she was and what she was doing, driving with the grim determination of a jailbreak fugitive or a refugee, toward what she hoped was the solution to a problem foisted on her by the deception and betrayal of the very society she'd been so proud of, and whose authority was, she had begun to realize, dead set on keeping women like herself in their place.

It was a new feeling, slightly scary but exciting, to be thinking about things like this. The only person she'd ever known who seemed to think along these same lines was Emmie. Lorinda wondered if Emmie had always thought this way, but was too scared to talk about it even to her closest friend — until that closest friend's recent indiscretion with Brad had caused Emmie to throw caution to the wind and open up. In any case, it was good to have something complicated and absorbing to think about at the outset of a long, boring drive with nothing to listen to but the official CCSA radio station and the occasional unwelcome blast of a billboard's audio. Speaking of which, when the air was clear enough to see through, there was nothing to look at in the flat landscape of farmland and pasture except those lurid electronic billboards.

These days they were mainly showing ads for the two candidates for the nation's Chief Executive Officership, in heavy rotation with the usual commercial fodder. Lorinda passed one displaying the grinning-bullfrog face of the incumbent, Ezra Ferrell McWeeny, over the blinking caption: I'M MORE RELIGIOUS THAN HIM — AND NOT INSANE! His booming voice filled the DragonFire's cabin, and there was nothing Lorinda could do about it: "Friends, so-called Reverend Waldrip says God speaks to him. But how does he know it's God? What if it's Satan? Meanwhile, I'm the one who knows how to run a business. And that's what government is, the Business of the Common Good."

A little farther down the road she came to an ad for his rival. The polished, silver-haired, expensively suited Oliver M. Waldrip was famously the more aggressively fundamentalist of the two, and proved it with his grim, God-sees-you visage side by side with a likeness of Jesus Himself—white, gaunt, bearded, vaguely troubled-looking—above the no-nonsense message: WOMEN DIDN'T VOTE IN JESUS'S TIME. LET'S GET BACK TO THAT BEFORE HE RETURNS. "We are a Christian nation." he yelled in Lorinda's ear. "Mr. McWeeny can scream all he wants to about 'defaults' and 'fiscal difficulties,' but when Jesus returns, He's going to take note about who voted for His representative here on Earth, and who didn't. Don't go to Hell. Vote Waldrip!"

Citing (and showing) Christ on a billboard like this was the opposite of anomalous. Everybody did it, everywhere, for everything. This was especially true in rural areas of the CCSA, such as the one Lorinda was now crossing. Some were ads for specific churches, essentially promising that the Prince of Peace would be making a personal appearance one day soon. But others advertised services as mundane as personal injury lawyers (e.g., the robed Christ, with a jaunty thumb's up and the slogan, ED FABER! BECAUSE THERE'S ONLY ONE GUY WHO WORKS HARDER FOR YOUR SALVATION!) or real estate agents (Kelly Tillis, a petite blonde in demure business suit and prom-queen hair, with her arm around the tall, dark, and handsome Savior and the message, BEFORE YOU GET YOUR LITTLE SLICE OF HEAVEN UP THERE, GET ONE DOWN HERE). And why not? Jesus, in the CCSA, was a cross between a founding father and a beloved pop star—and, best of all, you could get "His" endorsement for whatever goods or services you wanted to promote, without having to pay a thing.

Lorinda tried her best to ignore the ads, which wasn't so easy when they came right into your car. What she did ignore was the black Zhiguli pickup truck that occasionally crept up close enough for her to see in the rearview mirror. So lost in thought was she that she didn't even notice when it followed her into a rest-area gas station. (Her Ryonbong, though small and slow, always surprised her in its thirst for fuel. When paying she suppressed another spike of CCSA chauvinism: Without the nation's lavish petroleum subsidies, that tankful would probably have cost her the better part of a week's salary.)

And then, after hours of what, to Lorinda, was bleak nothingness punctuated by roaring billboards, the Austin skyline appeared beyond her windshield: its sail-shaped apartment high-rises and stacked-boxes-off-kilter Jenga condo towers, its abandoned tech towers (Salesforce, PayPal, Microsoft, Apple, Google, Meta-Facebook-YouTube, Adobe, Intel, Cisco, Tesla and the rest, electricity turned off, windows broken, signs askew), and then, like a frowzy governess chaperoning a gang of crazy kids, its Italian Renaissance Revival-style Texas state capitol building. This, in turn, was overshadowed — menaced, really — by the newest structure: the national capitol of the Confederation of Conservative States of America.

Texas had not been subtle in throwing its weight around to claim the New Country's capital. Once Austin was awarded the title, the Texas government commissioned a contest to design a magnificent structure to house the new bicameral legislature. Fairly quickly, however, the essential contradictions of the nation's fundamental principles ignited controversy. The constraints of "conservatism" and "tradition" clashed with the opportunities inherent in "freedom." The resulting edifice was nothing so much as a traditional super-tall rectangular compromise with, as its only design element, parallel vertical ribs designed to accentuate its height. Early on, some said it must have been built from the blueprints of New York City's martyred World Trade Center towers, but they were quickly accused of being traitors and were never heard from again.

It was about 8:30 — on what would have been a bright, sunny morning if not for the greenish haze in the air — when Brad, from behind the wheel of his shiny black Zhiguli pickup truck, watched Lorinda pull into the parking lot of the Cheryl B. and Oliver M. Waldrip Pavilion of the UT Austin Health Center. She found a spot not far from the building's entrance. Brad watched her park as he slowly navigated to within a few rows of her rusty Ryonbong and stopped between a lamp post and another Zhiguli truck, this one in matte green. Hunkering down, he managed to spy Lorinda get out of her car, lock the door, and start walking.

The building had a big sign on its portico reading GUNSHOT WOUND WING. Just next to it, with no irony stated or implied, stood an image of the national "crossed guns" flag. Brad wondered why she was going there, of all places. Considering the distance she'd just driven — and in the middle of the night — she walked vigorously, with excellent posture. So she obviously hadn't been shot by a gun. In fact, he thought, she looked really good. Maybe, he thought, she was there to visit a friend or a relative. Everybody either knew, or was, somebody who had suffered a gunshot wound or two. In fact, he thought, the only weird thing about her arrival here now was the lack of a line of customers waiting to get inside.

As she disappeared into the tunnel of the entryway, he got out of his truck, stretched, yawned, got back in, and immediately nodded off.

13 *In which Lorinda lashes out.*

LORINDA HESITATED BEFORE entering the hospital. The reception counter was about twenty feet behind the glass doors, and she could see three women back there answering phones and speaking to people across the counter. She glanced at the business card Emmie had given her even though she already knew what it said: Dr. Suzanne Fields, Rm. 3042. Waiting until all three receptionists were busy, she took a sharp breath and entered briskly. Once inside she saw a sign, WOMENS HEALTH THIRD FLOOR, and scooted down the corridor. An elevator door creaked open just as she arrived. She stepped in and pressed 3.

Stepping out of the elevator onto the third floor, she was hit by the noxious aroma of vomit, ammonia, and something unidentifiable and obviously toxic that caused Lorinda to cover her mouth and hold her breath. Two eleven-year-old kids, a boy and a girl, in too-big mint-green scrubs, were desultorily pushing mops around a nasty-looking puddle in the middle of the corridor. Two small plastic signs — one reading WET FLOOR, the other reading DANGER: BIO-HAZARD — warned Lorinda not to get too close. She skirted the mess, found room 3042, and knocked. "It's open," said a woman's voice from within. Lorinda opened the door and stepped into the small office. The light coming through the windows behind the desk was a dull green, but there was a lot of it, and it took her eyes a couple of seconds to adjust. The desk was spotless and shiny, with nothing on it but a keypad and a big screen. Sitting there, hands on the keys, was a woman in a white lab coat. She seemed to be in her late thirties, with straight black hair and striking green eyes. She would have been considered a beauty were it not for her mouth, which was contorted into a snarly frown amplified by a slash of vivid red lipstick. Lorinda didn't know whether to laugh or run.

"Doctor Suzanne Fields?"

"Come in, come in," said the woman. "Close the door, please. Have a seat."

Lorinda did as she was told.

"Now, what's your name?" the woman asked.

"I'm Lorinda. Lorinda Moon."

The keyboard went tic-tic-tic.

"And where are you from, Lorinda Moon?"

"I'm from Perfecton, Texas. I just drove here..."

More tic-tic-tic.

"Father Robert, mother Rita, brother Ezekiel," the woman read from her monitor. "Nice family." She didn't seem to mean it. "Your brother likes his manna, doesn't he?"

"Doctor Fields, I..."

"I'm Doctor Janelle Stark. Doctor Fields no longer works here. I've taken her place. Now, what can I do for you, Lorinda Moon? I assume you're looking for an abortion."

Lorinda was shocked to hear that word come out of the mouth of someone she'd just met. "I, well, I mean..." she stuttered.

Tic-tic-tic.

"Who's the lucky guy?" asked the woman behind the desk.

"Lucky?"

"Who did you fuck, Lorinda?" The woman looked sly. "Oh. Sorry. That was vulgar. I should have said, *whom* did you fuck?"

Chapter 13

"What is this?" demanded Lorinda, springing up from her chair.

"Sit down, Lorinda."

Lorinda reluctantly complied.

"Now, what's the man's name?"

"Why are you asking me that? I don't have to answer that question."

"Look, Lorinda, here's how it works." The woman leaned back in her chair and took a deep, satisfied breath. She seemed to be enjoying this. "You're not getting an abortion. It's against the law, sweetie! You're going to the beautiful new Austin Breeding Center. ABC! You'll be there for nine months, give or take. We'll feed you great food, you'll have fun, and you'll make a lot of friends."

"What—?"

"Oh, it's true. But it makes sense. You gals go through this wonderful experience together. I mean, the place has only been up and running for about three years, but we're already hearing that the moms that come out of there remain really close."

"So— "

"And best of all, you'll have that baby! We have excellent doctors." She shrugged. "Or so they tell me."

"They tell you?" Lorinda groped to understand. "Are you even a doctor?"

"You really shouldn't be talking to me like that," said Janelle Stark calmly. "As I said, you'll have your baby, you'll marry the father, and you'll have a nice family— "

"What happened to Dr. Fields?"

"That's really none of your business."

"It is my business! I have a referral to her!"

Janelle Stark seemed to find this interesting. She leaned forward and held her hands poised over the keyboard. "Really? From whom?"

"Where is Dr. Fields!?"

"I'm afraid that's something you don't need to know."

Lorinda clamped her mouth shut and looked away. This was really happening. It didn't take much insight to realize that this woman represented the same interests as whoever had sabotaged her condom. Lorinda had to make a decision, and she made it. Springing to her feet again, she said, "I'm not having a baby, and I'm not marrying some asshole."

Unfazed, sighing with patience, Stark stood up and leaned forward. "You don't have a choice, Lorinda. You have no power here. I have all the authority. You have nothing. You do what we tell you to do. Now give me your firearm."

Lorinda was panting. Adrenaline was kicking in. She shoved open her purse, thrust her hand inside, and came up with the gun. She looked at it for a second as though unsure what it was.

Stark sniggered. "Aww, isn't that cute. Pink! When you get out of ABC, you'll need a bigger gun." She leaned further over the desk and held out her hand, palm up.

Heart pounding, feeling herself start to sweat, Lorinda slowly pointed the gun at Stark.

"Moon! Don't do anything stupid. Give me your goddamned gun."

Lorinda shouted, "No!" and shut her eyes. At the last second she pointed it at the ceiling and pulled the trigger.

Its weak little click made Janelle Stark laugh. "Listen to me, Moon. I have total control over your life at the birthing center. I can put you in the Optimum Wing, with other nice girls. Or I can put you in the High-Security Wing, with nasty women and even nastier guards. Or I can throw you into Solitary. It's up to you." Stark leaned closer to Lorinda and again held out her palm. "Now fork it over, you stupid bitch."

Lorinda started to surrender the gun, hesitated, and then, half deliberately and half on blind, terrified impulse, with a mighty backhand swipe smashed the gun, grip-end first, into Janelle Stark's face. The older woman tumbled backward over her chair. Her head hit the window. Lorinda heard but didn't see it; she was already out the door and sprinting past the young janitors to the elevators.

14 *In which our heroine gets a taste of life in the big city.*

A PROFOUND, FULL-BODY snore juddered Brad out of his slumber. His back stiffened, he grabbed the steering wheel, he mashed the brake pedal to the floor. His adrenaline spiked. Strangling the wheel, crushing the pedal, he eventually calmed down enough to remember that he wasn't driving. His truck was parked. He was outside some hospital. In Austin. Lorinda Moon, lovely Lorinda, was inside that hospital. He looked around. His head was starting to clear. He looked over to where her Ryonbong was parked. Had been parked. The spot was now empty.

Lorinda drove like a lunatic away from the hospital and toward...she had no idea. She was unaccustomed to driving in populated areas, but that didn't slow her down. She just knew she had to get away.

After running a red light, it occurred to her that there were cops in Austin, and that she was going to be stopped if she kept this up. And then it occurred to her that the phony doctor, Janelle Stark, might still be alive, and if she was alive, she'd probably told the police what Lorinda had done. Told the police? She probably *was* the police. Her stomach knotted up as she realized that they would be looking for her car. Lorinda turned off the main street, drove for a minute on an industrial-looking side street, saw a shadowy alley, made a too-fast turn into it, and immediately jumped on the brake to avoid smashing into a dozen raggedy old men and women sitting — on chairs, boxes, upturned buckets, piles of trash — around a campfire. Those closest to the screeching car, and in the most danger, either froze or toppled off their perches. Some in the back stood up quickly and waved their fists; others had trouble standing and settled for hurling loud obscenities.

Eyes wide, Lorinda sat motionless behind the wheel for a good ten seconds, the prow of her car mere inches from her closest near-victim, a man with long gray hair and a bushy gray beard, with strikingly deep worry lines embossed on his dusty forehead. He managed to unfreeze himself, hoist himself to his feet using the hood of the car for leverage, and scream, "You coulda killed me you fucking fucking fuck!"

"Sorry! Sorry! Sorry!" Lorinda said out her open window "I didn't know y'all were there."

"No one does," cracked a woman with a dull red scarf over her head.

"I'm gonna break you in half," the bearded old man said, without showing any signs that he could actually do it.

"I said I'm sorry. I'm really sorry." Lorinda opened the door and stepped out of her car. The old man moved painfully to the side of the car and took a step toward her. Lorinda took her gun out her bag. She half-consciously noted that it seemed a little wet. Slippery.

"Hah," said the graybeard, his anger replaced by amusement. "You call that a gun?" He turned to the others. "Do you see that?"

"You need a bigger gun, sugar," said the woman with the red scarf.

Ignoring that, Lorinda did a quick scan of the sorry gathering, watching the ones who had fallen pick themselves up and the ones who were standing sit themselves back down. Then, selecting an old woman with a kind face who was wrapped in what appeared to be an old blanket, asked, "Is it okay if I leave my car here?"

"Leave the key," said the woman. "Leave the key and give us some money."

Lorinda slipped the gun back into her bag and started to dig for her wallet before remembering that she'd left home with only a few hundred dollars, barely enough for a half-decent breakfast. Her fingers grazed her phone and she realized that it was no doubt broadcasting her location to the authorities. "I don't have money," she said. "Can you use a phone?"

"Give it here," said a man in a tattered business suit. He extended a hand, palm up. It reminded her of Janelle Stark demanding her gun. Everybody is this city *wanted* something.

She tossed it to him.

He caught it with one hand. "You're being followed?" he said. "We can drive it around until the car runs out of gas. A joyride." He turned to the others. "Anyone remember how to drive?"

"Thank you," Lorinda said. She turned to walk back toward the street but stopped and turned back to the group. "What are you people doing here?"

The man who had caught her phone answered her as though she were a child. "We live here."

Lorinda had never heard of, let alone seen, anything like this. No one lived on the street in Perfecton. It was impossible and unthinkable. "But . . . why?" she asked.

"Why." He addressed the others. "I forget. Why are we here?"

"We don't like being comfortable," someone said.

"We keep forgetting where we live," someone else said.

Lorinda floundered. "And the fire. I mean, it's so warm out."

"It's something to look at," the woman with the red scarf said.

"What else are we gonna do?" said the man with her phone. "No money, no home, no family that wants us. So here we are. Staring at a fire."

"I'm sorry," Lorinda said lamely, then turned around and strode toward the street. She walked fast but, she hoped, not conspicuously so, keeping her head down, trying to decide what to do, trying not to think about the old people with no families and no money. It was upsetting. Maybe that was why, when she or Zeke had asked their parents if they could take a trip to "the big city," they had replied with variations of "We've got everything we need right here. They've got things there you don't need to see."

She passed another alley and saw a larger group of old people apparently living there. Same thing with a vacant lot she passed. She wondered if all the old people in Austin lived like this. Then she found herself wondering if one day she would live like this.

After passing another inhabited alley, this one with a few tents and lots of old people, she stopped in the shadow of a doorway to breathe deeply and try to focus on . . . focusing. Then she remembered her gun. She took it out of her purse. No, she hadn't imagined that it was slippery: there was a little drying blood on the bottom and sides of its pink grip. She decided it was probably a bad idea to walk around town with that woman's DNA on her gun. She fished in her purse and found a tissue she could use to wipe it clean.

Brad finally got out of his truck and walked to the entrance of the hospital. What else was there to do? He couldn't just turn around and drive the five hours back to Perfecton. At the reception counter he momentarily froze. What was he supposed to say?

"Are you all right, sir?" asked one of the receptionists.

"Hi, good morning," he said. "I wonder. I'm looking for a patient. Maybe she's a patient, I'm not sure..."

"Yes, sir?" said the receptionist.

"It's a girl. A woman. Her name is Lorinda Moon."

The receptionist tapped her keyboard and sat poised to enter information. "I'm sorry — her name again, sir?"

"Lorinda Moon," Brad said loudly, just as Janelle Stark rushed into the reception area, now wearing a black jumpsuit that had the squared-off, unflattering shape of a uniform. Her head was swathed in fresh bandages, some of which covered her right eye. Accompanying her, and huffing to keep up, was a small entourage of burly men, led by a gigantic bald goon with bulging muscles that threatened to burst the seams of his tight black T-shirt. A couple of the others were also in plain clothes, while the rest wore CCSA Domestic Security uniforms.

"Hold him!" she commanded. The big bald one stopped moving and allowed two of the Domestic Security men to grab Brad's arms and spin him around to face Stark.

"What's this?" Brad blurted. "What'd I do?"

"How do you know Lorinda Moon?" Stark growled, thrusting her grotesquely wrapped face to within inches of his.

"Lorinda Moon? I mean, I don't know — "

Stark grabbed him by the shirt, gave him a hard shake, then slapped his face. "How do you know her?"

"Who are you?!" There were tears in his eyes.

"I'm a Confederation security chief. And if you want to stay out of a jail cell tonight, you'll answer me *right now*." She raised her hand to slap him again. The others in her circle tried not to laugh. But not the bald one, who never laughed. Instead, belying his bulk, he moved quickly past Stark, grabbed Brad by the armpits, lifted him high in the air, and tossed him like a doll. Brad's trajectory was interrupted by a wall. He crumpled, moaning, to the floor.

"Skippy!" The bald thug was about to move in for the kill, but Stark's roar made him hesitate.

"Skippy!" she growled again. He continued to glare at Brad. "Edgar!" There was less volume but more menace in her voice this time. He took one hesitant step toward the young man on the floor. "Edgar," she said calmly. "We've talked about this before. You don't need to kill everyone. Now just stand down. He's mine."

Skippy — no one knew why this was Edgar's nickname — took a step back.

"Very good, Skippy." She approached Brad, who was trying to stand up. "Now where were we?" She kicked his shin.

"Oww," he moaned, scrambling to his feet. "Okay, okay. I know her from Perfecton. She's a bartender."

"That's better. Did you fuck her?"

"What?!"

She cocked her hand for another whack at his face. He flinched and blurted, "Yes! Okay, yes! Just once!"

"You come with us."

"But — "

"You're joining the team."

The two Domestic Security thugs manhandled him in the direction of the elevators as Stark and the others followed.

15 *In which our heroine meets a fellow bartender and has a drink.*

LORINDA TRIED TO stay in the shadows, tried to spot security cams, tried to make a plan. Getting arrested, tossed into a breeding center, being forced to marry Brad — whom, she now realized as she walked, she couldn't stand the sight of — was definitely not an option. But what was the alternative?

She crossed at an intersection. The streetscape on the other side was completely different. Instead of seedy industrial buildings, alleys, and vacant lots, there were gleaming, pre-fab modular stacks four, five, even six stories high. Dozens of multicolored stacks, maybe hundreds, stretched off into the distance. A tall barbed-wire fence separated their tidy little back yards from the sidewalk. She saw swing sets, bicycles and tricycles, small climbing structures, a miniature trampoline. In some of the yards there were little Black kids at play, along with some of their parents.

The block was endless. She finally came to an entryway over which an arched, wrought-iron sign announced

LITTLE HARLEM OF AUSTIN
Gateway To
Jewish Ghetto of Austin
Native Indian Reservation of Austin
Spanish Harlem Barrio of Austin
VISITORS WELCOME

Little Harlem. It was vaguely familiar. She must have heard or read about it somewhere. The name had something fantastical about it, like a magical place from a storybook, full of amusing, mischievous little people who got into scrapes and got up to shenanigans. But here it was, big as life and dead serious.

A hundred yards down the street, a police car slowly turned a corner and headed toward her. Ignoring her thudding heart, trying to look as normal as possible, she strolled in.

It was like another world. For one thing, there were two Black people walking ahead of her. She'd of course seen plenty of pictures of Black people. And videos and movies, and on the news. Pastor Doug occasionally invited Black musicians to join the house band for Sunday services, and they were always really good. And she vaguely remembered that she'd seen some Black jazz musicians playing in a park when her family vacationed in New Orleans. But she'd never seen one, much less two, just strolling along as if it was the most natural thing in the world. The thought that she should be afraid flickered through her mind, but she realized she was much more afraid of what could be coming after her from the direction of the hospital.

She picked up her pace, hurrying past the little stores carved out of the modular units that lined both sides of the street. A candy store. A burger-and-fried-chicken place. A clothing store. The Little Harlem Vintage Shop, with a window full of old junk. Another restaurant, this one called Bernice Soul Food. Little Italy Pizza. A hardware store. It was so interesting she almost forgot that she was on the run. An appliance-repair shop! A shop that repaired musical instruments! A place called the Harlem Jazz Club. Then a blues club. Then something called The R&B Club. She turned down a cross street and was surprised to see that Little Harlem was . . . big! It just kept going. The architecture was the same, but the storefronts were all different, each seemingly expressing the personality of the owner. A walk-in clinic! A shop that sold nothing but frozen foods! And then she came upon a double-wide storefront with a neon BAR sign in the window. It was ten o'clock in the morning, but the place was open. Without hesitating, Lorinda went in and immediately calmed down. The bar, the tables, the bottles, the glasses: She was back in her element. For the first time since she'd escaped from the hospital, she felt safe.

"All right, Brad," said Janelle Stark in the friendliest, least antagonistic voice she could manage. It was difficult enough to talk with all those bandages on her head; her anger only made it worse. "Now tell me again what we're going to do."

Brad, on the verge of throwing up, was trying with everything he had to keep it together. "You're driving me to this place Little Harlem because you know Lorinda went there because you have cameras everywhere."

"That's right. And what are you going to do there?"

"I'm going to find her and bring her back out to you and your crew. You'll be waiting by the entrance in two official G-Wagens because you can't go into Little Harlem — "

"We can go in if we need to, Brad. Keep that in mind. It's part of our unofficial agreement that we only go in for national security purposes. Do you love her, Brad?"

"Yes, I think I do. She's so beautiful."

"And what else?"

"And she's carrying my baby. Is she really pregnant?"

"She wants an abortion," said Stark sneering the best sneer she could muster with all those bandages around her face. "You don't want an abortion if you're not pregnant."

"Right, right. And I'm going to tell her how much I care for her and how great a life and family we'll have together and how she's trapped and better come out with me or..."

"Or there will be consequences."

"Right. Consequences."

"Close enough. All right, Brad, let's go. And remember, we'll be watching you."

The bar was expansive and dimly lit, which met with Lorinda's professional approval. It was empty, which did not. Of course, it was still before noon. Maybe the place wasn't even open to the public yet. PumpJack's opened at 5 p.m., although most days you could walk in the door before then. Of course you'd be asked to leave as soon as you encountered a member of the staff. The bar itself was a beaut: long, highly polished planks of dark wood with fifteen or twenty stools in front of it and a gorgeous mirrored back bar behind. Bottles lit from below. Very well stocked.

"Can I help you?" The woman who stood up from behind the bar was Black, early thirties, wearing a boldly colored print top, big hoop earrings, and the wildest hairdo Lorinda had ever seen, furrowed at the scalp, many long, skinny, beaded braids down the sides and back, all perfectly executed. Without realizing it, Lorinda was staring. "Can I help you, miss?"

"Oh, sorry," said Lorinda. "I haven't slept and I'm a little . . . your hair is just so amazing. And this bar. This bar is beautiful."

The woman gave her a skeptical smile.

"I'm a bartender," Lorinda went on, for some reason feeling slightly foolish. "In Perfecton. Actually, Head of Bartending Operations, or I will be soon. I know a good bar when I see one."

"Well, Miss Head of Bartending Operations," the woman said, "this beautiful bar isn't open yet. We'll be open in about forty-five minutes."

"Shit," said Lorinda, setting her purse on the bar with a clunk, slumping onto a barstool. "I don't know what to do. I've been up driving all night. I think I just killed someone. In a hospital."

The woman stared at her.

"Yeah, I know. I mean, do I look like a murderer? Don't answer that. My friend sent me to this doctor to talk about . . . a procedure. But the doctor wasn't a real doctor, she wanted to lock me up, and I mean I'm not going to get locked up for nine months, I have things to do, I have this promotion coming up, I'm not going to marry some dude I don't even like, they can't do that."

"Slow down, honey. Breathe deep. And never forget: They can do whatever they want to. I'm Crystal. Me and my family own this place. I think maybe you need a drink." She stuck out her hand for a shake.

Lorinda looked at it and hesitated.

Crystal's eyebrows went up. She said, with a lilt of surprise, "You ever meet a Black person before?"

Lorinda grimaced. "Not really, no."

"Well don't worry, honey, it won't rub off."

"Oh God. I'm sorry." Lorinda shook the hand. "I'm Lorinda Moon. Look — I just — "

"Forget it," Crystal said. "This is the country we live in now."

"Great. Thanks. So, yeah. A drink. I wasn't thinking of that, but, yeah, a drink."

"Or should you be drinking in your . . . condition?"

Lorinda shot her a look.

"Right," said Crystal. "You're working on making your condition go away. Were you followed here?"

"No. I kept turning around to look."

"Okay," said Crystal. "What about cameras?"

"I don't know," said Lorinda. "I tried to avoid them, but . . . who knows?"

"Tell me about it," Crystal said. "How did you kill this person?"

"Well, I don't know if I killed her, but with this." Lorinda took the little pink gun out of her purse. "I didn't shoot her. I hit her with it. In the face. Really hard."

"That's so cuuuuute," Crystal laughed. "You'd better get yourself a bigger cannon, so you can actually shoot someone next time. What are you drinking?"

Lorinda set the gun on the bar. "Can you make me a, let's see, oh, wait, I'm trying to remember . . . a Nineteen-Twenty Pick-Me-Up Cocktail. It's got — "

"Hold on, hold on. Okay. It's two-thirds Pernod, one-third gin, a dash of Angostura, a dash of orange bitters, a dash of sugar syrup, fill it with seltzer."

Lorinda was awestruck. "How do you know that?"

"You know how long I've been waiting for someone to order that drink?" Crystal reached under the bar and brought up a worn copy of *The Savoy Cocktail Book*.

"That's my Bible!" Lorinda cried. "I love that book!"

"It's the best, right? I must have read it a hundred times, going back seven, eight years," Crystal said, slipping it back under the bar. "I think I have it memorized." She started to prepare two glasses. "I need to try this drink. Research," Crystal said with a wink. "This might be my only chance."

She carefully poured and drizzled and dripped in the ingredients and finished by topping up each glass with bubbly water. Then she slid a glass to Lorinda, lifted her own, and said, "To bartenders. And weird cocktails."

Lorinda lifted her glass and clinked it against Crystal's. "To research," she said.

They each took a sip, rolled it around on their tongues, and closed their eyes in thought. Crystal spoke first.

"Kind of good. I like that anise-licorice thing. You don't get that a lot. And the way it goes all milky when the seltzer hits."

"Pernod," said Lorinda. "It's magic. And no one knows about it. 'Cept maybe in France."

"Ain't that true." Crystal took another small sip. "Now what are we going to do with you? You can't stay here. I'm sure they've seen you on their cameras. It's only a matter of time till they track you down. And, nothing personal, but you'll stick out like a sore thumb here."

Lorinda pondered her situation for a moment. "What about the other places," she said. "Spanish Harlem? The Jewish Ghetto?"

Crystal laughed. "No one's gonna put themselves and their families at risk with you. It's called harboring a fugitive. You've got to go far away."

"But," said Lorinda, "I need to get back. My promotion — "

"Baby doll. Lorinda. You have other things to think about now. Like saving your ass."

16 *In which Lorinda once again takes a swing with her little pink gun.*

TWO IMPECCABLY CLEAN military-style vehicles stopped in front of the Little Harlem entranceway through which Lorinda had gone. They were painted in CCSA colors, red, white, and blue. Emblazoned on the sides were the words "Domestic Security Administration Mercedes Gelandewagen Proudly Made in Alabama CCSA." The bright red and blue lights on top were flashing and strobing. All eight doors opened at the same time. Four large men spilled out of the rear vehicle. The driver of the front vehicle jumped out, as did Janelle Stark from the front passenger seat. Brad exited from the seat behind her as Skippy unfolded himself from the seat behind the driver.

Stark took Brad's shirt with both hands and pulled him close. "Don't let me down," she said. Skippy sidled up next to Brad and loomed menacingly over him. "Don't force me to let Skippy play with you."

He nodded repeatedly, trying not to look at Skippy. She let go and pushed him under the welcome sign and into Little Harlem.

"What can I do? I don't have a car; I don't have money. I have nothing." Lorinda took another sip of her drink. So did Crystal. "Can I ask you something? What's the story with this place. Are you stuck here? I mean in Little Harlem? Can you leave if you want to? How many people live here?"

Crystal considered how personal she was ready to get with this white stranger. "Look. When The Split happened I was in college. In the north. New York City. It was great. I was going to graduate and stay there. Be a journalist. In New York." She had another sip. "I'm not so sure about the bitters," she said, rolling it around on her tongue. "Anyway, my parents, they worked here at the University in Austin. Full professors, both of them. And my little sister, who was thinking of following me to New York. We had a nice house, lots of other professors in the neighborhood. Black, white. Then came The Split. They lost their jobs and were sent to this place. Along with all the other Black folk in Austin — and from all around the CCSA, too. I'm talking about the ones who didn't get out during the Great Moratorium. I don't know how many millions went to the USA, but at last count there was about a million of us in here."

"A million?!"

"This is the biggest Little Harlem in the whole CCSA. You want to know something? It's much bigger than the real Harlem in New York. Like almost ten times as many people. They should call this Big Harlem, not Little Harlem. It doesn't look like much from over here, but it goes back for miles. The New Country threw up these buildings as fast as they could, like a giant Lego set or something. They just pop together."

"How big is the Jewish Ghetto?"

Crystal laughed. "It's tiny. Five hundred people? The Jews, almost all of them left during the Moratorium. 'Lemme outta here!' I got some regulars from there. They like it in Little Harlem cause there's nothing to do over there on the West Side."

"So why didn't your parents leave?"

"It's not so easy," said Crystal. "What do you think about the bitters?"

Lorinda took another sip and swirled it around. "Yeah," Lorinda said, "I see what you mean. The orange is okay, but the Angostura is a little pushy. In France they drink it, Pernod, over ice with some water in it. Pastis, they call it. It's really popular. No bitters."

"And it turns white. I once had someone order a pastis here," Crystal said. "And he wasn't even French. Anyway, my parents had friends here, relatives. My sister had friends. They were optimists. They thought maybe they'd get their jobs back. It's not so easy to just leave your home. Even when, you know, you're being forced into . . . a ghetto. I mean, it's not bad as ghettos go, but it's a ghetto."

"So you came back to Texas."

"I came back. And look at me now. No journalism. Not that anyone does journalism here anymore. But," she looked around proudly, "I built this great place."

A man burst in, slammed the door behind him, and rushed toward the bar.

"What's the hurry, Leon?" Crystal said.

"Who's this?" the man said, glaring at Lorinda.

"This," said Crystal, "is my friend Lorinda. We're exchanging bartending tips. Lorinda, Leon. Leon, Lorinda."

"Well, it's gonna have to wait," said Leon. "We have visitors on the way. One visitor anyway."

"Damn," said Crystal. "How do you know?"

"The usual. Watching our cameras. And whatcha call it? Human intelligence."

"And what makes you think this visitor is coming here?"

"What makes me think it," said Leon, "is this white boy, he's asking people if anyone's seen some white girl around here."

"Shit," said Lorinda, and looked to Crystal for guidance.

"Okay," said Crystal, "we have to get you out of here. Fast."

Lorinda mouthed the words "cameras in here?"

Crystal shook her head. "Somehow they keep breaking down. But I'd better do this." She bent down and reached for something under the bar. Lorinda heard two loud metallic clicks. "There," said Crystal. "Government street cameras out front and back are off. They break down sometimes, too," she said, winking at Lorinda. "Leon, can you call the railroad boys, see if they're around?"

"For her?" Leon said, glaring at Lorinda with distaste.

"She's good, Leon. I'm telling, I'm not asking. And see if you can get Jalen and Amahl in here right away." Leon grudgingly moved down to the end of the bar, took out his phone, and started texting. "Now you," Crystal said to Lorinda, "you go take your drink and sit down way back in that booth."

Lorinda picked up her gun to put it back in her purse just as the front door opened and Brad timidly stepped into the bar. "That you, Lorinda?" he said, squinting as his eyes adjusted to the dim light.

"We're not open, sir," Crystal said sternly.

"Believe me, I'm not here to drink," he said. As Brad walked warily toward the bar, Leon finished texting, set down his phone, and edged closer to Lorinda and Crystal. "You heard the woman," Leon said in a calm, menacing voice. "Place is closed."

Brad replied with a look of mock-concern. "That's not very polite," he said. "For a tourist attraction."

"What are you doing here?" Lorinda said. "How did you get here? How did you find me? Are you working with *them* now?"

He took few small steps closer. "After you hit Janelle Stark — "

"You followed me to Austin, didn't you? I can't believe what a dickhole you are." Lorinda thought for a moment. "The black pickup truck. That's you."

"Lorinda," he pleaded, "I just want to be with you, that's all. Janelle Stark told me you're — " He suddenly stopped and leaned toward her. "Do we have to talk about this here? In front of... these people?"

Crystal gave Lorinda a look of utter disbelief. *"Him?"*

"Everybody makes mistakes," Lorinda said, still glaring at Brad. "She's alive?"

"Janelle Stark? Yeah. I mean she's all bandaged up — "

"Get out of here, Brad."

"Don't say that, Lorinda. We should be together, have a family. That's *my* baby you're carrying. They're here to get you, to get us..."

"Who's here?" demanded Lorinda.

"Janelle. And her people."

"Where they at?" Leon said.

"Out there, by the front gate. They said I had fifteen minutes — "

"They can't come into Little Harlem," said Leon. "That's the rules. Unless for national security."

"Janelle said fifteen minutes. She's nice, Lorinda. She sent me as a courtesy to you — "

"Courtesy!" said Lorinda and Crystal in unison.

Brad moved closer to Lorinda and reached out. Leon took a big step in his direction.

"Stay back, Brad," Lorinda said firmly.

"Look. Lorinda. That's *my* baby. Legally. And you're my girl. What are you gonna do," he said with a smirking glance at Crystal and Leon, "move in with your new... friends here? I'm offering you *marriage*.

Our baby's going to have a Mom *and* a Dad." He moved forward, then made a clumsy lunge to put his arms around her.

Her hand still clutching the gun, Lorinda took a big forehand swing. The stroke connected with his nose. He went down like a building imploding.

For what seemed like a long time the room was silent, with three pairs of eyes on the inert young man on the floor.

Finally, Crystal spoke: "That'll teach him."

"I never hit anyone in my life before today," Lorinda said to no one in particular.

"Here," said Crystal, tossing Leon a couple of bar towels. "Try to keep the blood off the floor. We gotta get him out of here."

The front door banged open and two large Black men charged in. They took in the scene and moved quickly to Leon's side. "A couple G-Wagens full of Confeds out there, outside the entrance," one of them blurted.

"Okay," said Crystal calmly. "Amahl, Jalen, get him out of here, please. Don't worry, I don't think he's dead. Bring him out near the G-Wagens. Say you found him in the street, must have tripped, fell on his face. Tell them they can get him to a hospital faster than an ambulance. He was never in this bar. Got it?" The two men nodded, picked up Brad by the arms and legs, and carried him out.

"Leon," Crystal said, "take her downstairs. Did you get hold of the white boys?"

Leon checked his phone. "Yeah," he said. "Be out back in fifteen, twenty minutes."

"Good," Crystal said. "Tell them cameras are off, they can pick her up behind Sharon's place. I'll tell her to dig up some kind of disguise for this one," nodding toward Lorinda.

"Thank you," Lorinda said to Crystal.

"You know, I like you just fine," Crystal said, "but I'm helping you 'cause I hate *them*. And believe me, this ain't over yet."

"Well, thanks anyway," Lorinda laughed. She and Crystal shook hands again across the bar. Lorinda used the end of one of the towels in Leon's hand to wipe the grip of her gun, dropped the gun in her purse, and slipped off the stool.

"This way," said Leon, dropping the towels and steering Lorinda across the room to a door bearing a small STAFF ONLY sign. He opened the door, flicked on a light switch, and went downstairs.

17 *In which our heroine prepares to escape.*

IN THE BASEMENT, Leon led Lorinda to a stack of booze boxes pushed up against a wall. He slid the boxes aside — they were empty — revealing a small door. "Watch your head," he said, opening it. They went through, crossed another basement to another stack of boxes concealing another little door. When opened, it revealed a staircase. Leon headed up. Lorinda followed.

The door above them opened when they were halfway upstairs. "Come on, come on, I ain't got all day," said the woman at the door.

"That's Sharon," Leon said over his shoulder to Lorinda. "You just ignore her." Leon got to the top, said to Sharon, "All right then, here she is, I've done my job, I'm back to Crystal's." He gave Sharon a slap on the ass and walked past her and out the back door.

"You're Lorinda," said Sharon as Lorinda reached the top step. She was around fifty, beautifully made-up and coiffed, lots of bangles on her wrists, a rather fancy dress. "Crystal says you're in trouble."

"Crystal's right. Hi." Lorinda reached out to shake hands.

Sharon ignored the hand and gave her a hug, then stepped back and looked Lorinda up and down. "No time to do a whole job on you," Sharon said, "but I can maybe do a little from the waist up. That's all they'll see through the truck windows. Stay here. Don't move." She reached around Lorinda to close and lock the basement door, then took off for the next room. When she opened its door, Lorinda heard some kind of unfamiliar music floating in.

"What do you do here?" Lorinda called.

"It's my beauty salon. Sharon's Salon. Best in Little Harlem. Best in the whole damn country."

She returned with a folding chair, which she opened and practically shoved Lorinda into. Then she ran out again and returned momentarily with three wigs, a pair of sunglasses, a green smock, and a hairbrush.

"What is that?" Lorinda said, thumbing upward and out, indicating the music.

"That?" Sharon smirked. "Yeah, that's right. You've probably never heard anything like that. That's a group called Outkast. They were big. For a while. Way before The Split. I don't know what y'all listen to now."

Sharon dumped all but the hairbrush on a shelf and immediately started brushing Lorinda's hair, securing it in back with an elastic she took off her wrist. Then she held each of the three wigs — one black, one blond, one red — up to Lorinda's face. "They'll be looking for a brunette," Sharon said. "I'm thinking you want to get as far from brunette as you can." She tossed the black one back on the shelf. "And you got that straight hair," she continued, "so I think we want to go a little afro on y'all." The blond wig was a big curly puffball. She fit it carefully over Lorinda's head, stepped back, stepped in again to adjust it, and said, "I think that's you. And by 'you' I mean someone who don't look nothin' like you. Stay right there."

She popped out and returned in a few seconds with a small mirror, which she passed to Lorinda. "Wow, amazing," said Lorinda. "I might just wear this forever."

"You might have to, darlin'." Sharon took the mirror back, set it on the shelf, and handed Lorinda the smock. "This ain't no designer blouse," she said, "but it's a different color than what you're wearing and that's what matters."

Lorinda stood and slipped into the smock. Sharon snapped the snap and tied the belt, then handed her the sunglasses. "Someone left these here last month," she said. "If she ever comes back for them I'll send her after you. Here, have a look." She held up the mirror.

The sunglasses were bigger than any Lorinda had ever worn before. She stared at herself in the mirror. "I look kind of... glamorous, I guess. Never thought I'd say that."

"Good. They won't be looking for a glamor queen."

"Hope so."

Sharon stepped over to the back door, opened it, looked out, gave a quick wave and returned to Lorinda. "Time for you to go. Your boys are here."

"Who are they?"

"They're your ticket out of here. Underground Railroad."

"Huh?"

"Don't worry. You'll find out soon enough."

Lorinda shrugged. "What do I owe you?"

"Nothing. You'll pay me when you can, which ain't now. You gotta get going. C'mon, get outta here."

Lorinda stood, scooped up her purse from the floor, and said, "Thank you, Sharon."

"Keep yourself safe," Sharon said, easing Lorinda out the door. "Oh, and take this." She tossed her the red wig. "One more thing." Sharon took both of Lorinda's hands and fixed her with a dead-serious stare. "You do what those boys tell you. Cause I don't think you know what you've gotten into with this. You attacked an agent. You may have a baby they want, but that's where their pro-life bullshit ends.

Those people coming after you — think about what kind of person takes that job. They ain't pediatricians, and they ain't nursery school teachers. They want the baby. They don't give a damn about you. So keep that in mind." She dropped Lorinda's hands and shooed her away. "Now get going. And good luck. You're gonna need it."

18

In which our heroine gets in a truck with a couple of slightly scary strangers.

A BEAT-UP OLD Ford pickup, in exhausted, rust-patched gray, waited in the alley behind the neatly manicured back yard of the brick-red pre-fab stack whose ground floor housed Sharon's Salon. The truck's passenger-side door, facing Lorinda, said PATRIOT FARM FRESH VEGETABLES. The pickup bed was loaded with crates of potatoes, carrots, and what Lorinda thought looked like beets. The engine grumbled, the exhaust pipe spewed smoke, the whole thing shuddered and rattled. A big automatic weapon hung on a rack outside the back window of the cab. The dark-haired young man in the passenger seat waved out the window for Lorinda to hurry up. As she approached, he opened the door, jumped out, and gestured with both hands toward the seat.

No sooner had she slid in across the ripped brown vinyl than he piled in next to her and slammed the door. She looked at the driver: another young man, late twenties, early thirties, bigger than the other one, with longish dirty-blond hair and a full beard. Without looking at her, he threw the truck into gear, drove quickly down the alley, and said, "She's onboard."

"Hi," she said, looking from one to the other. "I'm Lorinda Moon."

The dark-haired one shushed her, then whispered, "He's getting an update." Tapping the side of his head: "Earpiece."

"Right," said the driver. "See you in ten or fifteen." Then, not looking at Lorinda: "Do you have a phone on you?"

"Me? No. I got rid of it."

"Good. You need a reset?" said the driver, turning out of the alley onto a small street, still not looking at her.

"Reset?"

"Abortion," said the dark-haired one.

"Reset," she said. "That's good. Yeah, I need a reset. Where are we going?"

"Out of here," said the dark-haired one.

"Out of Little Harlem?"

"Out of the CCSA," the driver said.

Lorinda didn't know whether or not he was kidding. "Um... really?"

"What did you expect?"

It was a good question. "That... I don't know... That we'd find somebody else to do the... reset."

"Look," said the dark-haired one. "I don't think you understand what's happening. You're looking for an abortion. And you attacked a Federal official. They're coming after you. Even if we knew of another doctor—"

"Which we fucking *don't*," the driver huffed.

"Right. I mean, we couldn't just cruise on over to his—or her—place. They're going to be looking for this truck pretty soon. Our job is to get you out of the country."

For a few moments Lorinda said nothing. She tried to grasp the enormity of the situation, but felt a sort of emotional force field keeping her from it. Hitting that woman back at the hospital—that had been self-defense! Hadn't it? She had been about to be taken into custody and it wasn't fair. It was a violent act, but the woman had been mean to *her*. Lorinda was maybe sorry she did it—or, okay, she wasn't sorry. But it didn't mean she was a *criminal*. And it sure didn't mean she had to flee the entire country. How would she be able to come back? Or did they mean forever? And never see her parents or brother again? It was unimaginable. This whole thing had spun out of control.

"We have to go back," she said.

"Forget it," the driver said.

"I can't just leave the country."

"Listen," the dark-haired one said patiently. "If you insist on going back, we'll drop you off somewhere and we'll disappear. They'll pick you up off the street, or when you try to go home. You'll be arrested and tried for assaulting a government agent. You'll be found guilty. They'll put you in a breeding center until your baby is born, and then they'll put you in jail. Sound good?"

"How do you know all this?"

"Because," the driver sneered, "this is what we do. We've seen that happen. We're not going through what we're about to go through if you're not a hundred percent committed to it."

"What do you mean, you've done this before. Who are you guys?"

"I'm Ren," said the dark-haired one. "He's Stimpy."

"Those are your names?"

"Not our real names," said Ren.

"Which are?"

"Don't worry about it," said Stimpy, maneuvering the truck down one narrow Little Harlem street after another. The place was endless. Lorinda stewed, realizing that with every second, with every turn onto a new street, she was in fact committing to this overwhelming plan.

Finally, the truck left Little Harlem, exiting from a service accessway onto a desolate street somewhere in, or outside, Austin.

"But this is all wrong," Lorinda said. It sounded lame even to her. "I'm a nice person! I work as a bartender at PumpJack's Perfecton. In fact, I'm being promoted to Head of Bartending Operations."

"Not anymore," Stimpy said, as though lecturing a child. Then: "You're not being promoted. You're not going back to Perfecton. If you're really lucky you'll never have to come back to this shithole country." His attention flickered away from her as he listened to his earpiece. "Yo, what? Gotcha," he said, sounding almost friendly. "See you in a few."

Lorinda felt somehow under attack. So she tried to raise a feeble defense. "If it's so awful, why are *you* here?"

Neither man replied. Before she had time to pose a follow-up question, the truck turned into the nearly empty parking lot of an abandoned shopping mall. Stimpy slowed the truck to a crawl to avoid the larger cracks and potholes in the pavement. After a couple of minutes he parked about a dozen slots back from a defunct Skates 'N Sneakers 'N Beyond store. Three obese men rode their mobility scooters on the sidewalk in front of the corpse of the store. Stimpy got out and walked briskly toward the building. Ren opened his door, grabbed the red wig from Lorinda's lap, jumped out, and gestured for Lorinda to follow.

"Why is he so mean to me?" she said softly as she caught up to him.

"He's not really mean. He's just... serious. And paranoid. And, okay, a little fucked up. You'll like him when you get to know him."

Lorinda didn't buy it for a second.

She must have signaled that, because Ren added, "You'll see."

Next to the store, Stimpy ducked into a passageway marked by a barely legible RESTROOMS sign. Ren and Lorinda followed.

"No cameras in here?" Lorinda asked.

"Not anymore," said Stimpy over his shoulder.

Well, at least that was civil, Lorinda thought.

Down at the end of the corridor were two men — wearing the same jeans and plaid shirts as Stimpy and Ren — and a woman about the same size as Lorinda but a bit older. "Hi, guys," the woman said, as the men slapped hands with Stimpy and Ren. "Hi, Margaret," said the woman to Lorinda.

"Sorry," Lorinda said. "I'm Lorinda."

"You're Margaret until you reach the end of your journey," said the woman, undoing the belt and popping the snap of the green smock before Lorinda could fend her off. "The wig, please." Lorinda took off the blond wig and passed it to her. The woman slipped it over her own head and looked at her companions. "So?"

One of the men she was with — Lorinda realized that he was not only dressed the same but was roughly the same size as Stimpy, with similar hair and beard — reached out and adjusted it slightly. "Not too bad," said Stimpy 2.

The other man, who looked a lot like Ren, tossed Ren 1 some bunched-up fabric that, unfolded, turned out to be three shirts with collars. Ren gave the smallest, a light blue one, to Lorinda, who put it on and buttoned it up. Ren and Stimpy did the same with theirs, which were both white.

"Wig?" said the woman. Ren handed her the red wig. Lorinda took off the oversized sunglasses as the woman eased the wig over her head and straightened it out. Lorinda started to put the glasses back on. "Uh-uh," said the woman, holding out her hand, taking the glasses from Lorinda, and putting them on herself. She stepped out of the way as Stimpy 2 moved in and took a picture of Lorinda's face with some kind of small computer she'd never seen before. Twenty seconds later the device spit out a plastic Citizen Card bearing the name Margaret Melrose under Lorinda's picture. "There's a scanner in the car," the woman said to Stimpy. "Make sure she reads that right away so she knows who she is. And," turning to Lorinda, "I'll need your old card."

"My real card?"

"That's right," said the woman. "It can only get you in trouble now."

Lorinda opened her purse. "What's that?" the woman asked. Lorinda showed her the little pink gun. The woman looked vexed and shook her head as though in disappointment. "That's way too small." She looked at Stimpy. "She needs a bigger gun."

"Everyone says that," Lorinda said as she took out her Citizen Card and held it out to the woman. "This really makes me nervous."

"That's the last thing you should be nervous about," said Stimpy. "What you should be nervous about is — "

"Leave her alone," Ren said softly. Ren 2 gave Lorinda another pair of sunglasses, small and round with mirrored lenses. Lorinda put them on. The world looked blue. She wondered if she'd ever get used to seeing the world in blue.

"Good luck, Margaret," the woman said, handing Stimpy a car key. "It's a brown four-door Zhiguli Buckshot. Two stores down, five parking spots out."

"Not another piece of shit Zhiguli," said Ren, good-naturedly.

"We'll get you a Mercedes Q-Class next time," the woman said.

"I'm counting on it," Ren grinned.

"All right. You guys go first."

Stimpy gave a raised fist salute and left. Ren said, "Thanks, guys. See you at the farm," then took Lorinda's arm and followed Stimpy. They walked past Skates 'N Sneakers, past what was once a jewelry store, and stepped off the curb and into the parking lot as they passed the next broken-down store, which had a DIGITAL WORLD sign hanging at an angle behind the cracked plate-glass window. Lorinda couldn't take her eyes off the dozen or so worn-out looking old men and women who were aimlessly riffling through two tables of old clothes and broken-down appliances in front of the ex-computer store. She couldn't tell if they were buying or selling, or both, or if they were just there because they had no other place to be. *The world is a weird place outside Perfecton,* she thought.

19 *In which our heroine learns that she's got a long way to go.*

THERE WERE NO other cars in the vicinity, so it wasn't hard to find the brown Zhiguli. Stimpy unlocked the driver's door, then went around to the trunk, opened it, and took out an automatic weapon similar to the one they'd left on the truck. He opened the driver's-side back door, carefully placed the gun on the floor, closed the door, and took his place behind the steering wheel. Walking around to the other side of the car, Lorinda said, "I'm staying in the front with you guys. You're going to tell me your real names." Ren slid in next to her.

They drove in silence, on back streets, for a few minutes before Stimpy piloted the car onto a westbound highway.

"West," said Lorinda.

"You can read," said Stimpy.

Ignoring him, Lorinda said, "If you're going west we can stop off at my house in Perfecton and pick up some clothes. And leave a note for my parents."

"Your house is probably surrounded by Domestic Security by now," Stimpy said.

"So where are we going?"

"Seven hours west," Stimpy said. "And then you'll keep going."

"Without you?"

"We're not the ones who need a reset," Stimpy said.

"Where am I going?"

"Land of the free, home of the—" Ren said.

"Abortion," said Stimpy.

Lorinda's head was spinning. Yesterday everything was sort of normal. Today... "Seven hours!" she said. "Texas is big."

"The biggest," said Ren. "That's why the USA didn't want to lose it to the CCSA."

"Texas in the USA? That would be so weird," said Lorinda.

"They didn't teach you about that in school?" Stimpy said. "The Great Texas Debate? The Windsor Conference?"

"What's Windsor?"

"It's a city in Canada, across from Detroit," said Ren. "Neutral territory for a conference. It went on for three months. Almost started a shooting war."

"They taught us The Split was completely peaceful," said Lorinda. "The USA was afraid to fight us."

Stimpy laughed.

"They teach a lot of things that just ain't true," said Ren. "But, yeah, no shots were fired. I mean, people were firing guns all over the place of course. As usual. But nothing official. Nothing military. Just heavy negotiations. Other countries got involved, especially Germany and Japan. You really never heard this?"

"Never," Lorinda said. "I'm feeling a little stupid."

"Not stupid," said Ren, "Just ignorant. Every kid in the CCSA gets taught a lot of horseshit. It's the way countries like this work."

"Countries like this?"

"Totalitarian-moron states," Stimpy uttered under his breath.

"So," said Ren, "the deal was, the CCSA kept Texas in exchange for the Free Trade Zones, which mainly meant that the big foreign factories in the US South, like BMW in South Carolina and

Mercedes in Alabama and all the rest, got to export to the USA duty-free, just like before The Split."

"The geniuses behind CCSA," Stimpy said, "they thought this would screw the USA, because all those factories were staying here. What they didn't figure on was the exchange rate."

"Because the US dollar is worth so much more than ours?" Lorinda asked.

"They were worth exactly the same in the beginning," said Ren. "One US dollar equaled one CCSA dollar."

"That's crazy," said Lorinda "I never heard that."

"Yeah," said Stimpy, "that's another thing they don't talk about in school. Or anyplace else."

"So now," Ren concluded, "the CCSA is a Third World country — "

"Oh come on!" Lorinda was surprised at her own indignation. "We are *not* a Third World country!"

"Oh yeah?" Stimpy said. "Look around. At our infrastructure. At our life expectancy."

Lorinda took a breath. Did she really want to start arguing with this intense guy about her country's life expectancy? "Really?"

"Are you kidding?" Stimpy laughed. "The life expectancy in the CCSA has been going down since the ink dried on The Split deal. It's gone down something like 2.3 years so far."

Lorinda frowned. "That's not what we learned in school."

"No shit. You probably also learned that two plus two is five."

"Not only that," Ren said. "But the life expectancy in the USA has gone *up* by a year and a half."

"How? Why?"

Ren shrugged. "They're not sure. Maybe less pollution. Gun regulations. Workplace-safety rules — "

"— and the fucking fact that the statistics in the red states — you know, which became the CCSA — were bringing the stats of the rest of the country *down*," Stimpy said. "Subtract the red states from the old USA and the average life expectancy of the remaining states jumps up. Instantly." He paused for a breath. "And on top of that, here's *my* theory on why they're living longer in the USA: *less aggravation*. Two hundred million people, or whatever, finally could stop dealing with all the ignorance and hypocrisy and reactionary bullshit stupidity — "

Lorinda held up two hands in surrender. "Okay, okay, I get it."

"And so today," Ren said, "What the CCSA is good for is making stuff — for foreign companies — that they sell to the USA. And the rest of the world. Really good stuff, like BMWs and Mercedeses."

"And none of this Zhiguli crapola," said Stimpy. "This garbage stays here."

"They don't sell Zhigulis in the US?" Lorinda was confused. "But it was such a big deal when the Russians opened a factory in Texas. We had a school holiday!"

"They only sell them here in the CCSA. They're too shitty for the rest of the world," laughed Ren. "You can't give them away in the US."

"I can't believe I'm going there," said Lorinda, the reality of it suddenly hitting her in the gut. "I was born there, you know. In New York State. Upper State."

"Upstate," said Stimpy.

"Upstate?"

"That's how you say it. Upstate. Not Upper."

"How do you know?"

"Because that's where I'm from," Stimpy said softly. "Rochester."

"Wow," said Lorinda, "something personal. I hope that doesn't mean you have to kill me now with that big gun."

Stimpy didn't smile, but at least he didn't bark at her. Instead, he said, "You should study your nice new card in case we're stopped by a cop."

Ren pushed a button on the dashboard and opened the glove compartment door, which fell off in his hand. He tossed it casually into the back seat and removed a small tablet from the shallow cavity as Lorinda found her new fake Citizen Card in her bag and handed it to him.

"Thanks, Marge," he said.

"Margaret to you," said Lorinda. "Or maybe Peggy... Hey, what's that?" She pointed to what appeared to be an enormous single-story factory sprawled in a clearing a few hundred yards back from the road. Heat waves emanated from acres of light-colored roofing.

"That," said Stimpy, "is the biggest crypto-currency mining operation in the world, or so they claim. ConfediCoin. Owned by none other than Ezra Ferrell McWeeny."

"CEO McWeeny?" Lorinda didn't know why, but she was shocked. She'd heard the CEO talk about getting rid of regular money and turning the CCSA into a crypto-only nation, proving, he said, that the CCSA was the most advanced nation on the planet.

"None other," said Stimpy. "It's sort of a secret. Not that it matters. So he wants the government he runs to start doing business with the company he owns. It barely registers as corruption in this place."

"I never understood how that crypto stuff is supposed to work."

"No one does," said Ren.

"It's a cross between a Ponzi scheme and..." For once, Stimpy seemed at a loss for words.

"A lottery," Ren said, finishing the sentence.

"We don't even take it at PumpJack's."

"That's because PumpJacks's isn't in the business of money laundering or drug dealing," Stimpy said.

After a brief pause, Ren said, "All right, let's do this." He scanned the fake Citizen Card and held the scanner so Lorinda could read the screen.

"Okay," she said, "I'm from Perfecton — that's good, cause if it said I'm from Austin or Dallas . . . I don't know anything about those places."

"You know a little about Austin," Ren said.

"Yeah, right. And I'm a waitress at the General Lee. I know that restaurant. I went there with my parents once, so that's good. I have to memorize her address."

"Your address," Stimpy said.

"My address. And her parents' — *my* parents' — names." She read to the bottom of the screen, "Can you scroll down?" she asked Ren. He complied. There were only two more short lines of information, stating Margaret's blood type and allergies, or lack of allergies since there were none listed. "Margaret's a pretty boring person, isn't she?"

"We like to keep these things simple," said Stimpy. "The less info, the less you're going to forget."

"Who is 'we'?"

Silence from the two men.

"So," said Ren, handing back Lorinda's card, putting the scanner back in the doorless glove box, and steering the conversation in another direction, "what does it mean to be — what's the title? Queen of Bartending?"

"Head of Bartending Operations. It means . . ."

And for the next hour — until Lorinda fell asleep, her head on Ren's shoulder — the conversation ranged from how to successfully run a bar to favorite drinks to obscure cocktail ingredients to hangover stories to hangover cures to "annoying people we have known." Stimpy, frowning into his beard, kept his eyes on the road and brooded. The miles flew by, or as much as that was possible in a brown Zhiguli Buckshot.

Around 7:30 in the evening Lorinda was startled awake by the words: "Stimpy here." It took her a moment to remember where she was and another to remember that Stimpy had an earpiece. "Right. Confirming three overnight. Definitely another car if you have one. All right, we'll see you in a little bit."

"Where are we going?" Lorinda asked.

"To a very special gas station," said Ren.

20 *In which our heroine spends a night in a gas station.*

THE HAND-PAINTED SIGN on the building read:

ARTISANAL HOMEMADE GENUINE TEXAS GASOLINE
JESUS LOVES YOU & HATES COMMUNISTS

The building consisted of a store to the left and a two-bay garage to the right. Four dormered windows indicated a second story spanning the entire width, suggesting that the proprietors lived above their workplace. A pumpjack a short distance from the garage was pump-jacking away like a gigantic big-beaked water-bobber. A pipe leading back from the pumpjack to a dumpster-sized, smoke-belching mini-refinery behind it shuddered with each spurt of crude. A black hose ran from the mini-refinery to a fuel pump at the edge of the pitted blacktop apron that served as the front yard of the gas station. It was the petroleum-based equivalent of farm-to-table.

Lorinda was surprised when Stimpy didn't stop at the fuel pump. Instead, he aimed at the left-hand garage door, which opened as the car slowed down. The car continued into the garage and the door clacked down behind it. The chilly white lights overhead disclosed another CCSA-built Russian car, this one a dull gray Lada, parked in the right-hand bay. A man and a woman stood in the corner of the garage next to an open door, just beyond the left front fender of the Zhiguli. Both were remarkably tall and thin, both had long, stringy brown hair, and both wore identical denim overalls over fraying blue work shirts. They smiled weakly as Stimpy and Ren opened their doors and stepped out of the car. Lorinda slid out behind Ren, who said: "Bill and Hillary, meet Margaret."

"Hi, Margaret," they said in unenthusiastic unison.

"Oh, come on, you two," said Ren. "It can't be that bad."

The man, Bill, said, "You have no idea." Like Hillary, he could have been anywhere from his early thirties to his mid-fifties. Between their exhausted-looking clothing, their lined and fretful faces, and their general air of fatigue, it was hard to tell. Bill stepped through the door, followed by Hillary, Stimpy, Ren, and, finally, Lorinda. Instead of continuing into the store, Bill started a clanking trudge up a metal spiral staircase.

"They used to be called Mickey and Minnie," Ren said to Lorinda under his breath.

"I hated that," Hillary said. "We're not cartoon characters." Lorinda had no idea what she meant.

Upstairs they entered a combination living room, dining room, and kitchen. A couple of dilapidated chairs faced a cabinet beneath a screen on the wall. A scarred wooden dining table was set for five, with a big salad bowl in the middle. "Grilled chicken," Bill said. "Plus my special Caesar salad."

Hillary, directing her words to Stimpy, her voice trembling, said, "Listen, man. We've been here sixteen months. It's enough. Like, too much. If we don't get out of here soon I think we're going to kill each other. Or go insane. Or be poisoned by the fumes."

Just then the lights dimmed and flickered. In response to Stimpy's querulous look, Hillary said, "Looks like it's time to do a little crypto mining."

"ConfediCoin," said Bill, "They use more electricity than the rest of Texas combined. It's berserk. This — " He indicated the quivering lights. "— it's been known to cause epileptic fits. Among those so inclined."

When the lights stabilized fifteen seconds later, Stimpy stepped forward and hugged Hillary. "No promises, but I think we'll have a couple to replace you guys in the next few weeks. You've gone way above and beyond."

"I hope so," she said, patting his back and looking toward Ren and Lorinda. "The bathroom's right through there if you need it. Y'all must be starving."

"I need to call my parents." Lorinda said. "They must think I was shot or abducted or something. I just disappeared. And, oh, shit! My bar. PumpJack's. They're going to fire me."

The four others exchanged a glance. Ren spoke. "We'll get a message to them when we can. You've got to realize that everyone you know is being monitored now."

"I can't just tell them that I'm alive and okay?"

"You can't tell them anything," Stimpy said, trying not to sound too harsh. "Once we have a secure way to communicate with them, we will."

Hillary gently touched Lorinda's shoulder. "We've done this many times, Margaret. When it's safe you'll talk to them. Or we will. Now have some of Bill's salad. White wine or red?"

"Who is this 'we' who's doing all this for me?" Lorinda asked. "Who are you? I mean, I really appreciate it, but . . . who are you?"

No one answered.

Ren, the diplomat, smoothly changed channels. "So, Bill. What's happening with the road cameras tomorrow? A 'lightning strike' like last time?"

"I have something better," Bill smiled. "Before you leave I'll roll in a chunk of video from the same time today. It's an old trick but it works great."

"Bill's a genius hacker," Ren told Lorinda.

"Wasting my talents in the middle of nowhere," Bill muttered.

"So, Mr. Hacker," Stimpy said, "if anyone's paying attention they'll think our car pulled into the gas station and never left?"

Bill waved his hand, brushing aside that dumb idea. "No, no, no. They never saw the car arrive here. When you were about ten miles away there was some unfortunate static, or maybe electrical glitches, that took the picture down for, oh, maybe a half-hour. When it came back: Where did that Zhiguli go?"

Stimpy grinned.

"Hey," Ren said to Bill after they'd finished the surprisingly fine meal, "play Margaret something on your record player."

Lorinda looked puzzled. "Now your line," said Ren to Lorinda, "is 'What's a record player?'"

Bill didn't have to be asked twice. He jumped up from the table, took a big step over to the cabinet under the TV, turned the knob of an amp on the shelf below, flipped the lid of an old, once-expensive turntable on top, and prepared to drop the needle on the black disk that had started spinning.

"It's his hobby, fixing these things up," said Hillary, affectionately. A song blared from the big speakers on either side of the cabinet. Lorinda had never heard it, or, really, anything like it: a scratchy voice wailing "I see you got your / Brand new leopard-skin pill-box hat..." accompanied by a cacophony of honky-tonky music, whistles, and who knows what else.

Lorinda went over and stood next to Bill, staring at the spinning record and listening, rapt.

When it ended, Hillary gestured to Bill — her fingers symbolically cutting her throat — to turn it off. "I think we'd better get her to bed," she said.

"How does it work?" asked Lorinda, still staring at the record player.

"Well," said Bill, enthusiastically, "it's quite ingenious, really. They had to compress a wide frequency range into a tiny — "

"Uh, oh," Hillary interrupted.

"Okay, okay, keep it simple, Bill," said Bill. "Those little lines on the disk? That's actually a spiral that goes from the outer edge inward, and it has these little bumps in it — "

Hillary stopped him dead with a "not now" look, put her arm around Lorinda, said, "You'll get the lecture some other time," and guided her out of the kitchen toward a little bedroom a few steps down the hall.

A small window looked out onto a back yard of scrub and dirt. On another wall, in a modest chrome frame, hung a poster displaying the New York City subway system. Upon the neatly made bed sat a small stack of perfectly folded clothes — two pairs of jeans, four plaid shirts, some underwear, and a travel toothbrush. By this time Lorinda wasn't surprised. She just said, "For me? Thank you."

"You need clean clothes," said Hillary. "And you need to change your look."

Lorinda inhaled deeply. On the one hand, it felt...inappropriate to ask personal questions, with all these insiders using made-up aliases to keep outsiders in the dark. On the other, the rescue and escape mission on which they were all bound up could hardly have been more personal, at least to her. So she took a leap. "Can I ask you something?"

"Sure."

"Do you know Stimpy well?"

Hillary considered this. Maybe she'd been asked it before. Finally she said, "We've been working together for a long time."

Lorinda considered her words carefully. "He just seems…I don't know. He's…mean to me. He treats me like I'm an idiot. I mean, he's doing all of these amazing things, and I'm grateful but…"

"I shouldn't tell you this," Hillary whispered. "But it's not you. He wasn't always like this. But he is now. Ever since his wife died a couple of years ago. Ectopic pregnancy. She couldn't get a reset in the CCSA and she couldn't get out of the country. They prevented her from getting medical attention and it killed her. So this is all he does now. I mean, he was doing it before his wife…but he was doing a lot of other things too. He was one of the original organizers, after The Split. But now he's doing this one thing: helping pregnant women get out of the country to get care."

Whatever the cause — sheer relief to finally have a question taken seriously and answered; sympathy for the tragic background of her rescuer; exhaustion after the day's upheaval — Lorinda felt an unexpected wave of emotion and grasped Hillary in a hug. "Your organization — what is it?" she asked into Hillary's lank hair. It smelled like soap and gasoline.

"Well, put it this way," Hillary said when they disengaged. "We're part of a movement. Some people call us 'the Resistance,' but that's not really right. The French Resistance wanted to drive the Nazis *out* of France — "

"Who?"

Hillary paused. She gave a little laugh, rubbed her eyes, and shook her head in what was either mock or real despair. "You never learned about that? The French Resistance in World War II?"

Lorinda shrugged. "Not really. What we learned in high school was that the US beat the Germans and the Japanese."

"Did they mention the Soviet Union?"

"Who?"

With a sigh, Hillary said, "Never mind. Anyway, we're not here to destroy the CCSA. We just want to help people who want to get out. For whatever reason." She smiled. "Sometimes we refer to ourselves as the Rebel Alliance, but that's a joke."

"I don't get it."

"It's from this movie . . . never mind. What you have to do is get some sleep." Hillary pointed to the door. "Bathroom's right across the hall. We'll get you up around seven and give you some breakfast. Then you can get the hell out of this godforsaken place."

21 *In which our heroine learns about the enclaves of the CCSA.*

AS BAD AS the Lada looked, it was more solid and comfortable than the Zhiguli. It seemed faster and smoother, too, at least to Lorinda. Maybe it was just that she'd had a good night's sleep, a shower, a big breakfast, and had clean clothes that, surprisingly, fit her. "So what's our next stop?" she asked cheerily after they'd been on the road for a few minutes.

"Our last stop," Stimpy said, emphasizing "last."

Good-cop Ren immediately chimed in with: "We're almost there."

A few minutes later they came upon a billboard asserting itself in consecutive white-type-on-black-background messages:

SOCIALISM
CAUSES
CANCER DEATH
VOTE WALDRIP
THE CANDIDATE FOR THESE END TIMES!

It lingered on the last panel before launching its next ad. The image was of a curving road leading to a lustrous horizon, where a radiant capital L glowed with promise. Then came the text:

CONGRATULATIONS!
YOU'RE ON THE ROAD TO FREEDOM!
LIBERTYVILLE!

"Libertyville?" Lorinda asked. "What is that? Like, a resort?"

"That," said Ren, "is our destination."

"What is it?"

"It's possibly the stupidest place on the planet," said Stimpy.

"And how come we're not hearing the billboard in here?" Lorinda asked.

"Bill must have hacked the car," Ren laughed. "Did the impossible and turned off the SRBC."

Another billboard appeared. The first image was a gigantic closeup of the usual CCSA version of Jesus: white, gaunt, benign, Nordic-handsome. The caption read:

JESUS SAYS, "I'M COMING BACK SO I CAN
VOTE FOR OLIVER WALDRIP!"

Then Christ's face dissolved and was replaced by the pugnacious, bully-boy face of the candidate, silently mouthing the caption:

"CAN'T WAIT! THANKS, LORD!"

That ad faded, to be followed by another one for Libertyville: A white family of four (Dad, Mom, two kids) beamed up at the shining L that loomed over them. Then the words:

VISIT LIBERTYVILLE
AND BE
FREE
FREE
FREE AT LAST!

"It's the libertarian enclave," Ren said. "Founded by a bunch of asshole billionaires right after The Split."

"I know you think I'm stupid—"

"Ignorant, not stupid," Stimpy reminded her. "It's not your fault."

"All right," she said, "ignorant. What do you mean by 'enclave'?"

"What *do* they teach in Perfecton?" Stimpy mumbled.

The next billboard appeared: The family of four now stood, hand in hand, on a pretty town square, smiling as happy townspeople greeted them with merry waves of hello.

NO GOVERNMENT
NO TAXES
NO PROBLEM!
PURE FREEDOM
LIBERTYVILLE!

"Technically," Stimpy said, "it's 'self-governing enclave.' Some people say 'autonomous enclave.' There are maybe fifty of them, all over the country."

"You live in one," said Ren.

"Perfecton? We just call it a town. Or maybe a small city."

"Are there monthly homeowners' association dues?" Ren asked.

"Yeah. My parents pay them. They go up every year. Everyone complains about how expensive they are. But they do cover the church dues, too."

"So it's privately owned," Ren said. "Which means that legally it's a self-governing enclave. It's part of the CCSA, obviously, but it's also independent. Austin can't tell Perfecton what to do..."

"Unless they *really* want to," Stimpy snorted.

"Right," said Ren. "The CCSA federal government, if they really want to step in, they will. It almost never happens, but it can."

Lorinda found herself groping for an explanation. "I mean, why..."

"One of the purposes of The Split, at least from the CCSA point of view," Ren said, "was to privatize everything not nailed down. So the enclaves represent the privatization of the *idea* of a municipality. Of a town."

"After The Split," Stimpy said, "the brand new CCSA government had no money. Especially after they decided that the most important thing they needed to do was build their fucking walls. So they raised billions by selling off huge chunks of land to billionaires and their private companies and allowing them to act like separate entities — almost like separate *countries* — with their own governments, and police, and everything else."

"Except armies," Ren said. "And don't forget insurance."

"Right," said Stimpy, "that's huge. It's against the demented religion of our libertarian government to build a social-safety net, so how do you protect citizens from old age and tornadoes and life in general? Private insurance, of course! But the State isn't about to pay for private insurance, no no no: We don't help losers. So voila! Enclaves! Private corporations that can buy private insurance for their citizens!"

"Paid for by the citizens, of course," added Ren. "Through their homeowners association or some other sleazy invention. So if you don't live in an enclave and your house is destroyed by one of our regularly scheduled tornadoes — "

"Welcome to life on the street," said Stimpy. "And by the way, who started those insurance companies and who makes billions on them? Some of the same dicks who started the place we're headed to."

Lorinda, stunned, could only offer a weak, "Really?"

Stimpy snickered. "You never heard of this?"

Lorinda shook her head.

"Yeah," Stimpy said. "Really. Cause the government doesn't like to talk about not having any money after The Split. So that's why the little children of Perfecton don't know about it." He snorted. "Or the little children anywhere else in this fucked-up country."

Ren jerked his head toward Stimpy. "He was just starting on his PhD in history at UT Austin," he said. "Then came The Split."

"And suddenly teaching the humanities was illegal. And I went underground," Stimpy said softly.

"We both did," said Ren. "I was going to enter the same program. I never quite got there."

They reached another billboard: The family, each now wearing a bright orange life vest, stood at the railing of some kind of boat, their hair gently blown back by a pleasant off-shore breeze as they gazed expectantly across a placid body of water.

EXPERIENCE THE ULTIMATE FREEDOM!
SEASETTLING
AT LIBERTYVILLE

"I've heard of that!" Lorinda said. "Seasettling! You live on a big boat somewhere in the middle of the ocean, and it's like your own country. I didn't know that was real."

"It's not," Stimpy said. "And it's not a boat. It's like a giant platform. On pilings."

"Who's behind it?" Lorinda asked.

"The same Libertyville pricks," said Ren, as another billboard came into view. Here is where the promo people for the enclave, tasked with the challenge of illustrating "a family happily gazing at other people being happy," surpassed themselves. Now the image was of the family seated at an outdoor eatery, enjoying a pleasant lunch as, all around them, citizens of the enclave went about their happy everyday routine in work clothes, business suits, or exercise sweats, waving to each other, shaking hands, or pausing to chat.

YOU'LL COME FOR THE FREEDOM
YOU'LL STAY FOR THE PROSPERITY
YOU'RE 15 MINUTES AWAY FROM
LIBERTYVILLE!

"I don't understand," Lorinda said. "Do people actually live in these enclaves? I mean other than Perfecton?"

"If they can stand it," said Stimpy.

"So why are we going to Libertyville?"

"You'll see," said Ren.

Lorinda shook her head. "You two. So..." she stopped to think of a word. "Enigmatic! Okay, tell me about some other enclaves?"

"Well," said Ren, "you've got the recreational-vehicle people at R-V-Ville—"

"Is that really an enclave?" Stimpy asked. "It's more like a big parking lot."

"They registered as an enclave last year. With Alabama's approval."

"RVs? Big campers?" Lorinda was confused. "Enclaves can drive around?"

Ren laughed. "These people haven't driven anywhere for a long time. They're always threatening to go somewhere but they never do."

"They're lunatics," said Stimpy. "And their colony or enclave or whatever the fuck they call their parking lot, is growing. I just saw that there are about thirty-thousand of them now. They call themselves dissidents. To the *right* of the government." He smirked. "As if there's any room to the right."

"They make room," Ren said. "Remember, they accuse McWeeny

and Waldrip of being communists — "

"They call *everyone* a commie," said Stimpy. "Except themselves."

"I don't even know what a communist is," said Lorinda. "It's not like I've ever met one."

"They don't know what a commie is, either. Because commies don't exist," Stimpy said.

"Well, except in China," Ren said.

"Sure. But ever see one of them over here? It's a mythical creature that these fools conjure up from the depths of their poisoned souls."

Lorinda looked at him, slightly stunned by his unexpected eloquence.

"And they want to kill all the commies," said Ren, "which makes them insanely paranoid, thinking the commies must want to kill *them*. That's why they live in RVs. They want to be able to escape. When? When the commies finally attack, which will be never. Where to? They have no idea."

Stimpy laughed, a single, sharp "Hah!" "Still," he said, "when the time comes? When they *think* the commies are closing in? There'll be thirty thousand RV's trying to leave at once. I'd like to watch that from a helicopter."

Lorinda's face crumpled in on itself in disbelief. "But that's crazy!" Staring out the windshield, she muttered, "And now I bet you're going to tell me about more enclaves that are even weirder."

22 *In which our heroine learns way too much about the enclaves of the CCSA.*

"OH, THERE ARE lots more enclaves," Ren said. "I don't know about weirder — "

"The golf enclave!" Stimpy said, "where they worship Donald Trump."

"I thought he died a long time ago."

"Maybe he did," Stimpy crooned spookily. "Or maybe that's just what they *want* you to think."

"Well then how about Little Harlem?" Lorinda said. "Is that an enclave?"

Ren shook his head. "No. It's Confederal. The government built it and maintains it. The whole point of enclaves is, they're private property."

"And they force the people in Little Harlem to live there?" Lorinda said. "Wait a minute. What about 'freedom'?"

"Aha!" Stimpy shouted. *"Ding! We have a winner."*

Lorinda tried to metabolize this information. They drove in silence for a minute. Finally, Ren said, "There's also the conspiracy-theory enclave. Zone Z."

"There's Saucerville," Stimpy said. "People who say they've seen UFO's. Or been abducted by them."

"It's not called that anymore," Ren said. "Last year they split into two. Now it's called SaucerWorld, and the other one is called Reptilopolis. Folks who think that Lizard People live inside the Earth."

"The Rapture enclave," said Stimpy.

"I've heard of that," said Lorinda, "but I didn't know it was called an enclave."

"But which Rapture enclave?" Ren said. "There are three of them. Oh, and there's Civitas Dei. For Catholics."

"Wait," Lorinda said. "I thought all the Catholics moved to the USA."

"Oh come on!" Stimpy exploded. "There are still Catholics here. And Jews. And Muslims. And Blacks and Latinos and everything else. Not everybody who wanted to was able to emigrate."

"Okay!" Lorinda said. "Sorry! But...can I ask a question?"

"What."

"Are Catholics Christians?"

Stimpy took his hands off the wheel to slap his thighs in frustration. Ren said, "It depends on who you ask. Ask Ollie Waldrip and he'd probably say no. Ask me, or any other sane person: Yes, of course. They believe in Jesus, they're Christians."

The drove in silence for a few seconds. Finally, sounding apologetic and conciliatory, Stimpy said, "Oh, and there's Football Freehold. You can imagine what that's like."

"And The State of Swing," Ren said.

"State of Swing?" Lorinda was lost.

"Everyone there is married, but they have sex with everyone else," Stimpy said. "I think you get arrested if you refuse."

"Ick," said Lorinda. "Don't they get...?"

"Yeah," said Stimpy. "The hospital there is very busy. If there's any venereal-disease research done in this country, that's where they do it."

"The UnVirs sued to be allowed in there," Ren said.

Lorinda was utterly confused. "He just said you had to be married to live there."

"You do." Ren said. He was trying to play it straight and suppress his laughter. It wasn't easy.

"But," Lorinda said, "I thought the UnVirs were all men. Aren't they?"

"Yup."

"So — "

"Two of them tried to marry each other so they could live there," Ren said.

"But…that's illegal."

"Uh huh," Stimpy said.

"So, wait." Lorinda rubbed her eyes, as though that would help. "Two straight guys…who can't get laid…wanted to be able to marry each other…so they could live in an enclave full of married straight couples…so they could have sex with other men's wives?"

"You got it," Stimpy said.

"And that…worked?"

"I said they sued," Ren said. "I didn't say they won."

As Lorinda silently nodded in amazement, Stimpy added, "Then they tried to start their own enclave. Which is even more stupid, if you can believe it. If your whole *raison d'être* is to complain that you can't get laid, why would you want to be surrounded by other guys with the same problem?"

"Maybe complaining is the point," Lorinda said.

There followed a thoughtful silence as the two men traded approving nods at Lorinda's contribution.

"And then there's Noah's Ark," said Ren. "They have the world's largest petting zoo. Or they say they do." He looked at his partner. "Is the Penal Colony an enclave?"

"It's privately owned," said Stimpy, "so yeah. They have a really popular theme park. People get to pretend they're in jail. You can book a cell for the night. And they have the Museum of Punishment."

"Okay, *that* I know about," Lorinda said. "My seventh-grade teacher talked about it. People go there to . . . I don't know . . . experience something bad so they can value their freedom when they get out." She sighed. "That's what she said, anyway. I always thought it sounded like hitting yourself in the head with a hammer because it felt good when you stopped. But I never said anything."

"You probably got good grades in school," Stimpy said.

She looked at him with a combination of surprise, pride, defiance, and defensiveness. "Why do you say that?"

"Because that's how schools work in the good old CCSA. Pay attention to what they tell you, tell it back to them, and don't say anything too smart. Meaning, don't ask anything."

Lorinda wondered if she should take offense. Then it occurred to her that he was right: She *had* been a good student, and had always assumed that that entailed behaving in exactly the way he described. It was only over the past few days that she had begun to suspect that the world was far more complicated — and deceptive — than she had ever imagined.

"*Top of the Heap* is produced in the Penal Colony," Ren said.

"I saw that show once," Lorinda said, shuddering. "That's the worst thing I've ever seen. How is it even legal?"

Top of the Heap was a long-running program in which, every week, a number of men who were described as future mass murderers — always men — fought to the death. The one left standing — or, at least, alive — returned the following week to take on the next challengers. Sooner or later he, too, would succumb. It was legal because it took place in an enclave, where there were even more forms of freedom than those guaranteed by the country's, and the states', ultra-libertarian constitutions.

Before launching the show, the producers, including a son of the vice CEO of the country, made a sort of pilot that included interviews with some self-proclaimed legal experts claiming that a program in which a few people died every week not only did not contravene the laws that prohibited any contribution to population shrinkage, but actually helped maintain the population by taking would-be mass murderers out of circulation.

The methodology the producers described by which they intended to identify these future mass murderers was a load of academic-sounding doubletalk, but it hardly mattered. People ate it up. And after the first couple of episodes aired, all talk of methodology ceased. To everyone's astonishment (and the producers' delight), the number of applicants was overwhelming. (It should not have come as a surprise: The CCSA had the fourth highest suicide rate in the world, behind three South Asian nations that were underwater). Week after week, dozens, sometimes hundreds, of fame-and-death seekers from across the CCSA sent in audition vids or appeared at the studio door, begging for their big — and final — break.

"That's the beauty of an enclave," Stimpy said sarcastically. "If they want to do something, no one can stop them."

"I had no idea," said Lorinda. Then, abruptly changing the subject in an attempt to ambush them, she said, "What are your real names?"

"Okay, okay," Stimpy said. "They're not Ren and Stimpy." He paused. "They're Beavis and Butthead."

"Really?"

"No."

The car slowed down to pass under the flashing WELCOME VISITORS sign straddling the entrance to the Libertyville visitor-parking lot.

23 *In which our heroine experiences liberty run amok.*

THERE WEREN'T TOO many cars in the lot. Stimpy pulled up close to the gate and found a spot. They got out of the car, Ren grabbed the weapon from the floor in back, and they headed for the admissions gate. Somewhere beyond the gate a plume of thick black smoke rose to a bruise-colored sky. Stimpy paid at the turnstile with a Patriot Card in the name, Lorinda noticed, of Patrick Buchanan. The fee was $750-per-person, for a total of $2,250. She was surprised it wasn't more. They entered past a sign reading GUNS LOADED? WALLETS LOADED?

Ahead of them, Lorinda saw what looked like a midway. She hadn't expected that. It was as though Libertyville was trying to present itself as an amusement park. Or was it a theme park? Or a county fair? Just beyond the entrance, they passed a small vacant lot full of old people sitting around a fire, just like the ones Lorinda had seen in Austin.

"Welcome to Libertyville," said Ren.

"All you have to know about this place," Stimpy said, leaning toward Lorinda and speaking quietly, as though confiding a secret, "is that it was started as a community by people who didn't believe in community. These billionaires looked at CCSA — which is supposed to be like a huge fucking Wild West boom town — and decided, 'This place is too regimented.' So they started an enclave with no taxes — okay, ridiculously low taxes — no regulations, and no laws."

He gave her an obviously phony smile. "Brace yourself."

Beyond the vacant lot, the midway consisted of stores large and small, makeshift stands, and sketchy-looking people behind tables covered with junk. The larger establishments employed carney barkers out front — fast-talking young men or sexily clad young women all yakking into bullhorns and desperately trying to drum up business. There were storefronts for lawyers, stockbrokers, astrologers, betting parlors, game parlors, casinos, toy stores, brothels, cinemas, virtual-reality dens, fast-food restaurants, restaurants proudly touting their use of tablecloths and napkins, bars, liquor stores, pharmacies (ALL OPIATES ON SALE!), gun stores, shooting ranges, hotels, and an entranceway for a stadium, with an unpunctuated sign reading WELCOME TO LIBERTYVILLE HIGH SCHOOL STADIUM HOME OF THE LIBERTYVILLE SEASETTLERS FOOTBALL TEAM INC.

There were several crashed cars strewn about, and the more the trio walked, the more wrecked cars they saw. Lorinda was about to ask how cars had ended up in what was obviously a pedestrian mall, when she noticed a sudden sharp increase in the acrid smoke as well as many people wearing filtration masks or holding tissues or handkerchiefs up to their mouths, but seeming otherwise unperturbed.

Then they came upon the source of the murk overhead and the haze they'd seen in the parking lot: A store was on fire. A few tourists gawked, but only an uncoordinated bucket brigade of neighboring shopkeepers and their employees attempted to extinguish the blaze. There were no fire hydrants visible; the sight of men in various states of athletic incompetence huffing into and out of a nearby pizza shop, bearing buckets and cookpots, indicated that that was the source of the water.

As Lorinda coughed and tried to fan away the fumes with her hand, she noticed two of the bucket brigadiers suddenly square off against each other. Both were enormous. One wore an old, ragged black T-shirt the size of a pup tent featuring the faded image of a muscular, buff Donald Trump bearing a superhero shield and costume. The other's T-shirt displayed what looked like a photograph of the man himself, with his tiny wife and baffled-looking child standing on a lawn while, at their feet, upward of fifty handguns, automatic and semi-automatic rifles, and hunting rifles lay in a meticulously arranged pattern.

Trump Shirt said, "Stop pushing me! You're getting me all wet!"

Gun Shirt replied, "Then keep up! You're moving too slow!"

"This water is *heavy*, Fuckface!"

"Then get out of the line!"

"*You* get out of the line!"

They went back and forth like this a few more times, until suddenly Trump Shirt dropped his pot of water, grabbed the sloshing bucket from the other man and flung it to the ground. Gun Shirt balled up a meaty fist but, rather than actually punching his enemy with it, smacked him as though wielding a fly-swatter. Trump Shirt responded by putting up his dukes and swatting back. Someone yelled, "Take it out of here, assholes!" and shoved Trump Shirt out of the line. Gun Shirt stepped aside, panting.

Then out came the guns.

Stimpy and Ren instinctively put their arms around Lorinda's shoulders and whisked her away from the fracas just before two shots sounded simultaneously. Lorinda looked back to see both men lying in the street, bleeding, twitching, and moaning. They were ignored by the other pedestrians and bucket wielders.

With the fire raging behind them, the trio squeezed their way around two mammoth tow trucks and an ambulance inexplicably straddling the pavement, with engines thrumming and exhaust pipes spewing.

At the intersection where the pedestrian promenade ended, they could go no farther, stopped by the relentless traffic on the cross street. With no stoplight or stop sign or crossing guard, there were at least a dozen other pedestrians at each of the crossing points of the intersection, gauging the odds of surviving if they attempted to dodge the fast-moving trucks and cars. Fortunately for them, a car dared to turn left across traffic. The car — a tiny Pyeonghwa Peon— was instantly T-boned and accordioned by a bulky Shuanghuan Executive Suite coming the other way.

A predictable chain reaction of progressively less distressful crashes followed. Once the sounds of metal twisting, plastic snapping, and glass shattering had ceased, the impatient pedestrians bolted, some of them sliding right across the hoods of the mangled vehicles, ignoring the cries of those involved. Some drivers and passengers from lightly damaged vehicles, several car-lengths from the main impact site, jumped out and waved their guns, searching for someone to punish for this rude disruption.

Stimpy led the way across the street and past a luxury apartment building, then past a row of four shabby tenements. No storefronts or booths or carney barkers down here, just various forms of residential structures. At the next corner he turned right, following the arrow on the sign declaring FAMOUS SEASETTLING EXPERIENCE.

"That's where we're going," Ren said.

"But why?" Lorinda asked. "I mean, I'd like to see that and all, but why are we here?"

Now it was Ren's turn to lean in and speak in a confidential murmur. "We're going to get you to New Mexico, USA," Ren said softly. "We shouldn't talk about it in public, okay?"

Lorinda couldn't speak even if she'd wanted to. The reminder of her destination, and what she was doing — fleeing the country! Leaving her parents! Leaving her job! — hit her like a punch. That triggered a rapid and familiar emotional and intellectual loop: Maybe she should just go back and have the baby. But she couldn't go back. She had assaulted a Confederal agent. She had to keep going.

All she could do was nod to Ren and say nothing.

They were on a street of side-by-side mansions — big, multi-story monsters in a mismatched variety of styles: Colonial, Neo-Romantic, Pioneer/Frontier, Moderne, Space Age. Each sat at the center of its broad, landscaped — or formerly landscaped — yard. The grandest of them had a large brass plaque on a slab of granite standing beside its concrete walkway entrance proclaiming: LIBERTYVILLE FOUNDER PIERRE SPIELÉ FAMOUS HOME AND MUSEUM.

"That's one of the billionaires?" Lorinda asked

"The biggest," said Ren. "He stuck around here just long enough to set up this shithole enclave and the Seasettling thing. As soon as regular people started moving to Libertyville he couldn't stand it and moved out. Which is weird, since a lot of those people came here to be near him. Plus, what did he think would happen?"

"It's great to be a libertarian," said Stimpy, "when you're the only person in the world."

"Or," Ren added, "when you're fifteen, and think the world began the day you started reading Ayn Rand."

After two more short blocks of mansions they arrived at the shore of a big, and plainly artificial, lake. On an island in the middle sat a hodgepodge of small buildings — a geodesic dome, some A-frames, a couple of small log cabins, and a low-rise brick apartment building.

"Our guy is right there" said Stimpy, pointing at the dome.

"He'll take me to the USA?" Lorinda asked.

"He'll take us across the lake and hook us up with the people who'll drive us to our secret tunnel," Ren said. "You'll go through the tunnel and you'll meet your welcoming committee in New Mexico."

"And we go back home to save someone else," Stimpy said.

"Your guy *works* there?"

"Yeah," said Ren. "It's the perfect cover. He's the boss of the Seasettling showroom."

They approached a small ticket booth whose sign stated WORLD FAMOUS SEASETTLING EXPERIENCE VISIT NOW ONLY $250. Stimpy took out his card and stepped up to the window, then stopped: There was no one in the booth. He looked around for a ticket machine, but there was none to be found. Lorinda wandered out onto a dock, where she peered down at a dinghy tied to cleats on the dock.

"I can drive it," she said. She pointed to its outboard motor. "The key's in it." Stimpy gave her a skeptical look. She replied with some attitude. "I had a job the summer I was fifteen, driving one of these at Camp Perfect. We have to get over there to see your guy, so..." She lowered herself into the boat and expertly started the engine. "Don't just stand there," she said. "Undo the lines."

Ren and Stimpy walked across the dock, loosened the knots, tossed the lines into the little boat, gingerly stepped in, and sat on narrow thwarts across from each other, Ren being careful to keep the rifle off the wet deck. Lorinda lifted the steering handle and twisted the throttle cautiously. The boat started to glide across the mirror-smooth water, and in a few minutes they were approaching the dock on the island. A smallish, trim man wearing a somewhat fanciful fake naval-officer's outfit had come out of the dome to greet them. With his wavy white hair and beard, Lorinda took him for a wise, middle-aged sea captain. Then he spoke, and she realized he was around thirty. "What are you guys doing here?" he called.

"Keeping our appointment," Ren called back.

"You didn't get my message." It was a statement, not a question.

"What message?" Stimpy said as Lorinda feathered the boat up to the dock.

The fake naval officer caught the lines that Stimpy tossed him and secured the boat to the cleats. "Our com system must be down again," he said. Then, to Lorinda: "Hi. You must be Margaret. I'm Snoopy."

"Of course you are," said Lorinda.

24 *In which our heroine's escape is disastrously derailed.*

"NICE TO MEET you, Snoopy," Lorinda said. She turned off the engine and followed her companions onto the dock.

"What was the message," Stimpy asked more insistently.

"Please follow me to the orientation facility," said Snoopy, chuckling at his own officiousness. "Safer in there." He started walking back to the dome.

The building seemed bigger inside than it looked outside. It was full of table-top models and Seasettling dioramas: a mom, a dad, a boy, a girl — the handsome, happy family from the billboards, now joined by a dog — having a picnic on a lush lawn, surrounded by the sea; two men playing tennis on a platform in the middle of the ocean; a couple dining in a fancy looking restaurant; two couples playing golf, apparently on a floating golf course; a few dozen jolly people seated in a mid-century-modern community dining room; a cozy family living room with a fire blazing in a big brick fireplace. Freestanding posters trumpeted

FIVE-STAR RESTAURANTS
HYDROPONIC FOOD AND CANNABIS FARMS
NO EXTERNAL GOVERNMENTS — WE'RE OUR OWN NATION
WORLD'S FREEST MONETARY SYSTEM
NO TAXES EVER!
EXCELLENT MEDICAL CARE
PERFECT WEATHER IN THE MIDDLE OF THE BEAUTIFUL OCEAN
UNIQUE FLOATING GOLF COURSES

LOW ENTRANCE AND MAINTENANCE FEES
A SOCIETY OF PEOPLE JUST LIKE YOU

"So what's the deal? Are we safe in here?" Stimpy seemed agitated.

"Yeah," said Snoopy. "That's the thing — there's no one out here. My colleagues have all evacuated. We haven't had a single visitor since...I can't remember when. I sweep this dome twice a day for surveillance. But here's the big problem. We just learned, this morning, that Libertyville is about to explode."

"Like it's not exploding now?" Lorinda said.

Ren laughed. "Good point."

Turning to Snoopy, he said, "Seriously? How do you mean?"

"Have a seat," Snoopy said, indicating several chairs in front of a desk. He took the chair behind the desk. Clearly, this was where a Seasettling salesperson and potential Seasettlers were supposed to sit down and make a deal.

Ren gently rested the heavy automatic weapon on the table. He motioned Lorinda to one of the chairs, but she shook her head no, waved her hands in a gesture of nervousness, and walked around the room. Stimpy and Ren sat.

"All these people who moved to Libertyville from around the CCSA, looking for the libertarian life — no rules, no taxes, all that shit?" Snoopy said. "Well, you know that ever since the billionaires ran away, the place has been falling apart. No jobs, no nothing. And — "

"Of course there's no jobs!" Stimpy spat. "Who would open a factory here? Or a warehouse? Or anything? There's no taxes, so there's no infrastructure. The roads are shit! The utilities are shit!"

Snoopy held out two open hands to signal "calm down." He said, "It's true. And even if there were jobs, there'd be no taxes to keep the place going. The people who moved here, they're pissed. Really pissed. Plus, they're idiots. I know — you're shocked. Thing is, they feel betrayed. With reason. Now there's a big faction in the western sector, along the New Mexico border, they want to take over the whole enclave."

"What do you mean, take over?" Ren asked. "Can they even do that?"

"Who knows? It's anarchy out here, man. They want to kick out the owners and investors — I mean, if there are any left — and all their minions, kick out whatever remains of the government, and start the place over. And they're on the march. And of course heavily armed. That's what my message was about."

Lorinda, only half listening to the conversation, was fascinated by the Seasettling displays. "So is anyone out there? Actually sea-settling?" Lorinda asked.

The three men looked at her, confused by the non-sequitur. Ren was the first to make sense of what she was asking.

"No," he said, "and no one ever will be. It's a total scam. They're not even building it."

"It didn't exactly start out that way," said Snoopy. "They tried to build it in the middle of the ocean, but they had to quit after a couple of months — it was way too hard, too many storms, too expensive, whatever."

"Too stupid," said Stimpy.

"The only thing they ever built," said Snoopy, "is this marketing operation here, which they somehow forgot to close down. I took someone's deposit as recently as maybe six weeks ago — for the good of the cause. Our cause." He laughed. "Anyway, we can't get you anywhere *near* New Mexico right now. It's like there's a war going on, and you have to go through the war to get to our tunnel." He turned to Stimpy. "I was telling you to stay far away from Libertyville. That was my message."

Lorinda looked crushed. "But . . . how will I get to New Mexico?"

"Fuck," said Stimpy. "We had this nice, simple mission."

"That's the only way into New Mexico," Ren said. "Unless the wall falls down. Looks like we're going the long way."

They heard a distant explosion, then another.

"They're coming," Snoopy said. "You have to get out of Libertyville. Fast."

"What about you?" Ren asked.

"I'm going to ground. I've got an airtight cover, I should be fine. But y'all need to get in the dinghy."

The sounds of explosions and gunfire continued as they returned from the island. They left the boat at the dock and, moving quickly, retraced their steps.

At the main street — the extension of the pedestrian mall — all hell was breaking loose. A caravan of pickup trucks was several blocks away and closing fast. You could see them, hear them, and — with their stacks belching black smoke, even as the store fire continued to rage — smell them approaching. People lined the street, some panicking, some cheering. Each burst of automatic gunfire seemed closer than the last. A nearby bullhorn blared: "We are the Libertyville Liberation Army, liberating Libertyville from the billionaires. If you're not with us, you die! If you're a billionaire, you die!"

A tall, sixtyish man with wavy salt-and-pepper hair and a neatly trimmed gray beard, wearing a silky blue track suit and, incongruously, brown leather dress shoes, and carrying a big automatic weapon similar to the one over Ren's shoulder, pushed his way past

Lorinda and looked toward the approaching trucks. "Goddammit!" he screamed. "This is *my* enclave. I'm a frickin billionaire! I *own* this place!" He pointed his gun to the sky and fired off a short, loud burst that made everyone around him, including Lorinda, Stimpy, and Ren jump. For a moment she thought her ears would never work again. The billionaire turned and looked around. His blue eyes, blazing with insanity, locked on Ren.

"Stay cool, man," Ren said gently.

The man thrust his gun into Ren's chest, screaming "You're one of *them*!" And he squeezed the trigger.

Ren and the woman pressed up behind him, craning her neck to see what was coming down the street, were both torn apart.

Lorinda screamed.

Stimpy reflexively grabbed the billionaire's gun and smashed him in the face with the butt, breaking his jaw and sending him sprawling to the pavement. Then he spun around and dropped to his knees next to Ren. One look told the story. Though he knew it was pointless, he slid a hand under Ren's chin and felt for a pulse. Lorinda watched, frozen in anguish and fear. Stimpy looked up at her and shook his head. He gently slid the gun out from under Ren. Then he stood facing Lorinda, holding both of the bulky guns.

"We've got to get out of here. There's nothing we can do for him," he said.

"But — "

"He's gone. We can't help him. If we hang around here we're next." He clicked the safeties on both guns.

Before he could hand her one, she fell to her knees and vomited on the ground. When she stood up again, Stimpy patiently gave her a gun and said, "If you need to use it, you do this." He demonstrated the safety catch. "Wear it like this." He put the strap over her shoulder and placed her hand on the stock. "Hold it like this or it'll bump into you every time you take a step. Let's go."

In a daze, Lorinda walked next to him. They were on the main street, striding fast to stay ahead of the pickup parade. He muttered, "fuck fuck fuck" under his breath as they threaded their way through the chaotic throng hustling in panic in all directions.

Finally they reached the front gate. As they entered the parking lot they heard a big explosion behind them. By the time they turned to look, flames were shooting up from the street of billionaires' mansions.

Exiting the parking lot was relatively easy. There hadn't been many cars there to begin with, and most of the tourists inside seemed too paralyzed — or too thrilled — to leave. With the guns on the floor in the back, Stimpy drove, Lorinda sat in the navigator's seat. They were both dazed. Their hearts were still pounding.

Lorinda finally spoke: "Where are we going?"

Silence.

"Tell me what's going on!"

Stimpy gave her a stonefaced look. It took all his strength to show nothing. He said, "I don't know," and pressed down hard on the gas pedal.

25 *In which our heroine finds herself back at the gas station.*

IT WAS THE same road on which they'd been heading west only a few hours earlier. The landscape and the highway were the same, but everything else had changed.

Lorinda reached out and lightly rested her hand on Stimpy's shoulder, as much to make sure he hadn't entered some kind of trance state as to offer comfort.

"Hold the wheel for a second," he said.

She moved her hand to the steering wheel as he fished his earpiece out of his pocket. Once he'd secured it in his ear, he took the wheel again and Lorinda let her hand drop to the seat.

"Yeah, it's me," he said. "We need to stop in and regroup. Can you kill the road cameras again?" And after a pause: "I'll fill you in when we get there."

"Bill and Hillary?" Lorinda asked.

It was a few seconds before he realized she had spoken. He nodded. They drove in silence until they reached the gas station. The right-hand garage door opened. Stimpy parked the Lada next to the Zhiguli. The door slid down behind them. Bill, in the office doorway, waited for Stimpy to kill the engine, then turned and went inside.

Once again they sat around the dining table. Hillary poured red wine into four mismatched juice glasses as Lorinda stared at the empty fifth chair. Bill said, "Are you okay?"

She must have zoned out, just gone somewhere in her misery and — she realized —guilt. "Everywhere I go," she said, as much to herself as to the others, "I get people in trouble. Those people in Little Harlem — who knows what will happen to them? And now this." She looked around the table. All eyes were red. All cheeks were glistening with tear tracks. "I can't put you people in danger. I should just turn myself in, get sent to that place, have the baby..."

"And then what?" said Hillary gently.

"I don't know," said Lorinda. "I don't know."

"We do this because we want to," Stimpy said. "Ren did it because he wanted to."

"He was a good man," Bill said.

"The best." Stimpy could barely squeeze the words out. "He was my best friend."

"You should take some time off," Hillary said to him. "We'll get someone else to take her to the border."

"*Which* border?" Bill said.

"I don't know!" Hillary snapped. "We'll figure it out." She looked at Stimpy. "But you...you've done enough. More than enough."

"She's my responsibility," Stimpy said.

"If I even want to go to the border," said Lorinda. "This is all too much. It's like a bad dream. I need to get back to my life. Or at least get out of yours."

"Unfortunately, your path has forked," Bill said to her. "This is your life now." She was sitting next to him with her hand on the table by his wine glass. He placed his hand gently on hers. Her eyes once again filled with tears. "We'll do everything we can to help," he said.

"I never even knew his real name. Ren." She pushed her chair back with a squeal of dragging wood. She stood up. Sitting seemed impossible. Walking seemed impossible. Everything seemed impossible. Lorinda's eyes strayed to the turntable on the shelf. She went to it and opened the lid. The odd black disk with the funny striated surface was still there, but it wasn't spinning. The round red label in the middle said

COLUMBIA
BLONDE ON BLONDE
Bob Dylan

"How does it work?" she asked, softly.

Hillary looked at Bill and jerked her head to prompt him to join Lorinda. He got up and stepped over.

"So," said Bill, "that spiral groove I told you about? With the tiny bumps in it." He picked up the tone arm so Lorinda could see its ventral side. "See that little needle? That needle goes in the groove, and rides in the groove, from the outside in, when the record is spinning. The tiny bumps in the groove correspond to sounds. So the needle is super-sensitive to those little bumps, and the movement of the needle on those bumps makes a small electrical current, and this amplifier, well, amplifies the current and sends it to the speakers. The speakers vibrate the air and the air vibrates our ear drums and... we hear the music!"

Lorinda continued staring at the black disk. Finally, she said, "Come on."

"What do you mean?"

"That's impossible. You expect me to believe that?"

"It's true!"

She took the tone arm and pointed to the needle. "So you're saying this little tiny thing" — she put the tone arm down and gestured to the entire room — "makes all that sound we hear?"

Bill thought about it for a second. "Sort of," he said. "That little thing, yes, when it goes through the ups and downs and ins and outs and back and forths of the record, with the help of everything connected to it. It starts small, riding those tiny bumps, making a tiny current, but by the end, when it's amplified, its effect is huge."

"And the people," said Hillary, smiling and mirroring Lorinda's room-embracing gesture, "are happy."

Lorinda caught Hillary's effort to cheer her up. She didn't see herself as a stubborn person, but for some reason it felt important to defend her position, and even her mood. Everything was so awful, and now they're screwing around with her, expecting her to go along with this silly story about the record player? "I don't believe it," she said flatly.

"Why not?" said Bill, surprised. He thought he'd done a good job explaining it.

"Because it can't be true."

"But it *is* true!" Bill looked to Hillary and Stimpy. "Guys, tell her."

Stimpy suppressed a laugh and said, with great solemnity, "Bill always tells the truth. That is definitely how it works."

Not knowing why, Lorinda said, "Shut up!"

"*You* shut up!" Stimpy said.

"No, *you* shut up! Everybody just *shut the fuck up*!" Yelling felt good to Lorinda. It brought some kind of release.

Hillary stood up and held out her palms. "Okay, now, look,

everybody — "

Lorinda and Stimpy looked at her and said, at the same time, "*Shut up!*"

Silence for a moment. Then Stimpy cracked up, followed by Hillary and Bill and, finally, Lorinda herself. She didn't know why she was laughing, which made her laugh even harder. Finally, amid sighs and wheezing and the drying of eyes, the storm of hilarity passed. Lorinda collapsed into her chair. She shook her head and said, "I hope Ren doesn't think we're disrespecting him."

"Are you kidding?" Stimpy said. "Wherever he is, he's laughing along with us."

"And telling us to *shut the fuck up,*" said Hillary, which triggered another wave of laughs.

"All right," Lorinda said as her laughter subsided. "I guess . . . " She took a sip of wine. "All right. I'm not turning myself in. But if New Mexico is out, where do we go?"

Bill sat down in one of the chairs by the turntable shelf and tapped on a keyboard. The screen on the wall came to life. A few more taps and the screen displayed a map of North America. Bill zoomed in on Texas and the adjoining states.

"What about that square one?" Lorinda asked. "That's in the US, right?"

"Yeah," said Bill, "that's Colorado. But you have to cross this little strip of Oklahoma to get there, and that little strip of the CCSA is filled with tanks and soldiers — "

"What?" Lorinda said.

"Yeah, it's called the Oklahoma Crossing. And the soldiers have automatic weapons, and there's land mines — "

"But *why?*"

"What do you mean, why?" Stimpy said. "For the same reason that we have all of our stupid walls."

"But the walls, they're supposed to keep people, like from the US and Canada and Mexico, from breaking *into* the CCSA."

Stimpy took a deep breath to keep himself calm. "Our famous walls? Their purpose is *not* to keep people out. It's to keep *us in.*"

Lorinda opened her mouth, but nothing came out. This was possibly the most shocking thing she had heard him say. She just shook her head.

"Gotta maintain the population," Hillary said.

"It's like the old wall between East and West Berlin," Stimpy said. "Which I bet you've never heard of."

"A lot of people have tried that Oklahoma crossing," Hillary added. "The ones who don't get killed, they get arrested."

"Call me crazy," said Bill, who had been fully focused on the map, "but I think the best way out is Georgia."

"Georgia! That's what? A thousand miles?" Stimpy said glumly.

"Yeah," said Bill, "but it's a relatively safe drive. A lot of back roads, so we've got a pretty good infrastructure for switching cars and all that. Plus some ability to hack cameras. And good people you can stay with. And the assholes probably won't be looking for you in that direction."

Lorinda gave an enormous sigh. She leaned toward Stimpy. "Look. It's like what Hillary said. You've done your share. Just give me a car and some money and I'll get there by myself. Even if it is a thousand miles. I need to do something about this. To get on with my life."

"We'll do it together," Stimpy said. When she started to object, he cut her off. "Like I said — I *want* to do this. Seriously."

"But — "

"Especially now. After . . ." He gestured vaguely. ". . . everything that's happened. I want to finish the fucking mission."

She nodded and half-smiled. "Okay." She took a sip, then looked to Hillary and held up her glass. "What is this? I love it. California? Zin?"

"That's right," Hillary said. "You're good."

"It's my job. I tasted it once before. Smuggled in. I really liked it."

"Friends gave us six bottles. I don't know how they got them into the CCSA, but, yeah. Really delicious. Helps make it bearable to be here."

26 *In which Stimpy, on the road to Revelation, reveals Ren's real name.*

AT SEVEN IN the morning, having each suffered a bad night's sleep, Lorinda and Stimpy were heading east again in the Lada.

Stimpy finally broke the silence, saying: "Yeah, I'm here."

Lorinda jumped. "Right. That's great. Thanks."

"What's happening?" she asked.

"Bill set up a car-switch for us."

"That's good, I guess." She reflected for a moment. "I like his record-player thingy. Does it really work like that? With the needle and the little bumps and everything?"

"Yep, believe it or not."

"Amazing."

"The latest in twentieth-century technology. Or maybe nineteenth."

A few miles down the road he slowed and turned off at an abandoned exit ramp that led to a derelict weigh station for trucks. Pieces of the massive scale were still there, some standing, some scattered about. There was also a crumbling little structure that, before The Split, provided shelter for the civil servants who worked there. It was as if she and Stimpy had arrived at the remnants of an isolated outpost of an ancient civilization. (The Split put an end to deep-state truck-weighing, of course. Why impose such burdensome regulations on transport companies when there were no taxes or fees to be collected, and no nanny-state weight limits on commercial vehicles?) A faded-blue Lada stood next to the ghost structure.

As their car pulled to a stop, a man and a woman jumped out of the blue car and ran over to Stimpy's door. The man flung the door open and started hugging Stimpy before he was halfway out of the car. "So sorry, man," the guy said. "So, so sorry."

The woman joined the hug, saying, "We love you, Stimpy. So terrible. Bill told us..."

"Fucking hideous," Stimpy said, his words muffled by the hugs. When he finally stepped back, there were tears in his eyes as he looked over to Lorinda, who was now standing a discreet distance from the huggers. "Margaret, these are my friends and colleagues, Popeye and Olive."

"Hi, Margaret," they both said.

"Please take good care of him," Olive said.

"I'll do my best," said Lorinda.

"We'd better get this show on the road," said Popeye, scurrying over to the blue car and grabbing a couple of bright plaid shirts from the back seat, lots of reds and yellows and greens. "Just to change your looks," he said, tossing the shirts to Stimpy and Lorinda.

"Just what we need," said Lorinda. "More plaid."

"I left an old atlas in front," said Popeye. "In case our great nation's GPS network conks out just when you need it. Oh, and Bill hacked the billboard thing on this car a few months ago, so you won't have to listen to that shit. Don't forget your guns."

After bidding good-bye to Popeye and Olive, Lorinda and Stimpy changed into the hideous shirts. Lorinda decided the two of them now resembled a brother-sister hillbilly country-western act her mother used to like on television. Sitting in the passenger seat next to Stimpy, on the verge of grousing about the shirts, Lorinda realized that this get-up was pretty closely related to the cowgirl duds she wore at PumpJack's another lifetime ago. If it made her unrecognizable to cameras and government agents, they were now her favorite shirts in the whole world.

She picked up the tattered, oversized paperback atlas Popeye had left in the car. "I've never seen one of these," she said, paging through it.

"It's called a 'book'," Stimpy said, keeping his eyes on the road.

"Thank you, Professor Wiseass. No, I mean maps from before The Split. When it was all one big country. And, yeah, I like that it's on paper. In a real book." Her finger traced a line from the middle of Texas to Georgia. "We've got a long way to go."

"It's even longer than that, since we're not going in a straight line. We need to zig and zag to stay safe. And stop to switch cars and change how we look."

"And what happens when we get to Georgia?"

Stimpy sighed. "That I don't know. I'm sure Bill and Hillary are sending the word out. Sooner or later someone will get back to me and tell me where we're crossing the border and where to drop you off."

Although Lorinda realized that of course that's how it would happen, the words came as a gut punch. "Oh," she said. "Right. And then you go back and help someone else."

"Something like that," said Stimpy, who was unsettled to find that the idea of dropping her off in Georgia didn't sit easily with him, either.

A dense cloud of silence settled over them. Finally, Lorinda spoke: "What's our next stop?"

Stimpy jumped on that, glad to have a change of subject. "We're making a pilgrimage to the holiest of holies, the enclave they call... Revelation! Also known as — "

"Rapture Town!"

"You've heard of it!"

"Are you kidding? Of course! I've always wanted to go on that Rapture Ride."

"Well," said Stimpy, "you might just get your chance. We'll see how it goes."

"Great." She sighed. "It'll help me get my mind off—"

"Roger."

"Roger?"

"Roger. That's Ren."

"His real name?"

"His real name," said Stimpy. "Roger Winters. I guess it's a little late to worry about keeping it a secret."

Lorinda teared up. "I don't know why," she said, "but knowing his name, his real name..."

"I know what you mean," Stimpy said.

Lorinda drove. The road wasn't great. Nothing like the semi-well-maintained boulevards and streets of Perfecton. Or even Austin. The four-lane highway was pitted and crumbly from weather extremes—*especially tornados,* Lorinda thought—and not enough Citizens Construction Corps recruits to stay ahead of the assaults of nature. Yet another reason to Maintain the Population. The electronic billboards, mercifully silent thanks to Bill having hacked the Lada's sound system, were poorly maintained, with lots of dead spots, and featured low-rent ads for hundred-dollar stores, pawn shops, gun shops, and personal-injury lawyers. Then Lorinda saw, popping up on the horizon, a billboard that was noticeably bigger and brighter than the others.

"Speak of the devil," Stimpy said. "You see it?"

"That billboard? I can't read it. I'm trying to drive."

"Give it a minute."

As they approached, Lorinda realized it was an ad for the Rapture Ride at Revelation. YOU'VE WAITED YOUR WHOLE LIFE FOR THE RAPTURE RIDE! it said, with an animation of a roller-coaster speeding down a steep incline and passengers young and old waving their hands in the air, with bright lightning bolts flashing above them.

"For once I wish we had the billboard sounds," Lorinda said.

"Believe me, you don't."

Around the next bend another bright new billboard appeared. This one was flashing garishly colored words, in sequence, each one quickly blossoming from tiny to gigantic:

I

WILL

MAKE

MASTURBATION

ILLEGAL

Lorinda and Stimpy briefly made eye contact: *Whaaaat?* Then the face of Oliver M. Waldrip, the Divine Party's candidate for CEO of the nation, filled the screen, seemingly yelling at the approaching motorists. Without missing a beat, Stimpy supplied the soundtrack, a surprisingly accurate rendition of Waldrip's angry, guttural voice: "I have never once in my life masturbated! And I don't plan to start now!"

Lorinda burst out laughing.

"Masturbation is the wholesale murder of precious sperm! Each sperm is a baby! A beautiful human baby who looks exactly like God! Masturbation should be called mass *murder,* because that's what it is!"

"Stop!" begged Lorinda, who was afraid her laughter would cause her to lose control of the car.

"Elect me and the punishment for masturbation will be at least five years in prison — aww, hell, make it ten! — with the masturbater's masturbatin' hands tied behind his back! Or death! Whichever comes first!"

They passed the billboard. Lorinda heaved her final hoot. "You are really funny, mister," she finally said.

"Monty Python, *The Meaning of Life,*" he said, under his breath. She didn't bother asking what he meant by that, and he didn't bother pursuing it.

27 *In which our heroine doesn't crash the car as she learns yet more about CCSA enclaves.*

FOR A WHILE there were no billboards. The landscape was bleak and flat; the shoulders were littered with random auto parts and trash, occasionally upstaged by a shrine in the form of a cross festooned with flowers (some brightly artificial, others long-faded) where someone had died in an accident. *Probably because their car fell into a pothole,* Lorinda thought.

Stimpy sent and received messages. At one point he instructed her to take an exit onto a two-lane country road paved with a nubbly asphalt that made it feel like they were driving on an endless rumble strip.

The landscape here was a little more pastoral. They passed family farms, the occasional hill, not-entirely-level acres of furrowed earth. Sometimes a fruit or vegetable stand would appear near the road, a simple booth made of planks or plywood, unmanned, with nothing on display, and featuring a hand-painted sign reading POTATOS OR PEPPERS + ONOINS. In the middle of one gone-to-seed farm field sat a sprawling six-story brutalist concrete slab of a building with a sign reading CENTRAL TEXAS REGIONAL POORHOUSE & WORK FARM painted on its side.

"It's like a hundred years ago out here," Stimpy muttered.

Lorinda indicated his device. "Are you sure they can't track you?" she asked.

"We have our own satellite network. Totally secure. Made in the USA, and maintained by them, too."

"Really? How does that work?"

"I've already told you too much," Stimpy said. "I'm actually much more worried about CCSA cameras. Bill says he's turned off the ones in this part of Texas, but you never know. Anyway, they usually don't bother with these back roads."

"So what's your real name?" Lorinda thought she might catch him off guard.

"We're about an hour out from Revelation," he said, ignoring the question. "You're a good driver."

Once again they were back on a decomposing highway. After a while the signs started to appear: small, low, amateurishly hand-painted signs. They all displayed the same style of not-quite-Gothic lettering and the same version of Jesus: tall, white, buff, handsome, ruggedly bearded, clad in loose "heavenly" robes and sandals. In one, under the text GET RIGHT WITH JESUS OR GET LEFT BEHIND, He held out his arms in an offer of a welcoming embrace. In another — ARE YOU READY FOR THE RAPTURE? — Jesus gazed at the viewer with let's-talk-turkey frankness. Finally, they came to one that read YOU'RE TWENTY MINUTES FROM REVELATION — AND AN ETERNITY IN HEAVEN, under which Jesus gestured toward a glowing city on a hill in the middle-distance, foiled in its attempt to be radiant and glowing by its sun-bleached, flaking paint. A couple of minutes later, a huge, blazing electronic billboard appeared. Against an image of a leather-covered book that proclaimed itself THE HOLY BIBLE in gilt letters, scrolled glowing red words in Gothic script:

TAKE NEXT EXIT FOR DOMINION DOMAIN THE SEVEN MOUNTAIN COMMUNITY "JUST FOLLOW THE SIGNS"

"Oh, God," Stimpy sighed. "Them."

"Who?"

"You'll notice they're inviting people. They need bodies and income like everywhere else."

"*Who?* I've never heard of it. Or them. Or whatever."

"It was one of the first enclaves. Totally theocratic. Way, way beyond Revelation. It's based on some crackpot, hyper-Christian horseshit, that everything — *everything* — in life should be run according to the fucking Bible."

"That's blasphemy," said Lorinda sternly.

"Is that you talking or Perfecton?"

"Neither," Lorinda laughed. "I was joking. Anyway, I thought we already had a theocracy, as you call it."

"The CCSA? Hah. This country, it's like a big contest, a competition to see who can come up with the most extreme ideas, the most extreme laws, government, everything. As long as those ideas are right-wing, authoritarian, fascistic, whatever you want to call it. So, yeah, the whole thing is a theocracy of course."

"And this Dominion Domain is . . . ?"

"It's got to be the most extremely theocratic enclave in the country. At least that was its original goal." He rubbed his face, as though what he was about to say caused him pain. "There's a line in Genesis that says that God gave man dominion over the earth. So some power-hungry Christo-fascist UnVir wankers in the 1970s decided that this meant Christians should control what they called the seven — not six, not eight — but seven aspects of society. Lemme see if I can remember." He ticked them off on his fingers. "Religion — because DUH — family, education, government..." He paused and laughed. "Oh, right: media, business, and entertainment. Because Adam and Eve were deeply into starting a wholesale fruit and vegetable business empire, and Jesus had strong opinions about entertainment."

Lorinda shot him a dry look. "This is another 'let's fool the naïve small-town girl' routine, right?"

"No! I swear! You have no idea how crazy these people are. Right after The Split a bunch of these clowns set up this enclave — with a couple of billionaire backers to buy the land for them — and ran it according to their idea of strict Christian principles. Women couldn't work and had to obey their husbands. No abortions, no contraception, no teaching science, history... no teaching of anything, really, except Scripture. All art and entertainment had to reflect their... what's the word? Oh, right: 'values.'"

"I guess women didn't get to vote."

"Vote?!" Stimpy laughed. "No one got to vote! They didn't even pretend it was a democracy. They had a Council of Elders. You can guess how many women were on it. I'll give you a hint: less than one."

"Well," said Lorinda, letting that sink in, "it's not *that* different from our government." She thought for a moment. "And it's still like this?"

Stimpy smiled. "Hah! No, not exactly. I guess you can sustain a community of religious zealots if it's surrounded by a healthy economy to mooch off, like the Hasidim in Brooklyn." Unable to stop himself, he added: "That's in New York. Your home state."

"I've heard of Brooklyn," she said, sidestepping the obvious confession that she'd never heard the word *Hasidim*.

"But of course," he continued, "the CCSA has never had a healthy economy."

She squelched a knee-jerk objection.

"So poor Dominion Domain ran out of money in, like, year three. Huge healthcare issues. People were just dropping dead. Of curable diseases! Their one hospital shut down. All the sane doctors left. Are you with me?"

"I'm with you," said Lorinda, who was intently focused on navigating through a particularly bad stretch of road. "I'm just trying to avoid destroying this car."

"Anyway, what happened next was a textbook example of what happens when religious lunatics try to run anything. They turned on each other. Everyone accused everyone else of not being pious enough. Or observant in the 'correct' way." Lorinda could feel him getting worked up. "What did they expect? It's irrational! It's all based on opinion and feeling and," he practically spat the word, "*faith*! Of course they were doomed to start disagreeing about everything. Including the meaning of that magic book of theirs. Written by cavemen thousands of years ago!"

Lorinda couldn't help smiling. "It wasn't cavemen who wrote the Bible. I do know a few things."

"Well," he said, "maybe I exaggerated. But just a little."

"Are you an atheist?"

"Ren — Roger — had this expression. He says . . ." He stopped. Took a labored breath. "He used to say, 'I'm not an atheist. I'm an *anti*-theist."

"Meaning *against* God?"

"Yeah. Against the whole idea of religion. I mean, look at this garbage-dump country. Religion at work."

"There's some good stuff in that caveman book. My parents like it."

"Don't get me started."

She laughed. "You're always started."

As he considered that, she saw a wide, deep gash in the road ahead and stepped on the brakes. The Lada slowed down, hit the fissure with a mighty thump, and emitted what seemed like a long death rattle. But it survived. Which is more than could be said for the upside-down pickup truck in a ditch just to the side of the distressed pavement.

Lorinda's thoughts quickly moved on from the hazards of driving in the CCSA. "I miss my parents," she said. "It feels like I've been gone a month. And my brother. My friend Emmie." Her eyes teared up again.

Stimpy finally spoke. "You all right?"

"I'm okay. Just sad. So what happened then?"

"In Dominion Domain? The billionaires who'd seeded the place saw that it was going to fall apart if they didn't do something fast. So what did they do? They threw a little more money at it and forced the Council of Elders to turn it into a theme park. Probably inspired by Revelation, right down the road, which was doing pretty well." He saw Lorinda's eyes widen. "Don't get excited. They don't have rides. It's more like, I guess you could call it a lifestyle theme park. Ever hear of Williamsburg, Virginia?"

Lorinda shook her head.

"Doesn't matter," he said.

"So did all the religious people leave?"

"They probably wanted to," Stimpy said, "but they had no place to go. Remember, these people were *too fundamentalist for the rest of the* CCSA. Nobody wanted ten thousand religious fascists for neighbors. Also, most of them had no money — they'd donated it all to their beloved enclave, which was also their church. So the residents, most of them, stayed and got jobs working for the theme park as actors, guards, cooks, hotel workers, janitors, whatever. Advertising. Someone's got to write the billboards."

"If they don't have rides, what do they have?"

"I'm not sure exactly," Stimpy said. "I haven't been there, and I'd like to keep it that way. I know the main thing is their Seven Mountains exhibit. It's seven crappy papier-mâché hills, and you go inside them one at a time and learn about that 'mountain' by watching little plays and lectures and," he rubbed his face again, "Christ, it's so stupid. Families — you know, religious families, or people who just can't figure out what else to do with their lives — go there to spend a day, or maybe a few days, and wander around the seven 'mountains' and soak up the indoctrination. Like that ark theme park in wherever-it-is . . . Kentucky? Oh, and they also have people pretending to be teachers and students in a make-believe Biblical school. And people working in some kind of fake Biblical factory."

"Where they make Bibles?"

"Hah. Funny idea: The Bible being printed while it's being written. 'Stop the presses! Paul just wrote an epistle!' No, it's supposed to be a factory from Biblical times. You know, a bunch of cavemen working in a factory. Perfectly historically accurate. I don't know what they're supposed to be making."

"Myrrh? Frankincense?" Lorinda and Stimpy both laughed.

"I've heard they even have their own caveman video studio," Stimpy said. "That's about all I know about the place. Don't make me think about it again, please."

"So," said Lorinda, ignoring his plea, "they turned their enclave into a make-believe place."

"Yeah, but remember, what they had before the theme park was also make believe. Pious, fundamentalist make believe." He was getting worked up again. "None of the paying customers, the dipshits who go there and take pictures of their kids posing with the fake Bible cavemen, ever bother to ask themselves, 'If this kind of life is so wonderful, why sell tickets? Why put on a show every day? Why not just fucking live it?'"

"And you care because?"

He looked at her for three full seconds before saying, "What?"

"Why does it make you so angry?"

"Because it's so fucking stupid!" He stuck his head out his window and let the air calm him down. Finally, he turned to her and said, "It's a legitimate question. I think it bothers me because... look, this country is controlled by ruthless and greedy people manipulating stupid and ignorant people. I've suffered the effects of that — and so have you! This Dominion Domain is like a little nuclear reactor of ignorance. Pumping it out every day. And the people who live there... if one of them pulled out a gun and shot you because you had sex without the blessing of holy matrimony, their fellow Seven Mountaineers would cheer him as a true Christian."

"What about 'Thou shalt not kill'?"

"Exactly."

Lorinda nodded. "I guess it *is* pretty fucking stupid." She frowned and shifted in her seat. "This country is... kind of full of stupid things, isn't it?"

"You are acquiring wisdom, Grasshopper."

"What?"

"Oh. Right. See, there w — "

"Look."

They had arrived at Revelation. It was not radiant and glowing.

28 *In which Lorinda and Stimpy enter Revelation.*

THERE WERE TWO arrow signs at the entrance to the parking lot. The one pointing right said RESIDENTS, the left one said VISITORS. Lorinda steered left. The lot was huge and nearly empty. Suspended over the ticket booth was a flashing sign, proclaiming:

WELCOME TO REVELATION, TEXAS!
THE PLACE TO BE WHEN IT'S TIME TO GO!
"WE WHO ARE STILL ALIVE AND ARE LEFT
WILL BE CAUGHT UP TOGETHER
WITH THEM IN THE CLOUDS
TO MEET THE LORD IN THE AIR.
AND SO WE WILL BE WITH THE LORD FOREVER"
1 Thessalonians 4:17

Lorinda parked the car several rows away from the ticket booth. She and Stimpy grabbed the automatic weapons and headed for the booth. Halfway there Stimpy stopped and stared beyond the ticket booth at the flashing lights of the wide arch over Revelation's entrance.

"Hey," said Lorinda. "What's up?"

"I've been here twice before," he said. "With..."

"With Roger."

"Right," Stimpy said. "Roger. We worked together for a long time. Did everything together, really. Roger. We never used our real names.

It would have been weird if I'd called him Roger. Like I was his mom or something."

"Well," she said, "today you're here with Lorinda. I mean Margaret." She took his arm and guided him to the ticket booth. There was a scraggly looking teenager inside, his upper lip dusted in green, intently playing some kind of raucous game on a small screen. They watched him grimace and lean one way and another, his thumbs working rapidly to the tinny rasp of recorded explosions.

Stimpy slapped his card down on the counter. "Two," he said.

The kid, surprised, looked up. It took a moment for his head to clear so he could do his job. "Show your guns please," he said.

Lorinda and Stimpy lifted up their guns. The kid was impressed. "Crushers!" he said, approvingly. "Righteous! So, it's $500 each. You paying both?"

"That's right," Stimpy said.

The kid scanned Stimpy's card, slid it back, then pushed a small, flat device toward Lorinda. Reciting his memorized script, he said: "This is your Rapture pager. You flip up that little red door and press the red button hard if you're certain the Rapture is upon us. It sets off sirens, fireworks, explosions, everything we need to get God's message out, praise the Lord. There's a $10,000 fine for a false alarm and a $2,500 fine for not returning your pager when you exit. Look up here." Lorinda looked at him, a puzzled expression on her face. "Security scan," he said. He pointed to a camera mounted above his head, then reached far to his right to push a button.

"Fuck," Stimpy said under his breath.

The kid grabbed another pager and shoved it toward Stimpy. "This is your Rapture pager — "

Stimpy cut him off: "I heard the speech."

"Okay," said the kid. "Look up." Stimpy looked up, then looked down and rapidly shook his head as the kid reached for the button. The kid didn't notice or didn't care. "May you have a blessed time in Revelation," he said as Stimpy practically shoved Lorinda toward the Revelation entranceway.

"What was that about?" Lorinda asked in a harsh whisper.

"I forgot the camera. I should have had you dodge it. I forgot what I was doing. I was . . . I don't know. Like, overcome by emotion. Maybe I'm getting too old for this."

"Maybe your best friend . . ." Lorinda let the thought hang in the air. She took his arm again. "Maybe you just need to let your emotions out."

They walked under the flashing archway and into what looked like a more wholesome version of Libertyville's midway. Perky young families strolled among dozens of storefronts and booths, which displayed everything from embroidered trucker caps to lavishly decorated Bibles to survival gear. Waving from a flagpole above one booth was a big banner saying BE SURE GOD SEES YOU IN THE RAPTURE EXCITEMENT! In the booth was a display of what seemed to be long underwear or pajamas covered with tiny flashing lights. Another booth, this one offering strobing electric jewelry, bore a sign declaring: STAND OUT FROM THE CROWD AND GET GOD'S ATTENTION AFTER YOU LOSE YOUR CLOTHING. Lorinda's eyes were flitting from one display to the next. "Keep your head down," Stimpy said. "They have your picture." Lorinda guiltily complied.

She was about to ask where they were going when a short, primly dressed woman, with long, graying, ponytailed hair, fell in with them. Throwing her arms around Stimpy, she kissed him on the cheek, saying, "Terrible, terrible, terrible. Their goddam guns." She let go of Stimpy and looked him and Lorinda up and down as they walked. "And look at you with *your* guns. A couple of real gangsters."

"Margaret," said Stimpy, "this is Wilma."

"Wilma Flintstone," the woman smiled, shaking Lorinda's hand. Then, to Stimpy: "We didn't have time to prep for you. I think we have a safe hotel room. For a couple of days, max. We're trying to find you a car."

"They got her picture at the ticket booth," Stimpy said.

Wilma sighed. "Damn. Okay, we'll have Archie change what you look like. Don't worry, we'll get you back on the road as soon as we can."

A grizzled, hobo-looking old man — who reminded Lorinda of the old men she'd seen in the alleys of Austin and that decrepit mall parking lot — came out from behind a flashing-jewelry booth and headed toward them. "Religion is the public-facing bureaucracy of capitalism," he growled. "God is an alias for 'money.' Aristotle said that." As he passed them, he whispered something to Wilma before he continued on his way, muttering about the Bible being a work of fan fiction.

"That's the Reverend" Wilma said. "There are lots of reverends in Revelation, but he's THE Reverend, and he's with us. Used to be an actual pastor here before..." She laughed. "Before he saw the light."

"They don't lock him up for talking like that?" Stimpy asked.

"I think they feel sorry for him," Wilma said. "They still see him as one of their own. They think he went mad — which I suppose from their point of view, he did. Anyway, they're too focused on the end of the world to care what he says. Probably if he stopped saying those things they'd get suspicious."

"What did he tell you?"

"He said he checked your hotel room and it's secure."

Lorinda smiled. "So he may be crazy, but he's not stupid." She tried to scope out her surroundings while keeping her head down. "There are no bars around here?" she asked.

Stimpy and Wilma just laughed.

"I miss PumpJack's," Lorinda said to herself.

29 *In which our heroine has pizza for the first time and readies herself to be an old fogey.*

"I WAS GOING to be his thesis advisor," Wilma said between bites of pizza. "He would have made a great professor. Whip those kids' brains into shape."

Stimpy gave her an affectionate smile. He said to Lorinda, "Wilma's the one behind everything we're doing. She made it all happen."

They were in a small hotel room. A pizza box occupied the middle of the bed. Lorinda sat cross-legged at the head while Stimpy sat on the edge to Lorinda's right, Wilma at the foot of the bed. "I've never had pizza like this," Lorinda said. "So good."

"You don't get good pizza in Perfecton?" Stimpy asked. "Isn't everything perfect there? By definition?"

"The only kind we get comes on little muffins. It's like: muffin, a slice of tomato, and some cheese on top. Open-faced."

"That's not pizza," Wilma said between bites. "That's not even a good *muffin*. And, by the way, this isn't such great pizza either. The man who runs the pizza parlor here, he owned a pizza joint in Brooklyn. New York City. Left during the Great Migration. Total religious nut. Like everyone here." She took another bite. "He's always complaining about mozzarella."

"Who's Mozzarella?" Lorinda asked.

"It's a kind of cheese."

"Tastes good to me," Lorinda said. "So you figured out how to get girls out of the country for a . . . reset?"

"She was doing it even before The Split," Stimpy said. "They were outlawing abortions way earlier."

"It wasn't an original idea," said Wilma. "The original Underground Railroad beat us to it in the nineteenth century. Not to imply that they were doing it for exactly the same reasons, mind you."

"This woman I met in Little Harlem used those words, 'Underground Railroad.' I never heard that before."

"Education in these here Confederated States," Wilma said, with a shake of her head. She picked up another slice of pizza.

"The nineteenth-century Underground Railroad," Stimpy explained, "was a secret network of people who brought slaves from the South, the slave states, up north to the free states."

"And Canada," Wilma added.

"Wow," said Lorinda. "Brave."

"When it was obvious that education was dead in this dumb New Country — and it was obvious right away — your boy Stimpy here got busy running all around Texas, and most of the rest of the CCSA. Rounding up people who felt the same way we did."

"It was all her," Stimpy said. "I was like her lieutenant. Support staff."

"He's way too modest."

"It's pretty... heroic," Lorinda said, then instantly felt foolish. "And all your funny names? What's that about?"

"I taught a class called The History of the American Cartoon," said Wilma. "Probably my favorite class of all time. Very close to my heart. When we started making plans to do this it was clear that we'd be in danger, and that as a precaution we should adopt aliases. To me it seemed natural to use cartoon names — the names of cartoon characters — and that's what we did. Of course, not everyone loved the idea."

"She's met Bill and Hillary," Stimpy said.

"Ahh, Bill and Hillary. So much more dignified than Mickey and Minnie." Then, to Lorinda: "Do you have the vaguest idea who the real Ren and Stimpy are? Or were?"

Lorinda shrugged.

Wilma reached down and grabbed a screen pad from her bag on the floor. "Ren and Stimpy," she said to the pad.

A moment later she passed it to Lorinda, who started giggling almost immediately as she watched two surreal animals — what they were supposed to be she couldn't tell — beat the living hell out of each other. "Stimpy's the one on the right," Wilma said.

"I see why you gave them those names," she said to Wilma as the clip ended and the next one began with Ren saying, "*Steempy, you eedjit . . .*"

"We picked those names ourselves." Stimpy tried to laugh, but some deeper feeling overwhelmed him and choked it off. He looked away, eyes tearing. Lorinda put down the pad and started to move toward him, but Wilma got there first, sliding over and enveloping him with a hug. Head on her shoulder, he wept until he was out of tears, finally saying: "I didn't do anything. I could have saved him."

"You didn't know that guy was a lunatic," Lorinda said. "You couldn't know he was going to shoot."

"I should have known."

"No," Lorinda said firmly. "You couldn't. Crazy is crazy and unpredictable."

"He was a wonderful man," Wilma said, patting Stimpy's back. "He loved you dearly. And he died for the cause."

Stimpy heaved a great sigh, then stood and wordlessly headed to the bathroom to splash some water on his face.

Wilma also stood, picked up her pad, dropped it into her bag, and looked intensely at Lorinda. "How do you feel?"

"I'm okay," Lorinda said. "I mean, I can't believe what happened to Ren. Roger..."

"Physically," Wilma said. "How are you physically?"

"Oh, that. I don't feel anything at all yet. I mean, it's so early. I feel normal."

"Good."

"I can't believe I *did* that," Lorinda continued. "He was just some random guy at the bar — "

"It doesn't matter," said Wilma. "These things happen. We'll help you deal with it." Then, projecting her voice so Stimpy could hear her over the running water, she said "Don't go anywhere tonight. I'll be back in the morning with Archie. He'll finish you up — costumes, hair, makeup, the whole deal. When he's done, you'll look like old fogeys. You won't recognize yourselves. There's a bed and a couch. You can figure out who sleeps where."

"You can have the bed," Lorinda and Stimpy called out at the same time.

Lorinda laughed and hollered: "Steempy, you eedjit!"

"You'll work it out," Wilma said. "Try to get some sleep. You'll need it."

"I have one question," Lorinda said. "Would a couple of old fogeys take the Rapture Ride?"

"Definitely," said Wilma. "That's a fogey ride." Then, whispering: "Take good care of him. He's a little fragile right now." With that, she left.

Wilma and Archie arrived at 6:30 the next morning. Although only in his mid-thirties, Archie's hair was white. Crewcut. He was almost unhealthily thin and wore a tight white tee-shirt, tight white pants, and white sneakers. Having finished with Stimpy, he was standing and staring at Lorinda. "You don't want your hair as white as mine," he said. "You don't want to stand out. And anyway, it's too much work." He jerked his head toward Wilma, sitting on the side of the bed. "Maybe something like hers. A nice, dull gray."

"Fuck you," Wilma said.

"Language!"

Lorinda sat in the room's only chair, backed up against a small chest of drawers. Archie plopped down on the bed next to Stimpy and continued studying Lorinda.

Meanwhile, Lorinda was gazing at Stimpy and shaking her head. "I literally don't recognize you," she said to him. His hair was a distinguished steely gray and quite a bit shorter than it had been. The beard was gone, replaced by realistic-looking creases and crinkles.

"Wait till I get done with *you*," Archie said to Lorinda. "And we haven't even talked about your boring costumes yet."

Wilma, turning to Stimpy, said, "You should shuffle around a little. Get used to walking *old*."

Stimpy stood and hobbled in a circle in the small patch of available floor space.

Wilma laughed. "You can loosen up a bit," she said. "You look like a little kid playing old."

He shuffled past Wilma. "I think the secret is to walk *careful*," he said. "How's this?"

"Better."

Stimpy stopped at the small night table by the head of the bed.

"Think you can get us another car before we leave tomorrow?" he asked while opening the night table drawer and extracting a book that said *Holy Bible* on its cover.

"Working on it," said Wilma.

"I've been meaning to ask," said Lorinda. "What's with the lit-up underwear and flashing jewelry and all that?"

"I guess you're not a Rapturist," Stimpy said. "The idea is, when the Rapture arrives — "

"You'd better get naked!" Archie interjected. "Looking forward to it!"

"Only those who are pure of heart get swept up to heaven," Stimpy said. "Meaning, those who have accepted Jesus. But somehow it's better if you're not wearing any clothes."

"Everything's better without clothes," Archie said.

Wilma took over the lecture. "Some people believe that's nonsense about the clothing. Others say that God'll undress you automatically, because only your natural body can make the journey. No clothes, no tattoos, or dental fillings, or jewelry, or prostheses, or fake boobs. Nothing you weren't born with. You sometimes see people arguing, right out on the street, about what happens if you don't take off your clothes. *You go straight to hell! No you don't! Jesus rejects you! No! He loves you whether you're wearing clothes or not!* They go on and on. It's fucking insane. Just a couple of months ago two women were arguing about it in a store, right down the street from here, and one of them ended up with a bullet in her head."

"She was shot because of a stupid argument?" Lorinda asked, eyes wide.

"Stone cold dead," said Wilma. "And the shooter wasn't arrested! She said they were having a doctrinal dispute. No one, not the security force, not the Council of Elders, was willing to call it a crime."

"What happened to Maintain the Population?" Lorinda said.

"This is an enclave," Wilma said. "They make up the laws as they go along."

"Wait a minute," Stimpy said. "They still have a Council of Elders?"

"Hell, yeah," Wilma said. "It wouldn't be Revelation without those loonies. But they're just figureheads. It's the Richie Riches in Austin who run the place."

Stimpy suddenly remembered the book he had in his hand. "This can't be *THE Bible*!" he said. "It's too thin!" He held it open so the others could see. "It says *Holy Bible* but it's, like, fifteen pages long. And it's illustrated. It's a fucking comic book!" He flipped through it before looking at Wilma. "There's just one chapter: Revelation!"

"Whadja expect?" Archie cracked. "You think people around here can read?"

30 *In which our heroine finally gets to experience the Rapture Ride.*

ARCHIE FINISHED HIS work by ten-thirty. He took a step back and regarded Lorinda, then Stimpy. He nodded in mock respect. "Grandma. Pops."

Wilma handed him the same kind of device Lorinda had seen before. Archie quickly took her picture, followed by Stimpy's. In a half-minute it dispensed two new Citizen Cards. Archie handed one to each of them.

"Whoa," said Lorinda, "I'm fifty-seven years old!" She thrust her hand toward Stimpy. "I'm Randi Howland from Barronville. Pleased to meet you."

"Edward Chapman," Stimpy said. "Sixty-one years young. Odessa's my hometown. Texas. Not Russia." They ceremoniously shook hands as Archie printed out two strips of paper and handed them to the newly minted senior citizens.

"Better look those over before you leave," Wilma said, "if you want to know who you are. Okay, so let's work on your walks for a few minutes, and then we're out of here."

After a bit of "walk old" coaching, Wilma cautioned them to wait fifteen minutes after she and Archie left, to avoid any possibility of being spotted together. Then she hugged them, said she'd be back in the morning, and left with Archie in tow.

It was a gorgeous day. By the time Lorinda and Stimpy exited the dark hotel lobby, the sun was blasting, momentarily immobilizing them as their eyes adjusted. They looked like a dull, squinty, aging couple, wearing faded jeans, faded plaid shirts, and faded baseball caps. No one gave them a second glance. They were effectively invisible. The only mildly distinctive thing about them was that they were each wearing a big automatic weapon, while most of the other pedestrians toted lighter, more convenient jumbo handguns. Not that the sight of a middle-aged couple packing military-spec people-shredders caused even a ripple of interest. That was one of the great things about living in the CCSA: You could walk down the street brandishing a handheld rocket launcher and no one would say boo. Lorinda and Stimpy were just another older couple — slightly over-armed, perhaps, but understandably so, given the caution or paranoia or dementia that came with their advanced years.

They put on the boring sunglasses Archie had provided. Arm-in-arm, they walked — Stimpy with a cane — toward the place Archie had told them served a pretty good breakfast. It also happened to be on the way to the Rapture Ride, which was Lorinda's project for the day. By the time they reached the diner, their old-fogey gaits were synchronized, and convincing.

They were the sole occupants of the place. The teenaged waiter treated them with the condescending respect due to oldsters. The breakfast was better than expected, for which they were grateful.

They left and resumed their slow trudge down the street. As they approached it, an electronic mini-billboard that had been pointing the way to the Rapture Ride abruptly flashed NEWS BULLETIN, followed by USA CAVES TO POWERFUL CCSA. They stopped to watch.

The flashing title cut abruptly to CEO McWeeny at a lectern, apparently in the middle of a speech, saying: "...the USA is begging to be allowed to crawl back to the CCSA. Look what she said just a few minutes ago." At which point the picture switched to a shot of an attractive, stylishly dressed, fiftyish woman with dark, lustrous hair sitting at a big desk, speaking confidently to the camera; it was captioned ANITA FLORES GULDEN PRESIDENT OF THE USA, WHITE HOUSE, WASHINGTON DC.

"We already have some mutually beneficial commercial relations," President Gulden said, "but I look forward to more. I hope that one day the CCSA will change its attitude and do what it takes to join us in the United Nations and NATO. I hope our sports teams will one day compete. I hope our citizens will be free to visit their relatives and friends across the border. I can even imagine that one day we'll get rid of that border. To paraphrase a former occupant of this office: Mr. McWeeny, tear down that wall."

The picture switched back to McWeeny, now red-faced, jowls glistening, ready to explode. "See? What did I tell you? They're desperate! Their economy is failing, their citizens are dropping dead as they try to scale the wall — the wall that *they* built — to take advantage of *our* freedoms! And she's saying that *we're* the ones that need to change! That bitch has a lot of nerve! God bless y'all, and God bless the Confederation of Conservative States of America." The screen flashed THANK YOU CEO MCWEENY, then switched back to pointing the way to the Rapture Ride.

"That was weird," Lorinda whispered as they started walking again.

"Every word he said was a lie," Stimpy spat. "And people eat it up. They actually think the US built the walls. Fucking morons."

"I mean, you can't really blame them. It's what they get taught in school — "

"Please. Okay, if you're seven years old you can't be expected to know how to think for yourself. But for fuck's sake, just watching that bag of shit talk, you can see he's lying. It just oozes out of his pores — "

"All *right*." She didn't like cutting him off. But sometimes his little rants made her feel... diminished, somehow. Like a naïve child. It wasn't *her* fault she had been almost entirely raised with — or maybe indoctrinated in — the CCSA version of things. And she was doing her best, now, to catch up with what kept revealing itself as the truth. Still... She stopped walking and squeezed his arm. "Sorry."

"Forget it," he said. "I get carried away. Y — "

"*Oh my God.*" She was suddenly aware of what they were standing in front of. "We're here!"

Lorinda gazed in wonder at the ride she'd been hearing about since she was a kid. It was enormous, not so much high as endlessly wide. It was like an entire amusement park in a single ride. The grand entrance consisted of a line of glass double-doors, above which stretched a gigantic arched sign of thousands of tiny lights reading THE RAPTURE EXPERIENCE.

"It's six or seven big rollercoasters the billionaires behind this place bought up from all over the CCSA," Stimpy said. "They disassembled them, carted them here, and put them back together — with Rapture-ready modifications."

"Have you ever been on it?"

"Nah," said Stimpy, pretending he wasn't at all interested. "But I'm glad we're doing it," he said. "It'll be good research."

"Research my ass," Lorinda said. They both laughed, then approached the ticket machine. Stimpy paid $2,500 for two tickets and they passed through the turnstile and — remembering to walk old — lined up behind a few dozen eager, mostly middle-aged, people. A big electronic sign on the wall flashed:

GET READY FOR
THE CREATION OF ISRAEL AND SIGNS OF THE END TIMES
THE RAPTURE
RISE OF THE ANTI-CHRIST
THE SEVEN SEALS
THE THIRD TEMPLE
WAR
FAMINE
THE TWO WITNESSES
DEATH
THE TRIBULATION MARTYRS CRY OUT IN HEAVEN
EARTHQUAKE
THE SUN BECOMES BLACK
THE STARS FALL TO EARTH
144,000 JEWISH VIRGINS PROSELYTIZE FOR CHRIST

And there was more. "Holy shit," said Lorinda. "I never heard of any of this. Except the Rapture."

"You're not stupid. Just ignorant."

"Don't forget uneducated"

"Yeah," laughed Stimpy, "that too. And a bad Christian."

"Thanks. I appreciate it."

The little roller-coaster train trundled up and squealed to a halt at the start-finish line. The passengers getting off — again, mostly middle-aged, with a sprinkling of kids and fogeys — were clearly shaken-up and exhilarated by the ride. They climbed and shimmied and clambered away, loudly laughing off the terror they'd felt at the top of the big drops, praising the ride, and speculating about when they would be Raptured up to heaven for real. The gate opened once the train was empty and the new load scrambled in — Stimpy and Lorinda remembering to walk old and struggle a bit to fit themselves into their seats. They gently set their weapons, along with Stimpy's cane, on the floor.

As Lorinda and Stimpy clicked the security bar in place across their laps, a voice said, "I bet you two have been here before." It took Lorinda a moment to realize that the young woman sitting in the car in front of them had turned around and was addressing them.

"No," Lorinda said. "Actually, this is our first time."

"We live way out west," Stimpy said. "We never get this far east."

"We're on vacation," Lorinda added unnecessarily. "Driving around Texas."

"Texas is real big," said the woman, whose hair was like a huge, bright yellow, fuzzy bubble. "Usually the old people — old*er* people — on the ride have been coming here, like, every year since the place opened. Not that you're old."

"How long is the ride?" Lorinda asked.

"Oh," said the woman, "maybe forty-five minutes. Or an hour."

"Or eternity," said the woman's husband, who had turned to face them. He was rather short, and all they could see of him was his heavily bearded face and his tall black cowboy hat. Lorinda briefly entertained the hope that the hat wouldn't obscure her view of what was to come. The little train started moving. "We're lucky," he said. "We live right here in Revelation. Well," he said as he turned to face forward, "God bless."

"This is our thirty-seventh time on this ride, and we see new things every time," the woman said. "Have fun. You'll love it." As she turned around to face the front, Lorinda heard her say, "Now hold onto that stupid hat. You don't want it blowing off like last time."

31 *In which our heroine's long-awaited Rapture Ride experience is interrupted.*

THE CARS CLIMBED the first rise, enclosed on both sides by walls of cartoony murals depicting the Bible's greatest hits, some easily identifiable, like the Garden of Eden and the Great Flood, and some that were mystifying to Lorinda and Stimpy. The train climbed and climbed, the angle of incline growing increasingly steep. It finally emerged from the murals, accompanied by a cry of surprise from the first-timers, amazed by how high up they were. Although it was a little dizzy-making for Lorinda — enough so that she reflexively grabbed Stimpy's arm — she had the presence of mind to survey the scene down below, noting how many white church steeples were sticking up above the level of Revelation's houses, apartment buildings, schools, and commercial structures. As it crested the peak, the train passed under an arched sign captioned THE CREATION OF ISRAEL AND SIGNS OF THE END TIMES.

Then the coaster started downhill. Straight down. It was almost a ninety-degree drop. As it gained speed, the helpless passengers, including Lorinda, couldn't help but scream. It was virtual freefall; those who hadn't experienced the ride before assumed something had gone terribly wrong and they were all about to die. After a brief eternity of terror, the little train plunged into darkness, the tracks flattened out, the wheels screeched, and heavy g-force shoved the riders down into their seats. Then the tracks curved back up again and the coaster emerged into daylight. But it wasn't just going up. It was going up and over: a full, dizzying, 360-degree vertical loop.

After which the train was once again in darkness. It smelled to Lorinda like her basement in Perfecton. The train shuddered to a full stop, accompanied by a different kind of screech and the smell of hot metal (or possibly asbestos) dust from its crude braking system. A booming voice intoned "Welcome to the creation of Israel and signs of the End Times." Then, accompanied by a thunderclap that caused the riders to jump, thighs colliding with security bars, a diorama next to the coaster was blasted by bright lights. A classic Shylock-looking man with an exaggerated hooked nose sat at a desk piled with paperwork. On a wall behind him, a sign proclaimed WELCOME HOME JEWS. A small gaggle of big-nosed men and women, dressed in their shtetl finery, leaned eagerly toward the desk.

"The stage is set for the End Times," the announcer's voice boomed, "when, in May of 1948, the state of Israel is founded. Christians the world over happily await the return of all the world's Jews to their homeland."

Klezmer music blasted as the diorama came to life. The man behind the desk stood up jerkily and lip-synced "Welcome to Israel" in the voice of the same announcer. The shtetl people, moving clumsily, swarmed him and, one by one, shook his outstretched hand.

The coaster-train inched forward. The diorama went dark.

"Those are good robots," Lorinda whispered.

"They're not robots," Stimpy whispered back. "They're actors pretending to be robots."

"What? Why?"

"It's cheaper than buying robots."

"Why not just have them be people?"

"Because people aren't cool. Robots are cool."

"That's crazy."

"Shhh."

As the train rolled slowly forward, another loud thunderclap scared the riders. The announcer hissed, "Godlessness!" just as the second diorama lit up: a combination opium den, gay bar, and cheesy Roman orgy. To the sound of corny hootchie-kootchie jazz, partly clad actors — again moving robotically — rubbed against each other. "The modern world continues to decline into godlessness," said the announcer. "As Paul's second epistle to Timothy says, 'Men are lovers of their own selves, covetous, boasters, proud, blasphemous, disobedient to parents, unthankful, and unholy.' Christians the world over gaze upon this in dismay, happily awaiting the return of Jesus."

Three seconds later the music abruptly ended and the lights went out again.

"Pastor Doug never talks about this stuff," Lorinda said.

"Who the fuck is Pastor Doug?"

"Shhh."

"False messiahs and prophets," yelled the announcer. On the other side of the tracks, a wall of old-looking television sets lit up showing popular-culture icons from the USA, familiar only to the older CCSA citizens: music stars, movie stars, comedians, news presenters — accompanied by a tinny version of a song whose words sounded to Lorinda like "Yummy yummy yummy I've got love in my tummy." As the train moved past the screens, the announcer shouted over the music: "As Matthew said, there will be false messiahs and false prophets, deceiving many. Do not follow them! And do not let your children follow them!"

The music stopped, the televisions went dark, and the train plunged nearly straight down, eliciting another nervous scream from the riders. As the train leveled out and stopped, the sound of a martial snare drum faded in and the announcer growled, "Matthew also tells of wars and rumors of wars." A warmly illuminated, cozy living room appeared, with a mother, a father, an eight-year-old boy, and a six-year-old girl — all immobile, all with frozen grins on their faces — gathered around a screen watching a football game. At the sound of an electronic beep, the two children and the mother turned robotically to look at the father. Dad robotically fished a device out of his pocket, turned to his family, and said: "It's Dave. He says there's going to be another war next week." All but strong, stoic dad started sobbing robotically.

The scene went dark and the train lurched forward and braked sharply three times before it came to rest again. An unidentifiable sound faded in. Was it a heavy wind? An earthquake? A volcano erupting? When the sound reached its peak, a curved wall displaying pictures of natural disasters slowly lit up, one fading into the next as the announcer gravely said: "Famine, pestilences, earthquakes."

The wall of disaster reached its full illumination. The riders became slowly aware that there was someone else looking at it — a dark, brooding figure in a sort of monk's robe, with the hood up. The figure slowly — robotically — turned to face the spectators and let the hood fall back as a heavenly choir started to sing on the soundtrack. It was Jesus! A classic blond, long-haired, Nordic Jesus, who lifted his arms up and out as if to embrace his flock. Then, lip-syncing to the announcer's voice, he said, "I am ready to summon you." Sobbing could be heard from a few cars of the coaster-train.

"Look," whispered Stimpy, gesturing toward the Christ figure. "He's sixteen years old. His beard's slipping off!" As the young actor attempted, robotically, to straighten out the beard, his blond wig started falling to one side. Lorinda and Stimpy did their best to keep from laughing.

The lights went out and the little train began to roll. In a moment it was straining and juddering uphill at a steep angle, approaching daylight. The area surrounding the ride came into view. They were three or four stories up. People down below were strolling, chatting, and occasionally looking up and waving to the Rapture riders.

"I can't believe there's another forty-five minutes of this," Lorinda said. She gazed past Stimpy, scanning life down below. Then her expression changed to one of sheer terror. She bent over and tried to bury her face in his lap, bumping her head on the security bar in the process.

"What?" he said.

"It's her! Down there!"

"Who?"

"Janelle Stark!"

Stimpy casually turned and looked down. He saw Stark immediately, a woman in a black jumpsuit, her head heavily bandaged, surrounded by conspicuously armed thugs, all in CCSA Domestic Security uniforms except for the huge one standing next to her, who was in a tight-fitting suit. On the fringe of the group was a nervous-looking young man in street clothes, also with a bandaged face.

Lorinda, her head still low, reached into her purse, took out the Rapture pager she'd been given by the ticket kid, and held it up so Stimpy could see it. "Good idea, but not yet," he said. He looked forward, saw that the lead car was just approaching the peak, then saw the service ladder he was hoping to see. When he looked back down to the Confederals, the woman appeared to be ordering her minions to disperse in various directions.

"Okay," Stimpy said. "*Now!*"

32 *In which our heroine triggers the Rapture... or something.*

LORINDA FLIPPED THE little red hatch open and pushed the red button. Nothing. She pushed harder. A tiny red light on the alarm glowed red and something exploded very close to the ride. Everyone lurched forward as the train stopped abruptly, with the first car just under a sign for THE RAPTURE. There were more explosions, many more, near and far, seemingly from all over the enclave. They made a lot of noise but didn't seem to do any actual damage. Then came the sirens. A recorded voice — the voice of the ride's narrator— boomed and echoed: "And He will send His angels and gather His elect from the four winds, from the ends of the earth to the ends of the heavens. Mark 13:27." Fireworks shot into the air from each of the many alarm towers. They were loud but, except for their black puffs of pyrotechnic smoke, nearly invisible in the bright daylight.

The woman in front of them released her security bar, stood up, and screamed to no one in particular: "This is it! Praise Him!" She yanked off her blond bubble of a wig and tossed it overboard, where it drifted down like some bizarre deep-sea creature. This exposed a sweaty mop of short brown hair on the woman's head. She then frantically started tearing off her clothes. The buttons popped off her loose pink blouse, revealing the white bra underneath.

"Maybe this is just a new part of the ride?" her husband said hopefully.

"It's real, you idiot!" she screamed. "Take off your clothes!" He stood and reluctantly began unbuttoning his shirt. She ferociously grabbed his collar, yanked it hard enough to pop all *his* buttons, then started clawing at his belt.

Lorinda and Stimpy also stood and surveyed the chaos around and below them. Many people were yelling "Take off your clothes!" as they shed shirts, blouses, skirts, slacks, and shorts. A few cars behind them, a squat, plump guy in his thirties, already naked, was dangling from the sill of the low wall that looked out onto the grounds. Lorinda thought: *Why is he trying to get out? Doesn't he think God can find him right here?*

Unable to hang on, he fell, crashing through the roof of the "Famine, Pestilences, Earthquakes" exhibit. Those on the ground, who themselves were yelling and panicking, dodged badly aimed fireworks, not to mention discarded items raining down from the Rapture Ride — clothes, shoes, com devices, Rapture pagers, guns. Some got distracted from removing their clothes by the sight of discarded valuables — wallets, jewelry, watches — that they ran to retrieve, then drop again as they remembered that they were about to be sucked up to a place where those trinkets would be worthless.

Stimpy gently took hold of Lorinda's shoulder and pointed. "We're going there," he said, indicating the front car.

"Where?" She spotted the narrow ladder next to where the front car was parked. Curved hand-holds rose up from it like the ladders in swimming pools. "That?"

"That's how we get down."

Since Janelle and her crew were busy dodging flying detritus along with everyone else on the ground, Lorinda figured she and Stimpy could get down without being seen — if they could reach the ladder. But the train cars were hemmed in on either side by the low walls, with no catwalk beside it. Before she could ask how they were going to get to the ladder, Stimpy said: "I wanted to stop the ride here, before it started going downhill. We'll climb over these people. They're a little preoccupied."

So saying, he picked up the guns, handed one to Lorinda and strapped on the other, stood on the seat, put a foot on the front of their car, and took a big step onto the seat of the car in front — where the naked couple was too busy looking to the sky, waving their arms, and shrieking, "Here, God! We're here! God! We're here!" They took no notice of Stimpy standing on the seat between them.

He reached back, grabbed Lorinda's hand, and helped her make the move. They did this four more times — passing riders who were ripping their clothes off or digging in their backpacks for their light-up garments and jewelry — until Stimpy reached the front car, where a nude man and woman were madly bedecking themselves with flashing necklaces, bracelets, and headbands. He kicked their clothes and a six-shooter in a fancy leather holster off the seat and gave Lorinda a hand into the car. She accidentally clunked the woman's head with the butt of her gun, but the woman didn't notice.

"Let's hope it goes all the way to the bottom," Stimpy said. He squeezed past the oblivious man and moved within the hand-holds. Gripping them, he threw a leg over the wall, felt for a rung, found one, and started down. Lorinda followed.

"Stay still!" Janelle Stark yelled at her crew. But it was an impossible order to follow: Those who weren't standing next to her couldn't hear over the din, and the chaos surrounding them — the madly screaming people, the objects falling from the ride (including two madly screaming falling people) — was beyond distracting.

Near her, a Domestic Security goon nervously swiveled his head to take in the full scope of the action. "It's the Rapture," he said out loud, more to himself than anyone else. Then, louder: "The Rapture! The Rapture! The Rapture!" He started unbuttoning his shirt.

"Stop that!" Stark growled.

Stimpy and Lorinda reached ground level. "Shit," Stimpy said, "I forgot my cane."

"You'll survive," Lorinda said. "Can you see her?"

The foot of the ladder had deposited them within the framework of the ride's structure. They ducked behind a vertical I-beam and cautiously peered out across the grounds. Stimpy quickly homed in on the Domestic Security contingent: They were the only ones who weren't screaming and waving their arms around, or naked, or wearing flashing lights. His eyes quickly found the bandaged-headed woman in the center of the cluster. She appeared to be yelling at one of them, who was shirtless and gazing up at the sky while he unbuckled his belt. Suddenly there was a pistol in her hand. The shirtless man dropped his pants, which pooled around his feet. He stood there, now clad only in red and white striped boxer shorts, continuing to gaze at the sky and wave his hands in the air. Janelle Stark pressed the gun to his temple and shouted at him. He didn't respond.

The sound of the gunshot — a sharp crack — was loud enough to be heard over the pandemonium. The Confeds closest to the action jumped back in shock as their colleague, head spurting blood, collapsed to the ground. *Well, that's one way to get to Heaven,* Stimpy thought. It gave him a clear view of the huge thug in the civilian suit. He was laughing, possibly for the first time in his life.

"She's dangerous," Stimpy said. "Insane and dangerous. Let's go. And walk *old*."

33 *In which Lorinda and Stimpy slip out of Revelation under cover of pandemonium.*

LORINDA AND STIMPY understood, without speaking, that although they needed to walk old, they had to move faster than they had on the way to the Rapture Ride, both because it would be noticeably weird to be walking slowly in the midst of this chaos and because they had to get out of there as quickly as possible. So they had to walk slow but fast.

Lorinda couldn't help herself — as she scooted past one of the ride's pilings she looked toward Janelle's little army. She gasped at what she saw.

Janelle, gun in hand, was pushing her way through her men until she stood in front of Brad, who was still bandaged, and now shirtless, sitting on the ground and working on his belt. She grabbed his chin, yanked him to a standing position, and jammed the gun into his forehead.

Lorinda froze, horrified by what she thought she was about to see. But then Brad said something, Janelle lowered the gun, and Brad scooped up his shirt.

"Hurry up," Stimpy urged. Following closely, Lorinda found herself wondering if Brad had been planning to remove the bandage for smoother Rapturing. But did God really want that? To see everyone's icky, unhealed wounds? She gave a little laugh — and then stifled it. This wasn't funny.

They emerged from behind the ride and, facing away from Janelle's crew, walking old but fast past frenzied naked CCSA citizens and piles of their discards, headed toward the parking lot. She suddenly wrinkled her face in disgust. "What. Is. That. *Smell?*"

Without looking at her, Stimpy said, "People are shitting themselves."

"Fear?"

"I guess. Fear? Excitement? They're trying to leave their bodies behind? Who the fuck knows with these people. C'mon."

They hobbled on. When she came to an automatic weapon similar to theirs lying on the ground in front of her, Lorinda bent down and scooped it up. Stimpy gave her a nod of approval, then spotted a few handguns on the ground and did the same. Soon they were lugging as many guns as they could carry, cradling rifles in outstretched arms like firewood and dangling pistols from their fingers. When Stimpy came upon a shopping cart full of recently purchased food, he emptied it on the ground and gently lowered his weapons into it, indicating that Lorinda's collection should go in there as well.

"I know I started this," Lorinda said, "but why do we need these? How many can we shoot at once?"

"They might come in handy," Stimpy said.

She shrugged and placed her guns in the cart on top of his. Glancing back and seeing no sign of Janelle or her crewmembers, they resumed their hike to the parking lot, now with Stimpy pushing the gun-filled shopping cart. A moment later, despite the swirling anarchy around them, they heard a woman yelling, "No, Jeffrey! Put them back down on the ground! Gently!" They turned just in time to see a young mother and father, both naked, glaring at their young son (How old could he be? Four? Five?). He was also naked, and was grinning as he pointed two pistols at them.

"We're about to go to Heaven," the father said, taking a step toward his child. "Put the guns down! This is the Rapture!" Giggling playfully, the little kid pulled a trigger just as his father's hands reached out for the weapons. The recoil knocked the kid over backward. He burst into tears as the bullet shredded the father's left hand and passed into his heart.

Lorinda was already springing forward to help, but Stimpy grabbed her arm, saying: "No! We have to get out of here."

"But — " She pointed. The mother was on her knees, screaming.

"They are reaping what they have sown," Stimpy said sternly. Then he hesitated. "Sowed. No, have sown."

Lorinda sighed and, reluctantly, nodded. They walked quickly toward the gate. "I guess we don't have to walk old anymore," she said. "No one's looking at us."

"The cameras," said Stimpy. "But, yeah. The main thing is, we need to get the fuck out."

They passed into the parking lot. The noise was all behind them, except for the ticket-booth kid, who was on the roof of the booth, naked, screaming, "Take me, God! Take me! Take me! I'm here! It's me, Cord! Take me . . . !"

"Shit," said Stimpy. He stopped pushing the cart and indicated with his head for Lorinda to look beyond the booth.

"Fuck," she said. There was a uniformed Domestic Security officer, no doubt one of Janelle's, standing near their car.

Leaving the shopping cart in place, Stimpy took Lorinda's arm and walked her to the side of the ticket booth, where they couldn't be seen by Janelle's man. He took his device out of his pocket and made a call. It went quickly: "Yes, we pushed the button . . . we spotted

Confeds looking for us . . . we're in the parking lot, and there's one of them on our car . . . yeah, we'll deal with it . . . perfect, thanks."

"Wilma?"

"Yeah," Stimpy said, re-pocketing his device. "Wait here." The kid was still raving on top of the booth. Stimpy shoved the shopping cart toward Lorinda. "I'll be right back."

He clicked the safety off his weapon and walked his best old-man walk toward the Zhiguli. The security man eyed him suspiciously. In his creakiest voice, Stimpy said, "You see what's going on in there?" He turned toward the enclave, then, in one slick move, spun back to face the Confed, unshouldered the weapon, dropped to one knee, and let loose a burst that cut the man's legs out from under him. In a second he was standing over the moaning figure who, despite the excruciating pain, was clumsily trying to unholster his gun. Stimpy put an end to that with a hard kick to the man's temple. "Have a nice Rapture," he muttered before taking the man's gun and hustling back to Lorinda.

"Oh, God, are you all right?" said Lorinda, throwing her arms around him. "I heard . . ."

"I was the shooter," Stimpy said.

Slightly embarrassed, she released her hug. "Now what?" she said.

"Wilma's setting up a car switch, but we're in this one for now. You have your Rapture pager?" Lorinda took it out of her bag. "Just drop it here." She dropped it. He did the same with his. "We don't want to be fined $2,500 each, do we? Okay, let's go."

With Lorinda by his side, he pushed the shopping cart to the car.

"Oh my God," Lorinda said when they came upon the crumpled tangle of limbs in a puddle of blood.

"It was him or us," Stimpy said. "If he's unlucky he might even live."

He opened the driver's-side back door and carefully placed the guns on the floor. "You drive." As Lorinda slipped in behind the wheel, he rammed the shopping cart hard into the inert Domestic Security officer, walked around the car, and got into the passenger seat.

34 *In which our heroine trades arms for freedom.*

LORINDA DROVE AS fast as she dared on old, pitted, badly maintained back roads, keeping an eye on the rear-view mirror to see if they were being followed. Stimpy navigated and messaged. Their ears were still ringing from the explosions and gunshots.

Finally, after a particularly long, involved message, Stimpy looked at her and said, "You play golf?"

Lorinda wasn't sure she heard him right. "What?"

"Golf. Do you play?"

She laughed. "Do I look like I play golf?"

"At the moment? You look like you barely play shuffleboard. But — "

"Why are you asking me that?"

"I just want to get to know you better, that's all."

"Fuck you."

They both laughed.

"You'll see," said Stimpy. "It'll be a surprise."

"Let me guess. It's my next fake identity: professional golfer." Then she pointed to a crappy-looking billboard ahead of them. All it said was "1000 YEARS REICH" above a big faded-red swastika in a black circle. "What the hell?"

"We must be close to the Nazi place." He hesitated before asking, "You know about Nazis, right?"

She briefly glared at him. "I've heard of them."

"I don't know if those jerks can even *afford* to be Nazis anymore," Stimpy said, ignoring her sarcasm. "You need serious money to actually start an enclave."

"From billionaires. Right?"

"Exactly." He laughed. "'Job creators.'" He sighed. "Turned out the financial degenerates — that's what Roger called the billionaire class — couldn't see a way to monetize a bunch of dumb anti-Semite fascists. Not that they didn't think about it. So instead of an actual enclave, they ended up with just a few dozen shacks in the middle of nowhere. All these clowns had was a pile of fake Nazi uniforms and some flags. I've seen videos of them practicing goose-stepping. It's hilarious. Like the world's worst marching band. Without instruments. They — "

"Wait a minute. They walked around stepping over geese?" It seemed improbable, but so did everything these days.

"*Hah!* No. Sorry. You know the way a goose literally walks?" He marched two stiff fingers along the dashboard. "With those little straight legs? And no knees? That's how the original Nazis marched. The German ones. With stiff legs. God knows why. I mean, if there actually was a God. Anyway, these idiots practiced marching like Nazis while they waited for their Hitler to arrive and tell them how to own the world for a thousand years." He laughed again.

"I know about Hitler, too," Lorinda said. "So they were sort of waiting for their messiah?"

"Very good, Lorinda Moon from Perfecton! But of course their messiah never showed up. At one point they thought it might be Donald Trump Junior. But you saw how *that* turned out. So their dreams of a thousand-year Reich died. Now all they do is hustle their Nazi schtick in whatever ways they can think of. And they're not too good at thinking." His amusement suddenly disappeared as the Zhiguli rounded a curve. "Fuck."

"Uh oh," Lorinda said. Ahead was a line of motionless vehicles, at the far end of which, a hundred yards off, a geyser of black smoke spewed heavenward. "Gotta be police up there." Lorinda slowed the car. She peered at the rear-view mirror. "Maybe I can turn around—"

"Forget it." Stimpy shook his head. "Too late. They'll see us and they'll come after us for sure. Shitfuck."

As, one by one, the cars ahead of them were released to resume their journeys, Lorinda eased the Zhiguli forward. Soon enough, they saw sitting athwart the road a black and white police pickup truck—with flashing blue lights, a big red swastika sloppily hand-painted on its door, and enormous vertical chrome exhaust pipes projecting well above the roof of the cab. In the bed of the pickup, visible when the black smoke wasn't drifting down and obscuring it, was a makeshift easel supporting a crudely painted sign:

GUN CHECK!!!!!!!
$2,500 FINE IF YOUR NOT CARRYING!!!!!!!

They sat in silence as the minutes ticked by. Finally, Lorinda rolled the Zhiguli up to the front of the queue and stopped level with a paunchy police officer in a threadbare, generic "official" police-uniform costume, with swastika patches on the shoulders and, on his breast, a couple of obviously fake plastic badges that might well have said OFFICIAL BIKINI INSPECTOR and BEER TASTERS OF CCSA. He leaned over to conduct an interrogation through Lorinda's open window. "Loyalty oath," the cop growled, eyes darting suspiciously back and forth between her and her passenger.

"I re-pledge my loyalty to Jesus Christ... or, wait, is it the sacred memory of Donald J. Trump? Darn. I always switch those around. Can I start over?"

"Sure," the cop said. "After you pay me a five hundred dollar fine and give me your Citizen Cards."

"I bet we pass the gun check, though," Lorinda said, flashing her best PumpJack's smile and indicating with a toss of her head that he should look behind her.

The cop's eyes went wide as they focused on the treasure trove behind the front seat. He slid to his right and flattened his face against the rear driver's-side window. Lorinda gave Stimpy a quick wink, then stuck her head out her window. "You can take a closer look if you like, sir. Mind if I jump out?"

"Sure, okay," the cop muttered, opening the back door.

Lorinda got out, glided over, and pressed herself lightly against him. "You can touch them if you like."

"Y'all sure have a lot of nice firearms," the cop said. He bent over and ran his hands over the guns on the floor.

"We love our guns. They keep us safe. You can hold them. Go on! Pick 'em up."

The cop picked two handguns, one a vintage revolver, the other a gleaming, streamlined North Korean job. He straightened up and held the guns lovingly, one in each hand, hefting their weight, his eyes darting hungrily from one to the other. "They're beauties," he said.

"We really have more than we need," Lorinda said. "We were thinking of donating a couple to your police department. If you want to take them and save us the trip, that would be great."

"What about one of them big doggies?" he asked, now seeming more like a child in a toy store than a police officer with swastikas on his shoulders. "I've always wanted one of them."

"Of course, sir," said Lorinda. "I'm sure your department can make good use of it."

"Right," said the cop. "My department." He gently set the two handguns on the roof of the car, bent back down, and came up with two automatic rifles. Like a kid asking for cookies, he said, "How about these two? Can I have two? We could really use these two."

In the cutest voice she could manage, Lorinda chirped, "Sure thing! As long as we're free to go."

He snugged the rifles under his left arm, carefully took the handguns off the roof with his right hand, and started toward his truck.

"We can go now, sir?"

He nodded and grunted without looking back at her.

"Thank you, officer," Lorinda called after him. "Have a blessed day, now. Sir."

She closed the back door, slipped into the driver's seat, shut her door, and slowly drove around the pickup truck. She flashed a big smile and waved at the cop, who was carefully setting his new arms collection on the truck's passenger-side floor. He took no notice of Lorinda.

"Fucker took four of our guns!" Stimpy said once they were out of range. "How do we even know he's a real cop? I doubt that those fake Nazis have their own police force. I mean, did you see his uniform? Or his truck?"

Lorinda laughed. "First," she said, "I wouldn't exactly say they're *our* guns. Second, did he check our credentials? Did he take us to fake-Nazi jail? Are we driving to . . . wherever we're supposed to be driving to? And third, you're welcome."

Stimpy nodded in apology. "Thank you. You were great," he conceded. "You're getting good at this."

"I better be. I'll be needing a new career."

"And you're an excellent driver."

"Stop. You'll make me blush. So where are we heading?"

"We stay on this road for another . . ." he checked his device. "Maybe twenty minutes. Then we change cars again — at Wonders of the Old South."

"Another enclave?"

"Nah. It's just . . . a place."

"Wait. Don't tell me. Is it a golf course?"

"That comes later. This one's just a place. A fucked-up place."

35 *In which our heroine does a bit of tactical shooting.*

SOON THEY WERE seeing animated billboards for "Wonders of the Old South": Beautiful people dancing under flashing lights, surrounded by walls displaying old-fashioned stuff like plows and sickles! Chaotic Civil War battle re-enactments, with drunken men in crude Johnny Reb gray and Yankee blue uniforms, wielding rifles and charging each other and falling down as women and children on the sidelines cheered! Elaborate wedding scenes, the brides in big poofy dresses like Scarlett O'Hara and the grooms in Rhett Butler waistcoats and vests, with a million bridesmaids and a preacher all in black! Happy families sitting at picnic tables, waving hot dogs or hamburgers in one hand and Confederate — not CCSA — flags with the other!

Lorinda, who had never heard of the place, was baffled. "So if this isn't an enclave, what is it?"

"It's an amusement park."

"An amusement park?"

"That's right," Stimpy said. "A place where people go to amuse themselves."

"By celebrating a war?"

"That they lost. Yes." He laughed. "I don't know how to tell you this, but it takes all kinds."

The final billboard in the series was nothing but a huge arrow pointing right, flashing the words: TURN HERE FOR WONDERS OF THE OLD SOUTH.

Lorinda turned onto a narrow, winding driveway. She drove slowly, not sure what to expect. The first amusement they encountered was, according to its sign, the CIVIL WAR FIELD OF GLORY. The field of glory was a rectangle of dirt the size of a football gridiron. From a public address speaker mounted high on a pole came the announcement, "And now... The Battle of Manassas." A few dozen actors, some in blue uniforms, some in gray, clumsily stuffed their muzzleloaders, yelled a lot and shook their fists in righteous fury, then shot blanks at each other, and either spouted copious quantities of stage blood and tumbled theatrically to the ground (the blues) or performed elaborate victory dances and war whoops (the grays). A small, motley gaggle of spectators standing on the sidelines intermittently cheered (for the good grays) and booed (the bad blues) while gobbling unidentifiable comestibles out of paper bags.

Next they came to a big, festive tent behind a SQUARE DANCING sign. Fiddle music blasted, occasionally overwhelmed by a nasal caller announcing dance moves that sounded like, "HONNAYA PA-NAH, HONNAYA-KAH-NAH, ALAMMA LET LET LET..." The dance floor was empty.

"That's kind of sad," Lorinda said.

"You want to do some square dancing?"

"I think I'll pass."

"That's what everyone says."

A little way down the road was what appeared to be an oversized antebellum mansion. As they drew closer, they realized it was in fact a whitewashed cinderblock edifice masquerading as a bloated house and festooned with ersatz antebellum signifiers. Its sign said BLUNDERBUSS RESTAURANT AND COCKTAIL LOUNGE. A smaller fake-old-timey building next door identified itself as PLANTATION SPA AND HAIR-NAIL SALON.

"That's where we're going," Stimpy said.

"To the spa? Great! I could use — "

"No. Over there." He pointed to a sprawling single-story building that might at one time have been a warehouse or server farm. A billboard on the roof identified it as the DISCOTHEQUE OF THE OLD SOUTH, the bold words surrounded by a border of dancing Confederate flags and blinking musical notes. To Lorinda's surprise, the vast parking lot was at least a third full.

"What are all these people doing here in the middle of the day? Free bar?" Her question was quickly answered by a sign atop the entrance kiosk: 75% OFF ADMISSION IF YOU'RE UNEMPLOYED. PRESENT UNEMPLOYMENT CARD IN SLOT.

"I'm unemployed, I guess," Lorinda said, stopping at the kiosk. "But I didn't get my card yet."

"You forgot to ask that crazy woman for one," Stimpy said, handing her his money card.

"Janelle Stark. Yeah, why didn't I think of that instead of hitting her with my gun?" She paid and continued into the parking lot. "And why are we here?" she asked.

"For one thing, no cameras. We hacked them a couple of years ago and they never got it together to fix them. And no one's going to see us meet our contacts." He read the latest text on his device. "See how close you can get to that corner of the building."

Lorinda found a spot and parked the Zhiguli. She opened the trunk while Stimpy gathered up the remaining weapons from the back-seat floor and brought them around. Hanging onto the two machine guns they had had with them on the Rapture Ride, he eased the others into the trunk and slammed the lid.

Lorinda scowled at the rifles Stimpy was holding. "I'm sick of carrying that big thing. I've got this," she said, slipping her hand into her bag and bringing out the pink Lady SIG Sauer.

"In case you have to shoot a mosquito?"

"No, but — "

His tone turned apologetic. "We don't want to attract attention." He held out her rifle. "Consider this part of your costume."

Lorinda sighed, then dropped her little handgun back in her bag and took the rifle he was offering. Grumpily, she slung it over her shoulder, then tapped the key fob to lock the car, and passed it to Stimpy.

"You promise me there are no cameras?" she asked as they made their way to the nearest entrance.

"That's what my people tell me. And my people know their shit."

Inside it was vast and dark, with glowing signs pointing the way to four separate dance halls: GRAND OLE OPRY, LINE DANCE COUNTRY, METAL MANIA, and PSYCHEDELIA. A confusion of bass notes pulsing behind the walls caused Lorinda's stomach to clench. Stimpy guided her to Psychedelia.

The room was cavernous. The music — wailing fuzztone guitars, pounding bass and drums — was overwhelming. Illumination was provided by ultraviolet lights. The décor consisted of blacklight-reactive murals, stickers of stars and planets, and random slashes of orange, yellow, and red paint. A blue pencil-beam — not black-light — was aimed at a huge, mirrored disco ball hanging from the middle of the high ceiling.

Lorinda, who had never seen anything like it (not counting the small glitter-balls in the rec room of Pastor Doug's Church), stopped and stared at the massive, slowly rotating mirrored orb.

Stimpy took her by the arm and steered her across the floor between dancing couples, many wearing glow-in-the-dark clothes, hats, dangly accessories, and long-hair "hippie" wigs. When they were under the disco ball, she shook free of his grip, put her arms around him, and tried to get him dancing. He made a couple of perfunctory moves while attempting to keep their bulky guns from colliding, but his focus was on the far side of the room, and he continued gliding in that direction, taking her with him.

Then he spotted what he was looking for and changed direction by a few degrees. In a moment he and Lorinda were dancing next to, and practically rubbing shoulders with, a couple who had clearly spent some time preparing themselves for Psychedelia. The man, who was a head shorter than Stimpy, wore an obviously fake beard, a blond long-hair wig, a shirt covered with glowing palm trees, and radiant orange shorts. The woman, in a zigzag-striped shirt-dress, had UV-sensitive lightning bolts and swirly lines on her face that made it impossible for Lorinda to know what she actually looked like.

"What's your name again?" Stimpy asked Lorinda.

"I can't hear you."

He leaned down until his mouth was practically in her ear. "Your name. I forget."

She turned his head sideways and shouted into his ear, "Randi Something! Howling?" She brightened. "Howland!" She slapped his arm in triumph.

He turned her toward the other couple, who were standing and waiting patiently. "Randi, meet Sluggo and Nancy."

The new people didn't catch the name, but they gave her big smiles anyway. As Stimpy and Sluggo did an elaborate fist-bump-hand-shake thing, Lorinda saw Sluggo discreetly slip a small black object to Stimpy, then hug him and say a few words into his ear. Then Stimpy gave Nancy a quick kiss on the cheek. She and Sluggo resumed their dancing as Stimpy took Lorinda in his arms and started shimmying her toward a door with a glowing exit sign over it.

They were halfway there when she stopped and shouted in his ear, "You dance like an old fogey."

"Thank you."

Lorinda was just setting up to twirl him around when the pop of a gunshot cut through the throbbing music. The couples surrounding them either dove for the floor, turned toward the exit and prepared to flee, or brandished their own guns. One or two fired in the direction from which they thought the original shot had come—but, between the pounding din and the room's acoustics, it was impossible to know.

Then panic swept the room. Many more shots were fired—from different positions, toward different targets. Everyone who thought they were part of the solution became, to someone else, the problem. Stimpy tried to pull Lorinda toward the exit, but by then the rush in that direction had already become a pileup: Far more people were trying to get through the door than could fit. A man next to them started screaming and waving his gun around; then suddenly there was blood gushing from a bullet hole in his neck and he collapsed at their feet.

Somehow, Lorinda was angered more than distressed by this grisly chaos. She coolly unshouldered her weapon and racked the slide.

Stimpy's eyes went wide. "*No!*" he yelled.

But she had already aimed the gun toward the center of the ceiling. A short, deafening burst from her automatic sent dozens of bullets streaming at the chain holding up the disco ball. Understanding that there was no way to hit it if she simply aimed at it — she knew she wasn't that good — Lorinda waggled the gun back and forth, as though watering a garden with a hose, passing across the chain holding the disco ball just enough to ensure that at least some of the deadly little missiles would find and shred their target.

The recoil launched her backward, and Stimpy grabbed her around the waist to hold her steady. The deafening gunfire plus the percussive clatter of the bullets hitting the ceiling, the chain, and whatever else was in Lorinda's range caused a hush to fall over the crowd, accompanied by a de facto cease-fire.

The chain began to give. The disco ball jerked downward, halted for a breathless moment, and fell another few feet. Those directly under it were instantly screeching and scrambling. Before the crashing sphere ignited another phase of panicky gunplay, Lorinda and Stimpy managed — using their weapons as bludgeons when necessary, and stepping over quivering or, in three cases, permanently stationary bodies — to hack their way to the exit.

36 *In which our heroine heads for the greens in a chartreuse truck.*

LORINDA AND STIMPY burst through the exit and into the parking lot, not far from where they'd left the Zhiguli. In their wake spilled a mob fleeing the next wave of flying bullets. After running past a few rows of cars, they stopped and huddled behind a tall van.

"Good shooting," Stimpy said.

"You liked that?"

"I did. Very quick thinking. You didn't lose your cool. And minimal peripheral damage. I wouldn't have thought of it!"

"Oh." She felt pleased. "Thanks — "

"You got us out of there fast. Now put the safety on."

"Oh… Right," Lorinda said, flipping the safety. "My adrenaline…" She patted her heart.

"Now we need to find a green Xiaomi Lumberjax crew-cab," Stimpy said. "Should be right around here somewhere."

"Is that it?" Lorinda indicated a shiny, new-looking, sickly chartreuse pickup several slots over from where they stood.

Stimpy pushed a button on the fob Sluggo had given him. The truck's lights flashed, and the first five notes of the Xiaomi jingle blasted from all eight of its loudspeakers. "Afraid so," Stimpy said.

The first of the fleeing Psychedelia customers were already speeding away, honking their horns, far more likely to be injured in a parking-lot crash than by a stray bullet. Lorinda and Stimpy looked around. There were plenty of people who might see them.

"Fuck it," Stimpy said. "No one's looking."

Abandoning their old-person shuffle, they sprinted to their garish new ride, set their big automatics on the back-seat floor, and took their places in front, with Stimpy at the helm. He stopped the truck just behind the Zhiguli, and popped the trunk lid with its remote. "Don't go anywhere," he said as he jumped out.

"What are you doing?"

"Our guns."

After scooping up the remaining weapons from the Zhiguli's trunk and placing them carefully next to their machine guns, he closed up the Zhiguli, placed the key fob on top of the car's left rear tire, got back behind the wheel of the truck, and drove warily toward the exit.

"So much shooting everywhere we go," Lorinda finally said. It had been a good half-hour since either of them had said a word. "I don't think my heart rate will ever get back to normal."

"I guess you don't see much shooting in the bubble of Perfecton."

"Not too much."

"It's different out here in the real CCSA," Stimpy said. "Good thing Sluggo and Nancy were standing near the emergency exit." He smiled. "Well, not really standing. Dancing. Well, if you call that dancing— "

"That was deliberate? Being near the door?"

"Oh, yeah. We always meet near an exit door if we can. You never know when you'll have to make a run for it."

"Who exactly is we? I mean, who's *behind* we?"

Silence from Stimpy.

"All right," said Lorinda, "let me ask it this way. Who pays for all this? All these cars, this fancy truck — "

"Most of the cars are shit," Stimpy interrupted.

"Still! The hotel . . . the pizza . . . that gas station . . . your fancy communication system. All of it. It's kind of a big deal. Who pays?"

Stimpy nodded. "Okay, it's a fair question. But I can't answer it until you're out of this country. And then I won't be able to answer it because . . ."

"You'll still be here," she said softly.

He nodded, his eyes on the road, his hands on the wheel.

"But *why*? So secret!"

He sighed. "Think about it. If we don't make it . . . if I don't get you out of the CCSA, you'll end up in custody. That woman — "

"Janelle Stark."

"Right. And others just like her." He paused dramatically. "And you'll talk."

She waved a hand and scoffed. "No I won't. I won't tell them anything."

"You won't want to. But they don't ask politely. You get the picture?"

The image of that monstrous, sadistic thug Skippy flitted across her consciousness. Lorinda looked away and gnawed her lip as she considered this for about two seconds. "Fuck," she said. "You're right. I should have figured that out. Sorry for asking."

"No, no! Ask anything! Just don't always expect an answer."

She smiled and curled up in her seat. "It's funny. That's what my father always said. 'Ask me anything.' And I did. And he always had an answer. Turns out most of them were bullshit." She flipped down her sun visor to see if it was one of the fancy ones with a mirror. It wasn't. She flipped it back up. "Okay, one more question. What's your real name?"

Stimpy laughed.

The sun was starting to set behind them when they came upon the first golf billboard. It was electronic and animated, and showed nothing but a giant Donald Trump as a slim, muscular superhero repeatedly, and with perfect form, swinging an oversized driver and sending a glowing white ball soaring off into the distance. A startling voice boomed inside the truck: "*Congratulations! You're on the road to the President Donald J. Trump Memorial Christian Golf Course and Beautiful Residences!*"

"*That's* where we're going?"

"I told you," Stimpy said. "Golf."

"What the fuck — "

He held up a silencing hand. "You'll see."

Lorinda thought for a moment. "Speaking of Trump," she said, "When you made that comment about Donald Trump Junior? How the Nazis thought he'd be their messiah?"

"And I said that didn't turn out so well. Let me guess. You don't know how it turned out."

37 In which our heroine hears a ghastly story on the way to the enclave of golf.

"AHH, YOU KNOW me so well. No, I have no idea what happened to Donald Trump Junior," Lorinda admitted. "We don't see much news in our Perfecton bubble." She added, "Or only a certain kind of news."

They were interrupted by another loud announcement through the truck's sound system: *"Many people say this is the Christian golf capital of the world!"* And there was the billboard, showing a picture of Trump on a green lawn, wearing a biblical white robe and leaning jauntily on a golf club. The adjacent headline read:

LIVE THE CHRISTIAN LUXURY GOLF LIFESTYLE!

Before Stimpy could continue, he was interrupted by another blaring announcement: *"If you're rich and Christian, this could be your gated community!"* And there was the accompanying billboard showing a gigantic face of Donald Trump, perfectly bronzed and mischievously winking an eye, along with the proclamation:

MANY PEOPLE SAY
THIS IS THE CHRISTIAN GOLF CAPITAL OF THE WORLD!

"I mean," Lorinda continued, shaking her head as if to slough off the creepiness of the billboards, "we learned that Donald Trump had some children. I remember, let's see, Don Junior of course. Then there was...Edward?"

"Eric."

"Eric." And the girl. "Ivanka, right?"

"Right."

"But they didn't tell us what happened to them. I think there were some others too."

"Yeah, I can't remember them either. Maybe they changed their last name and disappeared. Anyway," Stimpy said, "Eric died in prison. In Connecticut, I think."

"Whoa. No one talks about that in Perfecton."

"They never did figure out what killed him. Or who. Ivanka, she divorced that creepy real-estate dude and married some Saudi prince. And converted to Islam. And then there's Donny Junior. You don't know anything about his story?"

"Not really."

"Okay. So he started out thinking he'd follow in his father's footsteps and one day be president of the USA. The budgies and dwaynes in the red states had elected his father, right? He was thinking: Why not me? It's my turn! Then came The Split. He figured he'd be a shoo-in as CEO of the brand-new CCSA. Nope. He had a little bit of a following among some old dementos who still worshipped his father, but the billionaires thought he was an asshole and a fool and a drug fiend, so that was out. And his father's so-called fortune, well, it turned out there *was* no Trump fortune. So he still needed a *job*— "

"Wait a minute. I thought Trump was a billionaire."

"Well guess what. He wasn't. So Donny Junior needed a job but he didn't know how to do anything. He'd already cozied-up to the Nazi morons, and he thought maybe if he couldn't be CEO of the country, he could at least be the Fuhrer of the Nazis. So he took five or six of the top Nazis out on one of his jerkoff safaris. He had this safari business in Louisiana — Trump Swamp Safaris or some shit. It was supposed to be a two-week vacation — "

"Hah!" Lorinda hooted. "Two weeks in a *swamp* is a vacation?"

"I guess it is if you're shooting things, yeah. Now, remember, he had spent his whole life being supported by Daddy, but he was somehow under the illusion that he was this Born Leader of Men. He figured the savvy way to conduct himself — and the way to be just like Daddy — was to bullshit and bully everybody. Except for dictators. Anyway, seven or eight days after the start of the safari, the Nazis showed up at a police station in some jerkwater town in Louisiana to report that their tour leader had somehow died while they were out there in the swamp."

"He died? On one of his own safaris?"

"Oh, it's worse than that. When they finally found the body — the parts the alligators didn't get to — and they had an autopsy? It turned out there were quite a few bullet holes and slugs in it."

"Someone *shot* him?"

"*Everyone* shot him. All the Nazis. The bullets came from different guns. But they'd conveniently lost all their weapons in the swamp, or at least the ones that could be matched to the bullets, so there were no ballistics matches. No evidence to tie anybody to the shooting. They all claimed to be surprised that he'd been shot. They said he'd had a heart attack or a stroke or something. Aneurism, maybe." Stimpy snickered. "Not that they knew that word."

"Wait. So how did these Nazis explain the bullet holes?"

"Good point! So maybe some *other* group of hunters came upon poor Junior and filled him full of lead. You know, after he died. That was their best theory."

She shook her head. The big world outside Perfecton kept revealing new forms of chaos, danger, and insanity. "Okay, so the Nazis shot him. But why?"

"They all claimed they didn't know nothin' about no shootin'. But remember, these people are stupider than anyone you've ever met. Of course they talked to all their Nazi pals, and soon the whole world knew that after a few days on the safari they just couldn't take any more of Don Junior. Hated his guts. Forget about him becoming their Hitler, the leader of their sacred crusade. They didn't want him leading them out of *the swamp*. They just wanted him gone, forever. Expunged. Wiped out."

"That's so weird!"

"It's sort of a variation of what happened in the war in Vietnam. Soldiers sometimes hated their own officers. I mean *really* hated them. So they killed them. Fragging, they called it. This is the modern, super-ultra-fucked-up version of that."

"How do you know these things?"

"I'm just a font of wisdom, and — "

"*You are about to enter the enclave for people just like yourself,*" the announcer interjected as the final billboard in the series came into view:

WELCOME TO THE GOLFCENTRIC GATED CHRISTIAN LIFE
DONALD J. TRUMP MEMORIAL CHRISTIAN GOLF COURSE
AND BEAUTIFUL RESIDENCES!
THE ENCLAVE FOR PEOPLE LIKE YOU!

Ethereal "heavenly" music filled the cabin of the truck. Stimpy slowed down and took a long look at Lorinda.

"What?" she said.

"I'm just checking your makeup. You still look sort of okay."

"You mean old?" she said.

"Yeah. But I don't think it'll make it through the night. How do I look?"

"Old, but getting younger all the time."

"The makeup's falling off?"

"Yeah. And the hair," she said. "Is it good news or bad news that you're not permanently old?"

"Whatever it is, we'll have to figure something out." He drove slowly toward an ornate golden gate in the middle of a tall brick wall topped by gleaming golden spikes. Over the gate, a sign blinked:

PRES. DONALD J. TRUMP
MEMORIAL CHRISTIAN GOLF RESORT
AND BEAUTIFUL RESIDENCES

On the other side of the gate they caught a glimpse of enormous golden crucifixes on both sides of the roadway. It looked like a line of glittery cartoon telephone poles, without the wires. Each featured, teed up atop its vertical member, an oversized, dimpled white golf ball, with the initials DJT in black Gothic script.

They stopped at the gate and fumbled around for their Citizen Cards as the uniformed guard in the gatehouse looked on.

38

In which our heroine begins a crash course in the plutocratic lifestyle.

"YOUR MANDATORY FACILITIES tour is at 9:30 tomorrow morning," the guard said, scanning Stimpy's perfectly counterfeited Citizen Card. "You're staying at the Trump Imperium Luxury Hotel. Prepaid for four days. Best hotel in the CCSA, that's what many people say." He seemed surprised by the next line of the readout. "You're in the Libertine Suite. Man, y'all's gonna have a lot of fun." He gave Stimpy a lewd wink and handed the card back with a surprisingly respectful little bow of his head. "Just follow the golden crosses up the path here and bear right, Mr. Chapman, sir. Can't miss it. Have an outstanding stay at our Christian golf resort."

"He didn't even look at my card," Lorinda said as they cruised slowly along the grand entrance drive.

"That's because you're with me, and I'm The Man."

"What's that supposed to mean?"

"Our friend Bill — I'm sure it was Bill — must've hacked our reservations and set me up as some kind of richy-rich oligarch dude. The ideal customer for this place."

As Lorinda stewed on this, she saw that, in contrast to the patchy brown scrubland they'd been driving through over the past four days (was it really only four? It felt like months), here they were, surrounded by a deeply vibrant, evenly trimmed carpet of green. Small rainbows were visible in the fine mist that hovered over the turf, apparently the product of an elaborate hidden sprinkler system. Off to the left, she noticed two brilliant white patches of sand forming parentheses around an elevated freeform shape that was a darker shade of green. A little flagpole poked up from the middle of it. "We're driving through a golf course," she muttered.

Before Stimpy could respond, there was a loud bang on the roof of the truck. Lorinda flinched, shouting "They're bombing us!"

Stimpy laughed.

"What's so funny?" she snapped.

"It was a golf ball," Stimpy said gently. "Just a little golf ball. You're right." He put a calming hand on her knee. "We're in the middle of a golf course. If I owned this truck I'd be pissed. Here we are. I'll explain this place…later."

He turned into the frilly, gilded porte cochère of the elaborately gilded entranceway of a pink-stucco ten-story building. In a robotic voice, he said: "Best hotel in the CCSA, that's what people say."

"Are we still walking old?" Lorinda asked.

Stimpy thought about it. "I think you can just walk normal," he said. "I mean, not *too* normal. No jumping around or anything. We don't want to attract attention."

"And what about you? You get to jump around?"

"I," he said, "will stay old. Old rich guy with cute, young sexy babe — we'll fit right in here."

The baseball caps Archie had issued were sitting on the console between them. He handed Lorinda hers. "This'll cover some of that gray."

Lorinda arranged the cap on her head. "So you think I'm a cute babe?" She was pleased, and a little surprised, that he would describe her that way.

A teenage boy, wearing a fanciful light-blue military-style uniform and a white pith helmet, scurried over and opened Lorinda's door before the truck had stopped moving. "Welcome to the Trump Imperium," he attempted to purr — despite his cracking voice — as he opened the door. "I'm Regis, your val-lay. It would sure be my pleasure to take your bags."

"O-kay..." Lorinda said uncertainly, not accustomed to being the target of fawning.

"No luggage," Stimpy affably called as he got out of the truck. "We're buying new clothes here. We understand you have terrific clothing stores in this enclave."

"The best golf clothes in the country, sir. Especially the stores right here in the hotel mall. That's what people say." The young valet bowed slightly as he closed Lorinda's door.

"When people say things, they usually know what they're talking about," said Stimpy, rounding the truck and dropping the key fob into the valet's hand. "We've got a pile of guns on the floor there," indicating the back door. "Could you rustle us up a cart so we can move them up to our room? We like to stay near our guns." Lorinda hadn't seen this sociable, charming-yet-assertive side of Stimpy before, and she was impressed

"Sure thing, sir," said the valet. He sprang over to a golden luggage cart, rolled it to the truck, and lovingly transferred the handguns to the cart's metal basket. "Hummin' sweet!" he said as he picked up one of the heavy automatics and laid it across the suitcase rails. He sounded more like the kid he was than the fake military officer he was dressed as.

Stimpy took Lorinda's arm and together they strolled into the hotel, Stimpy a bit stiffly, Lorinda — aware that she still was wearing the remnants of Archie's makeup and dowdy clothing—only a tad more spryly. The valet followed with the jangling cart. The lobby was all columns, gold bunting, fake orchids, overstuffed sofas, and big screens running CCSA-TV with the sound muted. Stimpy approached the elaborately carved and gilt desk. If the young valet was dressed as a lieutenant in some imaginary army, the middle-aged clerk behind the desk was decked out as a five-star general.

"Yes, sir, Mr. Chapman, sir," he said, snapping off a crisp salute. "Welcome to the finest hotel in the CCS of A. And welcome to you, Miss Howland. You're prepaid here for four days, it's your first visit here — well, y'all know that — so there's the mandatory facilities tour tomorrow morning, I know you'll enjoy it, your group meets right here in the lobby at 9:30 sharp, your room is the very special Libertine Suite up on the top floor, room ten-oh-one, I'm sure you'll enjoy it, your Citizen Cards are your room keys for the duration of your stay, and welcome again to the Trump Memorial." He paused for a breath. "Regis can bring that up for you if you like. And let me just say on a personal note that you two look very fetching together."

"Thank you kindly," Stimpy said. "C'mon, Regis." The valet, with the gun-laden luggage cart, followed Lorinda and Stimpy into the elevator. Lorinda made eye contact with Stimpy, wrinkled her face, and mouthed: "fetching?" He gave her a comic shrug as Regis pressed the button for 10 and the gleaming golden doors slid shut.

39 *In which our heroine continues her crash course, then crashes.*

THE GOLD-PAINTED DOOR to their room opened on more gold: two shiny gold canopy beds with gold-embroidered bedspreads, a gold-colored carpet, gold floor lamps radiating golden light through golden lampshades, a gold-painted desk and chair, and, between the beds, a gold wicker swing-chair suspended from the ceiling by gold-velvet-covered ropes. "What do you think of the Libertine Suite?" the eager valet asked as he wheeled the cart through the doorway. The room was big. Lorinda figured it must be the size of any two rooms on the lower floors.

"It's really something," Stimpy said.

"A swing?" Lorinda was puzzled.

"I'll tell you about that," said Regis, a bit nervously. "But where would you like the guns, Mr. Chapman? Oh, and by the way, there's a great ammunition store right downstairs in the mall, near the restaurants."

"Just put them on the floor, right by the wall there," Stimpy said.

The lad unloaded the artillery, then stood, more or less at attention next to the cart. Stimpy took out his wallet, removed a thick wad, peeled off five one-hundred dollar bills, and ceremoniously handed them over. The valet's eyes were practically popping out of their sockets as he took the cash.

"Sweet! Thank you so much, Mr. Chapman! And ma'am!" he gushed. "Just let me know if you need anything during your stay.

I'm here for you. Just ask for Regis. Oh, wait — the swing." He pocketed the bills, then pointed toward the swing, his face reddening. "You can use those little, like, buckle things at the bottom of the ropes to adjust it up or down, for your . . . you know, so it fits better, I guess." He bowed slightly, then, walking backward, pulled the cart to the open door, said, "Thanks again, thank you," and reached over the cart to close the door as he left.

"Big tip," Lorinda said. "I must be in the wrong line of work."

"It's an investment."

Lorinda looked puzzled.

"We don't have any people in this enclave," Stimpy said. "He's now our person."

"And how do you know that?"

"Five hundred dollars says he is."

Lorinda shrugged and looked around the room. There was a big gold crucifix — with a golf ball on top — on the wall over each of the beds; two small night tables with lamps and, presumably, with golden Bibles in the drawers; a small refrigerator; a screen sitting on top of the refrigerator; and, mounted on the wall above the screen, an elaborately framed reproduction of a painting of slim, orange Donald J. Trump (in golf shirt and slacks) and blond Jesus (in ancient robes), arms around each other's shoulders, beaming at the viewer from the seat of a golf cart parked next to the flag on a perfectly smooth golf green.

Stimpy, tracking her eyes, said, "That's a very, very bad picture."

She laughed. "Why? Because Christ wasn't alive then? Because he wasn't a golfer?"

"It's way beyond that," he said. "Everyone knows you don't drive a golf cart onto the green."

Lorinda laughed again, then continued surveilling the room. When her eyes lit upon the swing Stimpy said, "It's for sex."

"What?!"

"The swing. That's what it's for. See, the woman sits..."

"Ohhh-kay. I get it." She stared at the swing for a moment. Then, suddenly exhausted, she took a few steps to the nearest bed, tossed her hat to the floor, flopped on her back, and sighed deeply. "What's the deal with this place, anyway?"

"This enclave?"

"Yeah. And what are we doing here?"

"Too quiet for you? Not enough shooting?"

"C'mon. I'm being serious."

"Well," he said, sitting on the other bed, "the thing about this enclave is that pretty much every billionaire in the country is a member of the golf club."

"They live here?"

"A few of them live here. The others just come here a lot. To play golf, but mainly they come for secret meetings where they plot the future of the country. Which really means figuring out how to suck money out of the rest of us." He looked over at her. She was staring straight up at the ceiling. "They also bring their girlfriends here. Or get friendly with one or two of the many women who work here who specialize in...servicing them. Golf, secret meetings, secret girlfriends. It's the dream enclave for autocrats."

"Jeez," she said. "I wondered why they didn't check to make sure we're married. Like a regular hotel. In a regular place."

"This is definitely not a regular place. And now you're wondering: How does this help Lorinda Moon from Perfecton?

"Yeah. How?" She stopped as she realized what just happened. "You said my name," she whispered. "Isn't that risky?"

"The billionaires," he said, "don't want the rest of us to know what they're up to. So this is a camera-free and bug-free zone. The entire enclave, Lorinda Moon from Perfecton."

"Whoa!" Lorinda was incredulous. "That doesn't even seem possible."

"They built it and they own it, so it's exactly the way they want it," he said. "You saw that brick wall, right?"

"The fifty-foot-high wall we came through?"

"Forty, actually. And ten feet thick. It goes all the way around the enclave. It took them two years to build. They spent most of the CCSA's defense budget on it, and they had to stop building their stupid wall around the country until they finished it. Not enough money, not enough manpower."

"Wait. They were more interested in the security of this golf place than . . . than of the entire country?"

"Couldn't have said it better myself."

"Insane."

"Totally. We tried to hack the cameras here, and that's when we learned there are no cameras to hack."

"You — whoever y'all are — you went through the entire enclave looking for cameras?"

"The enclave's not that big. It's the size of three golf courses. And a driving range. And a couple of miniature-golf courses. Everything else — houses, churches, stores, hotels, schools, whatever — they're all packed inside the golf courses. The enclave can't get any bigger — there's a wall around it." Stimpy paused, considering how much to divulge to Lorinda. "And, just so you know, we didn't have to personally go over every inch of the enclave. We have sensing equipment, satellites . . ."

"Can I ask you something?"

"Who are *we*? That's what you want to ask, right?"

Lorinda laughed. "Yeah, but never mind that. Actually, I've been meaning to ask you something else. It's a complete non-sequitur. Is that the right word?"

"Depends on whether it's a sequitur or a non-sequitur."

She rolled her eyes without taking them off the ceiling. "So what is college like?"

"That's a non-sequitur, all right." He paused to absorb it. "You thinking of going to college instead of being on the lam?"

"Haha. No, I'm just . . . I've always been curious. Growing up in Perfecton, or maybe anywhere in this country, people like me — "

"Girls?"

"Girls, boys, anyone. It was like only the super-goobers got picked to go to college."

"And you thought it would be a good thing to do? But you didn't want to be a super-goober?"

"I wanted to learn things. I wanted to *study*. I mean, I never told anyone, except my friend Emmie. She at least went to nursing school . . . " Her eyes teared up. "I miss her. I miss everyone."

"College is like school, but much better."

She wiped a cheek with her hand. "Really?"

"Or at least it used to be. I'm sure it still is in other places. Maybe you can go to college in the United States when you get there."

"*If* I get there."

Stimpy ignored that and fell backward on the bed so that he, too, was looking at the ceiling. "What would you study?"

"I don't know," Lorinda said. "There's so much."

"So little time, so much to know," he chanted.

"What's that?"

"It's from a cartoon. The Beatles. *Yellow Submarine*."

"I've heard of the Beatles," she said. "I thought they were a band."

"Yup. And a cartoon."

She let that slide. "Where are we going next?"

"Another non-sequitur. We're paid for four days. I figure we'll stay for two or three. Rest up. Maybe take some golf lessons..."

"Get outta here!"

"And then make our final dash. To Georgia, USA!"

"No more stops?" Lorinda's exhaustion overwhelmed her. She tried to keep her eyes open but couldn't do it.

"We'll see. Maybe we'll switch cars a couple of times. Can't be too careful."

Lorinda slid into a dream about being in a classroom full of bright, eager fellow students. Emmie sat at the desk next to hers. Stimpy, standing in front of the class, was the teacher. Lorinda was ready to take the test! But thank goodness there wasn't going to be a test today. Instead, the teacher was narrating a long, enchanting story about what life is like in the USA...

40 *In which Lorinda and Stimpy tour the golf enclave.*

"WOULD YOU LIKE me to wrap up the clothes you wore?" asked the friendly, helpful cashier of the Trump Memorial Golf Shoppe. She was pretty, perky, and just about Lorinda's age, wearing red and black plaid golf slacks and a light green cardigan.

Stimpy now wore a turquoise polo shirt tucked into white baggy trousers over a pair of white leather walking shoes, while Lorinda showcased a pink mini-skirt, a cardigan like the cashier's but in white, plaid sneakers, a matching plaid baseball cap with an extra-long brim, and oversized sunglasses.

"No, thanks," said Stimpy. "You can just toss them. Or donate them. We're through with those old things."

"I understand," the cashier said. "Should I put this bill on your room, or would you like to pay here?"

"Oh, you can just put it on the room," Stimpy said. "It's room ten-oh-one, upstairs."

The young woman, blushing, couldn't help but look from Stimpy to Lorinda and back. She'd heard about that room.

Lorinda, who just then was adjusting her hatband, completely missed the cashier's embarrassment. "Do you play?" she asked as she put her hat back on her head and looked up at the cashier.

"Play?" The cashier gave a nervous laugh. "Oh, dear, no. I'm married!"

Lorinda's mouth fell open but nothing came out.

Stimpy laughed, saying, "She's just asking if you play golf."

The cashier visibly relaxed. "Oh, golf. No. You're not allowed to play here if you're not a member. But I know it's a great game. Sport. Whatever it is. And golf clothes, they're the best."

Agreeing that golf clothes were indeed the best, Stimpy and Lorinda exited the shop in their golf-adjacent attire and walked arm-in-arm through the hotel's mall. Stimpy checked the time on his device. "We have almost an hour until the facilities tour."

"Do we really have to do that?" Lorinda asked. "All I want to do is eat. I'm starving." They passed a store called Guns 'n Ammo 'n Such and arrived at the restaurant section of the mall.

"Me too," he said. "But we've got to do the tour. We don't want them to think we're weird. What about this?" They stopped in front of a big plate-glass window under a sign reading BugeRama Restaurant & Casino.

"Booj-rama?" Lorinda was confused.

"I think they want you to pronounce it "burger-rama."

"That's stupid," Lorinda said. "But they do serve breakfast. Look."

Sure enough, about half the tables were occupied — mainly by men, but there were a number of women and a smattering of kids. Everyone was forking up eggs or French toast with one hand while playing video poker or pulling the handle of a slot machine with the other.

"Ahh," said Stimpy. "I can't…I just can't." He peered down the corridor and brightened. "But look at that!" He pointed.

"Holy shit!" Lorinda said. "It's a PumpJack's!"

"It looks closed," Stimpy said.

"Yeah, if it's anything like mine it doesn't open till noon. And you can't get breakfast there anyway. Let's eat here and we'll have lunch there after the tour."

"Oh, all right. But don't make me gamble."

Fifteen or twenty people — mostly middle-aged men, three accompanying women, one couple with their two kids, everyone in golf attire — were puttering about in the hotel lobby when Lorinda and Stimpy returned. A moment later their guide came in the front door, a twentyish young man in a baggy business suit, an overly long red tie, and an ill-fitting orange-gold wig — apparently the official uniform of tour guides at the President Donald J. Trump Memorial Christian Golf Resort and Beautiful Residences.

"Hi, y'all," the guide said cheerily. "I'm guessing you're all here for the facilities tour. My name is Jared and I'll be your guide today. The tour takes about two hours, and I'll show you all around our miraculous luxury Christian golf community. And I should know, 'cause I grew up here. I'm a proud grad of Donald J. Trump High School. I even played on the junior varsity football team and our national-championship varsity golf team. I'm gonna try to give you such a great tour that by the end of it you'll want to move here and buy a villa. Or a condo. Or at least join the golf club as an associate member. Or maybe just a bunch of clothes and commemorative tee-shirts and whatnot. So let's go!"

"I think this 'facilities tour' is just about selling stuff," Lorinda whispered.

"That's the thing about billionaires," Stimpy whispered. "They always need more money."

The guide led the way out to the porte cochère, where ten gleaming white golf carts were parked, each emblazoned, in gold, with "Tesla" above the initials "P.D.J.T.M.C.G.R.A.B.R."

Chapter 40

"Just find yourselves a golf cart," said Jared the guide, "four folks in each, max. These are Teslas with Infallible Autopilot, and they're all programmed to follow mine, so you don't have to do a thing, just sit back and enjoy. I'll be talking to you through the speaker in your cart. If you have trouble hearing me just give a shout. Okay, climb aboard."

Lorinda and Stimpy sat in the last cart. Jared made sure everyone was in place, then hopped into the first cart. "Can y'all hear me?" he said into his microphone. His voice, coming through the air as well as from nine tiny speakers, was slightly surreal, but everyone waved and nodded happily. "All right, then." He tapped a button next to the base of his microphone and all the golf carts roared to life, their small gasoline engines sputtering and hiccupping black smoke for several seconds until they smoothed themselves out.

As the lead cart pulled away, the others fell in line behind it, two-by-two, other than Lorinda's and Stimpy's, which was a singleton at the end of the queue. A half-minute later the guide veered off the street and onto a narrow, golf-carts-only path beside a lush fairway. "You know," Stimpy said into Lorinda's ear, "Tesla started out making real cars in the USA. Nice electric cars. It was the most valuable automobile company in the world for a while."

"You're kidding. And now?"

"Now they're a joke. All they make are these internal-combustion golf carts, for sale only in the CCSA."

"Bizarre," Lorinda said. "What happened?"

"The guy who used to own the company was such a reptile-dick that everyone stopped buying his cars. And the people who liked him? They hated electric cars."

"Reptile-dick?"

"I just made that up. How about gator-dick? Crocadick?"

Lorinda laughed. "Is he the one who died on the way to Mars?"

"Very good!"

"I vaguely remember hearing that story. He built his own rocket? It exploded or something?"

"Actually, it got lost and veered off into deep space. He might still be alive out there somewhere."

"I guess you gotta give him credit for flying in his own rocket."

"Well," Stimpy said, "he tried for years to get other people to go first, but no one — "

"Here we have the world's greatest driving range," the guide interrupted. When he hit his brakes, the nine carts tailing his abruptly slammed on theirs, causing several of the riders to gasp and one to hit his forehead on the steering wheel. After a short, rote lecture about the driving range, and how great it was, the entourage churred on to the next attraction.

"You probably already know," said Jared, as the carts halted abruptly behind his, "that we have three famous golf courses here, the Blond, the Brunette, and the Redhead. Here we are at tee number-one of the Blond, the shortest and easiest of our links, with seven par-threes. It's the only one that ladies and children under fourteen are allowed on. Are there any lady golfers here?"

As all three women raised their hands, Lorinda whispered, "How nice that they allow ladies to play golf."

"Shh. They'll hear you."

"I'm sure you gals will love playing The Blond," said Jared the guide. "And remember, you get a complimentary thirty-six holes and a free lesson, because this is your first visit here." As he began to describe the rare and expensive constituent ingredients of the sand in the bunkers, the autonomous-golf-cart train took off again.

The next stop was in front of an elaborate miniature golf course filled with eerily quiet little kids and their teachers. The "hazards" of the course were scaled-down, highly detailed versions of stately old office buildings and hotels — except for the 18th hole, which featured a model of the White House in Washington DC, USA, with the glowing neon letters "DJT" filling the pediment above its stately portico.

"Miniature golf is a required course in our elementary school," the guide said, proudly. "We were the first school district in the whole country to make it a requirement. Every kid in this enclave plays golf, starting on our beautiful miniature courses!" His cart started moving again, followed by the others. "What do you say we check out some condos and villas?" A murmur of giddy anticipation swept through the carts ahead of Lorinda and Stimpy.

According to the guide, this slice of domiciles formed a several-block-deep semicircle behind the thirteenth green of the Brunette course. The vast ground-floor picture window of one of the houses, Lorinda noticed, was covered by unsightly sheets of plywood. In the middle of the house's lawn, which was contiguous with the apron of the golf green, several construction workers were putting the finishing touches on a tall fence of poultry netting, obviously meant to keep golf balls from smashing any more windows. "I should mention," said Jared, expertly ducking a small white sphere that was coming straight at his orange wig, "that there are villas available here for as little as nine-point-five million dollars, this week only! For the two-bed, one-bath."

The carts came around a bend and halted in front of a twenty-five-foot-high faux-marble statue of Donald J. Trump caressing a pair of golden tablets with glowing Roman numerals I through X on them. "I just want to stop here for a second for my own personal tribute to the man — the god, really — that this enclave and everything in it is named after. He was the inspiration behind The Split, and without The Split the CCSA wouldn't exist, and without the CCSA we wouldn't have — " he gestured expansively "— all this. Thank you, President Trump."

As he bowed his head, the guests in the golf carts clapped and cheered. Stimpy elbowed Lorinda. They joined in, even more enthusiastically than the others.

"I always get emotional around this statue," Jared said. "It's called 'The Ten Numbers.'" He sighed. "All right. Now, about the villas and condos. Did I mention that prices will never be lower than they are today? When we get back to the hotel at the end of this tour, there will be some great, terrific real estate people who will be happy to help you find the permanent or vacation home of your dreams, subject of course to board approval and a complete financial workup. Some terms and conditions may apply."

The visitors' golf carts trailed Jared's into a short stretch lined with mansions — each with a big golden cross (topped by an oversized golf ball) on its lawn, and with a front-row view of the third tee of the Redhead Course. A foursome of older men who were preparing to tee off paused their bantering to watch the little motorcade drone past them.

"This," said the guide in a low, confidential voice, "is some of the most primo real estate in the entire enclave. In the entire country! Sixty-five million and up! And worth it — for the best views of the best golf course in the world!" He sighed in admiration. "Look at them! They're castles!" As much as his audience wished he would stop so they could ogle the huge, turreted-and-crenelated residences, he took the first turn out of there, and they were back to looking at more conventional — though still enormous — houses.

The last villa they passed before emerging from this cluster was a big white one. On its lawn was a discreet sign reading "Dr. Jonas McFarland, Medical Doctor, By Appointment Only."

"Huh!" Lorinda said.

"What?"

"I've never seen that," she marveled. "A doctor in a private house."

"That doctor," Stimpy whispered, "is the billionaires' abortionist."

"*What?!*"

"Shhh."

She kept her eyes on the house as they chugged past it. "How do you know that?"

Stimpy paused to consider his answer. "Let's just say," he began in a near-whisper, "that we have friends and supporters among the people who work . . . in the various enclaves of the CCSA."

"That was nice and vague."

Stimpy smiled and continued. "And some of those members of the servant class have, let's say, been sent to this doctor by their billionaire boyfriends to avail themselves . . . of his medical specialty."

"So why don't I just go there? For my . . . problem?"

"You know what would happen if you walked in there and asked for a . . . reset? First, the receptionist or nurse or whoever works for him would say she didn't know what you were talking about. Then a minute later you'd be hauled away by the local blue boys and sent right back to what's-her-name. Your friend — "

"Janelle Stark. *Fake-doctor* Janelle Stark."

"Yeah. This Doc McFarland is definitely not for you," Stimpy said. "As far as you're concerned, he doesn't exist."

Lorinda looked away and digested this fresh piece of bitter news. Finally she whispered, "I hate this place."

"This enclave? Yeah, it's — "

"This whole fucking *nation*." She practically spat the last word.

Stimpy grinned and smacked her lightly on the thigh in congratulations. "That's the spirit!"

41 *In which our heroine has to leave the golf enclave right quick.*

THE ENTOURAGE TRUNDLED past a small, New Englandy clapboard church. A sign on the lawn read "Our Lady of the Greens Church & Casino."

A small animated billboard on the building rotated through a litany of phrases:

LET JESUS SHRINK YOUR HANDICAP
GOLF IS PRAYER
MAKE PAR WITH CHRIST
BE A SWINGER. PLAY GOLF EVERY DAY.
MAY EACH OF YOUR HOLES BE BLESSED
GOD IS IN EVERY ROLL OF THE DICE
WWDJTD?

"We have fourteen beautiful churches in our enclave," Jared said. "Wherever you live, you're never more than a three-minute golf-cart ride away from a church."

Just past the church stood an anomalous industrial-looking little brick building that appeared to be some kind of guardhouse, beside which was a sign pointing to a service entrance that passed through the enclave's brick wall. Chuffing up beside the building was an old yellow school bus — the word "school" obscured by a sloppy black paint stripe — blasting a murky column of smoke from a tall chrome stack. The bus stopped, the door flew open, and passengers immediately started filing out: men of various ages in casual or work clothes, young women, some in work clothes, most in heels and glittering tight dresses.

Jared said not a word.

In response to Lorinda's puzzled look, Stimpy whispered, "That's the servant class. They're not allowed to live here, and they couldn't afford it anyway. They have their own town five miles away."

"The women are what..." She groped for a guess. "Dancers? Blackjack dealers?"

"A billionaire gets very lonely playing golf and making evil plans all day long."

As their cart-train moved along, Lorinda saw three long — stretched — golf carts arriving at the guardhouse. The bus's former passengers clambered aboard.

"Of course I'm very excited about the next attraction," Jared gushed. "It's my high school, Trump Memorial High. I'm a graduate! You know, one of the things we're proudest of is the way we saved the taxpayers money by eliminating useless school programs, starting with music and art." The guests in the carts ahead of Lorinda's and Stimpy's chuckled knowingly. "Then, of course, came English..." the guide allowed a moment for his audience to boo. "Math." Another boo. "Languages, history and science!" A big boo, followed by cheers. "Which means we had much more of a budget for the golf and football programs. I'm super-proud that it was my school that invented the curriculum that was adopted throughout the CCSA!"

"That's not the way my high school worked," Lorinda whispered. "We had actual classes."

"No one adopted that curriculum," Stimpy whispered back. "He's just making that up."

"And here we are," Jared said, slowing down his cart.

Lorinda expected, at minimum, a stolid, Perfecton High-sized cinderblock school building, possibly with four or five pretentious columns guarding the entrance. Instead, what she saw was a cluster of doublewide mobile-homes with a sign in front proclaiming

DONALD J. TRUMP MEMORIAL HIGH SCHOOL
HOME OF THE TRUMP SWINGERS GOLF AND FOOTBALL TEAMS

Jared's cart stopped and, in sync, so did the other carts. But before the guide had a chance to speak, one of the carts in the middle of the pack emitted a grating mechanical howl, spun its rear wheels, clanked into the cart in front of it, wobbled, and took off, fast, toward the school. As Jared and his charges looked on in horror, the runaway cart gained speed, veered into a big tree, and violently tossed its four shrieking male passengers in four directions. Then it toppled onto its side and, with a muffled roar, erupted in flames.

Jared, so agitated that his orange wig flew off, grabbed his com from an interior pocket of his suit jacket and yelled into it: "Mayday! Mayday! Autopilot failure on the tour! Autopilot failure! By the high school! Autopilot failure!…"

On the slow, uneasy procession back to the hotel, Jared apologized profusely, explained that this was only the fifth Autopilot breakdown he'd ever witnessed, and reiterated that there would be authorized, friendly real estate agents waiting in the lobby for the group should anyone have an interest in purchasing a villa, condo, or club membership.

Lorinda and Stimpy avoided the real estate scrum in the lobby and headed straight to the PumpJack's in the hotel mall. A waitress, wearing the Western fringe outfit Lorinda knew so well, ushered them to a table and asked if they were ready for drinks. Stimpy ordered a Johnny Reb beer. Lorinda, declining to explain why that made her shudder, ordered a Nineteen-Twenty Pick-Me-Up Cocktail.

"A what?" The waitress gamely gave it a try: "A ninety-something pickup?"

"Tell you what. I'll just go up and talk to the bartender."

"I don't know..." the waitress said warily.

"It's okay," Lorinda said. She dropped her sunglasses on the table, stood, breezily said, "I'm a PumpJack's bartender too," and made a beeline for the bartender.

The bar was almost identical to Lorinda's. It was bracketed by two big screens, the left one showing a golf tournament, the right one football. The bartender was around thirty, a hunky dude in a regulation PumpJack's cowboy uniform, right down to the toy six-shooter strapped to his waist. "Hey," said Lorinda, plumping down on one of the barstools, "can you make me a Nineteen-Twenty Pick-Me-Up Cocktail?"

"Never heard of that one," the bartender said. "You want to give me the formula? I'm Chris, by the way."

"Nice to meet you. I'm Lor...I'm..." Why couldn't she remember her new name? "Just call me Emmie. I'm also a PumpJack's bartender. In...in Austin."

"Super! So what's this fabulous drink, Emmie?"

"So," she said, "you need a bottle of Pernod, some gin, Angostura bitters, orange bitters—"

"I'm out of that one. Or maybe we never had it."

"Okay, I guess we can live without it. Or just add a little orange juice. Then some sugar syrup and—" She was interrupted by a pair of hands on her waist. She spun on her stool. It was Stimpy. "What's up?"

"Don't look now," he whispered in her ear, "but you're on TV. Finish up with him. We need to go."

Straining to avoid looking at one of the screens, she said, "and soda."

"Sounds a little strange," said the bartender, nodding hello to Stimpy, "but, okay, let's try it." As he started gathering ingredients, Lorinda looked at the left-hand screen and stifled a gasp when she saw a bigger-than-life closeup of her face, undisguised, taken at the Revelation entrance booth. Below it a caption scrolled:

LORINDA MOON
DESPERATE FUGITIVE
ABORTION SEEKER AVOIDS JUSTICE!

Without giving Lorinda a chance to say a word, Stimpy firmly guided her off the stool. "Sorry," he said to the bartender. "We just remembered something."

"What's that?" the bartender said, grabbing a gin bottle off the back bar.

Relieved to see that Lorinda's picture was no longer on the screen, replaced by an ad for the reality-suicide show *Top of the Heap*, Stimpy said, "We have an important meeting." He handed Lorinda her jumbo sunglasses. "Gotta run now."

"We'll be back," Lorinda said, putting the glasses on, lowering the long brim of her plaid hat, lowering her head, and briskly following Stimpy past the confused waitress and out the door.

42 *In which our heroine hurtles toward another scary place.*

REGIS THE VALET was standing outside, in the porte cochère just past the hotel-lobby doorway, as Stimpy and Lorinda entered the lobby from the mall passageway. He saw them before they saw him. "Hey, Mr. Chapman, and ma'am!" he gushed, charging into the lobby.

Stimpy firmly took his arm and ushered him back out into the porte cochère. "Look, Regis," he said in a near-whisper, "the lady and I have run into a little situation and we have to move quickly." He pressed four hundred-dollar bills into the kid's hand, saying, "I'd like you to help us."

"Sure thing, sir," Regis said, peeking at the money and failing to suppress a grin.

"We need our truck, right out here, and we're going to need, let's say, six big sandwiches and a couple of big bottles of water or whatever kind of beverages you can get. In the next two minutes."

"What kind of sandwiches, sir? There's Nuclear's Submarines and there's — "

"It doesn't matter," Stimpy said. "Whatever's fastest, and whatever kind you think we'll like. You're the man! Keep the change, obviously."

"Okay, Mr. Chapman. I'll do my best. Thank you, sir. It might take a little more than two minutes."

"I know you'll do your best, Regis. Can you buzz us in our room when the truck's ready for us?"

"No problem," Regis said, snapping him a salute. "I'll put the food on the floor in the back seat?"

"Sure," said Stimpy, taking a few steps and grabbing a luggage cart, "but make sure there's room back there for the guns."

In the Libertine Suite, Lorinda loaded the guns onto the cart while Stimpy typed on his device. He was still typing as she pushed the loaded luggage cart over to the door, and sat on the swing while she waited. "I see how this could work," she said. "Although aiming might be hard — "

"Shit," he said, focused on his screen. "Shit, shit, shit."

"What?"

He finished and dropped the com back in his pocket. "We're screwed again. They'll have another car for us for in a couple of days, but they don't have one when we need it: right now! We'll just have to risk it in that big, conspicuous green truck."

"Where're we going?" she asked. "Georgia?"

"Alabama first. It's a ten- or twelve-hour drive. Depending on how we go."

"Long drive."

"It is. But it gets us pretty close to Georgia."

"And when can I get rid of this stupid makeup? I thought we'd be here for a few days . . . "

"We didn't expect to see your picture on every screen in the country."

"But," said Lorinda, trying out a little wishful thinking, "maybe it's just on the screens here in this enclave."

"If it's here," sighed Stimpy, "it's everywhere: CCSA TV. Grab one of those bedspreads."

"Okay," she said, hopping off the swing and sweeping up the bedspread she'd slept on top of. "What for?"

"To hide you in the truck. Roll it up so the gold side isn't showing. We don't want to get busted on the way out for stealing hotel property."

She did as he said and tossed it to him. He set it on top of the guns in the luggage cart just as the room phone rang. Lorinda picked it up. "Hello?"

"The truck's ready, ma'am."

"Hi, Regis. We'll be right down."

"Tell him to put the food on the front-passenger-side floor," Stimpy bellowed.

"I heard that, ma'am. Passenger side floor in front, not in the back. Will you be here for the séance with President Trump tonight at seven?"

"I don't know," Lorinda said. "Maybe."

"Just let me know if you want me to get you tickets, ma'am. Those séances are really popular." He clicked off.

"Why did you tell him to put the food in front under my feet?" Lorinda asked.

"You won't be sitting there," Stimpy said cryptically. "Let's go."

"I can't do this much longer," Lorinda said. She'd been lying across the back seat, completely covered by the bedspread, with its plain side up, for close to two hours. The a/c was blasting but, like most air conditioners in the CCSA, it was barely functional. She was hot. Sweaty. Sticking to the seat.

Stimpy, at the wheel, had trouble hearing her. "There's a place to pull over in ten minutes," he yelled. "We'll have a quick lunch and you can get some air."

"What?"

Sheltering behind a defunct gas station, they sat on the truck's tailgate and scarfed down their first round of hero sandwiches. Lorinda was holding back tears.

"What's up?" Stimpy asked, setting down his sandwich and giving her a quick little backrub.

"I just feel like I've made a mess of my life."

"It's this ridiculous country's that's messing up your life," he said gently. "It messes up a lot of people."

She shrugged. "My parents will see me on TV. They'll know I'm wanted by the police." She looked away, stricken. "They'll know I'm not a virgin."

Stimpy's attempt not to laugh turned into a snort. "At least they'll know you're alive."

"I guess that's something." She took a thoughtful bite of her sandwich. "This isn't bad, actually. Regis did a good job."

"That's why he gets the big bucks." They both laughed.

"I'm kind of surprised that we're driving on a main road," Lorinda said.

"I've been in touch with Bill — you've heard me talking to him, right?"

"I can't hear much under that bedspread."

"Anyway, he hacked the cameras on this highway the same way he did before — putting up an old video of the same road while we're passing through, so if they're watching their screens they don't see us." He took a sip of water. "The man's a genius. We couldn't do what we do without him."

"How did he learn that stuff? Did he go to school for it?"

"Yeah, and then he worked for CCSA Security, setting up their spy-camera network."

"So he's the perfect guy to hack it."

"Exactly." Stimpy finished his sandwich.

Lorinda took a few more bites and finished hers, then took a swig of water from the same bottle. "Ready for me to drive?"

Stimpy considered it. "It's safer if you don't. The cameras are okay for now, but we don't know how long that'll last."

Lorinda didn't hide her disappointment.

"I think it's safe enough for you to sit up in the back seat," Stimpy continued. "If you keep your back to the door, it'll be hard for a camera to get a good shot of you. Leave the bedspread nearby, so you can dive under right quick if you have to."

"Lucky they didn't get a shot of you, too," Lorinda said. "I have one demand."

"Okay," he said, "hit me."

"Tell me your real name."

Stimpy laughed.

For hours they drove through the bleakest landscape they'd encountered so far, passing more falling-down or boarded-up buildings than occupied houses and functioning businesses. They exchanged few words, which is why Lorinda jumped when Stimpy broke the silence: "Yeah, I'm here."

Before her mouth could form words to ask him why the hell he said that, she realized that he'd received a call on his earpiece. "And it's safe? Someone's been through there lately?"

Lorinda calmed herself down and eased back against the door.

"Yeah, sure," said Stimpy, "we can handle it. Good."

"What?" Lorinda asked the moment he finished his call.

"What what?"

"What's happening? Where are we going?"

In the spookiest voice he could muster, Stimpy said, "We are going...to Zone Z..."

"You're kidding!"

"Do I look like I'm kidding?"

"I don't know. I can only see the back of your head. Why are we going to *that* scary place?"

"It's only scary if you live there and you're one of *them*. Being scared is their way of life. They're always killing each other. They're fucking morons."

She laughed. "Half the people in the country are fucking morons."

"Well, then...they're fucking morons in their own fucking moronic way."

"Sounds great. Now why are we going there?"

"For one thing, it'll be safe for us."

"Like the last place?"

"Well, that was safe until you became a TV star."

"Haha."

"Zone Z is different. The people there, they don't watch TV, they don't get any outside news at all. They barely consider themselves citizens of the CCSA. And the feds almost never go in there. They're scared of the place."

"Oh great! And why aren't *we* scared of it?"

"Because," said Stimpy, "they love tourists, when they can get them. Or at least they love tourist dollars — they don't have much of a local economy. That's because — "

A booming voice filled the cabin: *"Jail the cannibals!"*

— as a small billboard, the first one they'd seen in hours, blinked the same words.

"What the hell?" Lorinda implored Stimpy.

"Speak of the devil," Stimpy said. "Cannibalism is a Zone Z obsession. You're supposed to know that's a Zone Z message. Look — there's more."

About a hundred yards down the road another billboard blinked, and the same voice boomed:

TRUMP AND JFK JR. WILL RETURN

And then another:

WHAT IF YOU ARE *ALREADY* IN HELL?

Followed in quick succession by a series that were no more than forty or fifty yards apart:

EDUCATION IS COMMUNISM
COMMUNISM CAUSES CANCER
SCIENCE IS COMMUNIST PROPAGANDA
OUR ENEMIES ARE ALL PEDOPHILES
ONLY COMPLICATED THEORIES ARE TRUE
GASOLINE IS THE FUEL OF THE FUTURE
ALL ELECTIONS ARE STOLLEN
ONLY 50 MILES TO FAMOUS ZONE Z

"Jesus Christ," Lorinda sighed and shook her head. "It's just one crazy community after another out here, isn't it. Did everybody know that except me?"

"Well — "

"No. It's not just me. My parents don't know it. The people I went to high school with don't know it. Probably nobody in Perfecton knows it! They think they're all normal, and that the whole country is just like them!"

Stimpy tried to sound soothing. "Not the whole country, but a lot of it is. Normal. Like them. Sort of. Of course it depends on what 'normal' means — "

"I don't know what it means anymore!" She was silent for a few seconds after her explosion. Then she gasped, her eyes went wide, and she said, urgently, *"Or maybe it depends on who's defining it!"*

Now he really did laugh. "Oh! Well, yeah! See — "

"Can you explain Zone Z to me before we get there?"

Stimpy opened his mouth to speak — and then shut it. Finally he said, "I don't know if that's possible. But I'll try."

The next sign they saw, just past the final Zone Z billboard, was a shabby little hand-painted road sign that was hanging at an angle from its wooden stake:

WELCOME TO ALABAMA
"The Haert of Dixie"
"The Haert of the CCSA"

Stimpy was silent for a good two minutes. "I'm just trying to figure out where to start with Zone Z, how far back to go." But before he could begin, another voice crackled through the sound system: *"Warning! This fugitive is armed and dangerous."* A moment later the associated billboard came into view. It was a big one, with a gigantic picture of Lorinda, the same one they'd seen on CCSA TV:

ABORTION SEEKER!
PUBLIC ENEMY LORINDA MOON
BIG CA$H REWARD FOR CAPTURE!
WARNING! THIS FUGITIVE IS ARMED AND DANGEROUS!

Stimpy looked grim. "I think you'd better get back under the bedspread.

43 *In which our heroine remains under a bedspread as her fame grows.*

"THEY'RE PUTTING LORINDA'S picture up on billboards," Stimpy said, then waited for a response through his earpiece. "No idea. We've got to assume they're everywhere. Listen, would you put me through to Bill?"

"What's going on?" Lorinda asked, poking her head out from under the bedspread.

"Get back underneath," Stimpy said harshly.

"How do you know I'm not underneath?"

"Because I can fucking hear you."

"It's impossible for cameras to see me," she said. "I'm too low, the windows are tinted, it's nighttime, don't worry about it."

"Bill! . . . I don't know if the billboards are everywhere. We passed one of them and I called it in right away . . . You see where we are, right? We're almost to Zone Z . . . That's great!"

"What's great?" Lorinda blurted.

"Bill can hack into the billboard system . . . No, I'm just talking to her . . . Yeah, she's covered up in the back seat . . . Okay, man. We'll check in when we're all cozy in Zone Z. Oh, right, good question."

"What's a good question?"

"Can I just finish this conversation?"

"I think I have the right to know what's going on," said Lorinda, indignantly. "It's *me* on the billboards. *I'm* the fugitive."

"Yeah," said Stimpy to Bill, "she wants to know what we're talking about." Then, to Lorinda: "He's going to hack the billboards and wants us to tell him what they should say."

"Something about . . . how what's happening to me could happen to anyone in this country."

Stimpy thought about it for a second, then said, "Maybe 'What's happening to Lorinda Moon could happen to you'?"

"Too long and boring," said Lorinda.

"Yeah," Stimpy said to Bill, "that's what Lorinda just said . . . all right. And if I think of anything better I'll let you know . . . Okay, bye." He half turned to the back seat. "He and Hillary are going to try to come up with something."

"Whatever it is, I'm sure it'll be embarrassing for me," Lorinda said.

"*That's* what's embarrassing for you? Not being called an abortion-seeking terrorist?"

"Not a terrorist," Lorinda laughed. "*Fugitive.*"

"Whatever," Stimpy said. "Is your head sticking up?"

Lorinda pulled the bedspread over her face. "No!"

Stimpy barely heard her. "That's better."

"I just figured it all out," Lorinda said.

"Get under the bedspread!"

"Don't worry. Nobody can see me."

"What do you mean, you figured it all out?"

"When you're under a bedspread for hours you think about stuff. And I figured out that it's all a big scam."

"What is?"

"This."

"This what?"

"This whole country! I've been thinking about that abortion doctor and how abortions are just for the rich. What do you call them? The authoritarians."

"Authoritarians. Oligarchs. The plutocracy. Rich fuckheads. They go by many names."

"It's all about money!"

"Well yes, but also — "

"Shh. Let me finish. The whole country is just for them. They own everything! They claim to be religious and all that, but — like in Perfecton! That huge stupid church! A guy who owns a drug company is standing up there? Like what's that got to do with Jesus? Or that stupid Libertyville!" She had a flash of Ren dying at her feet but shook it off and continued. "All that yelling about freedom? It's insane! There's . . . you can't . . . Or, holy shit, that disco! Everybody shooting at the same time! You know what they drilled into our heads in elementary school?"

They spoke in unison. "'If everyone has a gun, then everyone will be safe.'"

Lorinda was surprised. "You weren't in elementary school here. How do you know that?"

"I know shit."

She was instantly back on track. "But how can having guns make everybody safe? It's like saying, if everybody had a flame thrower, then everybody'll be safe. If everybody had a bomb! How can people believe that?"

Quietly, Stimpy said, "Everybody doesn't believe it."

"Everybody I know does." She thought of Emmy. "Well, mostly."

"People in the USA don't believe it."

That pulled her up short. All she could say was, "Huh."

"The thing about this country — " Stimpy began.

"And the golf enclave!" she went on. "Oh, man, that's the best." In a bitter tone that surprised even her, she said, "'Cheat on your sacred marriage and bring a girlfriend. Or we'll supply one for you! And if she gets pregnant, we have a full-time doctor to take care of it.' Meanwhile, *I'm* the criminal." Running low on venom, she sighed. "So is the whole country just a scam to trick people and take their money?"

"Not quite," Stimpy said. "To take their money, yes. You bet. But also to have control over them. Right? Because if you've tricked someone to take their money, and they find out, they may come after you." He laughed. "With their guns."

"But then what are the enclaves? There's not much control there. It's the opposite. They're fucking lunatic asylums." She paused, then completed the thought. "Run by the inmates."

"Here's another metaphor for you. The whole CCSA has cancer. It always has. The enclaves are tumors. Of one kind or another."

"Huh. And this all started with the Split?"

"Not really. It's always been this way. Before the Split the USA had laws that were supposed to keep these people from just, you know, taking whatever they wanted, whenever they wanted it. Which were sometimes even enforced! It's the main reason they dreamed of getting their greedy mitts on their own country."

"And now they have their own country but they pretend it's everybody's country. As if people like me have the same rights they have. It's a big fucking god-damned fucking scam. I hate them." She paused to catch her breath. "Okay. That's all I wanted to say."

"It's an excellent observation," Stimpy said calmly. "You're not the first one to make it, but I know you came to it on your own."

"Thanks to you for yelling at me all the time. You got me thinking."

"I do not 'yell' at you."

"Well, you did. At first."

"I'm sorry if it seemed that way."

"It didn't seem that way," she said. "It *was* that way." She giggled. "But you're nicer now. A little nicer." She paused. "Whatever your name is."

"Thanks. Now get under the bedspread. Excuse me: *please* get under the bedspread, ma'am."

For a few minutes, he drove in silence through the bleak landscape. Lorinda resumed her thinking until Stimpy broke the silence. "Are you experiencing morning sickness? Or any other symptoms?"

"It's much too soon," she said. "The test I used? It was some special new thing from the USA — Philadelphia, USA — that can figure out if you're pregnant much sooner than the ones we have here."

"How'd you get your hands on that?"

"We all have our secrets," she said with as much smugness as she could muster, lying under an itchy golden bedspread. Then, speaking softly, she asked a question that he didn't know she knew the answer to. "As long as we're getting all personal, have you ever been married?"

"Whoa!"

"What?" Lorinda said, poking her head out. "I'm sorry, I didn't mean — "

"It's not that. Look."

"I can sit up?"

"Just for a second."

Lorinda hiked herself up and peeked over his shoulder. A big billboard nearly filled the windshield. (Bill, who had hacked it, was opposed to billboard soundtracks. Hence, no soundtrack.) The background was a deep blue. Animated fireworks and shooting stars garlanded the periphery. The words in the center, in bold, shimmering, multi-colored type, sent her diving back under the bedspread:

WE ARE ALL LORINDA MOON

44 *In which our heroine finally emerges from under the golden bedspread.*

AS THEY BUMPED along the increasingly bad roads toward Zone Z, Lorinda brooded under the bedspread, her thoughts vibrating between an intense desire to escape from what she now saw clearly as the evil stupidity of the CCSA, grandiose fantasies about personally fixing the country so that no one would ever again have to go through what she was going through, and vague visions of what her life would be like in the USA. She was brought back to her present hot, itchy reality by a deep voice booming through the cabin speakers of the Xiaomi Lumberjax: *"Are you ready for Zone Z? You are getting close."*

Lorinda yanked the bedspread off her face, sat up—her feet noisily burrowing under the pile of guns—and said, "You still haven't told me about Zone Z." Two billboards appeared in quick succession, accompanied by the booming voice:

GO BACK WHERE YOU CAME FROM, SOCIALIST
WANT A VAX? TURN AROUND AND GO HOME.

"I was hoping you forgot," Stimpy sighed. "All right, the short version: Going way back before the Split, the USA was full of insane conspiracy theorists and their insane theories. The crazier they were, the more popular they were. After the Split, all those people—pretty much everyone who started the conspiracy theories or believed them or repeated them—they all ended up in the CCSA. At some point, early on, a character named Z, just the letter Z, popped up." He was interrupted by two more billboards and their soundtracks:

WE DON'T RECONIZE YOUR GOVERNMENT

NO COLLEGE GRADATES NEED APLY

"I guess they don't teach spelling in Zone Z," Lorinda said. "Was this Z a real person?"

"Nope," Stimpy said after thinking about it for a moment. "Pure horseshit. There was a rumor that counterintelligence people in the USA invented Z as a meme to spread chaos and stupidity in the CCSA." He shifted in his seat. "Not that it needed any help."

"Wow. Is that true? This Z was, like, a *character* invented in the USA?"

"Yes. It's true."

"How do you know?"

Stimpy paused before he spoke. "Don't ask. Maybe one day I'll tell you how I know," he finally said.

Two more small billboards appeared, along with that voice through the speakers:

SATAN IS A COMMIE

ONLY 5 MILES TO FAMOUS ZONE Z

"Jesus!" Lorinda said, "If I hear one more word I'm going to..."

"To what?"

"To start shooting." She laughed. "I've got a pile of guns here!"

"Just don't hit me," Stimpy said. "Aim out of the truck."

As they hit a series of potholes, the guns clattered, and the truck's headlights bounced over a simple road sign stating:

WELCOME TO ZONE Z

IF YOU CAN HANDLE "THE TRUTH"

"So how did a bunch of stupid conspiracy theories turn into an enclave?" Lorinda asked, now leaning up against the front seat. "More billionaires?"

"It might be the only enclave that didn't have billionaires behind it," Stimpy said, attempting to get his bearings as the truck entered Zone Z proper. "The true believers got together on their socials and contributed just enough money to establish their own enclave. They started some businesses to keep the place going. I think the biggest one was a tee-shirt factory. The enclave has always been on the verge of falling apart. They're not too good at, you know, real life."

"Can I stay out here? No more bedspread?"

"You're safe. The last time the CCSA tried to hang a camera in this enclave they killed the technicians, stuffed them in their official CCSA truck, towed it out of the enclave, and set it on fire."

"Who's 'they'?"

"Oh, just about everyone in the enclave. Men, women, children, dogs... Now I have to find our motel..."

They drove through streets lined with shabby two-story attached houses. It was a moonless night and streetlights were scarce, so it was hard to read the crackpot posters in the tiny front yards or figure out the symbolism of the many crazy-looking flags tacked to the fronts of the houses. When they reached a small commercial strip, Stimpy said, "Oh, look. There's a clothing store. Clothing Zone! Tomorrow we'll stop in there and — "

"It's makeover time for Lorinda and Stimpy!"

"Hah. And here we are." He turned past a sign reading "Zotel" and into the parking lot in front of a row of attached tiny white cabins, stopping in front of the one marked "Office." "I'll be right back," he said, leaving the engine running and jumping out. Less than a minute later he was in the driver's seat again. "No ID, no nothing," he marveled. "Here's your door code, thanks, goodnight. I could get to like this place. And we're in a back cabin, hidden away."

After finishing their remaining Regis sandwiches on the bed of their tight little room, Stimpy did a quick check-in with his people. "Tomorrow afternoon," he said to Lorinda, who had deposited the sandwich wrappings in the waste basket and was now looking for a comfortable position on the bed, "we'll have another car or truck or whatever they manage to find for us. Parked back here near our truck, key on the rear driver's-side tire. And then we'll be off to Georgia."

"And I suppose we just cruise into Georgia," Lorinda said. "Like, no problems."

"It's never *that* simple," Stimpy smiled. "We've got a little tunnel that goes under the wall between Alabama and Georgia, USA. We know we'll be able to get through this time — no riots, no wars. The tunnel's in the middle of nowhere. The last twenty miles or so is these tiny back roads — "

"You've been there before?"

"Oh, yeah," he said. "Four times. We have our own cameras on it, and on the roads leading to it. Maybe we'll even have a spy satellite on it when we get there."

"Satellite! Who *are* you people?"

He ignored the question. "The bad news is that once we leave Zone Z you'll have to hide under that bedspread again until we get to the tunnel."

"I was afraid you'd say that."

"So we get some sleep, in the morning we shower, wash off this makeup — "

"Finally!"

"Go to the clothing store, find a place to have breakfast, walk around, take in the sights of Zone Z, kill some time, get in our new car and we're on our way."

"Sounds good," Lorinda said. "I can't handle another last-minute escape." She snuggled her head into a pillow. It felt like it was stuffed with cardboard, but it was better than nothing. "I'm sick of being a fugitive." He was silent, but she sensed something was up. She lifted her head and saw him looking at her. "What?"

With difficulty, he said, "You've been an excellent fugitive. Believe me. You know I've done this before, and no one has been as brave and... *tough* as you. At first I thought you'd just be some pain-in-the-ass nice girl from some stupid middle-class enclave, but... I was wrong."

She felt a rush of heat. Maybe she was blushing. "Well, thanks..."

"So just... it'll all be over soon."

"Good." Knowing she was about to break into a silly grin, she pressed her face into the pillow. Soon, her mind drifting through the mad journey she'd been on since her violent encounter with the awful Janelle Stark, she tried to count how many days it had been since she'd left home. It felt like forever. Months? But, really... only five days?

With no need to wake up early, she slept profoundly until well after sunrise.

Sour green sunlight filtered through the streaky film of effluents that coated the office windows. The new bandage covered a bit less real estate on Janelle Stark's face than had the previous one, but it was still her most prominent feature. She scowled at her screen as her fingers danced on the keyboard: tic-tic-tic. The screen beeped twice. She hit a button and the face of a Domestic Security agent filled her screen. Withholding any kind of greeting, Stark stated: "You'd better have good news for me."

"Yes, I do, yes, boss." The agent was clearly terrified of Stark. His image shuddered on the screen.

"Hold your com steady!"

"Sorry, ma'am."

"What's your news?"

"We have custody of two people who collaborated with the fugitive. We think."

"Oh," Stark sneered, "you think."

"Yes, ma'am. We talked to a civilian who sighted them — "

"Who are these two people in your custody?"

"They call themselves — " he checked his notes "— Sluggo and Nancy, ma'am."

45 *In which our heroine unexpectedly encounters her nemesis.*

IT WAS AN unusually bright, clear day. Lorinda and Stimpy, looking refreshed and considerably younger than they'd looked twelve hours earlier, bounced out of the Clothing Zone and onto what the street signs identified as Commerze Ztreet.

Lorinda wore new white high-top sneakers, a faux-suede mini-dress, and the long-brimmed plaid baseball cap she'd bought — was it just yesterday? — at the Trump Memorial Golf Shoppe; Stimpy sported a red, white, and blue cowboy shirt, tight acid-washed jeans, black high-tops, and a black trucker cap with a Zone Z skull-and-crossbones logo on the front panel. Each had an automatic weapon dangling jauntily from a shoulder.

Lorinda was reaching into her bag for her oversized sunglasses when Stimpy stopped her. "You have the greenest eyes I've ever seen," he said.

"You've never seen my eyes before?"

"I guess not," he said. "They're amazing. Pure emerald. Maybe it's just this light."

Lorinda put on her sunglasses, saying, "The beautiful, pure sunlight of Zone Z."

Stimpy put on a new pair of mirrored wraparounds, moved his weapon to the other shoulder, and took Lorinda by her weaponless arm, saying, "We need a great big breakfast." Before they could take more than a couple of steps, he felt his com device vibrate in his pocket. He slipped it out, quickly read the screen, and said, "Confirmation about the car this afternoon. Georgia, here we come."

A family of six walked past them, a mom, a dad, and four kids ranging in age from about twelve down to about three. The parents were both carrying long guns, as were the three older kids. The little one had a toy automatic weapon, modeled after Stimpy's and Lorinda's real ones. They all, except the youngest, wore bulky bulletproof tunics over their military-inflected street clothes.

"Hi," said Lorinda pleasantly.

"Hail," all six of them said in unison as they continued on their way.

As soon as they were out of range, Lorinda whispered, "What was that?"

"Welcome to Zone Z," Stimpy said. "Now, which way should we go?"

"I think I've found our breakfast," Lorinda said, pointing a few blocks down Commerze Ztreet to what appeared to be several tables sheltered by jolly, brightly colored umbrellas.

"Wow," said Stimpy, "it looks like an actual restaurant."

"We've earned a little good luck."

"'Sluggo' and 'Nancy'?" Janelle Stark slammed her hand down on her desk and glared at her screen. "Don't screw around with me, agent."

"N-n-no, ma'am. Those are the names they gave us." The agent, a short, plump, sweaty young man, seemed like he was about to burst into tears.

"Hold your device steady, agent! You're shaking like a leaf."

"Sorry, ma'am," he said, attempting to steady himself. "We, we didn't get anything else out of them yet. But after the fugitive's picture went up, a civilian saw it and told us — "

"Yes, yes," barked Stark, way ahead of her subordinate. "The civilian saw Lorinda Moon with this Nancy and whatsisname. Where did this civilian see them?"

"At — " He checked his notes. "— at the, umm, Psychedelia disco dancing place. The witness thought Lorinda Moon was accompanied by a man."

"Disco?" Stark looked disgusted. "The little whore went *dancing*?"

"Yes, ma'am. That's where our witness saw her with them."

"And how did you locate these collaborators of hers?"

"There was a firearms incident at the Psychedelia and this witness ran out the door at the same time as Sluggo and Nancy and saw them get into a car — " checking his notes again "— a black late-model sedan, a . . . I'm never sure how to pronounce these words, ma'am . . . Pyeonghwa Satrap?"

"And you tracked them down because of their car?"

"Yes, ma'am. I mean, I didn't personally do it, but — "

"And where are these collaborators now?"

"They're right here, ma'am." He shakily turned his device to reveal a small shabby room in which Nancy and Sluggo, he in pajamas, she in a nightgown, both looking pretty roughed-up, were tied with ropes to metal chairs.

"We demand to see our lawyer," Sluggo yelled hoarsely.

"Very funny," Stark snapped. "No lawyers for garbage like you." Then, as the agent pointed the device back at himself, she asked, "How do you intend to get them to talk?"

At that moment, the sound of a door creaking open came through Stark's speaker. The agent aimed his device at the door just as a stooped older man with sparse gray hair, wearing a soiled white lab coat and brandishing an oversized hypodermic syringe, entered the room. "The doctor here is going to give them something that'll make them talk," he said.

"Perfect," said Stark. "I'll let the good doctor do his job, and you'll call me back as soon as you have some results. Won't you, agent?"

"Yes I will, boss, ma'am. I sure will."

"We need our lawyer!" Sluggo shouted off-camera.

"I'll expect your call within a half-hour. This doesn't need to be a full interrogation. You might not need anything more from them than the kind of car Lorinda Moon got into. If you get more, fine."

"Never! We'll never talk!" This time Nancy was shouting.

"Sure thing, boss. And I'll keep these two locked up — "

"Only until we apprehend the fugitive," Stark said. "After that they're disposable."

Once the gun-toting family was out of range, it was uncannily quiet on the street. On one side stood a row of two-story buildings of the type known as "taxpayers" in places where taxes were levied: commercial space downstairs, residential upstairs. Each storefront displayed a sign — commercially printed, identically designed — with one of four messages: Z IZ HERE; ALL IZ WELL; Z SEZ: "TRUST THE SCHEME"; and THE SCHEME IZ SUPREME. About a quarter of the storefronts also had "For Rent" signs in their windows.

"Is there any place outside of Perfecton that isn't weird?" Lorinda said.

Stimpy gave a loud, "Hah!" and said, "It's cute that you think Perfecton isn't weird."

They passed a bulletproof-clothing boutique, two gun-and-ammunition stores, a home-protection-equipment store, three real estate businesses trying to outdo each other in the size of their banners touting the availability of fully furnished family bunkers, a contractor who built both conventional homes and bunkers, a spy-equipment store, and a grocery store specializing in food guaranteed to last a hundred years.

Stimpy muttered, "We must be in the accessories-for-the-paranoid district."

In addition to the apparently official posters, most of these stores featured homemade signs and flags as well: Z'S STORM IS COMING; WHEREVER WE GO, WHATEVER WE DO, WE'RE GONNA GO THROUGH IT TOGETHER (or its abbreviation WWGWWDWGGTIT); NOTHING CAN STOP WHAT HAS ALREADY HAPPENED.

The other side of the street consisted mainly of dusty, paved vacant lots, punctuated by the occasional small house or tiny concrete shed located toward the back of its lot. "What's going on here?" Lorinda whispered. "Where is everyone?"

"I've heard about this," Stimpy said, his eyes sweeping the desolate landscape. "The underground bunkers of Zone Z. A lot of people here don't live in houses. They live underground."

"Because?"

"Fear."

"Of what?"

"Everything, I guess." Stimpy attempted, unsuccessfully, to laugh. "And I guess they spend a lot of time down there. Which would explain why there's no one here on the scary street."

As they approached the end of the block, Lorinda said, "Am I imagining that?" An impeccably white wooden church steeple rose from the dusty hard surface. There was no church. Just the steeple, its sharp point a good twenty feet above the ground.

They stopped when they reached it. Next to the steeple was a white concrete shed with a bombproof steel door in front and a rear that angled down to the ground, obviously housing a staircase. A sign on the door read "Church Entrance During Worship Hours." On the lower façade of the steeple, a big electronic sign said "First Christian Church of Zone Z," followed by the words "Daily Homily," beneath which flashed:

"CRAZY" IS IN THE MIND OF THE BEHOLDER

While attempting to digest that, Lorinda and Stimpy were startled by the sound of a vehicle approaching from the next side street and turning the corner. At first glance it looked like a jumbo toy car made of plywood, but they quickly realized that it was an actual car, a small one covered with thick, heavy sheets of rusting metal that clanged against the underlying bodywork and compressed the tires and suspension, so the poor thing was nearly dragging on the pavement.

"A homemade bulletproof car," Stimpy marveled as it lumbered past. "You wouldn't even have to shoot it. Just yell at it and it'll fall apart."

"Zone Z," Lorinda laughed. "It's all about the paranoia!"

The next two blocks consisted of more of the same, with storefronts on one side (their favorite: a place called End Times Financial Services) and dreary vacant lots — or bunker roofs — on the other, until they homed in on the restaurant at the end of Commerze.

Compared to everything they'd passed so far, Mimzy's Zeecrit Gourmet Café looked friendly and welcoming. Without needing to confer about it, they made a beeline for the terrace and sat across from each other on yellow plastic chairs at a blue table under a yellow umbrella. Almost immediately, a large middle-aged woman in a yellow dress wheezed out to the terrace, dropped two menus on the table, and said, "Mornin', y'all. Welcome to Mimzy's. I'm Mimzy. Need a couple of chemical-free cappuccinos?"

"That'd be great," said Lorinda.

"Just give me a minute," Mimzy said, shuffling back into the restaurant. Before she reemerged, the armored car loudly announced its return and grated to a stop in front of the restaurant. The two front doors and the near-side rear door opened simultaneously and disgorged their occupants: a thirty-ish couple in front, a pre-teen boy in back. All three wore military-adjacent outfits, bullet-studded bandolier belts across their shoulders, and shiny black hip-belted holsters cradling gleaming handguns. In a well-practiced move, they each faced a different direction and, in sync, slowly swiveled their heads until they had, with considerable overlap, scanned all 360 degrees of the horizon.

"Clear," said the man.

"Clear," said the woman.

"Clear," said the child.

At which point they relaxed and headed for a table as far away from Lorinda and Stimpy as possible. Since the terrace had room for only five tables, they weren't very far away.

"Good job getting those idiots Nancy and Sluggo to talk," said Janelle Stark to her subordinate on the screen. "Our satellite located Moon's vehicle in about ten minutes. She's in Zone Z."

"I'm an hour and a half from there," the agent said.

"I'm going to order a chopper right now. Gather as many agents as you can and meet me at the entrance to the enclave in ninety minutes. We can't bring the chopper right in there — they'll shoot us down, they have a few missiles. So bring an extra vehicle for me and my people."

"Just one extra vehicle?"

"I'm just bringing a skeleton crew. Plus your people is all we'll need," Stark said. "There's only two of them. They'll be easy to take down."

The nervous agent hesitated. "Ma'am, I only have a few agents I can grab that fast — "

"Three or four should do it. This operation's going to be a piece of cake."

"A, um…huh? What does that mean, ma'am?"

Stimpy and Lorinda lingered at their table, the remnants of their Cheeze Omelet Zpecials ("Z's Favorite!") before them. They were nursing their third chemical-free cappuccinos, which, after her first sip of the first one, Lorinda pronounced "weak coffee with whipped cream on top." Now sitting close together on the side nearest the family at the next table, she and Stimpy leaned on each other, and held hands, and sat in blissful silence, feigning romantic rapture so they could unobtrusively eavesdrop on the family's conversation.

BOY: But Mom! How can JFK Jr. be about to reappear *now?* I thought he died a long time ago.

WOMAN: That's just what they want you to believe, Clay.

MAN: Of course he didn't die.

BOY: But why do they lie about it? Why do they say he died when he didn't? Why does *he* lie about it?

WOMAN: First of all, Clay, it's not a lie. Z calls it a strategic fiction. There's a big difference. Second, JFK Jr. needed to go underground to accomplish all that he needed to do. Out of reach of the so-called media.

MAN: Just like Z.

BOY: Is that why Z lives in a bunker?

MAN: Not just one. He has lots of bunkers.

BOY: Did you ever see him?

MAN: No, but we know people who have. Jeanine and Everest.

BOY: Really? They've seen Z?!

MAN: I think so. Either that, or they know someone.

WOMAN: Z and JFK Jr. are best friends. Along with President Trump.

BOY: But he's dead, too. Right?

The man and the woman exchanged meaningful glances.

WOMAN: We've talked about this. Where did you hear that?

BOY: I don't know! From Duane.

WOMAN: Maybe think twice before believing Duane, sweetie.

MAN: President Trump also had to go underground, son.

BOY: But... wouldn't he be like a million years old?

MAN: Not with our doctors. And their special treatments.

WOMAN. This is why Zone Z is so important. One day you'll understand.

BOY: You always say that. [Crudely mimicking the woman] "Zone Z is the only safe place in the country." Is that why they live here? Z and JFK Jr. and President Trump?

WOMAN: Yes, but not just because it's safe. Because they need to be left alone to make their plans. Pretty soon Z is going to straighten everything out.

BOY: With JFK Jr. and President Trump?

MAN: That's right, Clay. "Nothing can stop what has already happened."

BOY: But what are they going to straighten out?

WOMAN: Lots of things. Like the Lizard People who run the USA. They're going to stop them from invading us.

MAN: The Jew bankers who bought up all the satellites to distribute . . . certain things.

BOY: You mean CHILD PORN?

WOMAN: Shh!

MAN: Who told you that?

BOY: I guess Duane.

MAN: Well —

BOY: But he didn't know what it was. What *is* child porn?

MAN: We'll talk about it later. [To his wife, pointing to the menu.] Check it out. The whole-wheat pancakes have gone up. Again.

WOMAN: And isn't it interesting that corn and wheat are expensive because of the drought, but beef is *also* expensive? I mean, coincidence? [Laughs.] If you believe that, I have some waterfront property in Galveston to sell you.

BOY: But don't the cows eat corn and wheat? So —

MAN: It's not that simple, Clay.

WOMAN: There are a lot of things *they* want you to believe. But Z's going to get them all. They're all going down. That's why it's time for JF —

"Can I get you anything else?" Lorinda and Stimpy hadn't noticed that Mimzy was back at their table. "A couple more cappuccinos?"

"Oh, no thanks," said Lorinda. "Any more coffee and I'll . . ." She made a "head exploding" gesture.

"We'd love to stay," Stimpy said, "but we don't want to take up your valuable table all day." Lorinda stifled a laugh: Other than the family at the next table, no one else had come anywhere near Mimzy's since they'd been there.

"Oh, don't worry about that," Mimzy said. "I like having y'all sit here. Makes it look like we're busy. Business attracts business, they say."

"Where *is* everybody?" Lorinda asked.

"I see y'all's not from around here. People are worried about things, so they don't come out much. At night is when they usually come out. If they come out at all."

"What are they worried about?" Lorinda asked.

"Oh," said Mimzy, lazily starting to stack their dishes, "Where to begin? The usual things, I guess. Newcular war. Pandemics. Communism. Socialism. Airplane crashes. Car crashes. Stray bullets. Immigrants. Muggers—"

"There are muggers in Zone Z?" Stimpy asked.

"Well, I've never seen one," Mimzy said, musing. "I heard of one once. I mean, it's possible, right?"

"Earthquakes," chimed in the boy at the next table, who was staring at the strangers. His father grabbed his arm, but the kid just kept staring.

"Can a bunker really protect you from an earthquake?" Lorinda kindly asked him. Both parents looked at Lorinda and subtly shook their heads. She couldn't tell whether they were signaling, "No, it can't" or "Don't encourage him."

"We do have two big parades every year," Mimzy said cheerily. "One on Christmas and one on Our Independence Day. That's when we all get to see each other out in the sunlight. I mean, unless there's a tornado or something. Or a public event, like a hanging."

"I love parades!" the boy said. "Last year we drove our car in the parade!"

"It's sad that it was interrupted," his mother said.

Lorinda's eyebrows went up. "Oh?"

"Tornado," the father said.

Two unmarked black G-Wagens stopped just short of the "Welcome to Zone Z" road sign. A minute later an ancient Kamov Ka-62 helicopter, devoid of military or civilian identification and painted incongruously in jungle camo, roared into view. Then, blowing dirt and trash in every direction, it set down dangerously close to the vehicles.

"That was insane," Lorinda said as they walked back along Commerze Ztreet.

"I know," Stimpy said. "'We all live underground and come out twice a year. And at night.' I'm not saying they're all vampires. But I'm not saying they're not."

Lorinda laughed. "Really. Meanwhile, how can anyone believe that stuff?"

"There's a lot of weird stuff that *you* believed. Maybe you still believe some of it."

Lorinda paused. "Not so much anymore." Then, changing the

subject slightly, "I have to say, those people were nice for not correcting their son about the earthquakes."

Stimpy considered that before saying, "Maybe. Or maybe they should be criticized for enabling his ignorance. Not to mention the antisemitism. Maybe one day he'll look back and think, 'My parents let me believe a lie about earthquakes. And bunkers.'" He paused. "'And bankers.'" He suddenly stopped walking, struck by a thought. "Although they don't think it's a lie. They think it's the truth. About the Lizard People and the Jews. Which makes it worse."

She took his arm and they resumed walking. "You can think that if you like," Lorinda said with a smile, "but I'm going with 'nice parents.'"

Stimpy grew melodramatic. "No! Bad parents!"

"Oh — "

"And then maybe that'll drive him to devote his life to overthrowing the fascist rulers of the CCSA. If the country still even exists." Lorinda gave him a look and rolled her eyes. "Ya gotta dream," he said with a grin. "Should we go back to the motel? Or do some more sightseeing first?"

"I don't think there are any sights to see," she said. "But I don't mind walking for a bit. I can get in some more fresh air before — you know, the bedspread."

The only interesting sight they came upon was the Zone Z Sheriff's Office And Jailhouse, a freestanding building in the middle of a dusty stretch of bunker roofs. The Sheriff's Office, with its name in an old-timey font on a wooden sign, a little boardwalk along its front, and vertical bars across its small window, looked like something out of an old cowboy movie.

"That's not an old building," Stimpy said as they walked past it. "This enclave isn't old enough for that building to be real. They built it to look old. It's, like, *art directed*. Very weird in the middle of all..." He gestured at the dusty bunker flatlands.

"Oh my God!" Lorinda pointed across the street from the sheriff's office. Instead of houses or stores, there was a small park or plaza in the middle of the block, in the center of which sat a wooden stage or platform, with two substantial uprights connected by a horizontal crosspiece about ten feet above the floor of the platform. A man wearing a tan uniform and a cowboy hat was standing on a ladder, meticulously attaching a heavy rope to the middle of the crosspiece.

"It's a gallows," Stimpy said huskily.

Lorinda shuddered. "I hope it's not for us."

They walked a little faster back to their hotel.

"I might take a nap before we head for Georgia," Lorinda said as they entered the Zotel parking lot.

"Good plan," said Stimpy. "I'll try to figure out where to grab a few sandwiches before we leave. Maybe just go back to Mimzy's."

"Where's Regis when we need him?"

They had just turned the corner of the cabins to head for their room in back, when two people with raised guns jumped out from the shadows: Janelle Stark and the enormous Skippy. "Drop your weapons and get down on the ground," Stark commanded, "Do it!"

Lorinda and Stimpy spun around to flee just as four agents closed in on them from behind.

"Drop your weapons now! Or we start shooting!"

"Fuck," said Stimpy. He slowly removed the rifle from his shoulder and set it gently on the ground. Lorinda, following his lead, did the same.

46 *In which our heroine is set free, then captured again.*

JANELLE STARK WAS in an expansive mood as she steered Lorinda around the side of the Zotel toward the rear parking lot. "I'm happy to see you graduated up to a real weapon," Stark said. "That little pink thing you had..." She trailed off into a mirthless chuckle.

"Your bandage looks good," Lorinda said.

Stark ignored that as she pushed her captive in the direction of the nearer of the two black Gelandewagens parked on the far side of the Chartreuse Xiaomi Lumberjax. "That's a nice truck you have, Moon," Stark said, giving the plastic cuffs securing Lorinda's wrists behind her back a nasty little shake. "Too bad for you our satellite found it in about ten seconds."

"Fuck you," Lorinda spat.

"Oh, my, my, my," Stark said. "You're a lucky girl. If you weren't with child I'd be slapping you silly."

If I weren't with child, Lorinda thought, *I'd be behind the bar at PumpJack's and not out here in the middle of nowhere.*

Just then Stimpy, his hands also cuffed behind his back, half ran, half stumbled past her, barely managing to avoid falling on his face. She turned to see that big ghoul Skippy grinning with sadistic satisfaction.

"Of course," said Stark, "there's no reason Skippy can't have his way with your little friend here, whoever the hell he is."

The big guy mimed dusting off the lapels of his dark suit, caught up to Stimpy, and yanked up on the plastic cuffs, causing Stimpy to yip in pain.

"You take him in the other truck," Stark said. "She'll come with me in this one."

Lorinda, nearly in tears, locked eyes with Stimpy and mouthed "I'm sorry" just as Brad opened the rear door of the first G-Wagen, popped his still-bandaged head out, and shouted, "Who is *he*, Lorinda?"

"Oh, Jesus," Lorinda said. Stimpy laughed. Skippy gave him another yank.

"Move over," said Stark to Brad, pushing down on Lorinda's head and easing her into the back seat. "And don't touch her."

"But I love her," Brad whined.

"Shut up, Brad," Lorinda and Stark said in unison.

"I'm bringing you and your friend to the local jail for a day or two," Stark said, turning to face Lorinda from the front seat as the two unmarked but unmistakably obvious CCSA vehicles burbled slowly toward the sheriff's office. "Of course I could extract you right now. I have a chopper waiting just outside of this stupid enclave. But I want to do it right. I want to have a big procession, a parade, if you will, all the way from here to the breeding center in Baton Rouge. The BRBC. It's probably even nicer than the one in Austin. You'll love it there. Here's the thing, Moon. You're getting famous. Your picture's on billboards all over the country."

"Some of them are calling you a hero," Brad said. He frowned and looked at Stark. "I guess those were hacked, huh?"

"Shut up, Brad," Stark said through gritted teeth. She turned back to Lorinda. "But yes, some of them think you're heroic for endangering innocent life and breaking the law, and I want to correct that misunderstanding. I want everybody in the country to see what happens when wicked young women get out of line. So I need a little time to advertise this. I want thousands — millions — of people looking at you along the parade route." Then, almost to herself, "Maybe I'll have to leave you in jail here for a week to get it organized." She gave Lorinda a cold smile. "You might find it interesting here. These people are insane. I wonder what they'll make of you..."

The trucks stopped in front of the sheriff's office. Out the window Lorinda could see that a crowd of sixty people, maybe even eighty or a hundred, had gathered around the gallows across the street. *They came out of their bunkers for this*, she thought. A man of around thirty, in torn black pants and a black tee-shirt, his hands, like hers, secured behind his back, stood straight and still in the center of the platform. Lorinda's driver stepped out, opened her door, and gestured — surprisingly politely, she thought — for her to get out. As she stood up, she saw a man in a tan law-enforcement uniform mount the platform, approach the prisoner, grab the dangling rope, and fit the noose at the end of the rope around the young man's neck. "Y'all know I'm innocent," the young man yelled, his voice easily carrying to Lorinda and beyond. "Just remember this when they come for you." He said more but Lorinda couldn't hear him as he was drowned out by the crowd hissing and booing and yelling "Shut up!" Finally, he nodded at the other man, who stepped down from the platform, pulled the rope taut, and reached for a big lever attached to the side of the platform.

"That could be you," said Stark, who had come around the truck. She grabbed Lorinda's shoulder and guided her toward the sheriff's office. But her curiosity got the better of her: She stopped and turned to face the gallows. Lorinda studied her captor's face, which lit up with joy at the sound of a wooden thud followed by a softer thud. A moment later came the collective gasp of the crowd, followed instantly by cheers. Still grinning, Stark stepped behind Lorinda, grabbed the plastic cuffs, and frog-marched her forward.

"By what authority are y'all here?" The sheriff had emerged from his office. A lanky man with a big white mustache, he wore a tan uniform, a big, shiny, five-pointed star on his chest, a tan cowboy hat, and a pair of gleaming six-shooters in the holsters on his hips. Whoever designed the Wild West building had apparently designed him as well. He came to a halt in front of Lorinda and addressed Stark, making it obvious that, in the unfolding scenario, his was the only authority that mattered.

"By the authority vested in me as a Senior Domestic Security Officer of the Confederation of Conservative States of America," Janelle Stark said contemptuously. "I and my team have full overriding authority to be here."

The sheriff theatrically spat on the ground before speaking. "Full overriding authority?" He smiled. "Full overriding authority. Enforced by what? How many are you, four? Five?" He noticed the towering Skippy. "Or is it three and a circus freak? Don't really matter, does it?"

He looked past the black trucks and nodded approvingly.

Stark followed his gaze. Behind her, the gallows crowd was scuttling across the street. They were all waving guns. As if they'd rehearsed it, they spread out until they formed a dense semicircle around the trucks, the CCSA security crew, Lorinda and Stimpy, and the sheriff. Many of them aimed their guns at Janelle Stark, quickly figuring out that she was the commander-in-chief of the invasion.

"Now," said the sheriff to Janelle, "I suggest you explain what the hell you're doing in our precious enclave. The only enclave, I ought to remind you, that don't take no shit from the CCSA government or any other government."

"I'm here to arrest this woman for..." Stark seemed to have trouble putting her words together in this unaccustomed situation. "To arrest this woman for seeking to terminate her pregnancy. To bring her to one of our breeding centers. And likewise to arrest her accomplice."

"I see. Well, that's very interesting because that's not the way the law works here in Zone Z."

"What are *you* going to do with them?" Stark said, apparently realizing that there was no point arguing with a crazy person, or a whole enclave of crazy people.

"I'm going to keep them here in protective custody, in my jailhouse, while we figure out what this is all about. Now remove their cuffs and get the hell out of my enclave."

Stark was frozen in indecision.

"Or," said the sheriff, "we can walk you across the street..." he paused for effect "... and hang the whole lot of you. Although" — here he rubbed the back of his neck, seemingly in thought — "we only got one noose up there right now. So it might take a while." Then he brightened, grinned at his townspeople, and said, "But we got plenty of time."

The crowd of armed Zone Z citizens cheered wildly.

"And I'll tell you what," the sheriff continued, clearly enjoying this, "just set down those nice new military weapons you got, right down in front of you. Real gentle-like. We could always use a few more weapons around here. 'Specially when folks like y'all come nosing around."

The townspeople cheered again and crowded in a little closer. Stark signaled to her people that they should do as the sheriff said. She placed her gun on the ground, patted it goodbye, stood up, and gave Lorinda's handcuffs a painful little twist that caused her to yelp in pain. In retribution, Lorinda fiercely clapped her wrists together, mashing Stark's fingers between the two sides of the sturdy plastic cuffs.

Now it was Stark's turn to yelp. She jumped back, and gaped at the blood oozing out of her left index finger. "You little bitch!" she snapped.

The same sweaty agent with whom she'd video-conferenced this operation to life stepped forward with a pair of small hedge shears and cut off first Lorinda's plastic handcuffs, then Stimpy's.

"I'll be back. And with a lot more firepower," Janelle growled. "Maybe tomorrow," she added as she skulked off toward the shiny black G-Wagens. Her people fell in line behind her.

The crowd stepped aside, just a tiny bit, to let them pass. "And fuck you!" someone yelled. Fifteen or twenty more townsfolk joined in the "Fuck you!" chorus, along with the odd "Fuck the CCSA."

As Lorinda watched them leave, she noticed a tearful Brad taking it all in from the back seat of one of the official vehicles. Across the street, the limp body of the hanged man lazily spun one way, then the other on the thick rope.

"I let you down." Stimpy, looking physically deflated, had slouched over to Lorinda's side as she watched the G-Wagens drive away and the mob lower their guns and start to disperse.

"What are you talking about? You're a hero." She put her arms around him and hugged him tightly. "Are you okay?"

"I'll be okay."

Lorinda felt a strong hand grip her arm. "Let's go, missy," the sheriff said harshly. He looked at Stimpy. "You, too, bub. I'm Sheriff Jesse Flint, and you're in my custody now."

As the sheriff guided them toward his office, Lorinda said, "Thanks."

The sheriff stopped and looked at her deadpan. "For what?"

"For… I don't know… getting rid of those people."

"They'll be back, with more of 'em next time. And I bet it's all your fault. They followed *you*. *You* lured 'em here."

"I didn't… we didn't mean to — "

"So now we gotta deal with them *and* with you. And your boyfriend."

"You could just let us go," Stimpy said. "You'd never see us again."

"Yeah? And get caught up in their aiding-and-abetting-a-fugitive bullshit? Have them send in the army and tear the enclave apart looking for you? Not happening." The sheriff drew a deep breath and looked off into the distance. "Course, I could just throw up another noose and hang the both of you, leave you dangling till they come back."

He stroked his mustache and his eyes went dreamy as he said, "What would Z do?"

47 *In which our heroine has a brush with Zone Z justice and makes a shocking announcement.*

AS THEY STEPPED onto the little boardwalk, Lorinda asked, "What did he do?" It was more to establish some kind of conversational rapport with the sheriff than to have her question answered.

"What did who do?" said the sheriff, temporarily halting the march into his office.

"Him. Back there," Lorinda said, jerking her head toward the gallows.

"Oh, him," said the sheriff. "That one was a sad case. He coulda gone far here. But he committed a capital heresy and paid the price. As you can see."

"A capital heresy?" Stimpy asked. That was a new one on him.

"Yep, a capital heresy," said the sheriff. "Class A, the worst kind. He denied the existence of Z, orally, verbally, in writing, and in the so-called media. We gave him the opportunity to retract his statements. Many times. But he refused. Gave us no choice but to string him up. Stubborn, stupid bastard."

"Have you ever met Z?" Lorinda asked.

"You don't want to meet Z," he snorted cryptically. Resuming his forward motion, he firmly guided her and Stimpy into the building.

The interior perfectly matched the exterior. The "office" part, on the right-hand side of the room, consisted of two wooden desks, a wooden chair behind each of the desks, two chairs in front of the near desk, and several wooden file cabinets. In bold red letters on a white background, a poster on the wall behind the desks said:

INDEPENDENZ FOR ZONE Z
Z SAYS
IT'S TIME TO ZECEDE FROM THE CCSA

Past the office were some rooms, presumably washrooms, closets, and the like. On the left side, facing the office, was a line of four small jail cells that extended to the rear wall. More accurately, it was one large cell divided into four smaller cells by floor-to-ceiling vertical bars, with each of the small cells having its own barred door facing the office side of the room. Sturdy, beat-up wooden benches were bolted to the floor around the three doorless sides of each cell.

Only the first cell, the one directly across from the office, was inhabited. The prisoners, seven men and four women, were a scraggly bunch. As the sheriff and his two new charges entered, most of the prisoners in the crowded cell — those who weren't nodding-out on a bench — scrambled up to the front of the cell to have a better look at the fresh meat.

"Calm down and back off y'all," barked the sheriff. The prisoners eased away from the cell bars while keeping their eyes on the action.

"Now," said Sheriff Flint, "first I gotta read you your Sacred Rights Warning."

Just then the deputy sheriff — the man Lorinda and Stimpy had seen stringing up the noose and who later pulled the lever — came through the front door.

"Did the clean-up squad come, Lukas?"

"Nah," said the deputy, "the dude's still hanging out there. Just twisting in the breeze."

"Damn. Why are they always so slow? We may need that gallows tonight for our new prisoners here." Then, to Lorinda and Stimpy, "This here's my deputy, Deputy Lukas."

Lorinda turned to the deputy, flashed her eyes, and said, "I'm...I'm Randi Howland. Nice to meet you."

"I'm Edward Chapman," Stimpy muttered reluctantly.

"Search 'em, Lukas," the sheriff said, sitting down behind the desk, opening a drawer, and grabbing a rumpled sheet of paper, a pencil, and a small, brightly colored packet.

"You got anything in your pockets, sir?" Deputy Lukas asked Stimpy, who took out his wallet and his com device. As he passed the com to the deputy, he stole a glance at the sheriff who, after removing a small square patch from the packet, peeled off the backing and slapped the patch on the side of his neck. "Lordy," said the deputy, fondling and staring at Stimpy's com. "I never seen one like this before. What is it?"

"Oh, it's just, like, a music player," Stimpy lied, as he deftly slipped his Citizen Card out of his wallet and into his pocket.

"You ain't carrying some kind of communicator on you?"

"The CCSA security people took it. They also took our Citizen Cards." He held out his wallet while sneaking a glance at Lorinda, who instantly caught what he was telling her: Our Citizen Cards say we're old fogeys, so we'd better try not to show them.

"We don't use CCSA credentials here," said the deputy, ignoring the wallet and handing the com back to Stimpy. "And you, ma'am? What's in there?" Lorinda held her bag open for him. He went right for the pink Lady SIG Sauer .22 and held it up in front of his face. "Hey, sheriff, check it out."

The sheriff, now writing on the sheet of paper, looked up. "What the hell?"

A woman in the cell shouted, "I want that little toy!"

"And I guess them CCSA folks took your communicator too?" the deputy said.

"That's right," said Lorinda.

"Okay," the deputy said, dropping the pink gun back into Lorinda's bag. "Can't see you doing any harm with that thing."

"Sit down," Sheriff Flint said. Lorinda and Stimpy sat on the chairs in front of his desk. The sheriff opened the drawer again, found a length of heavy white string and two pairs of handcuffs, and slid the handcuffs across the desk. Lukas cuffed Lorinda's left wrist to her chair and Stimpy's right wrist to his. "Fix up cell two for them," the sheriff said. "I think they'll be here for a while if I don't hang 'em first." Deputy Lukas moseyed off to a closet. Closing his eyes, the sheriff said, "This stuff is the best."

The woman who'd shouted about the gun now shouted, "Give me a patch!" Everyone ignored her.

The sheriff opened his eyes and held up the little packet so Lorinda and Stimpy could read its swirly logo: ZTONED THC PATCHES XTRA ZTRONG. "We just started a new manufacturing operation here. Closed down the tee-shirt factory and put everyone to work on this fine product. Pretty soon we hope to be shipping all over the CCSA." He closed his eyes again. "It's the strongest and the quickest anyone's ever seen. And I'm proud to say that I helped with the formulation."

"He owns the company!" the deputy chimed in.

"Well, I'm a part-owner. It's only right, since I thought of it. Also, I'm the top law-enforcement and legal authority here in this enclave, so I'm owed a piece of the action. Don't you agree?"

"Absolutely," Lorinda said. Stimpy nodded and tried to smile.

"He's like the CEO of Zone Z," the deputy said proudly.

The sheriff nodded to Lukas, then addressed Lorinda and Stimpy. "Down to business. You should know that this is just a little jailhouse, not a real prison. It's more what you call a drunk tank."

This was instantly met by catcalls from the cell and one deep voice grumbling, "I ain't drunk no more."

"Zip it, Howie," the sheriff shot back. Then, to Lorinda and Stimpy: "We don't believe in long-term incarceration here in Zone Z." He paused for effect. "That gallows out there gets a lot of use."

"Don't forget the firing squad," one of the women interjected.

"Yeah, well we don't do that so much anymore," said Sheriff Flint. "Ammunition ain't cheap."

"Also, we had that accident," called the deputy from behind the closet door.

"So what I'm saying," said the sheriff, "is that one way or the other you won't be here long. I'll either send you back to the CCSA, hang you by the neck, or..." He thought about it for a moment, then, surprisingly, giggled. "I don't know what I might do. Maybe I'll give you a loyalty oath and make you my deputies." He cracked up, as did some of the prisoners. "But," he said, pulling himself together, "I'll probably just hang you. Anyway, I need to read you your Sacred Rights Warning." To Deputy Lukas, he called, "I put some new stuff in the Sacred Rights, Lukas. You should listen."

Turning his eyes to the sheet of paper on his desk, he read aloud: "'You have the right to an attorney if you can afford one and if you can find one who will work for you. You have the right to remain silent. I have the right and obligation to do whatever is necessary to make you talk. Anything you say will be used against you in a court of law or right here in my jailhouse. Irregardless of your guilt or innocence, any blasphemy against Z will incur the death penalty.' That's why we had today's hanging. Did I tell you that already? 'And aside from everything else, I, Sheriff Jesse Flint, am sovereign in my jailhouse and throughout this Zone Z, and, under the auspices of our leader Z, have the right to do whatever I deem necessary to preserve our freedom and our way of life here in our precious enclave, up to and including doing whatever I deem necessary to prisoner's name here' — you know your names, I don't need to say 'em '—including, as heretofore mentioned or suggested, hanging you with a noose until you are legally dead. Z is here, there is nothing to fear, live the dream, believe in the Scheme. Amen.' Now put your right hands over your hearts and repeat after me."

Stimpy and Lorinda glanced dubiously at each other, then covered their hearts with their right hands.

"I swear to Z and Jesus Christ that I agree," the sheriff intoned.

"I swear to Z and Jesus Christ that I agree," Lorinda and Stimpy repeated, struggling to keep from laughing.

Several of the prisoners clapped and cheered. "That was a good one, sheriff," the deputy said as he opened the door to cell number two. "I like your new material. It gets better every time." He tossed two rubber pads and some sheets onto a bench in the cell.

"So," said the sheriff, "tell me what you did to get the CCSA so pissed off at y'all?"

Stimpy cleared his throat, cast a glimpse at Lorinda, and nervously began, "Randi and I, we... she got pregnant, you see, and she had just gotten a job promotion, she was about to get very busy, and she really wasn't ready to have a baby. So then the CCSA Domestic Security Force grabbed her because... they were worried that she wanted to have a reset. An abortion." He paused, not sure which way to take the story.

The prisoners who were standing were now pressed against the bars staring at the back of Stimpy's head. Those who were sitting were getting up and migrating toward the bars; those still on a bench were rubbing the sleep out of their eyes and trying to focus.

Lorinda looked over her shoulder at the prisoners. They were obviously sympathetic, and a few gave her big grins, affirmative nods, or thumbs-up. She gave them a wan smile.

"We don't even know how they knew," Stimpy said.

"Oh they know!" one of the women prisoners said. The crowd mumbled its agreement.

Lorinda's gaze had slid off the prisoners and was now aimed at the floor. Her expression went blank. She was contemplating an idea that — like all her best ideas — had come of its own accord, out of nowhere, seeming both superficially crazy…and absolutely brilliant.

"They caught her," Stimpy continued. Then he paused to swallow hard as he noticed the sheriff absentmindedly fashioning the piece of string into a noose. Stimpy resumed, "but…but she's an incredibly strong person, and she escaped. Which isn't easy to do. And that's when I decided to help her get out of the CCSA — "

"Hold on, Johnny," Lorinda interrupted.

Stimpy looked at her. There was a touch of panic in his eyes.

"Johnny?" The sheriff looked up, suddenly alert. "What happened to whatsisname, Edward Chap-thingy?"

Lorinda turned back to the sheriff and said, "Can I be honest with you, Sheriff Flint?"

"You better be."

"Can you keep a secret?"

"Only if it don't involve breaking one of Z's rules," he said with a smile.

She turned to the cell and addressed the prisoners: "Can you guys keep our secret?" They roared in affirmation. She turned back to the sheriff. "We've been lying for so long. I'm just tired of lying. I need to be honest. To finally be honest. My real name..." She turned to look at the prisoners, then looked back at the sheriff.

"What's your real name?" another voice called out.

"My real name," Lorinda said, "is Lorinda. Lorinda Moon." Stimpy gasped. "It's all right, honey. I know that these people are our friends." She gave the sheriff her biggest "Welcome to PumpJack's" smile, then turned and flashed it at the prisoners. "Yes," she said, leaning her head in Stimpy's direction. "He's right. I'm pregnant. It's *his* baby. This man, this beautiful man, is my husband. His name is..."

She looked at Stimpy, whose eyes were wide. She looked back at the prisoners, who were rapt.

"No," she said, letting her head sag. "I'm sorry," she stage-whispered. "This is all a mistake. I really...I can't say any more."

The prisoners exploded in "Say more"s and "Please"s and "Tell us"s and "Don't stop"s and, from Howie, the man with the basso profundo voice, "You can trust us, dear."

"Can you really *really* keep a secret?" Lorinda asked. They nodded and cheered. "Do you *really* mean it." They cheered much louder.

Deputy Lukas was now standing in front of the prisoners, cheering along with them.

"All right," she said, turning back to Sheriff Flint. "My husband's name is..." She turned to Stimpy, saying, "Don't worry, Johnny. I know we can trust the people of Zone Z."

Then, loud and clear, she said: "My husband's name is...John Fitzgerald Kennedy Junior!"

48 *In which our heroine continues her journey in a Cadillac limousine.*

"JOHN FITZGERALD KENNEDY Junior! That's JFK Junior!" a female prisoner bellowed. "He's JFK Junior! It's him!" The prisoners went wild, shouting "JFK Junior!" and "Johnny!" "Junior!" and "It's really him!"

Deputy Lukas's eyes were bouncing from the prisoners to Stimpy and back. Sheriff Flint got all squinty, stared at Lorinda, stared at Stimpy, and finally opened his little packet and slapped a second THC patch on the other side of his neck.

Stimpy did his best to hold himself steady and stare with a noble, self-effacing-but-proud, Man-of-Destiny look into the middle distance.

"You're wondering why he looks so young," Lorinda said, anticipating the sheriff's question.

"That's what I'm thinking," said the sheriff. "He must be, I don't know, sixty, seventy, eighty years old."

"You don't look much like JFK Junior," the deputy ventured. "I seen your picture."

"That's the whole point! You all," said Lorinda, sweeping the room with her smile, "you're the only people in the country who know what my husband, JFK Junior — my Johnny — looks like *now*."

"We have access to the greatest doctors in the world," said Stimpy in a husky, confidential voice. "Plastic surgeons, gerontologists — that's old-age doctors — every kind of doctor and scientist."

"He takes a bath in nuclear-stem-cell youth serum every week," Lorinda said. "He gets special radiation treatments. His bones are titanium and aluminum and carbon fiber. And look into his eyes."

Following her lead, Stimpy took a long, soulful look at the prisoners, then the deputy, then the sheriff.

"Those are not the eyes of a young man," said Lorinda in a hushed voice. "Those are the eyes of wisdom. I'm proud to say that he is . . ." And here she faltered — out of modesty? Love? Divine inspiration? Her voice broke, perhaps from sheer emotion. ". . . my soulmate."

The prisoners erupted in a cacophony of affirmation.

Waiting until they calmed down a bit, Stimpy said, "You should also know that my lungs and heart are new. They're only two years old. The doctors and scientists tell me I can live another fifty or sixty years if . . . well, let's just say, God willing." The prisoners again burst into cheers.

"Now just hold on a minute," the sheriff said, slapping his hand on the desk. "Y'all quiet down," he growled at the prisoners, "or I'm gonna move you to the back cell." They went silent. "Now," said the sheriff, looking at Lorinda, "what about you? If he's JFK Junior, who the hell are you?"

"I told you," she said. "I'm Lorinda Moon. What I didn't tell you is that I'm the daughter of — " Here she looked over at the prisoners, who were silent with anticipation. She paused, as though struggling with conflicting impulses. Should she tell the truth? Or maintain an easy, familiar deception? The truth won out. "Okay — I'm the *love child* of the late Donald Trump Junior and a very famous lady that I can't talk about because it would put her life — my mother's life — in great danger." She patted her stomach. "The Prophet of Revelation prophesized that our baby will be the reincarnation of President Donald Trump. Only better. And Z himself will be our baby's godfather."

Stimpy jumped in before the others could digest all of that. "That's why the CCSA fascists want to capture us. They know that our baby, our child, will grow up to lead the revolution that overthrows the rulers — the billionaires and trillionaires — who are destroying this nation with their corruption." And, as an afterthought, "And their pederasty." He tried, unsuccessfully, to remember one or two plot points from the old movie *The Terminator* to use in illustration of how their child would save the world.

"Why didn't they just hang you?" the sheriff blurted. "Or shoot you? Or poison you? And why are they accusing *you*," he looked at Lorinda, "of wanting an abortion?"

"Because they're liars," Lorinda said. "And because they want to make us look bad and make an example of me and Johnny. If they killed us right away, we'd be martyrs. So they want to put us in parades and on billboards and on CCSA broadcasts." She paused and swept the room for eye contact. "They want to keep us alive until everyone hates us."

"And then," Stimpy said, "they'll find the place in the CCSA where we're the most hated, and they'll release us there. They'll say we escaped — right into a murderous mob. And they'll make sure there are plenty of cameras around to show how much the people hated us. And they'll have some fake footage showing how they tried to protect us and bring us to safety so we could get a fair trial or some horseshit, but, sadly, the angry mob killed us."

The sheriff cracked up. "That's a damn good plan," he said as his laughter subsided. "Pure evil." He laughed again.

For a second Lorinda thought the sheriff was going to adopt

Stimpy's fantasy on the spot, march them across the street, and hang them in front of an angry mob. "You know," she said, hoping to change the subject, "we've been all over the country in the last two years. We believe people start out good, but then they're twisted by the billionaires' propaganda. Isn't that right, Johnny?"

"Absolutely," Stimpy agreed. "Propaganda is powerful."

"And that's why we have to get to Georgia right away," Lorinda said emphatically. "Tomorrow if possible." Stimpy tried to camouflage his shock with a fake cough.

"Georgia?" Sheriff Flint said. "Last I looked, that was in the USA."

"People can't go to the USA!" Deputy Lukas said.

"Why would you want to go to the USA?" the sheriff said. "How would you even get in? How do you know they'd let you in?"

"We *have* to go there," Lorinda said. "It's the prophecy." She leaned toward the sheriff as if they were having an intimate conversation, but her voice was clear enough to carry to the prisoners in the cell. "The prophet said that our baby must be born in Georgia, in the USA. That's the whole point! The baby has to be born in the most unlikely place. Like Moses in the bullrushes, and Baby Jesus in the manger. And the USA will welcome us." She altered her voice as though reciting Scripture. "'As soon as they behold the Mother, even then will they Know.' In fact, they won't be *able* to stop us from entering and having our baby there. And with the power of our child, combined with the power of Z and the power of Jesus Christ, the USA will leave us alone until the child is strong enough to come back here with his army of crusaders to save us all. And to return Georgia to the CCSA, where it belongs!"

An awed hush fell over the assembled. Finally, the sheriff said, "Wow." He sat back in his chair. "Just wow."

"But we can't do it without your help," Lorinda said urgently. "The prophet told us we will meet a tall, strong stranger with a mustache and a badge who will take us to the promised land."

"The prophet said that?" Sheriff Flint was now stroking his mustache thoughtfully. "And you think he meant me? I'm the one to take you to the promised land?"

"Of course it's you!" Lorinda said. "Who else could it be? We've been all over this country and there's no one else it could be. Until now. It's you!"

"You're the one, Sheriff," Stimpy said. "Don't you remember? Z himself posted something about this last year." He raised his eyes toward the ceiling, as though trying to recall the quote. "'And hey. Make sure the Vessel and the Father get to Georgia. Let them be helped by a Man of the Law. A man of patches.'"

"Sheriff!" the deputy cried, pointing to his boss's neck. "Patches!"

"You are the Man of Patches," Stimpy said.

"Oh yeah?" The Sheriff looked skeptical. "Then how come you two waited so long to tell us this?"

"Because," Stimpy said, "we couldn't be sure we could trust you. But now we know we can. You are... the chosen one." He couldn't remember what movie that was from, but it sounded right.

The prisoners cheered, called the sheriff's name. Some of them chanted "You're the one! You're the one!"

The sheriff closed his eyes and rubbed his temples. For a long time, he appeared to be deep in thought. When he opened his eyes there was a new look of determination on his face. He was practically yelling. "We'll get you there! We'll pull out of here by four in the morning! Lukas!"

"Yes, sheriff sir!"

"Get the word to everybody in the enclave. We'll form a convoy in front of the office here at three-thirty in the morning. Anyone who doesn't show up will be hanged when we get back." He closed his eyes again, re-opening them in a matter of seconds. "I'll get my cousin Hudson and his limo for these two," he said in his normal conversational voice. "They need special conveyance. Oh, and all of you," he said to the prisoners. "You're free. Let 'em out, Lukas. I hereby deputize all y'all to go tell everybody you know — your friends and relatives and everybody else — you go tell them what's happening, and that I'll hang 'em if they don't cooperate. I expect to see you back here at three-thirty, with your cars and trucks. Full tanks! Lukas, wake up Andy, tell him to open his gas station. You got that everybody? And no slacking off or . . ." He grabbed his neck, stuck out his tongue, and made a loud gagging sound.

Deputy Lukas promptly unlocked the cell door, and the prisoners piled out, thanking the sheriff profusely. Some of them shyly touched Lorinda or Stimpy before charging out the door.

"Up and at 'em!" the sheriff called, clanking the cell door a couple of times to make sure his message got through. But Lorinda and Stimpy were already awake. After a fitful, uncomfortable sleep on the narrow cell bench, they'd been woken up ten minutes earlier by the sounds of the first vehicles arriving out front, including the low-frequency rumbling of some big trucks.

"What time is it?" Stimpy asked.

"Three-thirty-five," the sheriff said. "And here's your breakfast."

Deputy Lukas sailed into the cell with a bag of take-out containers. "I had Mimzy, from the restaurant over there, make you something. She says hi. She remembers you from yesterday. She says she knew you were JFK Junior, but I don't believe it."

"You better eat quick," said the sheriff. "We want to get rolling in twenty minutes."

"What's that sound?" Lorinda asked. The rumbling had started again.

"Oh, that's just a missile-launcher truck," the sheriff said. "We got three of them. They're getting themselves in position for the convoy."

Two Kamov Ka-62 helicopters touched down near the WELCOME TO ZONE Z IF YOU CAN HANDLE THE TRUTH road sign, nearly blowing it over with their rotor downwash. A minute later a single file of eight gleaming, unmarked black Gelandwagens slowed down and stopped just before the first one reached the choppers. The hulking Skippy, now in a skin-tight black tee-shirt and jungle-camouflage stretch jeans, jumped out of the lead Kamov, turned around, and gave Janelle Stark — in a black jumpsuit, still with a bandage on her head — his hand to ease her leap to the ground. Out of the second helicopter poured ten uniformed CCSA Domestic Security warriors, followed by one dazed-looking civilian wearing plaid shorts, a yellow polo shirt, and a bandage on his head.

The uniformed drivers of the first three G-Wagens were already out and opening the doors for the helicopter passengers' load-in. The other five vehicles were stuffed with Domestic Security enforcers.

"Brad," Janelle Stark called to the civilian in shorts, "get in the third car." She and Skippy proceeded to the first G-Wagen, while the others segregated themselves into the second and third.

The procession, resembling a fancy funeral motorcade, stopped in front of the sheriff's office. Skippy leveraged himself out of a rear door of the first vehicle just as Deputy Lukas stepped out of the building and onto the little boardwalk.

"Why, look who's back," Lukas said cheerfully.

"Give me her," Skippy snarled. It was like listening to a rock try to talk.

"Give you who?" said the deputy, screwing his face into what he hoped would look like confusion.

Janelle Stark emerged from the other rear door, marched over to the building, and looked up at the deputy. She pulled a folded sheet of paper out of an inner pocket, thrust it at Lukas, and said, "By order of the Domestic Security Administration of the Confederation of Conservative States of America, you are to remand Lorinda Moon to my custody at once, motherfucker!"

"No need to cuss, ma'am," the deputy said laconically. "I'd love to hand her over to you, but she ain't here."

"What do you mean?"

"They all left here about two and a half, three hours ago."

"What do you mean, they left? And who's *they*?"

"*They* is everybody in Zone Z, pretty much. They ain't here. They left in a big convoy. Maybe, I don't know, fifty vehicles. Sixty? Seventy? Like a big parade, sorta, I guess…"

"Where did they go?!"

"Oh, jeez, ma'am. They didn't tell me that. I wasn't even awake when they left."

"Where's that sheriff? I need to talk to the sheriff!"

"Well, ma'am, he went with them, a-course. Yep. I guess that makes it an official Zone Z convoy."

Lunkhead Skippy stomped his foot on the pavement, like an angry bull.

"Traveling in a car going east again," Stimpy said dreamily.

Lorinda opened her eyes. "Hmmm? Was I asleep?" She was slumped against Stimpy, who was slumped on the seat. She tried to sit up, but it wasn't easy. Stimpy helped with a gentle push on her shoulder.

"I think I was asleep," Stimpy said, "and I think I said 'Traveling in a car going east again,' and woke myself up." He looked out the window. "But it's true. We are traveling in a car going east. I *hope* we're going east." He leaned forward, hit the window button, stuck his head out, and checked the whereabouts of the sun. "Yep, we're going east. And I'm not driving. That's the best part. And it's still early." He rolled the window back up and looked at the screen of his com. "Only seven-thirty."

"In the morning?" Lorinda said.

"Wow, you were *really* asleep!" Stimpy laughed.

"You're awake!" said the driver, rolling down the window that separated his compartment from theirs and looking at them in the rear-view mirror. His name was Hudson, Lorinda remembered, "Like the old car, which is maybe why I got into old cars," he'd offered by way of introduction as he stood by his impeccable black car in front of the sheriff's office. Lorinda had no idea what he meant, but she'd smiled anyway. Stimpy later explained that Hudson was a car from the USA that hadn't been produced since the middle of the twentieth century.

"We'll be to Georgia pretty soon," Hudson said, rolling the privacy window back up.

Stimpy felt his com vibrate. He looked at it and said, softly, to Lorinda, "It's all set." She gave him a big, drowsy smile. He scootched forward and tapped on the window, which Hudson rolled back down. "Route 80 to 280 right to Georgia," Stimpy said.

"Your prophet spoke to you, Mr. Kennedy?"

"Sure did," said Stimpy cheerfully. "Loud and clear."

"I'll tell the sheriff." He was already saying "Ten-four, Jesse..." as the window slid up.

After they'd wolfed down their Mimzy's breakfasts — scrambled eggs, Confed-fried potatoes, toast, chemical-free cappuccinos — they'd been hustled out of their cell by Deputy Lukas. The gathering convoy was impressive, starting with the three big rigs, each blasting black smoke and trailing a flatbed loaded with a vintage Iranian rocket launcher and many sharp-nosed, neatly strapped-down missiles. There were already thirty or forty cars and trucks jockeying for position, with more arriving from both directions. Some of the cars were waving hastily made flags or signs in their windows: ZONE Z TO THE RESCUE; BABY TRUMP IS OUR SAVIOR; JFK JR OUR HERO; LORINDA MOTHER OF LIBERTY. It was likely the biggest traffic jam in the history of the enclave.

And then Hudson's car had purred into view, stopping right in front of them. Lorinda had never seen anything like it. After introducing himself, and saying what an honor it was to make their acquaintance, Hudson—who bore a striking resemblance to Sheriff Flint—had proudly explained that it was a 1960 Cadillac Fleetwood limousine, that the car was his, and that he personally had restored it and did all maintenance himself, including fabricating parts if he had to.

"Does that include polishing it?" Stimpy had asked.

"Damn right. I detail it once a month, whether or not it's seen any use. When the sun comes up you'll see how beautiful she shines." A cloud had passed over his expression. "Not that there are that many special events around here lately."

"That's what you use it for?" Lorinda had asked. "Special events?"

"Yeah, weddings and things. It's not much good for anything else. Too damn long to park anywhere. Course, it's perfect for driving celebrities like yourselves to Georgia."

Down the street, the sheriff had been showing people how to line up their vehicles for the procession.

"Sheriff Flint said he was going to ask his cousin to bring out his limousine," Stimpy said. "I guess that makes you his cousin."

Hudson beamed. "Yes sir. My cousin, the big boss of the enclave. He wants me to ask you where we're going. I mean, he knows you need to get to Georgia, but where? And, you know, we can't just drive into Georgia. We'll probably have to drop you off or something."

"Let's just head east the fastest way possible," Stimpy said. "After we're moving the prophet will tell me the details. Is this car leading the parade?"

"No way. You don't want to put the celebrities right at the tip of the arrow, you want 'em in the middle, so they're protected."

Just then the little armored car — the one they'd seen the day before — clanged up and parked in front of the limo. The family — mom, dad, Clay — emerged and called a friendly "Hail!" to Stimpy, Lorinda, and Hudson. "We're here for you," said the father. "And, of course, for . . ." He looked at Lorinda and patted his own belly.

"See?" said Hudson. "The main thing is, one of the missile launchers will be near the front, one a few cars ahead of us, one at the rear. My cousin Jesse will be up front in his patrol truck, and me and him, we can talk to each other. I got a police CB radio! So you'll tell me the directions — you know, when you hear from the prophet — and I'll tell him."

"What are those things sticking up?" Lorinda asked, pointing to the rear of the Cadillac.

"That's called tail fins," Hudson said fondly.

Lorinda gazed out the side window at the flat, practically featureless landscape. "Do you really have a farm?" she asked.

"What?" Stimpy, who had been exchanging messages with Wilma in Revelation, looked up from his com.

"That old truck you had. When you guys picked me up in Little Harlem. With vegetables in back? And the name of a farm on the side?"

"Patriot Farm," Stimpy said. He was smiling, but his smile instantly curdled as he pictured Ren — Roger — with him in the truck, and then the catastrophe in Libertyville. "Yeah, it's a real farm. We're not great farmers, but we do grow some nice stuff. It's mainly a base camp, and an escape when we need to regroup between missions. And we've got some communications equipment there. And a small server farm. We'll have a memorial service for Roger. Snoopy recovered his body. I'll probably go there after, you know, you're safe in the USA."

Silence, other than the clanging of the armored car up ahead, hung heavily in the air between them. It was interrupted by a distant buzzing. Lorinda craned her neck and looked out the side window. "What the hell?"

Stimpy turned to see two ancient-looking biplanes, one red, one green, circling each other at low altitude. Trailing from the red plane was a banner reading FURIOUS FYODOR 6 WEEK CHAMPION; the banner on the green plane said ALEX THE AVENGING ANGEL. A loud air horn squawked, apparently a signal to the pilots. The planes instantly veered radically from their paths and the pilots — their heads and shoulders sticking up out of the cockpits — started shooting at each other with hand-held automatic weapons. Stimpy tapped on the window of the chauffeur's compartment again and loudly said, "What's going on there?"

Hudson stole a glance at the biplanes and rolled down the window. "No idea," he said. "Maybe the End Times? Or something from the Penal Colony? There's the exit." He pointed to an exit ramp whose sign read PENAL COLONY ENCLAVE.

"Thanks," said Stimpy as the window went back up. Lorinda looked puzzled. "It's the enclave where they produce that show, *Top of the Heap,*" he said. "I think we're seeing two contestants trying to kill each other."

Just at that moment, as the green plane was heading upward at a steep angle, they saw puffs of smoke emanating from the red plane, followed immediately by the sound of its gun, followed by the starboard horizontal stabilizer and the top two-thirds of the vertical stabilizer of the green plane disintegrating.

"I think we have a winner," Stimpy said. The green plane continued its upward trajectory for a few seconds before it started a slow spin; soon it started falling tail-first. Then the nose snapped violently down, and the old plane entered a spinning dive. Both wings on the starboard side were starting to detach when it crashed dead-center into the top of the red plane. There was an instant explosion. Flames enveloped both of the plummeting aircraft.

The limo was suddenly bouncing. Stimpy looked through to the front compartment and saw their driver bent over and staring out the passenger-side window at the chaos in the sky. "Hudson!" he yelled.

Hudson instantly sat up and steered the car back onto the road. He lowered the window just enough to say, "Sorry, boss," then raised it again.

The multiple concussions of the planes crashing into the ground nearby were terrifying. Lorinda was speechless.

"You think the show taught them how to fly those planes?" Stimpy asked after they'd left the raging flames behind them. "Or did they recruit two suicidal pilots?"

"What will they do next week if there's no winner from this week?" Lorinda said. "I guess they'll use last week's runner-up?"

"Last week's runner up is dead," Stimpy said. "By definition."

"Second runner-up?" Lorinda said. "Good thing we don't have to run that show. And I can't believe we're having this conversation."

They traded a look of horror and disbelief — then laughed.

That's when they passed the first of the newly hacked billboards: MAKE WAY FOR LORINDA AND JFK JR. Followed by several more with the same message. "I guess Bill didn't have time to get creative," Stimpy said. Then they came upon a group of young people lined up at the side of the road, waving and holding handmade posters:

WE LOVE YOU JFK, JR.
TAKE ME WITH YOU!!!!!!
PROTECT BABY TRUMP!
WE ARE ALL LORIDNA MOON
GO JOHNNY GO!

Several paces away from the rest of the group, two young men were kicking and trying to punch each other while still holding onto their posters, one of which said WELCOME BABY TRUMP! and the other WELCOME BABY JESUS!

Hudson rolled down the window and said, "What is wrong with people?"

"Is that a rhetorical question?" Stimpy said.

"Nah... But... I mean, everybody *knows* the baby isn't going to be Jesus. Right?"

Lorinda and Stimpy looked at each other and nodded. They looked back at Hudson in the mirror and nodded again.

"So, yeah..." Hudson said. He shook his head at the folly of mankind. "Anyway, what I really wanted to say is that we'll reach Georgia in, like, five or ten minutes. Hope we don't see no lizard people coming for us." The window flew back up.

And then they heard the helicopters.

49 *In which our heroine makes her exit from the CCSA.*

STIMPY COULD SEE them out the side window, two old Kamov helicopters — painted bright yellow, with the CCSA trademark visible in several places on their unwieldy bodies — approaching the convoy. "They found us," he said. But before the choppers could get uncomfortably close and low, he saw something else: a dark, smoky wind blowing toward them, fast, from the direction of Georgia. It rocked the choppers sideways, almost causing them to crash.

As Lorinda leaned over next to him and peered up, another wave of the dark wind forced the helicopters to veer off and head away from the Zone Z convoy. "What the hell was that?" said Lorinda. "A micro-tornado? I really don't need another midair collision. One a day is pretty much my limit."

Before Stimpy could venture an opinion, Hudson rolled down the window and said: "Looks like we'll be a little delayed. We're stuck behind a bunch of car transports heading to Georgia. That's what all this smoke is." The limousine, and the entire convoy, came to a halt.

Through the windshield and off to the left, Stimpy and Lorinda made out a heavy chain-link fence behind which appeared to be a big parking lot full of automobile transporters pumping black exhaust fumes through vertical chrome stacks into the sky. But the fumes weren't going straight up; they seemed to be heading toward the convoy. "Fans," said Stimpy.

"Yup," said Hudson. "Fans."

"What?" said Lorinda. For a second she thought, *Fans of who?*

"See those towers?" Stimpy pointed over the tops of the transporters.

It took Lorinda a moment, but then she saw the three tall, thin, white towers and the blurs of their enormous rotating blades. "Oh. So, like, electricity windmills?"

"The opposite," Stimpy said. "They're not catching wind. They're making wind."

Hudson nodded. "Blowing that smoke back into the CCSA, sons of bitches."

"But what are all these trucks doing here?" Lorinda asked. Just then a queue of automobile transporters spewing black smoke passed them on the left, packed bumper-to-bumper with high-end German and Japanese all-wheel-drivers manufactured in the CCSA: two trailers full of Mercedes SUVs, a trailer of Gelandwagens, two trailers' worth of BMW wagons, a trailerful of Audis, a trailer of Lexus pickup trucks.

"I've never seen any of these cars before," Lorinda said. "Except for those G-buggies or whatever they're called."

"You can't buy any of them in the CCSA," said Stimpy, "even though they're made here. I mean, except for the G-Wagen — if you're the government." He tried to see beyond the front line of transporters in the parking lot, but the air wasn't clear enough. "You can't see from here, but what they do is, they take the trailers off these filthy diesel trucks and hook them onto clean ones before they enter the USA." His face suddenly went grim. "Oh, shit. They're back."

They heard the helicopters again, a relentless drone getting louder and higher in pitch, as if from giant mosquitoes. Then they heard new sounds: several permutations of mechanical whining, some heavy mechanism squealing up and around and into position.

"Oh boy," Hudson said, more or less to himself. "Look out now."

"What's that?" Stimpy asked.

"That's the missile launchers taking aim."

A moment later a rocket spewing flames and smoke roared deafeningly into the sky from the flatbed a few cars ahead of the limo. It flew just to the left of the Kamovs, missing by a dozen yards. Then from the rear of the convoy came another one, this one zooming just to the right of the helicopters. As if frozen in fear, the helicopters hovered in place for a couple of seconds before lowering their noses and hightailing toward the horizon. A couple of miles off, easily visible across the scrubby terrain, the two missiles hit the ground at almost the same time and exploded, throwing up two bursts of orange flame and small mushroom clouds of dirt and vegetation. The helicopters wavered in their low trajectory, then landed not far from the convoy behind a mound with a big hand-painted sign in front stating "Toxic Refuse Garbage Dump."

"Those were warning shots," said Hudson soberly. "They missed on purpose. If they wanted to hit 'em, they would have hit 'em." His CB radio crackled. It was Sheriff Flint telling Hudson to swing around the other Zone Z vehicles and meet him in front.

Hudson drove carefully along the margin of the road. When he'd passed all the other Zone Z vehicles, he was surprised to see that his cousin's truck was no longer where he expected it to be, at the front of the convoy, but up ahead inside the area defined by the multi-layer chain-link fence.

"It's my job to protect the citizens of Zone Z, even if they're not our citizens. I mean even if they're just visiting. We want to protect all people whose hearts are in the right place, and who acknowledge that 'Z's Rulez Rule,' as we say. 'Rulez' spelled with a 'Z.' R-U-L-E-Z. That's important." Sheriff Flint, leaning casually against a USA Customs Service truck, gazed earnestly into the lens of the tiny camera attached to the shoulder of a uniformed USA Customs Service officer. "I took an oath to my enclave — and to Z," he continued. "And I always stand by it. Even when it means fighting the evil forces of the CCSA billionaires. They don't scare us."

As Flint spoke, two USA Customs Service officers waved Hudson's limo past signs reading "International Zone Co-Administered by CCSA and USA" and through a gate in the fence that, it was clear from this angle, defined a vast rectangular area that was no more than fifty yards deep but, from Lorinda's perspective, an unknowable distance wide. The tall white pylons with their rotating blades stood behind the fencing on the side across from the gate; between two of the pylons stood a tall flagpole with a giant, 25-star USA flag flapping in the wind produced by the fans.

Flint's truck was nuzzled up to five red, white, and blue SUVs labeled "USA Customs Service." Several yards away stood a lone red, white, and blue Gelandwagen labeled "Domestic Security Administration Mercedes Gelandwagen Proudly Made in Alabama CCSA," next to which stood two forlorn-looking uniformed CCSA Domestic Security officers. Off in the distance to the left, and still within the International Zone, a big crew unhitched smoke-spewing front-end tractors from car trailers and waved them away. As they roared and rumbled off, USA tractors pulled in to replace them. These trucks — newer, cleaner, quieter, elaborately decorated in bright, shiny colors — were then hitched to the trailers for the trip into Georgia and north into the rest of the USA. Spaced throughout the area were USA armored military vehicles and groups of USA soldiers, on full alert. As the limousine entered the International Zone, the gate slid closed behind it.

Flint approached the rear of the driver's side of the Cadillac, followed by the officer with the camera. Lorinda found the button and lowered her window as the sheriff bent over to look in. "You two doing okay?" he asked.

"We're good, thanks," said Lorinda. Stimpy noticed the officer with the camera, and quickly turned to show only the back of his head. Indicating the cameraman, Lorinda asked, "What's going on here?"

"Oh," said the sheriff, "they make movies of everything. The USA is weird. You okay, Mr. — " he stopped himself before he uttered the famous last name. "You okay, sir?" Stimpy nodded without turning around and held up a hand in greeting. "Gotcha," said the sheriff. "You two should just set here until they say you should come out." Then, turning to the officer with the camera: "C'mon, let's leave them be." He grabbed one of the officer's shoulders and started pushing him back to where they'd started. After a few steps he paused, then quickly returned to the limo, leaned in, and said quietly, "Your prophet was telling the truth. You got a good prophet. These people, they were expecting y'all. Don't ask me how, but they were. It was an honor meeting you two. I hope you'll remember what Zone Z did for you when you . . . you know. And make sure your child knows all about it."

"Oh, we will," said Lorinda. "It will be inscribed in all our holy books."

"That's what I want to hear," the sheriff said. "I'll see y'all on your triumphant march back." Then, louder: "Great work, Hudson." He returned to the cameraman and continued herding him away from the limousine.

From the near corner of the USA side of the International Zone, another gate opened and two khaki-green unmarked sedans silently approached, the first one stopping inches from the massive front bumper of the Cadillac. One of the rear doors opened and out stepped a dark-skinned woman in shiny hiking boots, black pants, and a black bomber jacket with a small embroidered USA flag on the left side over the inscription "Serena Ndiaye, Secretary of Health & Border Integrity." She gazed intently through the windshield of the limo.

"Serena!" Stimpy exclaimed, opening his door and jumping out. The woman grinned and opened her arms as Stimpy jogged over to her. They exchanged a big, warm embrace.

"It's so good to see you," she said. "It's been a long, long time."

"Too long," Stimpy said.

"I'm so sorry about — " here she whispered, "Roger."

"It's okay. You don't have to whisper."

The woman glanced over his shoulder at Lorinda, who was heading toward them. "Does she know your name?"

"Not yet," Stimpy whispered.

"Aha! The famous Lorinda Moon!" the woman said as Lorinda approached. "I'm Serena Ndiaye, and I'd like to be the first to welcome you to the United States of America. Well, not exactly the USA yet, but the International Zone. The main thing is, you're out of the CCSA. Hug?"

It took a moment for the last word to penetrate Lorinda's

brain. Before she had a chance to initiate a hug, Serena's arms were enveloping her. "Have you ever been hugged by a Black woman before?"

"Just once," Lorinda said, stepping back from the hug. "But... I'm famous? In the USA? How is that possible?"

"Oh, yeah! I mean, you weren't last week. But you are now. 'We are all Lorinda Moon.' My daughter has that tee-shirt!"

"What?" Lorinda was stunned. "How?"

"Oh, we follow the daily insanities of the CCSA pretty closely. It's like a depraved sitcom."

Lorinda wasn't sure what a "sitcom" was, but she let it go. "So, wait," she said. "You two know each other?"

"Oh, we go way back," said Serena. "Stew... Stimpy's a gem. I know how difficult it was for him to get you here, but he didn't waver — "

The conversation was halted by the sound of a small — but loud — combustion engine, accompanied by a range of mechanical groans, getting closer.

"Well, look who's back," Sheriff Flint yelled.

Across the scrubland beyond the fence came a little all-terrain vehicle. On the back of the seat, holding on for dear life and looking ludicrous, sat Janelle Stark. In front of her, grasping the handlebars, his massive bulk dwarfing the ATV, sat Skippy. A dozen USA soldiers instantly converged on the gate, their weapons hoisted; four of the armored vehicles moved quickly and almost silently into position behind them. The all-terrain vehicle groaned to a halt and Stark slid off sideways. After regaining her balance, and some of her dignity, she strutted toward the gate. She found a sheet of folded and crumpled paper in one of her pockets, waved it in the air, and shouted: "In the name of the government of the Confederation of

Conservative States of America, I insist that you remand Lorinda Moon to my custody immediately."

No one reacted in any way until Sheriff Flint called: "Maybe you have to ask nice."

"Goddammit," she yelled, "give her to me! She's mine!"

Serena walked slowly to the gate, gave Stark the once over, and said, "I don't believe we've been introduced. I'm Serena Ndiaye. I'm in charge here. And you are?"

"Janelle Stark, Confederation Security."

"Show me," Serena said. Stark rolled up the sheet of paper and thrust it through the chain-link. Serena took it, read it slowly, and said, "Well, my dear, I'm afraid this is nothing," tore it in half, and handed the pieces back to her. Stark furiously snatched them and Serena turned and walked back toward Stimpy and Lorinda.

Skippy huffed toward the gate, threw himself against it, and was about to start bellowing, when two of the soldiers jammed the tips of their rifles, hard, though the mesh and into his midsection.

"Shoot them if they don't leave at once," Serena called over her shoulder. "This is a hostile act, and they've been warned."

Reluctantly, Stark and Skippy turned and, grumbling to each other, stalked back to their ATV.

"Scat! Go home! Git!" the sheriff called after them.

"'Let's get you out of here," Serena said, putting her arms around Lorinda's and Stimpy's shoulders and walking them to the car that followed hers in. "We're blocking all these trucks that need to get in here."

"Where are we going?" Lorinda asked. "And what is that guy doing?" She indicated the Customs Service officer with the camera, who was closely following them.

"Oh, don't mind him. He's with me. We like to document everything for the legal record."

Stimpy abruptly stopped and turned toward Serena. "My face could get people killed in the CCSA," he said grimly.

She held up a hand in reassurance. "We know. Don't worry. No one will see your face unless you give us the green light."

She patted his back and turned to Lorinda. "We have a compound about five miles from here, away from all this noise and pollution. We'll do a debriefing, you'll spend the night, and tomorrow we'll bring you up north."

That was a little vague for Lorinda. "Up north where?"

The driver, a Black woman in a military uniform who stood by the car, opened the door for them. "Honestly," said Serena, "we're not sure where — it's one of the things we'll figure out in the debrief. I'll see you guys there," she said as they slid into the back seat. "I've got a bunch of calls I need to make, which I'll do in there — " pointing to her car, "so I don't bother you." The driver closed the door behind them.

No sooner had their car driven through the open gate to Georgia than the driver turned and said, "Welcome to the United States of America." She turned back to face the road ahead. "I'm Michelle, by the way. I usually work with Secretary Ndiaye when she's here. We'll be there in ten minutes."

For the first time in a week, Lorinda felt herself begin to relax. "I can't believe I'm here." Stimpy was looking intently at her. She smiled at him. "What?"

"You were fantastic," Stimpy said, not caring if their driver could hear him.

Lorinda was puzzled but happy. "At what?"

"You made this happen. You figured it out. Ten-dimensional chess. Pushing all their buttons. JFK Junior! You were . . . you are just . . . amazing."

Lorinda felt her cheeks starting to glow. "It's about time you recognized that . . . *Johnny.*" She took a breath. "But, I mean, it wasn't just me. You were right there. We did it together."

"It was your plan. I just followed your lead." He shook his head in amazement and looked away. "'Soulmates.' I loved that." He turned back toward her. "Remember when you said th — "

And then she was kissing him, and he was kissing her back. Michelle caught a glimpse of them in the rear-view mirror, then scrupulously kept her eyes on the road ahead.

50 *In which our heroine takes a short trip up The Corridor.*

LORINDA, STIMPY, SECRETARY Serena Ndiaye, and a young man Serena introduced as "Jonathan, my Chief of Staff," sat in comfortable office chairs at a round, dark-wood table in a small, elegant conference room. Lorinda faced a wall that was covered with floor-to-ceiling dark-wood cabinets and bookshelves; another wall displayed a screen on which a series of gorgeous color pictures of scenic attractions in the USA cycled through. Below the screen was a marble-topped cabinet that, Lorinda thought, very likely housed a magnificent assortment of expensive — and unobtainable in the CCSA — wines and liquors. The third wall was paneled in dark wood with two doors cut in it. One of those was the door they had entered through; the other, Lorinda figured, a washroom that only the occupants of the conference room could use. The fourth wall was nothing but that same lovely dark-wood paneling, which Lorinda briefly thought could be a screen displaying a perfect image of dark-wood paneling.

On the table in front of them were china plates, each of which featured, at the twelve o'clock position, the red, white, blue, and gold seal of the Department of Health & Border Integrity. A uniformed soldier entered quietly with a rolling cart and, without fuss, served each of the participants four delicious looking small sandwiches and a frosty glass of iced tea. When the soldier left, Serena said, "You two must be starving." She took a bite of one of her sandwiches, signaling that it was fine to dig in.

They were, Lorinda, thought, the best sandwiches she'd ever had, and she had to keep telling herself (in her mother's voice) to slow down.

"The most important question," Serena said between sandwiches, "is whether there's anyone in the USA you'd like to stay with for the first little while. Relatives? Close friends? We've done some research, and we couldn't find anyone except — "

"My aunt Helen," Lorinda said through a mouthful of open-faced smoked salmon (which she'd never had before) on black bread (which she'd never had before) topped with crème fraiche (ditto) and dill fronds (same).

"Yes, your aunt Helen," Serena smiled, looking down at the pad that Jonathan had slid in front of her. "It seems that she's — "

"She's a doctor, at John Hopkins hospital somewhere up north. This is so delicious."

"Johns Hopkins," Serena gently corrected. "Johns with an S on the end, for some reason. In Baltimore, Maryland. Looks like she's a nephrologist."

"Kidney doctor," Lorinda said. "She's my mother's younger sister. I haven't seen her since the Great Moratorium."

"What do you think?" asked Serena. "Would you like to visit her? Do you think she'd be willing to take you in for a while?"

"Sure, I'd love to see her," said Lorinda. "It's been so long. I remember her being really nice, but I was just a little girl. She has a couple of children now. My cousins, who I've never met. I mean, I don't know if she wants me to come stay with her."

"Why don't we give her a try?" Serena quickly typed on the pad and fired off a message. Lorinda noticed that Stimpy was looking particularly glum, but she was too excited to think about it. Serena's pad dinged almost immediately. Serena read the message and smiled. "Your aunt needs proof that I'm who I say I am and that you're really with me. Smart woman."

She tapped a button. They heard some electronic beeps and boops. A woman in a white lab coat, at a desk, in front of a board covered with scribbles and stick-on notes, appeared on the screen. She said, "Hello?"

Jonathan reached over, lifted the edge of the pad off the table, and popped open the easel so Serena didn't have to hold it up. "Hello," said Serena.

"Oh, my gosh! It's really you," the woman said. "Good afternoon, or good morning, Madame Secretary. I'm Dr. Helen Branch."

"Hello, Dr. Branch," Serena said. "It's so good to meet you. I'm here in Georgia with your niece Lorinda."

Dr. Branch squinted in doubt. "Really?"

"Really."

"I…I…um…" said Dr. Branch. "I mean, I saw some news about her. It was kind of amazing. But I didn't know if I should believe it." Serena swiveled the pad so the screen was pointing at Lorinda. "Oh my God! Lorinda! I'd recognize you anywhere."

"Hi, Aunt Helen. It's been so long." Her aunt, to Lorinda, looked a good twenty years younger than her sister, Rita, Lorinda's mother, even though she was only three years younger.

"Are you really pregnant, honey?"

"I'm afraid so."

"Well, I'm glad you're all right." Aunt Helen looked mischievous. "I understand you've become an enemy of the state down there."

Lorinda laughed. "Yeah, something like that. They found out I wanted to get a . . ." she reflexively hesitated on the word ". . . an abortion."

"Sweetie, you should come here to Baltimore. We have great doctors at Johns Hopkins, you'll be in and out before you know it, and you can stay with us for a while. Unless you have someplace else . . ."

"No. We were just talking about that." Then she laughed a little. "I'm a fugitive. I have nothing."

"Well it's about time you left that Margaret Atwood dystopia," Dr. Helen Branch said.

Lorinda was puzzled. "Who's Margaret Atwood?"

"Oh, you poor dear. We have some work to do. Listen, Lorinda, Mike and Tina, your cousins, they'd love to meet you. And Lloyd, my husband."

"Hey — he's my uncle!"

Helen was almost in tears. "That's right! Oh, honey, you've got to come stay with us for a while. I've missed you so much. All of you. It's so terrible . . ."

"Well, I got out," said Lorinda. "Maybe we can figure out how to get the rest of them out. Except I don't think they want to leave." Serena signaled that she had something to say her aunt. "Okay, Aunt Helen. I'm so excited. I'll see you soon. I'm not sure when, but, here's Serena, I mean, sorry, Madame Secretary. Love you!" She turned the pad back to Serena.

"Dr. Branch, I'll have my assistant give you our contact information," Serena said. "We'll be in touch very soon. We'll be driving her up the Corridor later today or tomorrow."

No sooner had Serena ended the call with Lorinda's aunt than her pad bleeped with a message. "By the time we finish lunch," she said to Lorinda, "your ride will be ready and waiting."

"Whoa. I'm not sure if I'm ready. I mean..."

"It's not as if you have to pack."

"Can I ask you something, Serena?" Stimpy said. "Her *ride?* Why aren't you flying her up north? It's not as if you don't have the entire USA Air Force at your disposal."

Serena thought about it for a moment. "I could give you a bullshit answer, like we don't have a plane available at the moment, or we think driving is more secure for some reason. But I'll tell you the truth. And—" to Lorinda "— I hope you take this the right way. You're not just another random refugee fleeing from the CCSA to the USA, Lorinda. Whether you want it or not, you've suddenly become a symbol to many young people, in both countries. Older people, too. We want—and, again, I'm probably being more honest than I should be—we want to make sure your story gets out there, and that it's told properly, in the form of a little documentary. We've tested the alternatives with cyber-algorithmic focus panels, and it turns out the most credible way for us to represent your journey and, shall we say, your metamorphosis into a liberated citizen of the USA, is to show you riding up The Corridor in an automobile. With one of our officers at the wheel. Talking to each other. In a plane, you're in and out. Cut to you getting on the plane, cut to you getting off the plane. This way people will see you taking in the new landscape, talking about how it feels to be in the USA with a smart, compassionate representative of our country. Gradually easing into your new life..."

Stimpy looked dour. To Serena he said, carefully, "I take it this was your idea."

"You know me too well," Serena said. "Mine and President Gulden's. Of course there were a few others involved. But not many. This obviously came together too quickly to take it to a committee."

"I bet," Stimpy said, reminding Lorinda of the surly Stimpy she met in the Patriot Farms pickup truck — could that have been only a week ago? "And what if she doesn't want to be the subject of a celebrity documentary?"

"Of course, if she doesn't want to — "

"I like it," Lorinda said. "I want to do it. I think it's a good idea."

"I'm so glad to hear that. Look, Stimpy, I — "

"Stewart," Stimpy interrupted. "We're among friends here."

"Stewart?" Lorinda was stunned. "That's your real name? You're telling me your real name?"

"With an E-W," Stimpy said, "Not a U." For a long moment he and Lorinda locked eyes.

"Well," said Serena, "I guess this is it for now. "Tomorrow morning you'll be in Maryland with your aunt."

They stood, alongside Stimpy — Stewart! — and Serena's Chief of Staff, Jonathan, in front of a small white building, one of many in the compound. A shiny white sedan, marked "USA Department of Health & Border Integrity," slowed to a halt in front of them. Michelle emerged from behind the wheel, smiling. "Hey, Lorinda Moon! I didn't realize I'd be seeing you again so soon," she called cheerily.

"Oh, good. I was hoping it would be you," Lorinda said. Then, turning to Stimpy-Stewart, "Maybe we . . . " she began. "I mean, are you going back to Texas?"

He shrugged. "I don't know. Probably."

She was about to say more but, instead, put her arms around him. He hugged her back, looking like he wanted to say something but thinking better of it. After an uncomfortably long time they broke the hug.

Barely able to speak, Lorinda said, "Nice meeting you, Serena, and thank you. Nice meeting you, Jonathan."

"Nice meeting you, too," Jonathan said. "Just ignore the cameras in the car."

Lorinda exchanged one last glance with Stewart and headed for the car. "I'd like to sit in front," she said to Michelle. "Is that allowed? Or do I have to hide under a blanket?"

"That would make for a very bad video," Michelle said.

They drove north toward the Georgia-Tennessee border. It was a nice day — bright blue sky, puffy white clouds. Everything — the trees along the highway, the very sunlight itself — seemed more vivid and colorful than the bleak CCSA landscape she had spent the last week crossing. The cars and trucks around them were clean and undented and quiet, without a black-smoke-spewing exhaust stack to be seen. All this reminded her of something, and when she spotted a little black dog in the back window of another car she realized what: a movie she saw when she was a little kid, before The Split, before she and her family moved to the CCSA. She felt like Dorothy in *The Wizard of Oz*, arriving at the Emerald City, wide-eyed and awed by its magnificence.

"So," she said, not bothering to wonder if it was a forbidden topic, "I guess the whole Underground Railroad thing is funded by the USA. Is that right?"

Michelle laughed. "Shh! I think they'll have to edit that out of the video. We don't want to cause an international incident."

"They're shooting... everything? Where are the cameras?"

"We've got three hidden cameras inside the car and a three-sixty camera outside. Really good microphones, too. Everything that happens on our way to Baltimore will be recorded. And only about three people will ever see all of it."

"Three..." said Lorinda. "Serena, President Gulden, and... who else?"

"Whoever the editor is," said Michelle. "Okay, maybe a couple of other people will see it. Like maybe their Chiefs of Staff."

"So anyway, am I right?"

"About the USA secretly funding the Underground Railroad in the CCSA? Tell me why you think that."

Lorinda laughed. "Okay, I see how this goes. I'll tell you why I think that. Mainly, they seem to have lots of money. And as far as I know, the only ways they have of getting money back in the CCSA are a little farm and a gas station. I mean, maybe they have some huge companies or crypto mines, but I didn't hear anything like that. They have their own *satellites,* for gosh sakes. They have their own com devices no one's ever seen before. They seem to have lots of people. They can hack electronic signs all over the country. And now I learn that Stimpy — Stewart — and the Secretary of Health & Border Whatever are old friends."

"They went to undergrad school together," Michelle said.

"Secretary means, like, in the White House in Washington DC, or something, right?"

"Something like that."

"Isn't she young for that kind of job? And do they even let women have jobs like that? Oh, right—I mean if a woman is president..."

"You're not in the CCSA anymore, Dorothy," Michelle said.

"*The Wizard of Oz!*" Lorinda cried with joy.

"Very good," Michelle beamed. "And you're right, she's the second youngest ever. She's a genius, in my opinion. But okay, even if those Underground Railroad people really are being funded by the USA, you'll never get anyone to admit it. And by the way, what you and I are saying right now? Right on the cutting-room floor, as they used to say."

"Hey, I don't have a problem with it. I was just wondering," Lorinda said. "Actually, I'm glad your country gives them money. It's really important. And, I mean...here I am!" Lorinda looked out the windshield and realized that not only were the cars splendid looking, but the road itself was, too. "Big road," she said. "It's so *nice*. I'm used to roads that are falling apart."

"It's a miracle what a tax base can do for a country," Michelle said.

Lorinda looked at her for a moment. "I'm not sure how to say this," she said with a big smile, "but you seem really...smart...to be, you know, working as a driver for the government."

Michelle laughed. "I guess that's a compliment. I only drive by special request of Madame Secretary. She thought the two of us would have a fascinating conversation on the way up to Baltimore. You know, for the documentary. That bit, by the way, is for the cutting-room floor. Normally I'm on her team working on...other matters." She looked briefly at Lorinda. "I guess I'm not used to bartenders being so smart."

"Oh, they're not," said Lorinda. "It's my secret weapon. I'm sure it's why I got a promotion." She sighed. "Or I would have gotten a promotion..."

Then she saw the monumental stainless-steel arch up ahead: huge, gleaming, with bold, electronically glowing red-white-and-blue letters spelling out

WELCOME TO THE CORRIDOR — GATEWAY TO VIRGINIA USA

"Holy...!" Lorinda muttered.

"So what do you know about The Corridor?" Michelle asked. "I expect they don't talk about it much where you come from."

"I mean, I've heard about it, and not just because Stewart and... Roger mentioned it."

"Poor Roger," Michelle said.

They drove in silence for a minute. As they approached the arch, Lorinda saw that a high cement-block wall extended out from both sides of the arch. Maybe not as high as the wall around the Trump golf enclave, but pretty high. Two big billboards, one in front of the wall extending from the northbound side of the arch, the other next to the southbound side, repeatedly flashed the words

BEHIND THIS WALL IS BEAUTIFUL NORTH CAROLINA CCSA

In front of each billboard, partially blocking it, was an enormous white tower with a giant fan on top, just like the ones at the International Zone, blowing pollution back toward its source, the CCSA.

"What an annoying billboard," Lorinda said.

"We're the only ones who can see it," Michelle said. "Citizens of the USA driving into The Corridor. Its only purpose is to annoy us."

"Good thing you put those fans there," said Lorinda. "So tell me what I need to know about The Corridor."

"It's very simple, really. Georgia's this island of the USA in the middle of the CCSA. The Corridor is a highway that runs through North Carolina connecting Georgia with Virginia, the closest USA state, which means connecting with the whole eastern half of the USA. And of course, The Corridor itself is part of the USA."

Lorinda pondered that. "So how do people in North Carolina get from one side of The Corridor to the other without going through the USA?" As they passed under the arch, she saw high walls that seemed to be made of fancy stone rising on both sides of the highway. Between highway and wall there was a wide margin of grass that looked as nice as the grass in the golf enclave.

"See that?" Michelle pointed to an overpass about a half-mile down the highway. "There are lots of them along The Corridor. Maybe one every five miles. It's the only way people from the CCSA can get across. There's one thing about these overpasses. Look at it when we go under."

Lorinda duly focused on it as they approached. The overpass had high glass walls, with a number of pedestrians gazing down at the traffic below as cars and trucks drove beneath them. "I guess it looks normal, except for the glass sides."

"Now why would you build an overpass with glass sides?" Michelle asked.

"So the people going across it can see what's going on down here? And we can see them?"

"You have to remember that the USA built and paid for The Corridor and all these overpasses," Michelle explained. "It was the first major public-works project of the post-Split USA. The people who planned this knew that the USA was going to have a much better economy than the CCSA, and they also knew that the CCSA would quickly become an authoritarian shithole. They wanted to make sure there were ways that citizens of the CCSA could peek into the USA and see what they were missing."

"That sounds mean," Lorinda said. "But kind of funny. What's the big deal? They're just looking down at a lot of cars driving by."

"Nice cars, though. Right? And, like you said, a nice road."

"Well, yeah."

"Anyway, give it a few minutes," Michelle said.

Beyond the overpass they came upon an elegant little road sign stating "Corridor Luxury Outlet Mall in 1 Mile." The mall, which they soon could see, was wedged in between the highway and the wall, which meant it was only as deep as a single store. It made up for its shallowness with its length. It was like — in fact, it *was* — an upscale strip mall a couple of miles long. Lorinda was dazzled by the stores, all of which were of necessity facing the highway, and equally dazzled when she realized there was an identical mall on the southbound side of The Corridor. She recognized only twenty- or thirty-percent of the brand names, but it didn't matter. It was clear that they all carried super-high-quality merchandise, much of it from Europe and Japan. The mall was busy; its numerous entrance and exit ramps to the highway were packed with shiny vehicles.

"I don't suppose we could..." Lorinda stopped herself before finishing the sentence.

"Not this time, honey. I've got to get you up north. But look. Here's what I'm talking about."

They were approaching a second overpass. It was just like the first one, but because it passed over the twin malls on each side of the highway, there were pedestrians lined up all across its expanse, noses pressed against the glass, gazing eagerly down into a world as glittery and dreamlike to them as Oz was to Dorothy.

"So mean!" Lorinda laughed.

"All's fair in love and war," Michelle said.

They'd had to slow down while passing the mall, to allow traffic to exit or enter the highway, but once past it, the car returned automatically to cruise speed. After a few miles, Lorinda was about to ask if there were any more malls to look forward to when they heard a far-off explosion. All the brake lights ahead of them came on at once as satellite traffic control slowed down the cars, soon bringing them all to a full stop. "Damn," said Michelle. "I hoped we could get away without this happening."

"What?"

"Probably another bridge bombing. Watch the other side."

Sure enough, after a couple of minutes a final pack of cars drove down the southbound side; behind them there was no more southbound traffic. Black smoke was rising in the distance.

"So it's the next overpass," said Michelle, "a couple of miles ahead."

Suddenly, with an abruptness that made Lorinda lurch in her seat, a male voice barked from the car's speakers, "Ryerson. Dispatch."

"What's up, Ernie?" Michelle said.

"You'd better spin around and come back to base, Lieutenant."

"Bridge bombing?" Michelle asked.

"Yes, ma'am. What else is new?"

"Copy. I guess they'd better set up an overnight room for my passenger. She's not going anywhere today."

"They're already on it, ma'am."

"Okay, Ernie. We'll be back in . . . however long it takes."

"Roger, ma'am."

"This might be a little bumpy," Michelle said to Lorinda. "Hang on."

She turned on her siren and flashing lights, disconnected from the satellite, cranked the wheel to the left, and with a rude thump drove up on the curb. The tires spun with a whine for a second until they got traction on the grass, whereupon the car charged across the median between northbound and southbound lanes before bumping down off the curb into the southbound side. Michelle wheeled it expertly through a sharp left, and they took off incredibly fast — until she had to slow down when she reached the last of the southbound cars that had made it through the overpass before it crashed down.

Still tense, Lorinda tried to settle in. "Who does that?" she said. "Who bombs these bridges?"

"Your fellow CCSA citizens."

Lorinda thought about it, then threw her hands up and slapped them down in her lap in frustration. "*Why?*"

"Oh," said Michelle, "no good reason. Jealousy? Boredom? Who knows. They like to mess up our traffic, I suppose. They just like to stick it to us. They don't know what else to do. Those are my best theories. My real theory? Don't quote me now: They're fucking morons." Loudly, she said, "Edit that out, guys!" Then, quietly: "Or leave it in. I don't care."

"But ... what if there are people on the bridge? And doesn't it also mess up *their* traffic? How do they cross The Corridor?"

"Sometimes they warn people off the bridges, sometimes they don't. And, you're right, if they blow up an overpass, they can't cross the corridor, doh!" Michelle laughed. "I mean, they have to go the long way round, to the next closest overpass. Which means having to drive farther, and then getting stuck in traffic with all the other people doing the same thing. And of course they blame it all on the USA."

Lorinda thought about it for a moment. "Okay," she said, "I get blaming it on the USA, but how come…"

"How come you never heard about it in Texas?"

"Yeah. How come?"

"Some of their propaganda they like to keep local," Michelle said. "The CCSA government doesn't want citizens who don't live near The Corridor thinking about The Corridor. You start thinking about The Corridor and maybe you start thinking about escaping from the CCSA."

"That's ridiculous," Lorinda said.

"Tell me about it," Michelle said.

"I still don't get it. What is the point of bombing a bridge?"

"Why do some people do spiteful, destructive things that are against their own self-interest? Let me give you a brief summary of my theory, which I believe I mentioned a minute ago: They're morons." She paused. "It's the best I can do."

"I don't know," said Lorinda.

"Actually, there's another theory I've heard," said Michelle, "which doesn't contradict that. The theory is that blowing up overpasses, and letting the occasional pedestrian die, keeps at least some CCSA citizens from standing up there and seeing what a real economy looks like."

"Isn't bombing the bridge of another country an act of war or something?"

"Now that's a good question," Michelle said. "Here's the problem. The perpetrators aren't CCSA agents or military or anything official. They're private citizens. Private terrorists. We know they're often funded by the government. Or at least partially reimbursed. Almost no one in the country can afford to blow up overpasses as a hobby. Except the billionaire class, and they have other interests."

"This is crazy!" Lorinda said. She paused, then added, "I mean, it's not the craziest thing I've heard in the last week, but it's pretty crazy." She fell silent.

"Of course," Michelle began, "the simple answer could be — "

"They're fucking morons," she and Lorinda said in unison, then burst into laughter.

"So what does the USA do about it?" Lorinda asked.

"Not much," Michelle said. "We do the repairs — we have fulltime crews on standby up and down The Corridor. Of course we make the CCSA pay for it. Which they do quietly, without informing their citizens. Occasionally, if they blow up one too many overpasses, we have to threaten to bomb the living shit out of Austin or Miami. That gets their attention."

The return trip, as return trips always do, felt much faster. In what seemed like no time the car was back in the compound, approaching a row of neat little bungalows.

"He's waiting for you," Michelle said.

It took Lorinda a moment to see who she was talking about. There was Stimpy — Stewart — standing next to Serena in front of one of the little houses. Her heart thudding, Lorinda jumped out of the car before it had come to a complete stop and ran toward him. He took a few big steps forward and opened his arms wide. She crashed into him. Their lips came together at a slightly safer velocity.

51 *In which our heroine participates in a battle at sea.*

THE SMALL ROOM was starting to glow from the early-morning light leaking in around the window shades. Lorinda, on her back, opened her eyes and stared up at the ceiling, trying to remember where in the world she could possibly be. As her memory returned, a smile bloomed on her face. With her eyes still fixed on the ceiling, she reached out and found what she'd hoped she would find: Stewart, or at least his bare shoulder.

"You're awake," he said.

"More or less."

"And here we are."

"And here we are," she echoed. "I have an idea. What if I take a quick shower and put on the nice new clothes they got me. Then I can go next door and get the nice new clothes out of your room while you take a shower. Then we can have some breakfast — "

"And go to that nice meeting they promised us," he said sarcastically.

"I like them, and I like their country, I think. And I like what they're doing for me. Look," she said, abruptly sitting up. "I'm here!"

"I'm looking," he said, with no remaining traces of sarcasm.

"Remind me what it was that we were working on last night," she said, flopping on top of him.

"We'd like to propose an interesting new plan," said Serena Ndiaye.

It was an hour and a half later, and Lorinda, Stewart, Serena, and Jonathan were once again seated at the table in the elegant little conference room.

"Uh oh," Stewart muttered.

Flashing him a smile, Serena continued. "I'd spell it out for you, but there's someone else who can do it better than I."

Jonathan tapped a button on the pad in front of him and the wall of beauty shots of the USA dissolved to a bright, wall-sized representation of the seal of the President of the USA. Then, to Lorinda's and Stewart's surprise, upbeat martial music started pouring out of the opposite wall — the blank, wood-paneled wall facing the one with the glowing Presidential Seal — and the paneling turned out to be (as Lorinda suspected) a huge screen, now displaying a shot of the Oval Office of the White House, in Washington DC, with President Anita Flores Gulden seated majestically behind the Resolute Desk. She wore a crisp white suit which perfectly set off her long black hair, and Lorinda's immediate thought was that President Gulden looked a lot better here than she did in any images she'd ever seen before. For what seemed like the millionth time since this wild adventure began, Lorinda had a type of thought that would have been unimaginable before: Maybe the CCSA lies to its citizens; maybe the images of the USA President you get in the CCSA are designed to make her look bad on purpose.

"Good morning, Lorinda! Stewart — excellent work. Serena, Jonathan, nice to see you. Lorinda and Stewart, I'm Anita. I especially want to welcome you, Lorinda, to the USA. Or should I say, *back* to the USA — I know you were born here, and of course you never lost your citizenship. Same with you, of course, Stewart — we never wanted to punish people who migrated to the other side during the Moratorium, especially if they were children at the time. But in any case, Lorinda, you probably know that over the course of this week the CCSA has turned you into the poster-girl for everything that, in their opinion, is wrong with the world."

"It's crazy," Lorinda said. "But why? I'm just one little person."

"Oh, I don't know about 'little,'" the President said. "From what I've seen, you've been remarkably brave, resourceful, and clever. Why do they do it? To create a distraction. The CCSA demonizes a woman who needs an abortion to keep its citizens from noticing that the country is falling apart because its leaders are corrupt and incompetent. But you've also become a hero to many in the CCSA. We have a couple of clips . . ." She nodded to someone off camera and the image of her in the Oval Office was replaced by a shot in which a McWeeny campaign pitch on an electronic billboard suddenly blinked off and was replaced by the words WE ARE ALL LORINDA MOON, followed by shots of young people rallying in the street, chanting and carrying posters defending Lorinda Moon. The picture switched back to the Oval Office.

"I've seen the billboards," Lorinda said, glancing at Stewart, "and we saw some people with signs on the way here, but I had no idea . . ."

"Oh, it's all over the CCSA," Gulden said. "But of course it will be suppressed in a day or two, and in a couple of weeks — down the memory hole! You'll go from Public Enemy Number One to Lorinda Who? Unless . . ." Here she seemed to look directly at Lorinda. "Unless we play this right. And unless you're willing to help us."

"What can I do?" Lorinda asked. "Please don't tell me I have to go back there."

President Gulden laughed. "No, no, that would be cruel and unusual punishment. What I'm asking you to do, Lorinda, is to let us bring you up to Maryland by *water*."

Lorinda frowned. Until that moment she had assumed that, after the failure of their attempt to drive her north through the Corridor, they would just fly her to Baltimore and be done with it. Now...

"Excuse me, Madame President," Stewart said, "but are you saying you intend to bring her north *on a boat?*"

"A *ship*, to be precise," Gulden said. "One of the excellent vessels of the USA Navy. And we'll continue making the documentary we started in the car on the way up The Corridor. Only it'll be more... *interesting* now." She paused. "How did one of my speechwriters put it? *'More compelling visually.'*"

"A ship? Meaning, like, on the ocean?" Lorinda said.

The President laughed. The question took her by surprise. "Exactly. The world-famous Atlantic Ocean itself."

"I've never seen the ocean," Lorinda said, as much to herself as to the others. Stewart was about to interject but Lorinda said, "I'll do it —" here she put her hand on Stewart's arm "— but only if he comes with me." She faced Stewart. "If he wants to."

"To the shipyard?" Serena asked.

"To Baltimore," Lorinda said.

Stewart couldn't help but grin.

No one objected.

"Kings Bay, on the east coast of Georgia, is one of the most outstanding naval bases in the world," their handler said. Although Lorinda and Stewart were wearing military-spec noise-suppressing headphones, it was still oppressively loud inside the big, almost empty helicopter, which contained only the two of them, their handler — a handsome navy commander in an impeccable white dress uniform, with a constellation of medals and a plaque with the name Charles Trout pinned to his chest — plus the two pilots up front. Trout was clearly in his element, and completely unfazed by the background din. "Specifically," he continued, "it's acknowledged to be the finest submarine base on the planet. Well, maybe the CCSA doesn't acknowledge it, but that's to be expected."

"We're going in a *submarine?*" Stewart asked, looking worried.

"No, no," Commander Trout chuckled. "That would defeat the purpose of the whole mission. We'll be transporting you in a Tornado-class patrol craft, the USS Jamie Raskin. She's one-hundred-eighty-some-odd feet long. Cruising speed is classified, but I can tell you it's well over 30 knots. She carries a crew of twenty-five and a suite of classified weapons. You'll be to the port of Baltimore around this time tomorrow."

Lorinda frowned. "Overnight?"

"Oh, don't worry. You'll have your own bunkrooms for when you want to catch some Zs," he said, "but you might just want to stay up. Looks like glorious weather, and if you haven't seen the sea-sky on a clear night, you haven't lived."

"And what's the story with the documentary?" Lorinda asked.

"Right. Operation Damsel — "

"Noooo!" Stewart said, slapping his own forehead.

"It's just the working title," Trout said. "The ship is being outfitted with cameras to shoot everything that happens on deck and at least some of what happens below. There'll be a small video crew onboard following you around. They're also pulling together a crew to shoot from a small boat that I believe will be accompanying you all the way to Baltimore, and they'll have a drone or two following up above. Like sea gulls tailing a fishing boat. It's quite a production."

Lorinda was thrilled to see an ocean for the first time, even if — since she was a mile-and-a-half up in the air — she wasn't able to stick her toe in it. She'd seen lakes, but somehow this seemed more . . . profound.

Stewart, meanwhile, was impressed by the vastness of the naval base below and, as they reduced altitude, the sight of dozens of submarines, as well as other types of military vessels, resting in their docks.

The helicopter dropped them off and flew away, leaving behind the blessing of lower-decibel rumbling and clattering of a busy shipyard. Commander Trout led them away from the helipad and toward the dock where their ship awaited, explaining that they'd be leaving on their voyage as soon as the provisioning — which in this case mainly meant setting up the video arrangements — was complete.

As they approached the dock, Stewart took Lorinda's arm, leaned close to her, and said, "To answer your question: Yes, once upon a time I was married. She died. Killed by the CCSA."

She already knew this, from Hillary back at the gas station. But it was different hearing it from him. Lorinda stopped walking. Her eyes filled with tears. This triggered a matching response in Stewart. "I'm so, so sorry," she said.

"Yeah," was all he could say. They hugged. Then, arms around each other, they hurried to catch up to Trout.

He stood before the sparkling white vessel that awaited them. But it wasn't just the ship that awaited them. A woman on the dock in a tan jump suit with lots of zippers and pockets was aiming a camera at them. She was accompanied by a man in a tartan flannel shirt and baggy jeans, holding a long boom with a microphone at the end of it, pointed in their direction, and another man wearing a dark green athletic suit, with a large pack strapped to his back and a big com-pad in his hands.

"Oh, shit," Stewart whispered. "Here we go." Without quite knowing why, they quickly detached from each other and put businesslike expressions on their faces.

"I fully expect this to be a routine trip up the coast," said Captain Frank Molina, the officer in charge of the Raskin. "A particularly pleasant one, with terrific weather and a nice flat sea."

Lorinda and Stewart, standing with the captain on the deck of the ship, had been guided into their positions by Commander Trout, who was now standing behind the three-person documentary crew. Like Trout, Captain Molina was a good-looking specimen. Lorinda wondered if the two men hadn't been assigned to this duty so much as cast for roles in the documentary. But was Trout even in the documentary? In any event, it felt unnatural to her to be having a conversation while lined up side-by-side, and even more unnatural to know that what they said was going to end up in a movie, but she supposed the USA government knew what it was doing.

"We'll be accompanied by a small vessel with another documentary crew onboard — you'll see it once we're out of the harbor," the captain continued. "We'll be navigating out to international waters as we approach the latitude of the southern edge of South Carolina, and we'll stay out until we hit the southern latitude of Virginia, USA. Are either of you susceptible to seasickness?"

"I should be fine," Stewart said.

"I've never been on a big boat on an ocean before," Lorinda said, "but I'm good in little boats on lakes and things."

"Well," the captain smiled, "if you feel even the slightest twinge just grab the nearest crewmember. We have a medic onboard who'll give you something that'll settle you right down. Besides, like I said, we're expecting smooth sailing. We'll be launching in a couple of minutes, so I suggest you two make your way up to the bow and enjoy the view. This trip is all about you, so if there's anything you need just give a holler. And just pretend these people — " indicating the film crew "— aren't here."

Commander Trout wished them good luck, saluted them and the captain, and took his leave.

The classified cruising speed of the USS Jamie Raskin was fast enough to cause the wind to burn and water droplets to sting. After twenty minutes on the bow, Lorinda and Stimpy decided they'd had enough and made their way into the cabin — followed by the video crew — which gave them the same majestic view but from behind the shelter of large panes of safety glass. They continued gazing, in a near-hypnotic state, at the vast, empty sea, ignoring the three documentarians hovering around them and the much smaller boat, containing the other documentary crew, that was buzzing around the Raskin. Eventually Stewart started speaking quietly — practically whispering — to avoid having his conversation recorded. In an uncharacteristic autobiographical mood, he told the sad story of his wife's completely preventable death, which resulted directly from the CCSA's ironclad commitment to withhold healthcare from pregnant women in distress (with the exception, as Lorinda had learned in the golf enclave, of women who happen to be "attached" to members of the oligarchy). They both managed to suppress their tears, if only to avoid the possibility of having to explain themselves to the camera at some point.

A couple of hours in, a crew member — perfectly okay looking, but not Trout- or Molina-handsome — entered with a tray containing a thermos of coffee, two mugs, and a plate of fresh fruit and cheese, which he set on a folding shelf he pulled down from the wall opposite the forward-facing windows. "Something for you two," he said. "By the way, we're about to enter international waters." He saluted them and exited.

Lorinda had just bitten into the best pear she had ever tasted, when something caught her eye. "What's that?" she said, pointing out the port-side window. Stewart and the utility guy from the film crew stepped up to look.

"Oh, shit," the utility guy said. They were watching a motley flotilla of about ten mismatched speedboats rapidly bouncing across the water toward the Raskin.

"Who are they?" Stewart asked.

"Damned if I know," said the utility guy, "but they're coming from the direction of South Carolina. Fucking CCSA. I think you want to get this," he called to his colleagues.

The camerawoman and the sound man stepped out of the compact cabin and onto the port-side deck to record whatever it was that was happening. The camera-boat crew obviously had the same idea — the little boat zipped around the stern of the Raskin and positioned itself between the Raskin and the approaching speedboats as its camera person clambered into a good shooting position. Two camera drones, which up to that point had kept their distance from the Raskin, swooped over to the camera boat and hovered.

The speedboats didn't slow down, veering to either side of the camera boat and almost swamping it with their wakes. As they approached the Raskin, Lorinda gasped. She couldn't make out the features of the face, but there was unmistakably a bandage on the head of the person sitting next to the enormous creature at the wheel of the lead boat.

"It's Janelle Stark!" Lorinda cried.

In a moment the boats were close enough that they had to slow down — and close enough for Lorinda to see that it was indeed Janelle Stark and her monstrous sidekick in the front seat, with two CCSA Domestic Security enforcers in the back seat, flanking a petrified-looking (and still head-bandaged) Brad. The other boats each contained four or five additional Domestic Security thugs. Everyone except Brad, who wore a baby-bib-like orange life jacket over his street clothes, was in a shiny black jumpsuit — or were they wetsuits? And everyone except Stark, Skippy, and Brad had an automatic weapon strapped on.

"This isn't possible," Stewart said. "How do they even know you're here?"

The first four boats, including Stark's, moved so close to the hull of the Raskin that Lorinda and Stewart lost sight of them. The camerawoman was now hanging over the rail to shoot straight down at them. Stark's voice, loud and distorted through a powerful bullhorn, boomed: "Stop your forward motion or we'll blast a hole in your hull." A speedboat that had been hanging back moved out from the pack. A crewman in the back seat opened the lid of the hold behind him, removed a rocket-propelled-grenade launcher, rested it on his shoulder, and aimed it at the Raskin's bow. "Stop your forward motion immediately," Stark bellowed.

"This is insane," Stewart muttered.

Lorinda could feel and hear the ship powering down. Then she heard Captain Molina, his voice loud and sharp from a PA horn atop the bridge. "This is Captain Molina of the USS Jamie Raskin. Identify yourself and state your intention."

It sounded like Janelle Stark gave a little laugh. "We are a duly authorized law enforcement contingent from the CCSA."

"We are in international waters. You are in violation of maritime law."

"Tough shit," Stark said. "Prepare to be boarded. Or sunk."

Both drones were now visible about ten yards off the port side of the Raskin, shooting down at the action below. There was suddenly a loud clanking sound, followed by two more, then a fourth that sent the camerawoman reeling backward, crying in pain, and banging her head, and her camera, into the shatterproof side window of the cabin. One tentacle of a grappling hook was now wrapped around the rail the camerawoman had been leaning on. A moment later the first wave of CCSA goons was scrambling up the rope ladders attached to the grappling hooks, over the rail, and onto the deck.

Two of them fired ammo-bursts into the air just to make some noise; the others fanned out on the deck. Janelle Stark jumped athletically over the rail, followed by Brad, who was shoved over the rail and tumbled onto his back. Next came Skippy, with a big grin on his face and Stark's megaphone clipped to his waist.

Lorinda and Stewart looked to the starboard side as a possible escape route, but by then Stark's flunkies were coming over that rail as well. Skippy spotted the couple through the window, charged into the cabin, grabbed an arm of each, and hauled them out onto the deck, just next to the fallen camerawoman.

Stark reached out to Skippy's belt, unclipped the megaphone, and announced: "Do what we say and no one will get hurt. We're just here to talk with the escaped fugitive."

One of the Raskin crewmembers, having broken through a CCSA contingent on the deck, came rushing toward Stark. Skippy let go of Lorinda's arm and, in one smooth move, grabbed the crewmember's neck and tossed him overboard. Lorinda instinctively kicked Skippy in the groin. He winced, let go of Stewart, and grabbed Lorinda by the throat with both hands.

"Skippy! No!" Stark yelled at deafening volume through the megaphone. He glared menacingly at Lorinda but reluctantly let her go. Stewart took a swing at his jaw. He connected, solidly. It rocked the beast for a moment, but before Stewart could follow up he found himself levitating: Skippy had hoisted him by the front of his shirt. "Drop him!" Stark honked through the megaphone. Skippy again complied.

A scuffle erupted in the cabin as three of Stark's squad, who had come up the starboard side, grabbed a Raskin crewmember as he emerged through a hatch in the cabin floor, yanked him onto his feet, and started smashing him with the butts of their automatic weapons.

"How did you find us?" Stewart shouted at Stark, who had momentarily turned to gaze approvingly through the glass and into the cabin behind him.

Turning back to her immediate problem, Stark said, "I don't believe we've been formally introduced."

"And we won't be," Stewart snarled.

Stark seemed to consider slapping him, only to decide he wasn't worth it. "We have the finest intelligence agencies on earth," she sniffed.

"That's fucking ridiculous," Stewart said.

With his baseball-glove-sized hand, Skippy grabbed Stewart's head and shoved it into the window, cracking the shatterproof glass. Stewart crumpled to the deck.

Lorinda gasped and dropped to her knees to... do what? See if he was all right? Comfort him? Kiss him? But Skippy was having none of it, and yanked her right back up by her shoulder. She yowled in pain as her bag, which she was still gripping, flew up and hit Skippy in the face. Her hands followed the bag's trajectory and she clawed furiously at his cheeks. He snapped his bald pumpkin head back and smashed it into a steel bracket sticking out of the cabin above the top of the window. Infuriated, with blood pouring down his face, he grabbed both of Lorinda's wrists with both of his hands, consolidated them into his left hand, gently felt his cheek, then his head, with his right hand, and examined his bloody fingers. Wiping them on her bag, glaring at her, he reached behind his back, grabbed his pistol from his waistband, and pointed it at her.

"No, Skippy," Stark purred in a low, ominous voice. "Put it away."

Skippy turned to face her and shook his head. Fresh drops of blood flew off his head and his gouged cheeks.

"Put it away, Edgar! *You will not kill anyone here.* Especially her."

Skippy grunted fiercely. Turning his back to Stark in defiance, he jerked the pistol up, scratching Lorinda's chin with the front sight, and pushed it against her forehead.

A thunderclap of a gunshot briefly filled the universe; blood gushed from both sides of Skippy's massive neck; his gun hit the deck but he remained standing for another five seconds, during which he bloodily burbled, "But . . . Janelle . . . love . . . Skippy," then sank slowly to the deck and collapsed on top of his gun.

"That's beside the point," Stark lectured the big corpse at her feet. "You're not allowed to ruin my work." She turned to Lorinda, who was covered with blood and screaming. "Stop it!" Stark yelled. She started to re-holster her gun behind her back, but something else caught her attention. She looked over her shoulder at Brad who, still on his back on the deck nearby, was blubbering loudly and uncontrollably. She pointed her still-smoking pistol at him, saying, "Stop that right now or I'll kill you." He stopped it. She put her gun away.

"All right," Stark said to Lorinda. "You and I and all my men, we're going to calmly climb down to my boats and get the hell back to South Carolina. Do you still have that cute little pink gun of yours in there?"

"What do you think?" Lorinda said, taking a couple of small steps toward Stark, who unconsciously, just to keep her distance, backed up a couple of small steps until she was almost against the rail.

"Hand it over," Stark said.

Lorinda reached into her bag.

"Hold the barrel," said Stark, quickly reaching behind and fetching her own gun again.

Lorinda took another small step forward as she took out the pink gun and started to pass it to Stark, who took another small step back and put out her hand. "Don't get clever," Stark said.

Lorinda set the handle of the gun onto Stark's palm. Stark grabbed it, popped it open, and took a quick look. "Still no ammunition, you stupid cow?"

"Oh, I have ammunition," said Lorinda in the steeliest voice she'd ever heard herself use. She reached into her bag, fished around, and came up with a rattling handful of small bullets. "Here's one," she said, and threw it hard right at the bandage. Stark yelped in surprise and pain. Lorinda took a small step closer and threw another bullet, this one bouncing off Stark's nose.

"Keep going," Stark said. "Each one is another month of confinement."

Lorinda threw another bullet, which hit Stark's cheek, then another to her forehead. Stark defiantly refused to defend herself. Lorinda was about to throw another when the air was filled with the loud, non-directional surf-crash sound of the Loch Ness monster emerging from the deep. Lorinda's eyes, which had been fixed on Stark's face, flitted to something behind Stark, then went wide. When Stark spun her head to see what it was, Lorinda took a big step forward and kicked Stark in the groin — just as she had kicked Skippy — then lowered her head, lunged forward, and rammed Stark hard, like a lineman blocking for a running back. It caused Stark to drop both guns and, arms flailing, sail backward into and over the rail. She fell between the USS Jamie Raskin and the much larger submarine that was rapidly surfacing immediately next to it. Athletic Stark managed to twist around and grab the gunwale on the way down, where she hung for perhaps a second. Lorinda had just steeled herself to stomp on the woman's hands, when an unexpected wave in the calm sea, perhaps a forward swell caused by one of the other USA submarines that were surfacing nearby, caused the hulls of the first sub — on whose flank could now be read "USS New London" — and the Raskin to briefly meet with a plangent clang and a mighty splash. Stark's legs were crushed by the meeting of the hulls. She lost her grip, let loose an unholy screech, and plummeted.

Another wave clanged the ships together again. Lorinda, struggling to mind her balance while still amped and panting from adrenaline, picked up the two guns, carefully approached the rail and peered over the side. She saw the crushed remains of some of Stark's speedboats mixed in with the crushed remains of Stark herself. Lorinda threw the guns — first Stark's and then, with a brief rush of affection, her own, down at what was left of Janelle Stark. Another wave, now from the opposite direction, lifted first the Raskin, then the sub. Lorinda was thrown painfully into the rail. Desperately she pushed herself away from it, slipped on a patch of water and blood, fell backward, and hit her head hard on the deck.

Dozens of USA Navy Seals swarmed off the submarine and onto the Raskin. They found Lorinda, unconscious and in a heap; Stewart, also out cold and bleeding from the head; the camerawoman, who was struggling to open her eyes; and Brad, who was blubbering again, on his back, his hands waving in the air in an attempt to symbolize his innocence.

The drones and the onboard cameras captured it all. The small camera boat had been swamped by the USS Groton as it surfaced behind the New London; its crew had been rescued and was drying off onboard the sub.

52 *In which our heroine reaches the last chapter of her journey to the USA.*

LORINDA'S LEFT EYE opened. That familiar deafening noise and vibration. Another helicopter ride! Pounding her head. Tried to look around. Couldn't move. Disembodied deep voice said "something something hospital VIP wing." Left eye closed.

Lorinda's eyelids fluttered open. She was in a bed, her back slightly elevated. A woman in blue scrubs with "Johns Hopkins Hospital" on one side and "Dr. Helen Branch" on a name tag clipped to the other sat on the bed, gazing at Lorinda's face.

"Lorinda, darling," Aunt Helen said in a near-whisper.

Lorinda's eyes pinballed in slow motion around the room. She blinked. She tried to focus. She rotated her head slightly. Then she broke into a big smile. "Aunt Helen!"

Helen leaned forward and gave Lorinda a gentle hug. Lorinda wrestled her arms out from under the covers, sat up, threw her arms around her aunt's waist, and hugged her fiercely. "Stimpy! Stewart!" she said when she saw him standing behind her aunt. His head was wrapped in a big, thick bandage, but other than that he looked good. She reached one of her hands out to him and he kissed it.

She glanced around, taking stock, getting oriented. She was in a large hospital room painted a relaxing shade of blue-green, and housing, in addition to the bed, a desk, a desk chair, and two thickly-upholstered visitors' chairs next to the desk. A whiteboard with names, phone numbers, and instructions (and a smiley face) in blue marker hung on the wall next to the doorway. A rolling bed tray stood nearby, holding several plastic cups and a pitcher of water. Bright daylight came in through a large window with half-shut blinds. Electronic beeps repeated somewhere off to the side.

Something was covering her forehead and wrapped around her head. She felt it: a rough, stretchable bandage.

Turning to Stewart, Helen said, "You're a true hero. Both of you. I'm so proud of you, Lorinda."

"Do I have an appointment?"

"Oh, honey," Helen said when she realized what Lorinda was talking about, "you don't need that appointment. You…" Helen paused, maybe not sure how to deliver this news. "Honey, you had a miscarriage from whatever you got involved in on that boat. I'll see that you get the follow-up care you'll need."

It took a moment for Lorinda to digest the news. "I just can't…"

When she tailed off, Stewart stepped in and said, "But they say you'll be fine. I mean, completely recovered."

"So. They put me through all that, and this is the result." Lorinda tried to laugh. "It's so…what's the word?" She looked at Stewart.

"Ironic?" Stewart said.

"That's it. Ironic. Thank you, Janelle Stark." To her aunt, who looked puzzled, Lorinda said, "Fake doctor Janelle Stark, the Confederation security creep who was chasing me, trying to lock me up and force me to have a baby." She shook her head. "Who I saw kill two people. Because she was so 'pro-life.'"

"Oh God, those bastards!" Helen said with surprising passion.

There was a knock on the door. A nurse standing discreetly next to it opened it a crack, letting in an unexpectedly loud burst of crowd hubbub. She saw who was knocking and opened the door a little further, allowing a compact man in his mid-thirties, in an impeccable suit and long brown hair, to enter the room. He was trailed by a younger woman toting a big com pad and a bulky leather bag over her shoulder. As the nurse closed the door behind them, the man made straight for Lorinda. Circumnavigating Dr. Helen Branch on the bed, he stuck out his hand, saying, "Lorinda Moon! I'm thrilled to meet you! I'm Connor Feldman, President Gulden's Chief of Staff."

"Wow," said Lorinda, shaking his hand.

"This is my assistant, Mindy," he said. "The president is on her way over. I wonder if we can get a few pictures for the media before she gets here." He looked at Stewart. "Stewart Roderick, right?"

"That's right," said Stewart, not looking too happy about it.

"Stewart Roderick," Lorinda said under her breath, wondering how it was that this stranger knew Stewart's last name and she didn't. Well, she did now.

"What's going on out there?" Stewart said. "I thought this was a hospital."

"Oh, it's just the media," Connor said. "The hallway's a sort of holding pen for them. This is the VIP wing, you know." He looked from Stewart to Lorinda. "You guys are just amazing." He turned to Helen. "We should get you in some of the pictures too, Doctor."

"Oh," she said, "I'm not her doctor. I mean, I'm a doctor, but I'm at Johns Hopkins, not here at Walter Reed. I'm Lorinda's aunt, Dr. Helen Branch, and I really think you ought to let them recover a bit before you start taking pictures. Don't you?"

"Sure," said Connor smoothly, "in a perfect world. But the president really wants to get the news about them out right away." He spoke directly to Lorinda. "Millions of people in the USA are following your amazing journey, and they want to know that you're okay."

"I feel pretty good," Lorinda said, touching the bandage on her head. "I mean, I could live without this, and I have a little headache. They must have given me some drugs, right?" Her aunt nodded. "It's a headache . . . but it feels like someone else's headache." She looked at Stewart. "How are you?"

"Pretty much the same," he said.

"All right," said Helen affably, "I can see that I'm outgunned here. Why don't I go, and when this business is over we'll figure everything out."

"Hold on," Lorinda said to Connor. "I'll do the pictures, but first I need to talk to my parents, and my brother if you can find him. And I want Aunt Helen with me."

"You drive a hard bargain," Connor said with a smile and a nod to his assistant, who instantly started typing on her pad. "We anticipated this, so we already set up a secure connection. Are they ready?" Mindy nodded and tapped her pad. Most of the wall across from the bed lit up, revealing Lorinda's nervous mother and her glowering brother, in their living room, looking straight into the camera.

"Mom! Zeke!" Lorinda cried. "I'm so happy to see you! This is so great!"

"You killed dad!" Zeke yelled.

"What are you saying?!"

"He didn't die," Rita said. "He had a small heart attack."

"And it's your fault!" Zeke was practically foaming at the mouth. On the huge screen, Lorinda could see that the tip of his nose was green. Manna.

"He's in the hospital," Rita said flatly. "Recovering. Maybe."

"It's because of you," Zeke said heatedly. "These police coming to our house all the time, tearing it apart, pushing us around. You should see what they did to your room. It's your fault, Lorinda! You're the antichrist! You're going to hell! You can't hide in the USA! They'll get you!" Rita put her arms around her son, who burst into tears on her shoulder.

"He had his heart attack here," she said to the camera. "Right there in the dining room. We had to drag him to the car, me and your brother, and bring him to his office parking lot."

"We left him there," Zeke sobbed. "In the parking lot."

"What?! Why, Mom?"

"So it looked like he had it at work. Otherwise, no insurance. Now at least it's covered by the business policy." It was Rita's turn to burst into tears, but she quickly composed herself, looked hard into the camera, and said, "Hello, Helen. Glad to see you're alive. You, too, Lorinda."

"You're a whore, Lorinda!" Zeke shouted.

"You need to have him treated for manna addiction, Mom," Lorinda said as calmly as she could manage. "That stuff is deadly."

"If your father lives, he'll never talk to you again," Rita said.

"Don't come back," Zeke said.

"It's nice seeing you, too," Lorinda said sadly.

"I miss you so much," Helen said. Rita and Zeke turned away from the camera and the screen went dark. A moment later the wall was back to looking like a wall.

Lorinda stared at it until Helen shrugged her shoulders, leaned in and kissed Lorinda's cheek. "I thought that went well," Helen said.

Lorinda cracked up and continued laughing, somewhat hysterically, until tears rolled down her cheeks. When she calmed down, Helen gave her a tissue. Lorinda daubed her cheeks, gave Stewart a wan smile, and took a deep breath. She turned to Connor, nodded decisively, and said, "Okay. Let's do it." Connor nodded at Mindy, who typed quickly on her pad.

A moment later the door opened, admitting both the crowd noise and a tall, thin, bald man with a goatee, in his forties, all in black, who carried a serious looking tripod on top of which was a serious looking camera. He was followed in by another man, shorter and stouter, with a full head of hair and a full beard, also dressed in black and carrying a second tripod, this one with an array of small lights on top. "Our official image team," Connor said.

"Some stills?" the tall one said.

"Yeah," Connor replied. "A few of Lorinda in bed, a few with her aunt, a few with Mr. Roderick — "

"No, thanks," said Stewart. "No pictures of me. I don't want to put the people I work with in the CCSA at risk."

Conner gave him a quizzical look. "How — "

"There may be spy pictures of them with me. Face recognition, easy match, they might be able to track my friends down. You never know." He walked to the corner of the room, behind where the image team had set their tripods.

"Lorinda, honey, I think I'm going to go," Helen said. "They don't really need my picture. You'll come stay with us as soon as they release you." She looked across the room. "And you too, Stewart. We have plenty of room. Stay as long as you like." She and Lorinda hugged again.

"Mindy has all your info," Connor said to Helen as she stood up.

"I think they'll release her in a day or two."

"I think so too," Helen said as she waved at Lorinda and Stewart. The nurse opened the door just enough to let her out — and keep the chatter and shouting to a minimum — and she slipped away.

"I must look terrible," Lorinda said, hoping to hear that a makeup person was about to burst through the door.

"Don't worry," said the camera guy. "The camera will fix you up." To Lorinda's skeptical look, he added, "It has excellent makeup software."

The lighting guy studied Lorinda, then said, "Can you sit up a little straighter?" Lorinda did as he said. "That's good. Great look. Have you modeled before?" He tweaked the lights a bit and nodded at his colleague, who took the camera off the tripod and circulated around the room for no more than fifteen seconds with the camera pointing at Lorinda.

"All right, that's great," he said, putting the camera back on the tripod. "When is she coming?" he asked Connor.

Connor looked to Mindy, who looked at her pad and said, "Right about now."

"I'll let you know when to come back in," Connor said to the camera and light guys, who left their equipment in place and started for the door — at which point the door opened and, as the noise in the hallway somehow got even louder, two big Secret Service men in dark suits entered, took a few steps in, gave the room a gimlet-eyed once-over, and followed the media crew out the door. Then the president of the USA entered. The nurse left and closed the door from the outside.

"Lorinda Moon and Stewart Roderick," Connor said, "it is my pleasure to introduce you to the president of the United States of America, Anita Flores Gulden."

Of course Lorinda and Stewart recognized her, but they were unprepared for her charisma, a force-field that nearly rendered them speechless. She was slim and of medium height, with long, dark hair. She wore a collarless beige blazer over a white blouse and matching beige trousers.

With some effort, Lorinda managed to say, "Hello, Madam President." Stewart echoed her.

"Please, call me Anita," the president said.

"Madam President," Connor said, "we thought it would look great if you were sitting right there next to the bed, so you and Lorinda are the same height — "

"That's good," President Gulden said. Without being told, Mindy rolled the desk chair over to the bed, then left the room, leaving only Lorinda, Stewart, Connor, and the president inside. As Gulden sat and adjusted the height of the chair, Connor said to Lorinda and Stewart, "We'll be doing a live feed to all outlets after this. But first..."

"First," said Gulden, "I'd like to talk to you about something important."

"Have a seat," Connor said to Stewart. "We're not shooting yet." To the president, Connor said, "He doesn't want his picture to get out. Security concerns about his people in the CCSA."

"Totally understood," Gulden said as Stewart sat on the side of the bed opposite the president's chair. "You know," she said to Stewart, "the woman whose *nom de guerre* is Wilma Flintstone — she and I went to college together."

"She told me that you were friends," Stewart said. "It's not the kind of thing you want to brag about in the CCSA."

"Understood. We were roommates from sophomore year on. Besties."

Stewart was surprised. "That, she didn't tell me."

"We've stayed in touch," Gulden continued. "It's not so easy with her behind the Iron Curtain, but we have our ways. She's the bravest person I know. She's told me all about you, Stewart. She holds you in the highest regard, which means I hold you in the highest regard. I just want to say that, in my opinion, you've done more than your share of work in the CCSA and we welcome you to the USA with open arms. I hope you'll stay. If there's anything you need from me, the line to Connor will always be open. Any idea what you'd do with yourself here?"

Stewart smiled. "The first thing I need to do is . . ." He looked at Lorinda. "Recover from what we've just been through. Do a little thinking. A little sleeping. Regroup."

"Do you ever consider finishing your PhD?"

"I've thought about it," Stewart said. "That was my original path."

"If that's what you want, I can write a very persuasive letter of recommendation when the time comes," the president said. "And I'm pretty close with the presidents of three Ivy League universities. Make that four. Plus Stanford." Lorinda was almost certain she saw Stewart blush. Gulden took a breath and closed her eyes for a moment. When she opened them, it was clear that she was ready to get down to business.

"So, Lorinda. And Stewart. As Connor knows, I've been accused of talking too much and too fast. I've tried to slow myself down when I give speeches and such, but right now I'm not going to rein myself in. I've got a lot I want to cover and we don't have a lot of time. So I'll start right in.

"What I say here is between us, understand? Completely off the record. And just so you know what I mean, you may hear me say things on the record that are different, or even that contradict, what I'm about to tell you. Sometimes being in politics means you have to trick some people into doing, or believing, the right thing. I'm afraid you sometimes have to lie to get to a higher truth. But I'm not going to lie to you. Because of who you are and what you've been through, I think of you as being untrickable. And even if I could, I wouldn't want to trick you. I respect you too much for that. And I want to earn *your* respect. I want you on my team for the right reasons. I trust you not to tell anyone what I tell you in private here. But you should know that if you slip and tell someone, and it gets out into the world, I'll deny it — and, to be blunt about it, I'll be the one who's believed. But I sincerely hope it never comes to that. Are you following so far?"

Lorinda and Stewart both nodded.

"Good. All right. The first thing I want to get out of the way is this. Do you have any idea how those CCSA security forces knew you were going to be on the USS Raskin?"

"Janelle Stark," Lorinda said, "the CCSA security person who was chasing us, she said they have the best — what did she say?"

"'The finest intelligence agencies on earth,'" Stewart said. "I told her that was ridiculous. It almost got me killed."

"You were right," Gulden said. "Their intelligence agencies suck. You know how they really found you? I told them." She paused to allow that to sink in.

"You… You told them we were there?" Stewart said. "Why?" Lorinda could see on his face that he was suddenly torn between respect for Gulden and anger about what she'd done.

"Well, not me personally," Gulden said. "But the buck stops here. I authorized the leak through a double agent, if you must know."

"But why?!"

"You weren't meant to be put in any danger, and I'm mortified that you were. And of course I apologize. The plan was for the subs to surface *before* those pirates boarded the Raskin. Or, preferably, while they were climbing up their rope ladders. You ask why, Stewart? We're making a propaganda film posing as a documentary, that's why. Lorinda is now famous in the CCSA. And here, too. Fame doesn't last if it's not tended and curated. Sure, we could have put you two in an airplane and flown you here, but no one wants to watch someone boarding an airplane. We wanted something memorable, a battle scene that no one would ever forget. We wanted to show the CCSA going to ludicrous lengths to chase down one pregnant woman. And we wanted to show them being crushed by the superior and much more powerful forces of the USA."

"Literally crushed," Lorinda said.

"That," said Gulden, "was not in the script. And you — I can't stress this enough — you were not meant to be put in harm's way. The submarines surfaced a few minutes late. I'm told there was some kind of communications snafu. Whatever it was, we've started an investigation and there will surely be consequences for whoever screwed up."

"They almost killed us," Stewart said. His voice was calm but his eyes were burning.

"But they didn't," Lorinda said. "I totally get it. The movie's going to be amazing. And us getting beaten up'll make it even more amazing."

Stewart's mouth fell open. He gave Lorinda a look of shocked disbelief, as though she had suddenly morphed into a bird. Or Joan of Arc.

"Again," the president said, "I apologize. And I'll never forget your sacrifice." She looked at Stewart, who was quietly seething. "Stewart," she said, "I know you're angry. And I don't blame you. You feel like you've been used, a pawn in a game you maybe didn't even know you were playing." To Connor she said, "Cancel my next meeting, and tell the shooting crew to hang tight — this could take a little longer than we scheduled."

Connor, seated in one of the guest chairs, took out his com and started tapping on it. Gulden continued. "I want to give you a little background on how we got here. How *I* got here. You may know a lot of this, Stewart, but I especially want you, Lorinda, to understand what's behind all this. I don't want you to think that we put you at risk for frivolous reasons.

"To back up… many years ago, before The Split, a group of wealthy and powerful citizens of the old USA came to the conclusion that there was no reconciling what at the time we called the red states and the blue states." She paused, thought for a second, then continued. "Actually, I want to start a little earlier than that. I think I was triggered by a slogan the GOP started using: 'It's not political, it's Biblical.' I was disgusted, of course. And I thought about how it was like the 1600s, when they kicked the worst of the religious assholes out of Europe, because no one could stand them, and sent them to North America."

"Excuse me," Lorinda interrupted. "What's the GOP?"

"The Republican Party," Stewart gently said. "The political party of the red states. They started out conservative, and gradually became crazy-religious and fascistic."

"And here they were, the spiritual descendants of the same people, hundreds of years later, still being intolerable reactionary assholes. But now we couldn't just send them to another continent that they could colonize — "

"And despoil," Stewart said.

"Exactly. Anyway, end of digression. So... before The Split, I was one of the youngest among a group of influential people who had concluded things had gone too far, that it was a waste of energy to try to patch up the cracks that had developed between red and blue.

"Many in the red states were talking about seceding — you know, The South Shall Rise Again and all that crap, reliving the Civil War. Most people in the blue states were appalled by that kind of talk, but after a while we in this — I'll use the word — *elite* group were surprised to find ourselves agreeing with them, that separation was the only way forward. We'd had it with them blocking legislation, screwing around with our courts, our politics, our elections, the very basis of our democracy. And we were blocked by our own Constitution from doing anything about it. Do you know about the Electoral College, Lorinda?"

Lorinda shook her head.

"Let's just say that it gave the red states a lot more voting power than the blue states."

"That's crazy," Lorinda said.

"I'm sure Stewart can tell you all about it if you're interested. In any event, we were also sick of carrying them financially. Money was always flowing from the blue states to the red states. And we were sick of the racism and the sexism. We'd had it with their cartel of fascist media demagogues who, for decades, had become the only source of news for thirty-five or forty percent of the country. It was a world that George Orwell could have invented — "

"If he'd had a better imagination," Stewart interjected.

Gulden laughed. "Right. He couldn't have imagined that there were a lot of people who *wanted* Big Brother to be watching them.

And so, in summary, we were sick of living like that. We had so many good ideas, there was so much we could accomplish, and they were holding us back. We came to the conclusion — we, this group of powerful, influential Americans—that we were *already* two separate countries. We had two different and distinct ideas of what 'America' meant. And even if we had to give up forty percent of the population, and a whole lot of dirt and trees, and a chunk of gross national product, we'd be better off making a clean break. Parenthetically, our economic projections indicated that it would take only fifteen or twenty years to grow back to the same size economy we had before ditching the red states.

"So what did we need from this divorce? When it was time to get specific it wasn't so easy to figure out. It was excruciating, in fact. We in this group banged heads for years. In a few cases we had to wait until some old-timer died to be able to move forward. But we finally came to a compromise we could all live with.

"During this time we were in touch with our counterparts in the red states, who had pretty much reached the same conclusion about getting a divorce. Of course, no one on either side wanted an actual war, a shooting war, aside from the most retrograde, dug-in, out-of-touch red-staters."

"Meaning," Steward said, "the gun nuts, and the Johnny Reb hotheads, and the idiots who think armed combat is glamorous."

"Don't forget the wannabe martyrs," the president said. "The next step was in some ways the hardest: to convince a majority of our own blue-state citizens that splitting up was a good idea. We launched a massive — here's that word again — propaganda campaign to get people to see things our way. Some of it was overt. Politicians talking about it, editorials and op-eds, straight-up advertising. Some of it was more subtle. I remember there was an old Janis Joplin song, 'Ball and Chain,' that you started hearing everywhere in the blue states. We pushed it out there and kept pushing it. The red states were our ball and chain, you see, and after a while everyone was singing along."

Lorinda had no idea who Janis Joplin was, but this didn't seem to be the time to ask.

"Finally, the majority of Americans — blue-staters and red-staters — had adjusted to the idea that splitting the country was not completely crazy. The red-staters came around first — because of course they did. After all those years of Civil War talk, and secession fantasies, and 'states' rights' , and Don't Tread On Me bluster, and their desire for a 'Christian' nation, they were sold!

"But after a while polling showed that blue-staters had also come around. At last we were ready to start over, new Constitution Two-Point-O and all. We finally had a couple of national referendums and there it was: a big majority for splitting up."

Stewart and Lorinda were rapt. It wasn't every day that you got to hear the inside story of a major world event from the lips of an actual participant. "I thought that a lot of blue-state politicians opposed The Split," Stewart said.

"Definitely — at first," said Gulden. "But we managed to flip most of them early on. After that, a lot of the resistance was for show. They were pretending to resist, waiting for public opinion to catch up. It was all part of the plan. They loudly resisted, then gradually — and very publicly — came around, starting to say that splitting up was better than remaining in an abusive marriage. The whole thing was scripted so it wouldn't look like a bunch of the rich and powerful jamming their ideas down everyone else's throat.

"Things finally got real and we started negotiating with our red-state counterparts. We made huge demands at first — *outrageous* demands. Gradually, we started caving in, or pretending to cave. At the risk of appearing immodest, I was the loudest voice for playing it that way, and I had to argue against many powerful, and much older, men, who didn't want our side to lose face by pretending to be weak. I said it was political jiu-jitsu: We needed to flatter them into submission, and that's exactly what we did. The conservative media swallowed the bait, and that meant that the entire red-state population swallowed the bait. Their media couldn't stop crowing about how strong they were and how weak we were. It was a classic 'don't throw me into the briar patch' strategy."

Once again, Lorinda looked confused. "Don't ... what?"

"Connor can talk to you about that after I leave," Gulden said. "Their media and their politicians started saying it proved that God was on their side. Hah! So finally the hard-core negotiations began. Skipping the small stuff, we insisted that Texas had to come with us, that it was a dealbreaker, that it was a natural blue state."

"The idea of Texas being in the USA ..." Lorinda said.

"I know," Gulden said. "Of course they stood firm. After a while all they cared about was making sure they got Texas. In the media it was 'The Great Texas Debate.' I was at the negotiating table in Windsor and I actually managed to cry a few times when we talked about Texas. I should get an Oscar for that."

"Windsor," Lorinda said to Stewart. "You mentioned that."

"Right," Stewart said. "Windsor, Ontario, Canada. The famous Windsor Conference where they negotiated The Split."

"In reality, we wanted nothing to do with Texas. When we finally threw in the towel on Texas, and hung our heads in make-believe shame, they were so exuberant they didn't notice that we'd walked away with everything we actually wanted, like the deal for the Free Trade Zones for manufacturing in the CCSA. And the floating exchange rate. We argued against that, you know. We *insisted* on a locked exchange rate, so that the USA dollar and the CCSA dollar were permanently linked: one US dollar equals one CCSA dollar, forever. The harder we argued, the more they were convinced that they needed to beat us, that their dollar would soon be much more valuable than ours. It was almost sad...they didn't have a single economist who could look at the big picture honestly and model the future movement of the two currencies."

"I had no idea you didn't really want Texas," Stewart said. "So all you had to do to get what you wanted was argue against it?"

"Pretty much. One day the history of all this will be written. Maybe," she said conspiratorially, "you'll be the one to write it. Well, P.S., within the first year after the Moratorium, the US dollar was worth around three CCSA dollars. A year later it was over six. Today it's much higher than we'd dared dream."

"You guys are not very nice to the poor old CCSA," Lorinda said mischievously.

"I guess we're not. You want to hear something brutal? We're secretly supporting Waldrip in the upcoming CCSA election. The guy's — excuse my language — out of his fucking mind. If you think the CCSA's in bad shape now, wait until you see what it'll be like under a Waldrip administration. We've done the economic modeling, and it's not a pretty picture. But whether or not he wins, we have exactly what we wanted: a Third World autocracy on our border churning out excellent, low-cost manufactured goods for us. It's very selfish, right? Realpolitik. Stewart knows what I mean.

"In the grand scheme of things, our never-ending skirmishes with the CCSA are minor annoyances. The real battle for us and our allies is the fight against fascism, all around the world. Can we crush it, once and for all? I don't know. There seems to be a permanent subset of humanity that consists of, to call it by its technical name, authoritarian personality types. They crave an authority figure — the more absurd the better — telling them what to do. For some reason, they need Big Daddy. I'm just glad that we have a captive supplier of excellent low-cost consumer goods, which keeps our citizens happy and helps our overall economy to focus on big issues like climate, peace, and dismantling global fascism.

"Does this mean we like having the CCSA as a neighbor? No! It's a terrible neighbor. Aside from its insane politics, there's the pollution. The annoyance attacks — like what you just experienced in The Corridor. The pandemics that flourish in a place where science is considered unpatriotic. And, of course, the fact that the continental USA is no longer a contiguous nation — you can't drive from Maine to California without going through Canada. The Canadians have been wonderfully cooperative, but still... Here's a secret for you. You've heard about the proposed North Dakota Purchase?"

"I saw CEO McWeeny and Waldrip debating about it," Lorinda said.

"The secret is — now don't tell anyone or we'll have to charge you with treason." She winked, just in case Lorinda didn't get that she was joking. "In a couple of weeks, you'll hear that it's a done deal. North Dakota will become our twenty-sixth state."

"And the CCSA will be down to twenty-four," Stewart said.

"Wait," Lorinda said. "You mean you're actually *buying* a state from us? From *them*, I mean."

"Why not?" Gulden said. "Thomas Jefferson bought Louisiana and the whole Midwest from the French. But yeah. It's wild, isn't it? Then again, it's business! We need the land, they need the money. And we're pretty far along in the negotiation to buy strips along the top borders of Montana and Idaho."

"Another Corridor," Stewart marveled.

"Correct!" she said, then cast a quick glance at Connor, who left his seat, scurried to the rolling bed tray, poured a cup of water, and handed it to Gulden. As she sipped it, he returned to his chair.

Lorinda took the opportunity to jump in. "Okay, but hold it," she said. "There's something I don't get. The Split happened a long time ago. It's a done deal. There's no need to sell people on it any more. Right?"

"Basically, yes," Gulden said.

"So why do you need to keep doing propaganda? Why are you doing this movie about me? Who are you going to show it to? Will you hack it into the CCSA to show how bad their government is? Or maybe you're going to show it to your own people here, to show them how good *you* are...?"

The President put her cup down, shut her eyes for a moment and nodded. "That's a good question. I'll tell you why," she said, opening her eyes. "Many years ago, long before The Split, politics was boring. The Left and the Right met somewhere in a reasonable middle, and stuff got done. The Left got progress, but slowly. The Right hated progress, but it was slow enough to be tolerable.

"The problem with the Left was that they were too *nice*. And self-satisfied. They grew complacent with the slow pace of progress. It was as if they didn't want to upset the people on the Right by pushing too hard. And they were so convinced that they were *correct*, they just assumed that sooner or later everyone else would see the light and come around to their world-view. In the meantime, the people on the Right, the conservatives, they weren't complacent. They felt... *aggrieved*. And they made up their minds that they were going to win, at any cost, and at every level. They became fanatics as the Left became lazy.

"Their work was practically invisible at first. They took over local school boards, state legislatures, the kinds of political races that had zero national media coverage. After a while, policies and platforms and *ideas* became irrelevant to them. All that mattered was winning. They won by injecting fear into the discourse. This wasn't new, but the scale of it was — especially once they'd built their own media ecosystem, independent of the media: their own TV, radio, newspapers, websites, even churches. Its job was to scare people about... well, about anything and everything. Especially about 'the other': foreigners, strangers, people who looked different and who maybe didn't speak English. It turned out that it wasn't hard to do in low-population-density areas, where people didn't get around much and had minimal contact with anyone who wasn't a mirror image of themselves. And — surprise! — it was exactly those places that got an extra voting boost from the Constitution.

"It took the Left forever to realize that the Right was winning. That a big chunk of the overall population had been propagandized to ignore the conditions of their actual lives, to vote not in their own interest but according their supposed *identity*. By the time the Left woke up, the Right was well on its way to owning the Supreme Court and Congress and the whole goddamn country. And, again, this was in the service of a political party that was confident enough to come right out and say that they had no ideas and no policies — that all they wanted was power and money, money and power.

"That's why The Split was such a triumph. It was a huge relief to be rid of them. No more ball and chain. But we don't — I certainly don't — want to squander what we gained with The Split. We can't be complacent. I thank them for teaching us how this has to work. I'm committed to a constant, permanent campaign to remind people in *both* countries that the USA has the right ideas and the CCSA is a fucking nightmare."

She sighed and gave Lorinda a little smile. "Well. You asked."

"I know there are people in the CCSA who secretly like the idea of re-uniting," Stewart finally said. "And McWeeny talks about it. I mean, he says that *you* talk about it, but I assume he's projecting."

President Gulden shrugged. "It could happen. Over time. But not until everyone — okay, let's say ninety-five percent of the population — in the CCSA realizes that it was founded on stupid premises by corrupt imbeciles who were intent on subjecting and stealing from their own citizens. Just like every other authoritarian regime. We need to crush them. Or should I say, we need to help the citizens of the CCSA crush the corrupt imbeciles who run the place. The battle doesn't end until we know the imbeciles are too far gone to rise from the dead."

She took a deep breath. "That was quite a download, wasn't it? Sorry I've gone on for so long, but I needed you to see what the stakes are here. So! Lorinda Moon! Are you with me?"

"I think I am," Lorinda said. She was inclined to give a more positive answer, but something inside told her to hold back a bit, leave a little room for negotiation.

"Stewart?"

"Madam President... Anita... you've made certain things very clear," he said, "and I appreciate that. Maybe I'm just not cut out to be a politician, but, to be honest, some of what you've said..."

"Makes you feel ill?" Gulden said with a smile.

Stewart laughed. "I don't know if I'd go that far. I'll just say that it makes me a little nervous."

"I advise you to get that PhD," she said. "Once a year I'll even come and give a guest lecture in your class. If you and your students can handle it."

"Thank you," he said. "Yes. I'm with you."

"Good. I have three more years in my administration. I want you two to be with me for those years. I want you to be available to tell your stories about your life in the CCSA. I want to have our people hack your media appearances into CCSA media when we have a message we want to send them. If there's anyone you want us to extract from there — parents, family, friends — we can often arrange that. You'll be my special envoys, not just to people here and people in the CCSA but around the world. You've never been to Paris? Rome? London? Tokyo? I'll give you some good luggage recommendations. We'll send you to spread the message that I think you already want to spread.

"Let me be clear about why you're perfect for our needs. First, we want to always be undermining the confidence that citizens of the CCSA have in their politicians, their government, their country. All you need to do is tell your true stories.

"Second, we need to keep the pressure on our own allies to maintain their boycotts of the CCSA — other than their manufacturing deals, which are similar to ours. Hearing from you, Lorinda, how you were brainwashed and persecuted, and from you, Stewart, about what you suffered — I know your story — and how you channeled your anger and sorrow into saving other women from . . . your wife's fate, hearing from you will keep reminding people around the world that the CCSA is a poisonous state. You are proof that the human spirit can outlive and outsmart fascism. But we can't just say it once and walk away. We have to say it every day until we win. I want you to be with me, with us, saying it every day."

"I'm afraid Lorinda will have to do all this without me," Stewart said. "If I don't keep a low profile I'm afraid I'll get people like Wilma into deep trouble."

"Of course," Gulden said. "It's just so easy for me to picture you next to Lorinda barnstorming the USA. But you're right — we can't put anyone in unnecessary danger."

"Thank you," Stewart said. "I was hoping I wouldn't have to argue with you about it. I can't imagine winning an argument with you."

"I appreciate that," she said. She nodded at her Chief of Staff.

"Ready for the camera?" Connor asked.

"I'd better be," she said. As Connor went to the door to signal the media crew to come back in, and Stewart retreated to his post behind the tripods, Gulden quickly explained to Lorinda that they were going to speak on camera for a little while, to be broadcast live around the USA — and even onto some billboards in the CCSA.

The two media guys entered, practically on the run. The first guy got behind his camera and fiddled with it, then put on a set of headphones. The other one approached Gulden and Lorinda with a couple of tiny microphones, which he stuck to the president's blazer and to Lorinda's hospital gown before returning to his station and slipping on his headphones. Connor and Mindy, who'd come in with the media guys, joined Stewart behind the camera. The president slid her chair a little closer to Lorinda, who raised the top part of the bed until it was almost vertical and she was sitting up straight. The cameraman cocked his head as he listened to directions coming through his headphones, then did a countdown with his fingers — five, four, three, two, one — and nodded at the president.

It was as if Anita Flores Gulden had been tapped by a magic wand, as if she were a cartoon everywoman who'd just swallowed the potion that turned her into a superhero, as if she were suddenly lit from within. Lorinda saw it. She felt it. And, somehow, she instantly incorporated whatever it was — a jolt of energy? a contact high from a charismatic leader? — until she, too, felt transformed. Suddenly she was calm and strong and, despite her banged-up head, feeling very smart.

"Good evening," President Gulden began, gazing warmly into the camera. "I'm here at the Walter Reed National Military Medical Center in Bethesda, Maryland, with a very special person. Her name is Lorinda Moon, and just yesterday, with the help of the USA Navy, she escaped from the CCSA, pursued by a gang of heavily armed CCSA security hoodlums in a fleet of stolen speedboats. There were camera crews on the scene, and you'll soon be able to see how it played out. The good news: Lorinda survived! Hello, Lorinda Moon."

"Hello, Madam President." Lorinda was beaming.

"How does your head feel?"

Lorinda patted her bandage, saying, "It's been better, but I'll live."

The president returned her smile. "Why were they chasing her? What was Lorinda's crime? All she wanted was a simple medical procedure, an abortion. As you know, that's illegal in the CCSA because, not to put too fine a point on it, it's a religious-authoritarian-misogynist state." She paused to give her words time to land. "Women there are second-class citizens who aren't trusted — aren't *allowed* — to make their own health decisions." Lorinda made eye contact with the camera and nodded knowingly. "And their war against women isn't the only thing that's wrong there. Their population is shrinking at an alarming rate, a result of poverty, terrible health care, and the stupidity of their enforced anti-science bias. And let's not forget the constant flow of people escaping the CCSA and seeking asylum here in the USA." She leaned forward and gave Lorinda a hug, then sat back and turned to the camera. "Welcome, Lorinda."

"It's so great to be in the USA," Lorinda said.

"You should know that when those CCSA zealots attacked her — physically attacked her — Lorinda suffered a miscarriage. That's right. In the course of trying to capture and force her to have a baby in one of their prisons for pregnant women, they injured her and caused a miscarriage. They could have killed her. The cruel stupidity of it!" She patted Lorinda's shoulder. Lorinda considered doing the same to the president, but thought better of it. "Once Lorinda fully recovers here at Walter Reed, we're going to help her get settled." She turned to Lorinda, making sure to hold a flattering three-quarter view for the camera. "When you're ready, if you're willing, I'd like to offer you a job."

"I'll need a job," Lorinda said enthusiastically. "What kind of job?"

"I'd like to send you on an extended tour of the USA, to tell your amazing story, answer questions about life behind the wall in the CCSA, and — "

"I can show that documentary you were talking about!" Lorinda exclaimed.

"I think that was a yes," Gulden said to the camera.

"Yes," Lorinda said. "Definitely. It's a yes."

"I'm so glad to hear that," the president said. She was about to launch into a little wrap-up speech, but Lorinda spoke first.

"You know, Madam President," she said, "my family moved to the CCSA during the Great Moratorium, when I was about seven, and after that we hardly went anywhere. Most people in the CCSA never travel. I can tell you just from this last week, when I was on the run from Texas all the way to Georgia, that travel is an eye-opening experience."

"Your enthusiasm is contagious," Gulden said.

"But, Madam President... Anita?" Lorinda started, before Gulden could get in another word, "I've thought of something else I can do after that tour of the USA. What if I become the host of a show where, every day, there are different guests, and they talk with me about all kinds of interesting things."

"A... talk show?" the president ventured.

"Yes! What a good thing to call it," said Lorinda. "Here's how it can work." She was obviously figuring it out as she spoke. "Every week I'll go to a different place around the USA, and each day of that week I'll host my show at a different bar or restaurant in that town. I could be standing or sitting behind the bar, and my guests could be, like, sitting on barstools across from me. There'd be no limit to what we could talk about."

She glanced over at Stewart, who was staring at her in amazement. "Well — "

"I think at first the guests would mainly be educating me about their town or city — remember, I grew up in a place that doesn't really believe in education, and we were given a very distorted view of this country. I mean, we were taught that everyone in the United

States is on the verge of starving to death because of all the poverty. That's obviously not true, so what else am I misinformed about? We'll find out on the show. And sometimes maybe I'd get a celebrity guest who grew up in that town, or has a house there, or always wanted to go there, and we'd talk about that. And maybe I can end every show with an interview of a local bartender who has a special cocktail recipe that no one's ever heard of before." She had a quick afterthought. "Or I can show them one!"

The president, who had marshaled all her will power to keep herself from making Lorinda stop talking, said, "That's a good idea for a show, Lorinda. Now — "

"So I spend a week in one town, and then the next week we'd go to a different town and set up shop there. You know, now that I think about it, Anita, maybe I don't even have to start out on that tour you were talking about."

"You're saying — "

"I can just start, on day one, with the talk show. I mean, we can run the documentary right there on a screen at the bar, and I can talk about it with the customers. We can keep doing the show for as long as people want to watch. Or until I've been all around the USA. Maybe we can call it 'Lorinda Moon's Bar Tour.'"

Lorinda paused. The President, stopping herself from responding immediately, waited a beat, and then said, "You're going to go far in this country."

"I just have one more thing I want to say, Madam President. When the USA Navy rescued me, they also rescued a very good friend of mine." She looked at Stewart, who was cringing. "He and the people he worked with got me all the way from Texas to Georgia while we were being chased by CCSA security people. If he wants to, he can be my co-host, and we can tell his story along with mine. I mean, as soon as it's safe for him to talk about it."

"That's all really great, Lorinda," Gulden said, desperate to regain control of the narrative. "We'll seriously consider helping you launch your show."

"Thank you, Madam President," Lorinda said. "Will you really be able to? Help me?"

"I think you have an excellent idea, and I'll certainly use whatever influence I have to help you get it off the ground. You really need to get some rest now. Thank you so much for inviting me to speak to you despite the pain you must be in. And on behalf of my fellow Americans, thank you for honoring us with your presence here. You're an extraordinary human being, Lorinda. I'm sure we'll be seeing a lot more of you in the coming months." She finished up with that warm gaze into the camera, saying, "Thanks for watching, everyone."

"And... out," said the cameraman. "Good work."

The instant the camera was off, so was Lorinda. It was as if she'd been disconnected from a power source. She was ready for a nice, long nap.

President Gulden stood up, straightened her suit, shook Lorinda's hand, and said, "Lorinda Moon, you're a real piece of work." Lorinda was puzzled by the expression, and Gulden picked up on it. "It means you're a lot more formidable than you look. In the best possible sense. You'll go far. And you'll have me as a fan."

"Thank you," said Lorinda. "I think."

As the sound-and-light guy inconspicuously scooped up the two microphones from the two women's clothes, Connor approached the president. "A word?" he said. As Stewart sat down on the bed, shaking his head in wonder at Lorinda's performance, Connor and Gulden moved as far as possible from everyone else. Connor held up his com so she could see the screen.

"What am I looking at?" Gulden whispered.

"It's the real-time ratings of the segment you just did, minute by minute."

"If I'm reading this right, they start out down around two-fifty K, then start to go — "

"They start rising two minutes in. Then they go through the roof. Twenty-five million, fifty-million . . . Lots of people recording it too. And here's the best part. In the InstaPoll after it was over? Yes or no to the statement 'Lorinda Moon should have her own talk show.' Close to a hundred percent said yes. I've never seen one-hundred percent before."

"Can't argue with numbers like that," Gulden whispered. "Looks like she'll be getting her show." Then, out loud, she said, "It was good to meet you, Stewart. We'll have you two over to the White House after you've recovered. I hope to see you very soon." Connor nodded to Mindy, who tapped on her pad. Two seconds later the door opened and the wave of hubbub rolled in, followed by the same two Secret Service men. They stood by the door, waited for President Gulden to exit, and followed her out. Those in the room heard the roar of "Madam President! Madam President!" even after the door closed.

"I've never seen anyone do that to her," Connor said to Lorinda.

"Do what?" Lorinda asked.

"Say so much before she interrupts. Talk before she does. Force her to do your bidding."

"What?! What did I force her to do?" Lorinda was truly puzzled.

"You're going to get your show," said Connor. "She supported you in a live feed. Now she has no choice. Polling shows that millions of people saw it and voted for you to have a show. She can't back out of it — she has to stand behind you. If she's behind you, it'll happen."

Stewart gave a little laugh and said to Lorinda, "You're the one with the best story. Your guests will want to interview you."

Lorinda grabbed Stewart's hand. "You'll be my first guest. You can wear a mask. We'll change your voice. You have to!"

Connor grinned. "You'll have the president's backing. It's a brilliant idea, and she'll get some credit for it. Remind me to buy stock in your production company." He reached for the doorknob, then remembered something. "'Please don't throw me into the briar patch.' It's from a folk tale passed down by slaves in the Old South. It's probably illegal to talk about it in the CCSA."

"Uncle Remus," said Stewart. "Book by Joel Chandler Harris, around 1880. A major piece of cultural appropriation. Arguably. And you're right: banned in the CCSA."

"You can talk about stuff like that," Lorinda said eagerly. "You can talk about whatever you want. I love this show!"

Connor smiled. "You two are full of surprises. I'll see you soon in the White House."

He opened the door and stepped into the fray.

— THE END —

About the Authors

STEVE RADLAUER was born in Brooklyn before Brooklyn was cool. He is the author or co-author of a bunch of books, including *Monsters of the Ivy League* (Little, Brown, with *The Split*'s own Ellis Weiner), *The Historic Shops & Restaurants of New York* (The Little Bookroom, with Ellen Williams), *Dan Quayle: Airhead Apparent* (Behind The News Press, with Paul Slansky), *Townie Planet* (auto-published), and *Special Moments* (Ballantine Books, with Joe Bodolai).

His byline has appeared in a plethora of periodicals, including *New York* magazine, *Spy*, *Esquire*, the *New York Times*, the *Los Angeles Times*, *Asian Art News*, *Cosmopolitan*, *Hamptons Country*, and the *Irrational Inquirer* and *Off The Wall Street Journal* parodies. He has worked in television as a writer and producer, is a founder of a travel-app developer, has been a creative on dozens of advertising campaigns and an officer of two non-profit arts organizations. A long time ago he owned a restaurant.

He lives in Manhattan.

ELLIS WEINER began as an editor with *National Lampoon*, moved on to freelancing for a thousand magazines back when they existed, and was one of the original columnists ("How to Be a Grownup") of the much-lamented *Spy* magazine. In 1980 he began contributing to the *New Yorker*, which still exists.

He is, with his late wife, Barbara Davilman, co-author of the best-selling *Yiddish With Dick and Jane,* as well as *How to Raise a Jewish Dog* and *How to Profit From the Coming Rapture* (Little, Brown).

Solo, he is author of many books, including *The Joy of Worry* (Chronicle) and the middle-grade series *The Templeton Twins Have an Idea* and *The Templeton Twins Make a Scene* (Chronicle).

And, of course, he is co-author, with Steve Radlauer, of *Monsters of the Ivy League* (Little, Brown).

He lives in Los Angeles.

Acknowledgments

WHEN WE COULDN'T find a so-called mainstream so-called book editor willing to publish a satire that included the terrifying satirical premise that, prior to the beginning of the tale, the red states and the blue states of the USA had peacefully and satirically split into separate countries, Rebecca Schoenkopf—editor and boss of the online, often satirical publication *Wonkette*—came to our rescue. Like modern-day Charles Dickenses, we serialized *The Split* in *Wonkette*, a chapter a week, from November 2023 to November 2024, the last chapter "dropping" just in time to distract our readers from the ghastly news about that year's presidential election. Thank you, Rebecca. We tried.

Our friend Liz Dubelman is a writer, a publishing consultant, and an expert on the mysterious (to us) workings of Substack, *Wonkette's* publishing platform. We thank Liz for unconfusing us and helping us focus on the Dickensian task of weekly chapter-writing.

We thank Yael Shahar and Don Radlauer, without whose formidable proofreading talents this edition would never have achieved liftoff. Beyond that, Yael designed, laid out, and did all the production prep for the book.

Ken Kobland's impeccable design sense helped us figure out how to make our book look nice, and for that we thank him profusely.

www.ingramcontent.com/pod-product-compliance
Lightning Source LLC
Chambersburg PA
CBHW020527110726
47899CB00004B/1280

* 9 7 9 8 9 9 2 8 0 4 4 0 9 *